THE DARK SIDE OF THE SUN

ALSO BY ELIZABETH PALMER

Scarlet Angel
Plucking the Apple
Old Money
Flowering Judas
The Golden Rule

THE DARK SIDE OF THE SUN

Elizabeth Palmer

THOMAS DUNNE BOOKS
St. Martin's Press
New York

THOMAS DUNNE BOOKS.
An imprint of St. Martin's Press.

www.stmartins.com

ISBN 0-312-26141-1

First published in the United Kingdom by Century,
The Random House Group Limited

First U.S. Edition: July 2000

10 9 8 7 6 5 4 3 2 1

For my mother

There are those who labour under the delusion that money and privilege go hand in hand with happiness but, never forget, there's a dark side to every sun.

Rafe Bartholomew

Part One

A Complicated Childhood

1

1928

Screaming and whooping, the four Harding children stormed along the hall, past Miss Halliday's room and thundered on down the uncarpeted oak staircase. The time was 7 a.m. It was not, thought Miss Halliday resuming her packing, that they were bad children. No, not *bad*. She groped for the word. *Untamed*, that was it. Primitive, even. But then, meeting the mother, who could fail to be surprised at that? Davina Harding was so unmaternal that it was difficult to imagine her having one child, let alone four. There was a vagueness, loopiness even, about her which meant that most of the time while she was there in sylph-like body, she was not there at all in spirit. So where was she? Not for the first time Miss Halliday gave up on it. Though, because Mrs Harding was habitually so distrait, childbirth must have come as a nasty, earthy shock, and not once but three times if you counted the twins as one ordeal rather than two.

Elfrida Halliday folded up two pairs of lisle stockings and placed them in the bottom of her valise together with assorted snip-clean shabby underwear and two nightdresses, all of which had been thriftily mended time and time again. Into the case also went a Bible, a silver-framed sepia photograph of her parents, long since dead, a bottle of eau-de-Cologne, a sponge bag and a small velvet pouch which contained all her jewellery, namely a garnet brooch and matching garnet earrings which had belonged to her mother. On top went two neat, serviceable skirts, together with two neat, serviceable blouses. Lastly, and carefully folded with tissue paper in between the layers, she added her attending interviews/going to church/funerals costume plus gloves. Shoes, two pairs, were destined for another holdall, along with her small collection of books. Shorn of her few personal possessions, the tiny room in which she had passed the last six months had a forlorn air, as though it did not know what to expect next. Elfrida wondered about the new incumbent as well. She also wondered if her four charges would miss her. Probably not. Like a litter of boisterous puppies they had each other, though not for long. As was the habit of the upper classes who, once they had sired their children, immediately looked for ways of getting rid of them, Godfrey was shortly to go to boarding-school whence he would be followed eventually by the twins. Not by Nettie though. Nettie would continue to be educated at home until she was finally sent off to be finished.

Elfrida shut the case and placed her hat which, in the interests of preservation, she intended to wear on the journey, beside it. The old, uncomfortable feeling of impermanence surfaced, accompanied by the frankly terrifying imponderable: What will I do when I'm too old to work? No doubt it was a question that governesses everywhere asked themselves. Better not to think of the future. Live for the moment. She suddenly became aware that the din downstairs had ceased, and that there was a deathly hush.

The cause of the silence was Geoffrey Harding, who had arrived at his country home late the previous night without any warning. An old-fashioned father of the 'Children Should Be Seen But Not Heard' variety, and veering moreover in the direction of 'And Not Seen Too Often Either', he was affronted when his own brood erupted into the drawing-room where he was sternly reading yesterday's *Times* in the gloaming of drawn curtains. The maid, who in common with everyone else did not know of her employer's sudden arrival, had not yet opened up the room or laid the fire and it did not strike Harding to pull back his own drapes when he had a servant to do it for him. During sojourns at home, he treated the drawing-room like his gentlemen's club in London. Wing armchairs, hushed tones and no interlopers was the form. And no women. Even Davina knocked before entering when Geoffrey was in residence. It did not occur to him that in a family house, albeit a large one, such behaviour was tyrannical.

'OUT! OUT!' roared Geoffrey Harding, rising unexpectedly out of the wing armchair in wrath, giving them all a fright. Without bothering to greet his offspring, whom he had not

4

seen for three weeks, he threw his newspaper at them. As though he had pointed a blunderbuss, in a group his children turned, rushed into the hall and then scattered.

'DOOR!' yelled Harding, after the last one through it. When they had gone he picked up the pages of his newspaper, put them back in order and resumed reading the foreign news pages.

Panting, they finally reassembled in the day nursery.

At first glance they looked very different. Godfrey was blond and willowy, like their mother. The twins, Jonathan and William, were sturdier and altogether more robust in appearance while Venetia, the plump youngest, all curls and dimples, was straight out of Mabel Lucie Atwell. It was almost as though the more children Davina Harding had had, the more the original blueprint had firmed up. All had the unusual turquoise-blue Harding eyes and dark eyebrows and all were victims of the upper-class compulsion to bestow nicknames, so that the respectably christened Godfrey, William, Jonathan and Venetia had become Dods, Wigs, Jonty and Nettie.

'When did Father come home?' asked Nettie.

'Must have been last night,' said the twins, answering together as they often did. There was a silence. Nobody liked it when their autocratic parent was *in situ*. Father, who sometimes mixed up his own children's names, alternated between taking no notice of them at all and taking too much notice of a destructive kind. What Mother's view of these visitations was, none of them knew. If anything she seemed to become even more removed from the real world when he was there. At lunchtime, a meal they frankly dreaded, nobody spoke until he did and, because they feared the sarcasm, all preferred it that way. When one or other of them was singled out for criticism, Mother would flutter her hands in a despairing sort of way, saying, 'Geoffrey! Geoffrey!' but that was as far as it went. None of them ever saw her stand up to Father. When the household arrangements broke down, which was quite frequently, he would voice his displeasure in front of all of them, the current governess included. In the face of such criticism, Mother remained meekly Geisha-like and mute, reacting with martyred patience and no discernible improvement in the running of the house. His overbearing presence produced uneven behaviour, and seasoned observers noticed that when he was in residence the children crept about like mice and, when he was not, ran riot. The mystery was, of course, why the Hardings had had any children. The answer was probably that everyone did.

Nettie said, 'Miss Halliday leaves today.' And then, very smug, 'I got her a present.'

Their interest caught by this, the others all chorused, 'Did you? What?'

'Soap!' said Nettie.

There was a silence. Nobody else had thought of doing such a thing.

'You can give it with me if you like,' offered Nettie generously.

Elfrida put on her hat and pinned it. She glanced at her watch. It was nearly time for the taxi to arrive. She decided to go downstairs and wait in the hall. It would be interesting to see if Mrs Harding came to say goodbye. On the whole, Elfrida did not think that she would. After one last glance around the room to make sure that she had not left anything behind, she opened the door and, carrying valise and grip, stepped out into the passage. At the head of the staircase she met Geoffrey Harding.

'Ah, Miss Halliday!' said her employer. And then, noting her hat, 'Are you going out?'

'I am leaving today, Mr Harding,' replied Elfrida. Perhaps his wife had not told him. In fact, since it was three weeks since he had last been in the country, it was quite likely that she had not.

'Are you? Well, good luck.' Without very much interest, he shook her gloved hand and then turned on his heel and walked along the landing in the direction of his dressing-room. Watching him go, Elfrida thought, I'm glad I'm getting out of here. She walked on down the stairs, across the hall and out through the massive front door into the porch where she was confronted for the last time by the park and a bold, brilliant winter morning. A new incarnation beckoned. She put down her bags. It was here that she was ambushed by her four charges.

'We bought you a present, Miss Halliday,' said Nettie, offering it. She smiled up at the governess. For the first time Elfrida noticed a sort of flirtatious coquetry about Nettie which momentarily caught her attention. With all of them watching, she opened the little parcel.

Soap. Very expensive soap. Chanel soap. It raised the question of where it had come from. Davina Harding's bathroom, perhaps?

'It's lovely, simply lovely,' said Elfrida. 'Thank you!'

A tear slid down her middle-aged cheek.

The taxi arrived. With all of them clustering around, she got in. As the cab drew away, she waved. Watching the tiny group receding, she wondered with a pang what would happen to them all. I've been in some odd households in the course of my job, thought Elfrida, but that was definitely the oddest.

The car turned a corner of the drive and the little Hardings were lost to sight.

2

Sitting opposite her prospective employer, Sibyl Fox uncharacteristically felt herself the victim of creeping exhaustion. It
was as though the extreme languor of the other was catching.
Or maybe it was that the only way Davina Harding seemed
to be able to function was by syphoning off other people's
energy. When words failed her, she simply waved her
hands balletically and then carried on speaking as though
the sentence had been properly finished and her audience
knew what it was she had intended to say. All the same,
in spite of the fits and starts, a lot of information came out
of the interview. Mrs Fox learnt that governesses had come
and gone with rapidity, the last having been a Miss Elfrida
Halliday who had departed three weeks earlier.

'So close to Christmas. So inconsiderate!'

So close to Christmas? It was only September.

'Since her departure, Dods has gone to boarding-school
leaving Wigs, Jonty and Nettie. In the fullness of time, by
which I mean next year, Jonty and Wigs will go as well,
leaving only Nettie in your charge.'

Dods and Wigs and Jonty and Nettie? With the exception
of Jonty, who seemed to have got off lightly when name
assassination was taking place, Mrs Fox wondered what on
earth they could all have been christened in the first place.
Aloud she said, 'And what about Nettie? When does Nettie
go to school?'

Davina Harding looked quite shocked.

'Nettie is a girl. Nettie will not go to school. No, no, Nettie
will remain at home until she goes to finishing-school, prior
to Coming Out. So, what do you say, Mrs Fox?'

This was the moment. Fortified by the knowledge that so
far the Harding forays into the governess market appeared
to have been disastrous, Mrs Fox said, 'I should like to take
the post, but there is one thing you should know.'

'Yes?' said Davina Harding, looking almost alert for the
first time.

8

'I am a widow and have a daughter who is the same age as Nettie. It would be impossible for me to accept this position unless I could bring her with me and educate her along with Nettie.'

Mrs Harding felt rather put out. However Mrs Fox, whose references had been adequate, though only that, seemed a ladylike person and, presumably, had a ladylike daughter. After a pause, she said, reluctantly, 'Oh, very well. I should like you to start as soon as you possibly can.'

'I shall be free to come to you at the end of this month.'

'Then that will have to do, I suppose.'

'May I be allowed to see the nursery wing?'

'Of course. I shall take you there myself.'

Following Davina Harding as she swayed, storklike, up the staircase, Mrs Fox looked around her. The house was well furnished with silk curtains, Persian rugs and impressive paintings and furniture. What Mrs Harding lacked in energy she appeared to have made up for in taste. The culture shock, then, going into the children's wing was immense. Beyond an oak door, polished floorboards gave way to grey lino and chipped paintwork.

'This is the day nursery,' said Mrs Harding, pushing open the door.

Spartan was the only word for it.

Outside the window the munificence of the park only served to point up the extreme spareness of the room in which they stood. Collapsing armchairs of the sort which might be seen on the back of totters' carts were haphazard and shelves overflowed with tattered books and jigsaws. There was what looked like an open scrapbook on the floor accompanied by a pot of paste and a pair of scissors, the whole surrounded by coloured pencils and crayons. Dominant was a huge rocking-horse with glass eyes whose tail was reduced to a few wispy strands and whose stuffing had partially disgorged itself through a hole in its bald leather stomach. There were no curtains.

'As you see, it's a large room,' said Davina Harding, encapsulating all there was to say about the wasteland that was the day nursery. 'And now, perhaps you would like to see the one that is to be your own.'

She turned and led the way. Watching her retreating back,

Mrs Fox was reminded of Edith Sitwell's lines *Jane, Jane, tall as a crane* . . . She followed. This room was medium-sized and prettier than she might have expected. The wallpaper was covered in a pattern of small deep-pink and red roses and the mahogany furniture was plain but acceptable. In one corner stood a washtand on which was a large flowered jug and bowl and beside that was a pedestal hand basin. A single bed was positioned along one wall and a *chaise-longue* which, although it had seen better days was still elegant in a faded sort of way, ran along the other. The only other piece of furniture was a small desk. There were no pictures or ornaments of any kind with the exception of a rectangular china plaque which bore the legend *Thou, God, seest me* and hung over the head of the bed. One for the back of the cupboard, thought Sibyl, eyeing it with disfavour.

She became aware that the room felt very cold.

Apparently able to read her thoughts, Davina said, 'In the winter, should you so wish it, the maid will lay the fire for you both here and in the day nursery where you will teach the children. In the normal course of events when my husband is in London you and they will have supper together. When Geoffrey is here he likes us all to eat together in the dining-room.'

A small moue and a ripple of transparent, blue-veined hands indicated incomprehension. Later Sibyl was to learn *Geoffrey likes us all to eat together* really meant *Geoffrey likes to hold forth and for that Geoffrey requires an audience.* The answer to another unspoken question followed.

'You and your daughter, whose name is . . . ?'

'Mary.'

'You and Mary will share a bathroom with the children. If you are agreeable, I suggest that Mary sleeps in the night nursery. Now, is there anything else you would like to ask me, Mrs Fox?'

Astounded that she and not the vague Mrs Harding was having to suggest it, she replied, 'Yes. I wonder if it would be possible to meet Nettie and Jonty and Wigs.'

'Of course. What a good idea! I have no idea where they are, however. We shall have to go in search of them!'

We shall have to go in search of them? It had occurred to Sibyl Fox to wonder who was supervising the three young children during the hiatus between one governess leaving and another arriving. The answer, it appeared, was that no one was. It reinforced her first impression that Davina Harding had very little idea of what was going on in her own household which, if it was indeed the case, opened up all sorts of interesting possibilities. She followed in the scented, limp wake. Eventually, with the aid of the cook, introduced as 'Mrs Boswell who has just joined us,' Nettie, Jonty and Wigs were run to ground helping the gardener, who was preparing to burn leaves. The light was just beginning to fade. Cobalt, sweet-smelling smoke swirled heavenwards. With a dangerous crackle, the fire caught hold and suddenly surged. Tongues of yellow flame snaked high into the air shedding a surprising amount of light all around. Far too close for their own safety, three small sturdy figures waving sticks whirled like little dervishes and screamed with delight, intoxicated by the blaze. Silhouetted against the radiance, they struck the burning leaves again and again, so that showers of sparks exploded all around them. None was aware of the approach of their mother and her companion.

Davina Harding and Mrs Fox reached the gardener first.

'This is Mr Patten, who started work here last week,' elucidated Mrs Harding, not seeming at all exercised by the fact that three of her offspring were practically dancing in the fire. Inwardly laughing, Mrs Fox thought, I *don't* believe it. *Another recent arrival!* She turned her attention back to the matter in hand.

'Come here, children!' commanded Mrs Harding, at the same time clapping her hands so that all her rings rattled. Reluctantly they complied, dropping their sticks as they did so. 'I wish you to meet Mrs Fox, who is going to become Miss Halliday.' The way this was said inferred that one governess was indistinguishable from another and provided a possible clue as to the brisk departure of hired help.

'How do you do, Mrs Fox!' chorussed Nettie, Wigs and Jonty. For children they had disconcertingly level stares. Shaking one grimy paw after the other, Sibyl Fox said, 'I gather you have an elder brother who is away at school.'

'Yes,' said Nettie, adding, 'Dods. I miss him. When Wigs and Jonty go I'll miss them too. I'll be on my own.'

Sulkily, she eyed her mother.

Registering her daughter's attitude, Davina Harding decided to replay to her own advantage the tiresome daughter card already dealt by Mrs Fox. 'Ah, so that's what you think, Nettie. Well, you're wrong, for Mrs Fox has a surprise for you. She has a daughter exactly the same age as you who is going to come and live here and be educated with you. There now!'

If ecstasy was looked for at the end of this arch speech, it was not to be forthcoming. Nettie scowled. 'What if I don't like her?'

'Well . . .' Davina Harding's voice trailed away uncertainly in the face of this vote of no confidence. Lowering her eyes, Sibyl Fox suppressed a smile. There was something almost endearing about such intractability in one so small. 'Oh, but I very much hope you will, Nettie,' she said, stepping in.

Nettie turned away from her parent and towards the new governess. Grudging interest replaced surliness. 'What's her name?'

'Mary. If Mrs Harding agrees, perhaps I could bring her over to meet you at the weekend. Then you could see if the two of you can be friends, because there is no point in me coming to live here if you can't.' It was a gamble but probably one worth taking.

Nettie considered Mrs Fox in silence for a minute. 'All right,' she said at last and then, to her mother, 'Can we go back to the fire now?'

As the two women walked back to the house, Davina Harding asked, 'What happens if they don't hit it off?' inwardly flinching at the thought of beginning the interviewing process all over again.

'Oh, of course they will!' answered Sibyl, 'I have no doubt about it. But it is only fair to let Nettie find out for herself. Otherwise we might have a problem on our hands. Children can be very stubborn. Better to get off on the right foot. And may I venture to suggest that Mary and Nettie spend some time getting to know one another without Jonty and Wigs since, at the end of the day, when the boys have gone away to school, it will be just the two of them?'

'I believe Jonty and Wigs are going to a birthday party on Saturday afternoon. Perhaps you would like to bring your daughter then.'

'I will.'
They stopped at the front door.
'Goodbye, Mrs Fox.'
'Goodbye, Mrs Harding.'

Extract from the day book of Davina Harding
September 12th 1928

*Today I interviewed Mrs Sibyl Fox, who answered my
advertisement in* The Lady *for the post of governess
in the wake of the very inconvenient departure of
Miss Halliday. Mrs Fox, who is a widow with a
small daughter, seems a demure, respectable person.
In looks, she is almost as tall as I am and slim. I
would think that she is my age. Alas, she wears no
make-up and her reddish-gold hair, of which she
appears to have a very great deal, is gathered into
a rather old-fashioned knot at the nape of the neck.
The shingle seems to have passed Mrs Fox by, though
it probably would have suited her. To sum up, apart
from the hair, she is unremarkable in every way and
should therefore prove to have been a wise choice. As
such let us hope she will be a perfect member of the
staff, who knows her place in this house as well as
her Geography. Her references, it's true, are somewhat
lacklustre but that is all the better. I do not want
flamboyance here and Geoffrey does not approve of
too much education for women. Which is just as well,
as I myself had hardly any, although Mother Eustacia
did believe in a surfeit of religion. But of what use has
religion ever been to me?*

Apart from a note of the salary she had agreed to pay Mrs
Fox and a summary of the terms of their agreement, this
uncharacteristically introspective question ended the entry.

The little girls got on very well. Sitting watching them
in the sparse surroundings of the day nursery, Sibyl Fox
thought that perhaps one of the keys to it was that they
were complete opposites. Certainly another had been giving

Nettie the option for Nettie, she divined, even at such a tender age, had a ferocious will and the stamina to sustain a very long vendetta. Nettie reminded her of herself at that age. The product of a privileged upbringing, used to the rough and tumble of life with brothers, she was robust and confident – in a word, very *physical*. Mary, however, had a tentativeness and reserve born of being an only child who had moved from post to post with her mother, an existence which had curtailed the putting down of any roots, either of friendship or of place. Sibyl wished her own daughter was more like Nettie.

The two of them were currently kneeling on the floor inspecting Nettie's scrapbook. Both were wearing white socks and frocks with Peter Pan collars, puffed sleeves and a bow at the back. Courtesy of the maid, no doubt, Nettie's was so comprehensively starched that it virtually crackled.

'I hate this dress,' said Nettie, stuffing it between her knees. 'It gets in the way.'

'Nettie, why don't you show Mary the garden?' suggested Sibyl.

'Can I?' said Nettie with alacrity, and then to Mary, 'Would you like to see it? And the wood? What about the wood?' She jumped to her feet. Her enthusiasm was catching.

'Oooh, yes!'

'Right, boots and coats,' ordered Sibyl, putting down her book and becoming a governess.

Watching them walk away across the lawn, her emotions were complex. Mary was taller and thinner than Nettie, with shoulder-length mouse-coloured hair which a ribbon prevented from falling into her eyes. Nettie strode out, marginally ahead. One needed toning down, one needed toning up. It would be interesting to see what happened.

What did happen in the short term was that both of them came back half an hour later exuding camaraderie and caked in mud. Nettie had torn her coat. It was not a very auspicious start.

'I'm so sorry about this,' said Sibyl to Davina Harding, who wandered around the corner at that moment presumably in search of a progress report, and whose eyes had opened very wide at the sight of the two ragamuffins.

14

With a dismissive wave, 'No matter,' responded her employer-to-be, very queenly, secure in the knowledge that the Elfrida Halliday replacement problem had been solved possibly for years to come. 'Girls will be girls! Now, assuming my daughter approves,' (long look at Nettie) 'when will you be joining us?'

Extract from the day book of Davina Harding
September 15th 1928

Such a relief. It is all signed and sealed, though at Mrs Fox's request I did increase my initial salary offer, which fact I shall not mention to Geoffrey. I look forward to her arrival in two weeks' time. I confess I had hoped that her appointment signalled the end of my staffing problems for the time being until, today, Mrs Causton the housekeeper handed in her resignation. So it's back to The Lady. *I wonder whether Geoffrey realizes what hard work running a house this size is!*

3

As Sibyl had hoped, with the passing of time Mary and Nettie
became close, no doubt partly because the rural isolation in
which they lived meant outside socializing was something
of a major excursion. A year after the arrival of the Foxes,
Jonty and William went to prep school. Uncerebral and very
sociable, for a week or two Nettie pined for her brothers'
boisterous company and then, with what Sibyl viewed as
admirable pragmatism, began to make the most of what
she had left. Nettie was emerging as a great survivor.
Ironically, apart from loneliness, it was what the girls did
not have in common which drew them together. Nettie was
fascinated and not a little envious of her friend's unorthodox
background and wanted to know all about it. What emerged
was that Mary herself knew almost nothing. To Nettie, who
came from a strata of society where every detail of family
history was known and chronicled, this was extraordinary.

'Why don't you ask your mother?'

Why didn't she? Mary was unsure of the answer to this
but was instinctively aware that the question would not
necessarily be a welcome one. Without directly answering,
she said in her own defence, 'Well, I do know some of it. I
mean I know the part about me. I know that my parents were
only married for a very short time before Father died.'

'What did he die of?' Nettie was curious. In the world of
a child, people died of old age. They did not die young.

Mary did have the answer to that one and it had to
be said that, in the face of Nettie's amazement, it was
a distinct relief to have the answer to something. 'He
collapsed in the street one day soon after I was born and
never regained consciousness. They said it was a heart
attack.'

For a brief moment Nettie allowed herself to contemplate
being half an orphan and, without a twinge of remorse,
confronted the fact that life without her own fearsome
father might be enhanced rather than the opposite. On

the other hand Father earned the money which was partly responsible for keeping her in luxury.

'What kind of person was he? What did he do?'

'His name was Charles. According to Mother he was very unpractical and at the same time very clever. By profession he was an engineer but in his spare time he loved inventing things. It was his hobby and his passion though he never made any money out of it. Nobody knew he had a heart condition. When he died we were left with virtually nothing and because he was an only child and both his parents were dead there was no one who could offer help.'

'Sometimes I wish I was an only child,' said Nettie.

'No, you don't, Nettie!' Mary spoke with feeling. 'You really don't.'

Aware of having hit a nerve but not prepared to back off all the same, Nettie persisted: 'And what about your mother? What sort of family did your mother come from? You must have some idea. Everyone knows that sort of thing!'

Well, no, apparently everyone didn't. Mary didn't. It was something her mother never harked back to, much less reminisced about. She experienced a sudden surge of anxiety. The old rootlessness surfaced again together with a terrifying sense of loss of identity. If the past, by which Nettie apparently set such store, was a void then what about the future? What did you base a future on if you hadn't got a past?

'You're right, I'll have to ask her,' conceded Mary with clouded brow, mentally shying away from doing any such thing and then, anxious to get off the subject of her own family history, or the lack of it, said, 'Tell me all about yours.'

'I've told you once already.'

'Tell me again.'

Nettie did.

As the girls' friendship grew, Nettie's lack of inhibition drew Mary out of the shell of her private, introspective world so that, Sibyl noted, her daughter became less serious, more like other children. Unlike Nettie, Mary was academically bright, a fact which became apparent despite the inadequacies of her mother's teaching. Her good brain manifested itself in the maturity of the compositions she wrote and her

17

quick grasp of anything mathematical. Jonty, who taught Mary how to play chess during one of the school holidays, was amazed at how quickly she picked it up and frankly miffed when she began to beat him. All this fired Nettie, who was naturally competitive, to try harder at her lessons in an effort to keep up, though the concentration required by the chessboard proved to be beyond her. As the years went by each of them acquired a new dimension from the personality of the other.

Stifled by country life, Sibyl fantasized that either Jonty or William would fall for Mary. Godfrey was out of the question, partly because he was the Harding son and heir and partly because in terms of eligibility and looks Mary was not in his league. Not even one of the landed county families would get a look in, Sibyl realized. Godfrey was clearly destined for a brittle London beauty with a very great deal of money.

Meanwhile life went on. As her pupils grew up teaching them became more interesting, and Sibyl devised their reading list according to her own (alas, unrealizable) tastes and aspirations. The motives of feisty, manipulative heroines such as Becky Sharpe, Kate Croy and Madame Merle were minutely examined and received the Fox seal of approval. Lily Bart and Tess of the D'Urbervilles were held up as unfortunate examples of those who had not stayed ahead of the game.

'Women have to take what they want out of this world,' declared Sibyl, a feminist before her time. 'Nobody's going to give it to them if they don't.' History got the same biased treatment, being full of useful role models such as Boadicea, Elizabeth the First, Catherine the Great and even, on a day when Sibyl was feeling particularly jaundiced, another Elisabeth, this time the Hungarian drinker of blood, Countess Báthory. Geography, with nothing along these lines to offer, was deemed worthy and therefore dull and dropped from the syllabus. If Sibyl had dared, arithmetic would have suffered the same fate. One of the most fertile sources for her propaganda was Shakespeare, though not the comedies which were considered too tame. Otherwise it was all there: lust, betrayal, torture and murder, and on the same topics the Old Testament was dependably graphic as well.

'The playing field on which both sexes operate is not a

level one,' opined Sibyl, 'and never has been. It therefore behoves women to be very vigilant where their own interests are concerned.'

'But what happened to Becky Sharpe couldn't happen to me, for instance,' argued Nettie, alluding to her own privileged society slot.

'Probably not, but just don't bank on it, Nettie,' her governess replied elliptically.

In the light of Sybil Fox's unusual educational approach, both girls discussed sex endlessly, though neither was exactly sure what it was they were talking about. Speculation got them part of the way but it was not until the day Nettie did what she had been told not to, and went through the contents of her father's desk looking for writing paper, that further light was shed on this tantalizing subject. Right at the bottom of one of the drawers she found a large, leather-covered book. Intrigued, Nettie lifted it out and opened it. On the title page was the legend *Forbidden Fruit*. It sounded too promising to not turn the page. Nettie did and found herself confronted by an engraving of buxom, partly-clothed ladies in what looked like a harem. Several pages further on, and by now unclothed, they had been joined by men in a similar state of undress. Nettie carried on flicking over the pages. By the time she got to the end of it there was not a lot she did not know. Well, well! Apart from the exotically erotic goings-on, it shed an interesting light on Father. And on Mother too, for that matter. Did they *really* do all that . . . ? Nettie supposed they must. Though presumably not in groups. Very carefully she replaced the book and put everything else back as she had found it and then shut the drawer. To say anything to anybody else about her find would be more than her life was worth. It must remain her secret.

4

1937

Mary was always to remember 1937 as the year she fell in love with Godfrey. Others would recall it for different reasons. For the moment however the activities of Hitler in the Rhineland and elsewhere, though they concerned Geoffrey Harding, did not as yet cast a shadow over day-to-day life in rural England. The boys came home for Easter but to everybody's unspoken relief it appeared that their father was not expected. The weather was unseasonably mild, diffused buttery light alternating with rain of such fineness that silver clouds of it drifted through the air.

At fifteen, though not yet a woman, Mary was sensitive enough to be more than just a naïve girl. With sensitivity went understanding and with understanding went pain. In her heart of hearts she knew that Godfrey was unattainable, although knowledge did not cure the longing. But that was not all: the old easy friendship had gone. The twins were the same but Godfrey was not. Godfrey was now almost nineteen and no longer enamoured of the country or, it seemed, of his own family. He spent a lot of time in his own room, and none of them knew how he passed his time. It was amazing that a few months could make so much difference, and yet it had to be said that even Byronic brooding suited him. Godfrey withdrawn and morose was as compelling as Godfrey open and charming. If anything the air of inaccessibility was more potent. *Noli me tangere.*

Watching her daughter's eyes dwelling on the unattainable eldest brother when she supposed nobody else to be looking, Sibyl Fox was baffled. It caused her to wonder how a child of hers could be both so intelligent and so obtuse, especially after all her strictures of the subject of female self-preservation. Up till now, despite their different stations in the life of the house, the co-existence of the Foxes and the Hardings had worked well because among themselves the

20

children perceived no boundaries. Love and adolescence, however, were likely to be a different kettle of fish. Of course, she reminded herself, Mary was only fifteen and (here Sibyl was aware of grasping at straws) this was the age of the crush. Hopefully, it would all pass and, when Godfrey went back to school, subside. If her daughter had confided in her, she might have been tempted to speak to her along these lines, even promote the idea of either William or Jonty instead, but Mary did not confide.

Although on the surface all seemed tranquil, other under-currents were becoming apparent. There was, for instance, the day Sibyl saw Nettie coming from the direction of the stables. Nettie, who appeared to be fiddling with the top button of her blouse, did not see Sibyl. There was a replete look of satisfaction about her, an air of someone who had been doing what they should not have been doing. It was hard to escape the feeling that Nettie had been up to no good, particularly because in the course of her teaching Sibyl had noticed that Nettie was slipping away. There was nothing in particular, just a sensation of detachment as if, during her lessons, her charge was there in body and not in spirit. Of course Nettie never had been studious. Stirring elopement poetry such as Sir Walter Scott's Young Lochinvar aside, she had always been able to take or leave academic pursuits. Maybe I'm imagining it, thought Sibyl. Or, on the other hand, perhaps, like Godfrey, Nettie was beginning to point towards a different horizon, one which no longer included life as she had so far known it.

The possible key to it came the day they commenced ; study of Tudor poetry beginning with that of Sir Thomas Wyatt.

> '. . . but once especiall,
> In thinne aray, after a pleasant gyse,
> When her loose gowne did from her shoulders fall,
> And she me caught in her arms both long and small,
> And therwithall, so swetely did me kysse,
> And softly sayd: deare hart, how like you this?'

Mary's voice was clear though low. She read with expression and appreciation.

'It was no dreame: for I lay broade awakyng . . .'

It was at this point that Sibyl looked up from the text and caught the expression on Nettie's face. Her look was knowing, redolent of hidden laughter. I have a secret, it said, and it's the same as Sir Thomas Wyatt's. A vision of the new stable hand, a muscular youth called Joshua, presented itself before Sibyl's inner eye. Whatever had or had not been going on, it raised the question of who was responsible for Nettie's moral welfare. Not me, thought Sibyl. I like Nettie but as far as I'm concerned this is one for Mrs Harding to sort out. That's supposing she even notices.

'But, sins that I unkyndly so am served:
How like you this, what hath she now deserved?' recited Mary in conclusion. She put down the book. 'What a wonderful poem!'

'Isn't it?' said Sibyl. 'There is a theory that he was referring to Anne Boleyn. If so, it was a dangerous liaison, for when she was disgraced and subsequently executed, other purported lovers went to the scaffold too.' There was a silence at the end of this speech. Mary was silent. Even Nettie was sobered. Both were struck by the savagery of such an end to the romantic delights of love.

All the same, Nettie was not deterred from keeping her assignation with Joshua in the tack-room of the stables. This was Joshua's little domain, and at a chilly time of year the windowless tack-room was surprisingly snug. The masculine fragrance of saddle-soaped leather pervaded the air in a small space which was full of the organized clutter of saddles, bridles, head collars, hats, boots and whips.

The first time the two of them had made inexpert love the tumble had taken place in the hay barn. Nettie found the hours spent removing the evidence, in the shape of millions of small darts of hay all over her clothing and her hair, a bore. At the next assignation, very practical, she disrobed in the doorway and advanced into the hay-barn naked under the mesmerized gaze of the more modest Joshua. Truth to tell, Joshua, who was the same age as Godfrey, had not at first wanted what had happened but Miss Nettie (as he still thought of her) had been very persistent. Now he found himself addicted. Well aware that, should they be discovered, he would be at most horse-whipped and at least sacked by the bellicose Mr Harding, Joshua nevertheless craved Nettie's peachy body and was prepared to risk a lot to go on enjoying it. Sometimes he wondered whether perhaps he was in love.

For Nettie herself the whole experience had a different slant. There could be no question of being in love with Joshua. In the world of the Hardings, class forbade it. Nettie might briefly deign but never commit. What she learnt from Joshua was the potential power of her own performance in bed or rather, in this case, under a horse blanket. As a result of it, Joshua was in thrall. She, on the other hand, while she found the lean hardness of a man's body against her own exciting, did not confuse physical engagement with romantic engagement. So far as Nettie could see the whole arrangement could go on until she went off to be finished. Since the boys had gone to boarding-school, nobody apart from the odd house guest rode these days, making the tack-room the perfect venue for such clandestine encounters.

Nettie's secret drove a wedge between herself and Mary. Hitherto the two girls had confided everything in one another but there could be no question of doing that in this case, and not just because the governess happened to be her best friend's mother. Mary was not only cleverer than she was, though as Nettie honestly acknowledged to herself this was not difficult, but there was a probity about Mary which, while it would not have suited herself, Nettie recognized and took into account. Mary would not, for instance, have used Joshua the way she was doing. Well, thought Nettie, neatly side-stepping the moral dimension, we are all different.

That afternoon Geoffrey Harding turned up without warning from London with a colleague. As he might have foreseen, this threw his wife into a panic, and likewise, when the news was relayed to her, Mrs Boswell the cook. Somehow, between the two of them, they did manage to cobble together four courses and by the time the family gathered in the drawing-room for drinks before dinner there was at least a semblance of calm.

Sibyl Fox self-effacingly remained on the fringe of the conversation and because she did so was able to observe Mr Harding, whom she hardly ever saw, and his house guest,

Rafe Bartholomew. Bartholomew, who was tall and dark, had a clever, aquiline face and a moustache. There was a studied elegance in his dress and the way he leant against the mantelpiece, and he listened more than he spoke. This was probably just as well since, as usual, Geoffrey Harding had a great deal to say. But Bartholomew was not just listening. He was assessing too. Watching his expressionless eye flick over the room and the other people in it, Sibyl was aware of a sudden resonance as though a subtle chord had been struck. It was a disturbing mental reverberation which she was at a loss to explain.

Mary and Nettie were sitting on one of the sofas whispering so Sybil decided to engage the twins, who were also on the edge of the group, in conversation. It was no longer part of her remit to teach them and so when Jonty and William were at home, apart from mealtimes during which the conversation was more general, she saw little of them. Both were still relatively uncomplicated, but no doubt this would change as it had with Godfrey. Physically Jonty had a look of his father about him these days and there was something else as well. Sibyl tried to put her finger on it and came up with the word impervious. As with Geoffrey Harding, subtlety would not be Jonty's forte. On the whole she preferred his twin. Turning to William she said, 'How's school these days? It's amazing to think that you'll soon be leaving.'

'Oh, it's all right, Mrs Fox,' said William, summoning all the eloquence normally associated with one rising eighteen.

'What sports have you been doing?'

'Fives and I'm hoping to row next half.'

Silence.

It really was like getting blood out of a stone. 'Did you see much of Godfrey when he was still there?' persevered Sibyl, sipping her dry sherry. 'Because you were in the same house, weren't you?'

The twins exchanged looks. There was a hesitation which might have been born out of a fervent wish that the question would go away. Probably was born out of just that, thought Sibyl, who was good at deciphering that sort of ambiguous nuance. She raised her eyebrows, indicating that she was still waiting for an answer. 'A bit,' said Jonty at last, speaking for the first time.

'But he *was* in your house, wasn't he?' persisted Sibyl, who was beginning to wonder if she had in fact got that right. She found their reluctance to talk about their brother extraordinary. Clearly something was going on.

William was just opening his mouth to frame some sort of reply when dinner was announced. His relief at the reprieve was obvious.

'Tonight,' said Davina Harding, as though announcing some arcane ritual to the accompaniment of a fanfare, 'there is a Placement.'

They all took their seats. Between his subtle, understated friend and his languid, etiolated wife, Geoffrey Harding looked larger than life, like an irascible, bucolic squire. Silence fell as they ate Mrs Boswell's excellent soup.

Rafe Bartholomew addressed Nettie. He did not condescend to her youth the way certain adults do. Smoothly he asked her about her life in the country. Just as seamlessly he drew her elder brother into the conversation and then he inclined to Mary, enmeshing her also in the fine net of his considerable charm. While he talked and listened he assessed. Nettie, Sibyl noticed, had become blatantly flirtatious, flashing her eyes at her father's guest. Probably because in common with the rest of them she had been drinking wine, her colour was high. That evening she was wearing dark green velvet, a product of Davina Harding's unerring dress sense. Mary, who owned nothing comparable, was wearing something similar in midnight blue which Nettie had lent her and looked distinctly less glamorous. However, while appearing to listen intently to Nettie's inconsequential chat, Bartholomew was in fact concentrating on Godfrey and Mary, opposite him. In Bartholomew's world moderately bright, moderately pretty, gently reared girls such as Nettie were ten a penny. Mary Fox he divined to be cast in a different mould, and because of this she interested him. One day, he decided, she might become a beauty but, because of her modesty, not one of the obvious variety. Her looks would be of the intelligent, luminous sort which come as much from within as without and would probably bloom later rather than sooner. Though as the daughter of a governess it was doubtful whether this would do her much good.

Answering a rather silly question of Nettie's, Bartholomew took in Jonty and William, though he could not hear the conversation they were having with Sibyl Fox. As a type, he sized up Jonty as being closer to Nettie in terms of character than William, despite the fact that they were twins. There was a confident aura of *I know who I am and what is due to me* about Jonty whereas William struck Rafe as altogether more reflective. The whole brood must have inherited their looks from Davina. Certainly it couldn't have been from old Geoffrey. Although the Harding children were all handsome, there was no doubt that Godfrey was the flower of them all. His beauty was quite startling. Bartholomew's mind rather than his eyes rested for a moment on his host with disdain and then, once more with appreciation, on his host's eldest son.

Feeling himself out of the conversation in his own house, Geoffrey was correspondingly irritable. In the absence of anything else to do he let his eye range along the table and was surprised to encounter the green gaze of the normally demure Mrs Fox. The look of frank invitation that she sent him occupied one split second before she modestly looked down at her plate again. All the same it had been unmistakable, but before he had time to consider it further the arrival of the next course diverted him and did not enhance his mood. His eyebrows drew together.

'What's this, what's this?' It was an accusation more than a question. 'It looks like rabbit but it can't be because, as you know, Davina, I abhor rabbit.'

The table fell silent. Sibyl Fox let the mask slip for an instant, revealing a sly glee which was noticed by Rafe Bartholomew. There was a distinctly vulpine quality about her pointed face.

'Yes. Yes it *is*. It *is* rabbit. You see, Geoffrey, you didn't give us . . .' The transparent hands began to writhe. 'We had no idea you and . . . and then suddenly here you both were . . .'

It was painful to behold. Suavely pretending that he had not heard the previous exchange in its entirety, Bartholomew said, 'Did I hear someone say rabbit? Excellent! It's my favourite. And now, Mrs Harding, you must allow me to compliment you on your exquisite house. It is not often one

26

encounters such impeccable taste. How lucky you are to have such a clever wife, Geoffrey.'

Dinner ground on. After it the two men retreated to the library with their brandies and cigars where they must have had a great deal to discuss for they remained closeted within until well beyond midnight.

The following day was Saturday. That meant lessons in the morning but a free afternoon.

'There's a market on the village green. Why don't we take a picnic and bicycle over there,' suggested Mary to Nettie.

Nettie, who had grown out of such simple pleasures the day she seduced Joshua, said, 'I'd love to except that I'm not feeling too well. I think I might lie down this afternoon.'

This was so unlike the normally resilient Nettie that Mary was astonished, but in the end she decided to go by herself. The bicycle was of the high-handlebarred, bone-shaker variety with a basket on the front. Rattling along on it, hair streaming and with the sun on her face, Mary temporarily put the agony of unrequited love to one side and prepared to enjoy the day. Out of the house and away from the proximity of Godfrey, optimism asserted itself over realism. Maybe Godfrey *would* fall in love with her. After all why not? Tennyson sprang to mind:

> *As shines the moon in clouded skies,*
> *She in her poor attire was seen:*
> *One praised her ankles, one her eyes,*
> *One her dark hair and lovesome mien.*
> *So sweet a face, such angel grace,*
> *In all that land had never been:*
> *Cophetua sware a royal oath:*
> *'This beggar maid shall be my queen!'*

However, even in her current hopeful mood, Mary had to admit that while the prospect of Godfrey as her King Cophetua was enticingly romantic, outside Tennyson's poetry the chance of such a thing happening was inherently unlikely. Gloom threatened to descend again. Resolutely she pedalled on. The sun had gone in for the moment but a high, light sky indicated that the rain might hold off. She rode through the village towards the duck pond and the green.

The market was mainly farm produce, some of it live. Mary loved the noise and the bustle. She wished Nettie could be here to share it with her. Life in the big house could be monotonous and sometimes she was aware of a restlessness, a need to spread her wings outside its protection. She propped the bike against a wall and walked around the stalls. She especially loved the eggs which were all different sizes, brown and speckled, some still with a small feather clinging to them and packed in straw. Their curved dull sheen reminded Mary of stones worn smooth by the sea. Beside them were vast farmhouse cheeses and large blocks of butter which had been beaten into shape by ridged wooden spatulas and now reposed on raised rectangular white china platters with the words PURE BUTTER printed on the front. She wandered on, eating a piece of cheese which the owner of one of the stalls had given her. On either side hung hams and poultry juxtaposed with horizontal sticks from which depended half a dozen dead rabbits at a time. Right at the end of the market, beyond the honey and preserves and homemade cake was the livestock in the form of a group of cacophonous chickens, some geese and a comatose pig. Time to start back and stop on the way to eat her sandwich. As if endorsing her plan the sun came out again.

By the time Mary got to her favourite picnic place by a stream the exercise had made her very hot. Anticipating a treat, she was more than a little put out to discover that someone else had got there before her. A small caravan whose gaudy paint was flaking was tucked into a small clearing some way off the road, beside which a narrow path wound through the undergrowth to the brook. Nearby an unharnessed and untethered piebald pony peacefully cropped the grass. The door of the caravan was shut. Mary skirted both as quietly as she could and followed the little track to the bank of the stream. This had been the setting for many other picnics through the years with cucumber sandwiches and ginger beer and cream soda, her mother presiding during the school holidays. Until they grew out of such childish pursuits, they had all fished for sticklebacks and when the nets dropped off the ends of the canes, which they all invariably did sooner

28

or later, William, who was a good sort, was the one deputed to wade in and get them. Today, because of the rain, the water was high and elegantly iridescent dragon-flies, natty as the sequinned chorus line of a Hollywood movie, swooped and darted.

Sitting among the celandine and buttercups, Mary opened the cardboard box which contained her sandwiches and began to eat with relish. By the time she had finished she was very thirsty and the sight of the sluggish stream exacerbated it. She should have brought a bottle of water with her. It occurred to her to wonder if the inhabitant of the caravan might not have some. She rose to her feet and, leaving the bicycle where it was, retraced her steps along the track. This time the front door (if it could be called a front door) was open.

'Hello?' called Mary, and was rewarded by a trusting 'Come in, dear!'

She climbed the wooden steps, bowed her head and entered. The tiny interior was cluttered. A narrow bed, a table and two chairs took up most of the floor space and every flat surface was covered with bric-à-brac. In the middle of it all sat a small person who appeared to be engaged in making artificial flowers.

'Sit down, sit down!' commanded her hostess, without desisting from what she was doing. 'My name's Rosa. What's yours? You didn't happen to notice what that horse is doing, by the way, did you?'

'Mary, and it seemed fine to me,' answered Mary. 'It's just standing about eating grass and being a horse. It isn't going anywhere. Look, I hope you don't think this is a cheek, but I wondered if I might trouble you for—'

'A glass of water,' said Rosa. 'Bless you dear, of course you can!' She gave her visitor a piercing look and then set aside the flower she had been working on and got up to get some out of a large billy can. Over one shoulder she said, 'But that's not what you're really here for, is it?'

Mary was astonished. 'What else would I be here for?'

'Knowledge, of course!' Disconcertingly, Rosa looked both at Mary and beyond her as she said the words. 'Secret knowledge. I've been waiting for you.'

Waiting for her?

Mary felt her flesh creep.

It was beginning to seem that nothing was straightforward in this world, not even asking for a glass of water. She stared. Patiently Rosa said, 'I'm a Romany. I have The Knowledge. I do sittings for the curious at summer fêtes and the like.'

A fortune teller.

Mary drank her water at a swallow. She would have liked to extract herself from the situation, which was becoming more bizarre by the minute, but did not know how to do so.

'Now,' Rosa was continuing, 'the point I'm making is that timing is all.' Surprised, and also wary, Mary said nothing. 'Why did you come today? If you hadn't, you wouldn't have seen me because I'm moving on tonight. *You* could say it's a coincidence but *I* don't. I say there is no such thing as coincidence. I say there is something you have to know and my job is to tell it to you and *that's* why you're here. Get down the square leather box on the shelf behind you, take out what you find inside and hold it in both hands for a minute or so. Then give it to me.'

Rosa's authority was not to be flouted. Mary obeyed. The crystal was warm, she noticed. Fascinated by its spherical perfection, she let it fall from hand to hand. It reflected the inverted interior of the caravan and then, disconcertingly and suddenly, it did not. It clouded. Watching her sharply, Rosa said, 'I'll take it now!'

Even though the door was still open to the bright normality of a summer day it was as though the two of them were sealed off. The silence within the caravan was all at once profound and the air dense as though there had been a distillation, a filtering out of the mundane.

'And now . . . now let us see what was, what is and what will be . . .'

Rosa's voice was dreamy, her eyes curiously opaque, like those of a blind person. It was as though her sight was temporarily turned inward so that the outside world was not there at all. Physically she seemed to alter too, as though she had grown in stature so that her presence, like that of a high priestess, dominated the small space within which they sat.

She began to speak. Even the voice was different. Other-worldly, she moved forwards and backwards down the years, apparently time travelling with ease.

What was . . . what is . . . what will be . . .

Some of her forays into the past were eerily accurate, others might have been. Mary had no way of knowing. One startling assertion in particular, connected with her mother, she was inclined to dismiss out of hand. It was inconceivable. All the same, the high degree of correctness where other matters were concerned was unsettling. The future was not a comfortable proposition either but that, for the moment, would have to take care of itself.

There followed quite a long silence and Mary was just starting to assume with relief that the unsolicited sitting was over when, unexpectedly and shockingly, it all tipped over into something altogether more sinister. Rosa's breathing started to escalate. Like an asthmatic, she began to pant. Her distress was palpable. Transfixed and frightened, Mary sat there looking at her, uncertain what to do. Panic reigned. The rasping, laboured breathing intensified, then, 'Where am I?' screamed Rosa. 'Water! There's water everywhere.'

Eyes closed, she threw back her head apparently sucking in lungfuls of air, flailing her arms as if trying to keep afloat and then shouted in a man's voice, 'I don't want to die! Dear God, don't let me drown!' Mary could feel the terrible fear. She felt mentally buffeted by it. It was invasive, all around, a suffocating, dreadful thing.

And then suddenly the tension dropped.

Rosa was ashen. She did not speak again but slumped in her chair. Slowly her breathing began to stabilize and it seemed to Mary that whatever it was she had just witnessed had quite literally run out of energy. There was an indefinable sensation of lightening all around and the air appeared to whiten, as though something dark was withdrawing.

Rosa shook her head and opened her eyes.

Mary found herself to be trembling violently. What to do next, apart from leave as quickly as possible?

'Are you all right, Rosa?' she ventured faintly at last.

Rosa looked surprised. 'Yes, dear.'

It was as though nothing had happened.

Am I going mad? Mary asked herself. Did I imagine the

whole thing? Should I offer to pay? Would Rosa be offended if I did or offended if I did not?

'No need to give me anything,' said Rosa, apparently still in clairvoyant mode but otherwise back to normal, adding more obscurely, 'After all, you didn't ask for it. That was in the interests of Fate not Commerce!' She stood up, no longer a priestess but a small, rather ordinary, black-haired, blue-eyed woman in a floral print dress who seemed all at once very tired. 'I hope that was useful. I don't know what I'm saying in trance, you know. You wouldn't like to give me a hand with the horse, would you?'

By the time Mary had done so, the weather was threatening to close in. Riding back to the house, she was in turmoil. It was not only the unnerving scene that she had just witnessed which disturbed her, but also, among other things, the extraordinary statement concerning her mother. She told herself to stop being ridiculous. It was, of course, all nonsense.

Because of the sensitive nature of some of what Rosa had said, Mary decided to tell no one, not even Nettie, about her strange experience. Nettie would want to know everything. She did, however, bring up the subject of Rosa with Mrs Boswell. 'You don't know anything about a gypsy called Rosa who sometimes does readings at the village fêtes, do you?'

'I should say so!' The answer was heartfelt enough to indicate that possibly Rosa's impact on the small community had been out of proportion when set beside her comparatively fleeting visits.

'Is she usually accurate?'

'Yes. Very! *Too* accurate in my view! What Rosa's said has caused a lot of trouble. Some sleeping dogs are best left to lie!'

Nettie arrived at the tack-room before Joshua. She threw a pile of rugs on the floor and was in the process of arranging them as a reasonably comfortable rustic bed when her lover arrived. She immediately desisted from housewifely fussing and got on with what she was really here for. Kissing Joshua, she undid the buttons of his shirt and then the buttons of his trousers.

'Come on.' Nettie was very impatient. 'What about me?'

With a start, Joshua, who could never quite believe this was happening to him, got on with undressing Nettie and finally there they stood, naked, an adolescent Adam and Eve. As his mesmerized eye took in her round, high breasts, small waist and plump hips which tapered into surprisingly slender legs, she was gratified by the immediate physical response.

'Oh, Miss . . . Oh, Nettie . . . You're *lovely*.' Her skin felt like velvet under his rough, boy's hands. He was afraid of hurting her.

'Let's get under the rugs,' said Nettie. 'I'm cold!' She pulled him down onto the makeshift bed, her animated face framed by auburn curls laughing up at him as she did so. She drew Joshua to her so that she could feel his young strong body against her own and his penis, hard and straight, between her thighs. This is bliss, thought Nettie, absolute bliss. Whoever would have thought making love was so easy? It was hard to imagine her parents indulging in such an act but obviously they must have. Well, three times, anyway.

When it was all over, Joshua tenderly covered his little mistress with one of the blankets. Still on certain levels a child, Nettie fell asleep almost immediately, her head on his shoulder. As he looked at her face and the rosy swell of her breasts, he was conscious of a surge of complex emotion but, had he been asked to articulate exactly what it was, could not have done so. Lying beside her, eyes open, Joshua mulled over what was happening between himself and Nettie and came to no useful conclusion whatsoever. Except that it was hugely enjoyable. And threatening. If his employers found out what he was up to he would lose his job. Better not to think too hard but just take every day as it came. He wondered what the time was. Joshua did not possess anything as expensive as a watch and usually relied on the stable clock during the course of his duties. Very slowly, trying not to disturb her, he eased his arm from under Nettie's head and got up. Unlike her he had work to do.

Geoffrey Harding and Rafe Bartholomew were once again sitting in the library. This departure from the usual was a huge relief to Davina who was used to doing without her own drawing-room for long periods of time when Geoffrey was at home. Reminiscent of a Mucha poster, art nouveau drifts of blue cigar smoke hung in the air. Bartholomew finished his whisky and went and stood by the window. A girl came bicycling up the drive as he watched and a closer look revealed that it was Mary Fox. As she arrived, rain began to silently fall on the park out of a lowering sky. She had made it just in time. He turned back to Harding.

'The question is, what do we do?' said Bartholomew.

'Nothing to do for the present,' replied Harding. 'And, of course, that might be the right course of action. It depends whether Herr Hitler is a man of his word. Chamberlain considers he is.'

Bartholomew, who thought Chamberlain was an ass and quite possibly a dangerous ass, privately doubted it.

'Winston Churchill doesn't think so,' he observed at last.

'Oh, *Churchill.*' Harding was dismissive. 'Man's a turn-coat.'

Since it was Bartholomew's view that Harding was an ass along with Chamberlain, albeit a powerful one, he was not impressed by this last declaration.

Mildly he said, 'Firstly he isn't the only one and secondly that doesn't stop him being right, and his view of what is currently happening in Germany is that it's a serious threat to future peace. And what about the occupation of the Rhineland? It's a blatant violation of both the Treaty of Locarno and the Treaty of Versailles and the League of Nations hasn't done a bloody thing about it. Next stop Austria.'

Harding frowned and did not immediately answer. There were times when he thought his high-flying younger companion was too clever for his own good. Bartholomew felt inclined to give up on it. The room in which they sat was airless and stuffy. Outside the streaming windows of the library the park was now all gusting rain and muted shades of green and grey, an English water-colour. He had a sudden urge to be out in the clean fresh air and to feel the weather in his face.

'I could do with some exercise. What about a walk?'

Harding stood up. 'All right.' He stared gloomily out at the weather. 'Let's get a couple of riding macs. That should do the trick.'

'Good idea.'

As they descended the stairs together, Harding put his hand on the other man's shoulder in an avuncular manner. 'You know, Rafe, courtesy of my age, I've had more experience of international politics than you have and my instinct tells me that things will settle down. After the last war, I think Germany has too much to lose to try and upset the European apple cart a second time. And if they try, the League of Nations will flex some muscle, make damn sure they don't succeed.'

The League of Nations? Flex some muscle? Christ almighty! In Bartholomew's opinion the League of Nations had no backbone at all. Look at the feeble response, if you could even call it that, to the Italian invasion of Abyssinia. It was probably watching Mussolini get away with it that had prompted Hitler to overrun the Rhineland.

Feeling patronized, as he was no doubt meant to, Bartholomew elected to say nothing. Given Geoffrey's unshakeable complacency, there seemed no point. It was becoming apparent that two days spent trying to alert him to the fact that European peace might be approaching flash point had been a complete waste of time.

Wrapped in the horse blanket, Nettie was standing kissing Joshua when she heard the sound of voices approaching the tack-room door. She froze. Years later, laughing about it, Nettie was to say, 'You read about people's hair standing on end in books. As a result of that day I know what it feels like!' Equally frightened was Joshua who, against his better instincts, had succumbed to his lover's plea to stay a little longer and who had been about to let himself out. They both looked around in desperation. There was nowhere to hide. Neither had thought to turn the key in the lock, which just might have saved the day. It was too late now.

At the house Mary went in search of Nettie but could not find her. She was not in her room so presumably whatever had been the matter earlier was no longer bothering her. In the course of looking for her she stumbled upon Godfrey. Hands behind his head, he was lying on his back on the shabby sofa in the day nursery where they had all spent so much time together, staring up at the ceiling. His air

35

of isolation was practically tangible. Betrayed by her own feelings, Mary blushed.

'Oh, I'm sorry, Godfrey, I didn't mean to disturb you. I was looking for Nettie.'

He shrugged. 'That's all right. But I'm afraid my sister isn't here.' Speaking the words, he turned his face slightly towards her for a moment, so that it briefly caught the fading light from the window and, as he did so, she saw with a shock that Godfrey had been crying. After the initial surprise, the impulse to take him in her arms was almost overwhelming.

Aware from her expression that she had seen his distress, he raised one hand, 'Look, don't say anything, Mary. There's nothing anybody can do. It's something I have to work out by myself.' That, to coin a phrase, had been that. As she was going, he said, 'Mary.'

She paused at the door.

'Yes?'

'Don't tell anyone else that I was . . . was upset, will you? Especially not Nettie.'

'No, of course I won't.'

'I want it to be our secret.'

'I know.'

So now she and Godfrey had a secret. But what was it? Why was he upset? In a few days the holiday would be over. After that she would not see him again until the summer. Then he would no doubt go to university and out of her orbit altogether. I must say something before he goes, thought Mary. I must know if there is any hope for me.

The tack-room door opened and the light snapped on. Godfrey Harding stood on the threshold with Rafe Bartholomew just behind him.

'Good God!'

A dreadful silence and then 'What's going on here?' It was a roar rather than a polite enquiry.

Nettie went scarlet. She opened her mouth but no words came.

It was perfectly obvious to Bartholomew what was going on there. Tactfully he stepped backwards, out of the light and into the shadows. From the rear he could see a flush the colour of one of his own bottles of vintage claret rising up the back of the other man's neck.

'Get out,' shouted Harding at Joshua. 'Get out! I'll deal with you later!'

Joshua fled.

'And you,' addressing Nettie and still shouting, 'you little whore, get your clothes on and then I want to see you in my study. Straight away! Understand?'

'Father, you don't understand –'

'Are you arguing with me? Are you?' He took a step towards his daughter and raised his hand. 'Get back to the house!'

Unedifying, thought Bartholomew listening to it. During the three years he had worked with Harding he had become familiar with the way his host bullied junior staff. The treatment of his family was in another dimension altogether.

'Yes, Father.' Nettie was weeping, all bravado gone.

Harding turned on his heel and slammed the door. He stood for a moment breathing heavily and then strode off, stiff-backed and bristling, a puce martinet, in the direction of the main house, past Bartholomew whom he seemed to have forgotten all about. Hardly surprising in the circumstances. A short while later he was followed by Nettie, now dressed and still sobbing, who did not see her father's house guest either. Knuckles pressed to her eyes, she looked absurdly young.

From the first, despite the breeding or maybe because of it, Bartholomew had marked Harding's daughter down as a primitive, and saw no reason to change his assessment of her after the scene he had just witnessed. For his own instinctive reasons he felt that this was useful knowledge. A superlative chess player, Bartholomew usually operated several moves ahead on all fronts. For the moment the potential usefulness of Nettie was beyond his game plan. All the same, he filed her away in his very good memory for future reference. There was no doubt in his mind that, on certain levels, Nettie would go far, though not necessarily in the direction her socially ossified parents had in mind.

Bartholomew permitted himself a sardonic smile.

When she had gone, he let himself into the tack-room and after some searching found what they had gone there for in the first place, namely a full-length riding mac. As he was putting it on, he eyed the pile of rugs on the floor and laughed to himself. 'Courage, Nettie,' said Bartholomew aloud to no one, after which he buttoned up the coat and went for a walk in the rain by himself.

On his return the darkness was beginning to gather. A swag of aubergine cloud shot with crimson looped the far horizon, forming a spectacular backdrop for a sinking sun the colour of a blood orange. There was a sombre, portentous magnificence about such a sky, a sense of the world stage being set. But for what? Bartholomew, who feared he knew, shuddered.

Back at the house there was no sign of Harding or his errant daughter. In search of company Bartholomew put his head around the library door and discovered Jonty and Mary, who must just have finished a game, resetting the chessboard.

He nodded to Mary and then said to Jonty, 'Have you just finished?'

'Yes, sir.' Jonty, who had just been trounced again, was getting fed up with it.

'Would you like to give me a game?'

Jonty felt he had enough ritual humiliation for one day. Good manners towards a guest, however, dictated that he should graciously acquiesce. There was only one way of getting out of it. Sounding more generous than he felt, he replied, 'Actually Mary would give you a better run for your money than I would. She's very good.'

If Bartholomew was surprised by this suggestion, he did not show it. He turned to her.

'Would you do me the honour?'

Unlike some young women Mary Fox did not blush or prevaricate but simply said, 'Yes, of course.'

'Excellent!'

They both sat down.

'Your move.'

She moved a pawn.

With his mind half on the game, which was unlikely to be exacting, and half on what he and Geoffrey Harding had been talking about earlier, Bartholomew moved one of his.

Mary moved her queen.

'Checkmate, I think!' she murmured.

What?

He put the threatening international situation to one side and concentrated totally on the board. Fool's mate! He must have been twelve when he last fell for that one.

'I'm sorry.' Mary smiled at him. 'You don't mind, do you?'

Only half in jest, he replied, 'Mind? Of course I mind! I'm supposed to be a classy chess player and Miss Mary Fox has just wiped me off the board in three moves. I demand an immediate return match to salvage what I can of my tattered reputation!'

They began again and this time he did not make the error of underestimating his charming adversary. On one level it was no contest. All the same, she was very good. A natural, in fact. Not as good as he was, of course, but still a worthy opponent. With experience and a more sophisticated teacher than Jonty, whom she had clearly already overtaken, she would in time be a truly formidable opponent. Her capacity to think several moves ahead was impressive and so was the concentration. Under siege Mary Fox did not panic.

Eventually, 'Checkmate,' said Rafe. Feeling honour was satisfied he sat back in his chair and studied her with respect for a moment. 'Tell me, Mary, what else do you know? You clearly understand the moves and have a grasp of strategy but what about the openings and variations?'

'Oh heavens, none of that,' relied Mary frankly. 'I don't think Jonty does either and he's the one who taught me how to play.' She began to put the pieces away in the box. 'I'd like to learn more though.'

And she should. He made a mental note to send her a book when he finally got back to London.

'Do you think you could find the time to play me again tomorrow?'

Secretly pleased and very flattered, this time Mary did blush. She nodded.

'And I owe you an apology.'

Surprised, she looked up.

'Yes. When I suggested a game I addressed Jonty and ignored you. It was unforgivable and not a mistake I shall make again.'

With a half bow he left her. Intrigued, she watched him go.

5

Wrapped in a white sheet which gave him a Roman look, Godfrey was sitting up in bed reading. It was almost one o'clock in the morning. Apart from the occasional bark of a dog fox in the park the silence was absolute. Topaz light diffused by the parchment shade of his bedside lamp enveloped him and formed a nimbus around his blond head. Outside its charmed circle the grape-coloured darkness was intense. This particular room was away from the main children's wing of the house, something for which Godfrey, who had long grown out of the communal spirit of the nursery end, was grateful.

The unmistakable sound, then, of a soft footfall in the corridor outside was alerting at this time of night. With a mixture of anticipation and apprehension he looked up from the book. Whoever it was did not knock but turned the brass knob and gently, eerily pushed the door so that it slowly swung open, revealing Godfrey half lying, like a young god, within the dazzle of light.

'I'm so sorry,' said the sable shadow on the threshold. 'I seem to have got the wrong room.'

This was the moment of truth and Godfrey recognized it as such. Fight it as he might, and he had been fighting it for years, either he confronted what he knew in his heart of hearts or he denied it and, in so doing, denied the essence of himself.

'No,' said Godfrey. 'No, you haven't got the wrong room.'

He closed his book and put it to one side.

And waited.

In another part of the house Geoffrey Harding was finding it difficult to sleep. The memory of Mrs Fox's predatory emerald gaze interlocking with his own was hard to shift. Its power still surprised him. Hitherto he had hardly noticed her, but then hitherto there had been nothing to notice. The unveiling of the eyes had been like a theatre curtain going up on a totally different production from the one he thought he had booked. Restlessly, he turned over and over in bed and finally consulted his watch. Quarter to one. There was one certain way of getting off to sleep. Harding got up, put on his dressing-gown, a tartan affair with a cord bought during the last shooting expedition in Scotland, opened his bedroom door and set off along the corridor. Padding along it he fancied he heard footsteps ahead of him. Perhaps someone else was unable to sleep. He stopped at his wife's bedroom door and softly knocked. There was no response. He knocked again, this time with more emphasis. Still no response. She was probably asleep. Davina needed a lot of sleep and, as he knew to his cost, was also prone to strategic headaches. No headaches allowed tonight. He turned the handle.

The door was locked.

It must be locked against him. There was nobody else likely to ravish his wife in the middle of the night. Short of beating it down and thereby causing a fracas, he could think of no way of gaining entry. Harding felt sorry for himself. What was a wife for if not to keep his bed warm for him when he required it and, given the way they lived, he scarcely ever required it. Now he did and it was not available to him. Well, he had done his best to be a good husband and, in the unsatisfactory circumstances, who could blame him if he looked elsewhere?

He set off towards the nursery wing of the house. Half way there it occurred to him that he did not know which was Mrs Fox's room. Dealing with the governess was Davina's job and he could hardly ask her. By now he was feeling so horny that giving up was unthinkable. Facing the array of doors in the corridor he took a chance, chose one of them and entered.

Nettie sat bolt upright in bed.

'Who is it? I'll scream if you touch me!'

Good God! His daughter!

'Don't scream, Nettie, whatever you do, don't scream!'

'Father?'

'Yes, I thought I heard an intruder,' improvised Harding in a stage whisper. 'I've come to make sure you're all right. And apparently you are, so go back to sleep.'

Sweating, he set off again along the threadbare Turkish

41

runner. Even if he never succeeded in locating the elusive Mrs Fox he should have no trouble getting back to sleep at the end of what was turning into a hike. Right at the end a door was ajar. Approaching it with caution in the light of the last *faux pas*, he put his head round. As he did so there was the sound of a match being struck and then the subdued glow of candlelight spread itself around the room. Sibyl Fox pushed back the bedclothes. She stood up and came towards him and, with a shock, he saw that she was stark naked. The light gave her slim body a golden bloom. When she was within a yard of him she released her hair. Red-gold, it sprang free as though charged with electricity and then slowly unravelled and fell in shining coils over her breasts and shoulders until it reached her waist.

His erection was instantaneous.

Harding had the presence of mind to lock the door. After he had done so, kissing him full on the lips, Sibyl undid the cord and slid the dressing-gown off his shoulders. Then she led him towards her narrow bed.

They had still not exchanged a word.

Much later, furtively returning to his own room remembering her voraciousness and her expertise, Harding felt dazed. He had literally never known anything like it. Her inventive performance certainly eclipsed anything to be found within the pages of *Forbidden Fruit*. As he entered his own corridor once again he thought he heard somebody else moving ahead of him but dismissed it as a figment of his imagination. Back in his own bed he fell into a sated sleep.

Two days later, Geoffrey Harding and Rafe Bartholomew left for London together.

'What charming children you have,' observed Bartholomew as they travelled up by train. Remembering Nettie in the horse blanket, Harding glowered. Noting this and hiding a smile, Rafe continued, 'Godfrey tells me he hopes to go to Oxford and, coincidentally, to my old college Christ Church.'

'Yes, he does.'

'If you approve, Geoffrey, I'd like to offer to take him under my wing. He can stay with me when he's in London and so on. Young men need some sort of guidance from time to time and, as I don't have to tell you, there's a lot of temptation around. Wine, women, gambling . . . you know the sort of thing.'

Geoffrey did, although in the light of what had just happened between himself and the libidinous Mrs Fox, he didn't feel he got tempted often enough. On the whole it seemed a good idea. His own flat was a *pied-à-terre* with one small bedroom. And as a Man About Town who knew everyone, Rafe would be a very useful connection for Godfrey and would keep him on the straight and narrow. After all, look at Nettie. Nettie had been led astray under his own roof with no help from either the fleshpots of the capital or Oxford. If that could happen, anything could.

'I think that's a good idea if it won't inconvenience you too much,' said Harding at last.

'Oh, it won't inconvenience me at all, I assure you. I won't let it.'

Harding lit a cigar and then picked up his newspaper. 'Well, that's very generous of you. I'll mention it to Godfrey the next time I talk to him.'

A week after this conversation took place, Godfrey went to London. All noticed that he seemed much more at one with himself but nobody knew how to account for the sudden change. Mary never saw him on his own again during the remainder of the holiday, so the carefully rehearsed conversation she had been nerving herself for (and quite possibly would not have had the courage to initiate anyway) never took place.

Joshua did not wait to be sacked but gathered up his few belongings and disappeared. His replacement was a strapping female. There was speculation among the children as to what had happened to him.

'One can never rely on that sort of person,' said Davina Harding, attempting to explain it away. Nettie, who had been very subdued lately, said nothing. Watching her employer narrowly, Sibyl Fox wondered if that was the whole story and was frankly sceptical. To her mother's inestimable relief, Nettie got her period. Now they need never refer to what had been a lamentable episode ever again. And hopefully

Geoffrey, whose ire had been dreadful to behold, would put it to the back of his mind too.

The one who never forgot was Joshua. Joshua, who had fallen more than a little in love with Nettie, was damaged. The Harding perception that his love was a sordid, unhealthy thing confused and wounded him. Of course, she was the daughter of his employer and he shouldn't have done it and *wouldn't* have done it if she hadn't pushed it. All the same, I would have died for Nettie, thought Joshua. Alone in his bed at night, remembering her vivacious, laughing face as she pulled him down onto the heap of rugs, Joshua wept.

6

1938

Nettie eventually told Mary all about the fling with Joshua. Not her mother's daughter for nothing, Mary was conscious of a vicarious sexual thrill and also something like envy. Nettie had crossed the divide between innocence and experience and in doing so had left her behind. One way of partially catching up might have been to tell Nettie about her secret love for Godfrey but here natural caution, engendered by an insecure childhood, won the day. Mary did not want her love to become public property.

'Weren't you afraid of becoming pregnant?'

'Not at the time,' her friend replied blithely, 'though it did cross my mind afterwards. And it certainly crossed Mother's. Anyway, it didn't happen.'

'Where did Joshua go?'

'I don't know!' Nettie did not sound too interested. 'He ran away I suppose. When he found out about it, Father beat me and, do you know, I think he enjoyed doing it.'

Mary, who had not been made privy to the goings-on between the covers of *Forbidden Fruit*, was shocked. 'Oh, Nettie, I'm sure he didn't.' Once again, the temptation to confide was almost irresistible and once again she shied away from it. It would have been different, Mary told herself, if Godfrey had not been Nettie's brother. These days he no longer came home unless press-ganged into it by some family celebration, such as his father's birthday, but stayed in London, often, according to Nettie, with Rafe Bartholomew. Rafe appeared to have become Godfrey's mentor.

On the whole, country life could be dull, but there were still some diversions. The twins occasionally brought friends home when they came but pleasant as most of them were, none of these birds of passage touched Mary's heart as Godfrey had done. Nettie pined for nobody. She loved male company and male company loved her. Without being a beauty, she had a certain sparkle and dash which was captivating. Usefully, this went hand in hand with an impressive emotional detachment which meant that, as with the Joshua incident, if anybody got hurt it would not be Nettie.

It was probably the contrast between his noisy sister and Sibyl Fox's daughter which caused William to look at Mary and really see her for the first time. Mary did not flirt like Nettie and, because of Nettie's exuberant personality, tended to get overlooked. Of the twins, William, who was studious, was also the quiet one. At the opposite end of the spectrum, Jonty was loud, sporty and gregarious. The disparity of their characters together with the similarity of their looks was frequently remarked upon.

On this particular day Mary was curled up in one of the large library armchairs reading a book. Her head was propped up on one hand and tilted so that the sweep of her straight shoulder-length hair followed the oval of her face on one side and fell away from it on the other in a shining curtain. But it was the sweet gravity, sadness even, of her expression that really caught his eye. Eyes downcast over the page, enraptured by whatever it was she was reading, she reminded him of nothing so much as a da Vinci madonna. Like Rafe Bartholomew before him, William suddenly saw the possibilities of such a face and wondered why it had taken him so long. At the same time, it occurred to him that, beyond the fact that she was the daughter of the governess, he knew next to nothing about her. Which was strange when one considered that she had been brought up as a member of his own family. Or rather, he corrected himself, almost a member of his own family.

All at once conscious of his gaze upon her, Mary looked up and smiled. The spell was broken.

'Oh, William! I didn't hear you come in.'

She closed her book with one finger keeping the place and he saw that it was *The Golden Bowl*. Uncertain what to do next, and at the same time feeling it necessary to explain to her why he had been standing looking at her silently for as long as he had, William said, 'I'm sorry, I was day-dreaming.' He coloured and hoped she had not noticed. An overwhelming desire to know how she spent her spare time prompted him to ask, 'Do you always read in here?'

'Quite often. Unless your father is using it. It's so peaceful and I love being surrounded by books.'

Through the open window they could hear shrieks and laughter coming from the tennis court where Nettie and Jonty were having a game. It was a chartreuse summer afternoon. The air vibrated with heat. Not a leaf moved. Under a darkly blue sky the garden smelt of freshly mown grass and roses. There was a sense of time standing still, of the world taking a breath. Languorous English summers such as this had been a dependable fact of William's childhood and there seemed no reason why this tranquil state of affairs should not continue. The day after tomorrow he and Jonty were due to go to university. Godfrey. Briefly William confronted Godfrey's school career and then looked away from it. Godfrey must hoe his own row.

On impulse he said, 'Mary!'

Mary, who had gone back to her book in the face of William's obvious distraction, looked up again. 'Yes?'

'Will you write to me while I'm away?'

Her face lit up with pleasure. It was the sort of request which made her feel properly part of the Harding family.

'Yes, I will!'

'Nettie always forgets,' said William, thinking as he spoke the words, Why am I talking about Nettie? Nettie's nothing to do with why I want Mary to write. He briefly wondered what it must be like to be a man of the world like Rafe Bartholomew. How long had it taken him to acquire that particular blend of sure charm and *savoir-faire*? Maybe one didn't acquire such qualities but was born with them. William dismissed that idea. Whoever heard of a baby with *savoir-faire*? There was hope for him yet. Elaborately casual, he said, 'Why don't you join me for a stroll in the garden?' and immediately felt a fool. I sound like a character from a bad film, he thought. Why on earth can't I just be natural? To his unconfident surprise, Mary put her book on the arm of the chair and swung her feet to the floor.

'I'd love to!'

It seemed he must be doing something right.

'Shall we walk to the tennis court?'

There was no doubt that if this happened he would no longer have Mary to himself and the moment of intimacy, if one could call it such a thing, would be lost.

'I had the lily pond in mind,' suggested William, adding, 'I promised Mother I would feed the fish.'

Mary looked amazed, as well she might. Mrs Harding had never to her knowledge shown the slightest interest in the fish. A clandestine fish-feeder, perhaps.

Outside the cool interior of the house the heat of the day was enervating. Mary and William dawdled their way to the pool. On their way they passed the tennis court where a friendly game had become acrimonious. Over the beech hedge Jonty could be heard accusing Nettie of gamesmanship. There was the sound of a tennis racket being thrown down. 'If you say that again I'm not going to play any more,' shouted Nettie, sounding furious.

'There are times,' remarked William, 'when I think my little sister is a spoilt brat.'

'Nobody likes to lose,' murmured Mary.

'Especially Nettie! And certainly not Jonty.'

Unwilling to criticize her friend even to her own brother, Mary did not respond to this. She sent William a sidelong glance. He was like Godfrey and at the same time not like Godfrey. The Harding eyes were there and the dark blond hair and, up to a point, the graceful carriage but, despite all these advantages, William did not produce the same effect on others as Godfrey did. William was more . . . (here Mary hesitated over the word and then allowed it) . . . ordinary. The unique extra dimension of flawless physical perfection was missing, and with it the unconscious princely arrogance of all great beauties. In Godfrey's case this was counterpointed by a sort of melancholy which made him appear both remote and vulnerable at the same time and, to her anyway, infinitely interesting. It would have been heavenly to have been walking through the garden on a summer afternoon with Godfrey rather than with William.

The pool, which was substantial, was round and constructed of stone. In the centre was a marble putto holding a dolphin. When the fountain was turned on, though today it was not, water poured from the mouth of the fish and cascaded over the mauve water hyacinths and carmine lilies which grew at the base of the statue. Though neither William nor Mary knew it, it was here, he sitting on the edge of the pool and she on one of the elegant cast-iron garden seats which surrounded it, that Geoffrey Harding had first proposed to Davina, in those days a haughty beauty in much the same mould as her eldest son. 'No,' said Davina, in charge at that early stage of their relationship, but a year later, on being asked again in exactly the same place (Geoffrey being a creature of habit), she had said Yes. Occasionally reflecting back on it, Davina felt that had she known then what she knew now the second reply would have been No as well. It was one of the reasons why she never went near the place.

Mary sat on the mossy lip of the pool just as Geoffrey Harding had all those years before. She leaned forward and dreamily studied her own reflection in the dark water. She put the tips of the fingers of one hand in the water and ruffled it. The insubstantial image of herself fragmented and then, as the surface calmed, drifted together again. Without appearing to, William observed her. It struck him that there was a sense of isolation about her, probably compounded by the fact that after all their years of childhood friendship, the romantic change in his perception of her made it suddenly impossible to talk to her naturally.

The two of them watched carp and koi as they slipped in and out of the long stalks of the lily pads. The lazy flow of perpetual movement was hypnotic. A combination of blanket weed and sheer depth made it impossible to see the bottom of the pool. Lower down the fish lost definition, and became blurs of red and yellow and orange curving through the blackness like comets.

'Where's the food?' asked Mary at last.

'Oh!' Since the food was not the point of this exercise William had forgotten all about it. 'It's here!'

He reached down into a large terracotta urn, one of a pair, and pulled out a rusty tin and opened it.

'Here, you do it.' He handed it to Mary. *Now I can't even call her by her name. What is the matter with me?*

Mary flung a handful into the pool. The pellets moved through the air in an arc and fell upon the water with a faint, dry rattle like rain. The fish converged on them, wheeling, turning, eating, retreating and returning. The shadow carp particularly fascinated Mary. She preferred them to their gaudier companions. When they turned over in the water, their pale bellies could be seen to be unexpectedly decorated with golden spots, rather like a fop's embroidered waistcoat. She was just going to point it out to William when there was a sudden interruption.

'So this is where you've been,' complained Nettie. 'I've been looking everywhere for you.'

'Oh, Christ!' muttered William under his breath. It was clearly the end of what might have become an idyll if he could only have got his act together in time. Too late now. On impulse he swooped towards the water and snapped the stem of a white water-lily. Disregarding Nettie, he handed the ivory bloom with its pale yellow interior to Mary.

'This is for you,' said William, haste and irritation with his sister producing the sort of spontaneity he had been trying to achieve all afternoon. 'Don't forget your promise.'

He went. Cupping the lily in her hands and reflecting that nobody had ever given her anything before, Mary looked down at it with delight.

'What's got into him?' asked Nettie crossly.

Sibyl Fox received a summons to Davina Harding's little private sitting-room. Jonty and William had returned to university, since when the house had gone back to its normal routine. Davina was doing *petit point* when Sibyl entered. She tucked away the needle.

'Do sit down, Mrs Fox.'

'Thank you, Mrs Harding.'

Mrs Fox. Mrs Harding. It was odd, reflected Sibyl, that the two of them had lived in the same house for ten years, their daughters had grown up together and yet, to each other, they were still Mrs Harding and Mrs Fox.

She prepared to listen.

Davina Harding looked distractedly out of the window for quite some time. Just when Sibyl was beginning to think her employer had forgotten what she had summoned her for, the other woman spoke.

'You remember, Mrs Fox, that when you first applied for this post I said that it would effectively last until Nettie went to finishing-school.'

Here it came. Sibyl nodded.

'Yes I do.'

'I'm afraid that time has come. Nettie is not academic . . .' That much was certainly true although it was Sibyl's view that a personality such as Nettie's would have been enhanced by as much education as she was prepared to tolerate, for Nettie was by no means unintelligent. '. . . and even if she was, it is Geoffrey's view that an overeducated woman is an undesirable thing.'

No danger of that where Nettie was concerned, thought Sibyl.

'You don't think it's perhaps a little early to end Nettie's formal education?' she ventured.

'Nettie will learn French as well as the social graces,' said Davina, side-stepping this with a half answer. Sibyl forbore to point out that Nettie was already learning French. Just. There was no point. The die, it seemed, was cast.

'You would like me to look for another post.' It was a statement, not a question.

'I am afraid so, yes.'

'When does Nettie leave?'

'That is yet to be decided. But soon. She will go to Switzerland to be socially honed by the estimable Madame Vernier.'

Sibyl wondered if Nettie had been told all this yet. If she had there had been no visible sign of it. She stood up. The time had clearly come to start putting pressure on Geoffrey.

'I shall start looking for another post straight away.'

Mrs Harding also stood up.

'Before you go, Mrs Fox, there is something I should like to say, and that is that I am well aware of what has been taking place between you and my husband.'

Oh!

There was a short dead silence of the sort commonly produced by a revelation of the completely unexpected.

Not so stupid after all.

Serenely continuing, with a flutter of the hands, 'Yes, but allow me to reassure you that on that level it is of no concern to me. I would prefer Geoffrey's hot hand to fall on any knee rather than mine. I do not begrudge you that particular delight at all. However, in case you harbour any thoughts of marriage I should warn you that he will never leave me for you. Geoffrey is hidebound by convention and draws a stern moral line between loose women and virtuous, though unelectrifying, wives. Loose Geoffrey is, of course, another matter. At the same time he does not see why he should not have both. And given the mutually sexually unsatisfying marriage that we have, nor do I. Furthermore, should you wish to go on gratifying his desires once you have left, I would have no objection. Otherwise I might have to do so until a new incumbent for the post of mistress is found.'

It was a rout.

Without a word, Sibyl prepared to leave.

'Would you please be kind enough to ask Nettie to come and see me,' requested Davina, picking up her needlepoint.

When Mrs Fox had left the room Davina considered her own less than enchanting future. For with no more children requiring supervision in the country, she would no doubt be expected to spend more time in London with Geoffrey in a small flat. While this did not appeal, it had to be said that the prospect of a revived social life did. Alas, it seemed one could not have everything in this world.

In a filthy temper, Sibyl went in search of Nettie and found her.

'Your mother would like to see you in her sitting-room immediately.'

Nettie, who was reading a novel and who did not like being interrupted, scowled. 'Why?'

'I have no idea, but if you do as you've been told and go there, no doubt you'll find out,' snapped Sibyl. When Nettie had gone she turned to Mary.

'What if I don't *want* to go?' Facing her mother, Nettie was mutinous.

Davina spread her hands helplessly. 'Of course you will go. *Everyone* goes off to be finished.'

'What about Mary? Does Mary go off to be finished?'

'Well, no,' Davina was forced to concede, 'Mary does not.'

'Well then!' Nettie was triumphant. 'Why should I?'

'Because your circumstances and hers are quite different.'

Then, getting to the crux of the matter, 'And your father has decreed it!'

'Mary and I are like sisters. We've grown up together. I don't want to be separated from her. She's my best friend.' Nettie could have added, but didn't, *and I don't want to be a lady either.*

Davina, who had shot her energy bolt seeing off Mrs Fox, felt unequal to it. There were times when her daughter's ferocious will and unreasonable insistence on her own way reminded her of Geoffrey. Better let the two of them fight it out. Surmising that that would be the end of the matter, she said, 'I suggest that if you have any complaints about the plans for your future you take the matter up with your father.'

She was right. It was the end of the matter. Nettie tossed her head and left.

Mary's reaction was one of shock. She received what her mother had to say in total silence. There was no sound in the room except that of a clock ticking, ticking as it had ticked away the last ten years of their life in this house. Finally she rose and moved across the room. This was the mellowest month, chrome yellow September whose leaves were already bronzing and curling. Shortly October would sashay in trailing orange, vermilion and old gold. Across the lawn the gardener was lifting exhausted annuals and generally clearing and shaping up the beds for a tranquil incarnation that she, Mary, would not be here to see. There was a ritualistic rhythm and timelessness about his movements which should have been reassuring but only underlined her own impermanence and acute sense of loss. *Nettie and I will be separated. I will never see Godfrey again.* Intending to be brave about it, she turned back to her mother and was ambushed by treacherous, scalding tears.

'What are we going to do?' wept Mary. 'And where are we going to go? Does *nobody* care what happens to us?'

Mary and Nettie lamented the end of childhood together.

'I don't want to go!' announced Nettie. 'I *won't* go!'

Both of them knew that she would. At Nettie's age there was no choice. She would do what her parents told her. But at least, thought Mary, there is a plan for Nettie. Heaven knows what will happen to me. I'd like to go to university and there isn't a hope of that. Most of all I don't want to leave here. It's the only security I've ever had.

'Where is the place they're sending you to?'

'I don't know.' Nettie was gloomy. 'Somewhere in Switzerland. It'll be full of women just like a prison.'

'This place is full of women most of the time,' pointed out Mary.

'It's freedom I'm talking about,' said Nettie, and then, brightening up, 'but I didn't tell you. Godfrey and William and Jonty are coming home next weekend for Father's birthday.'

Preoccupied with her own troubles, Mary had completely forgotten Geoffrey Harding's birthday. Now that she was going away for good, the prospect of meeting Godfrey again was both exhilarating and threatening. Her heart missed a beat. She blushed and hoped Nettie hadn't noticed.

After giving the matter a lot of thought, Sibyl Fox decided not to look for a post similar to the one she currently held. Ten years had elapsed since she had been first employed by the Hardings and situations like this one seemed hardly to exist these days. Even if she found one, the chances of such a family being prepared to take on her daughter at the same time were probably negligible. With Nettie and Mary being the same age, it had been different. Probably the best thing to do was to try and obtain some sort of live-in teaching job. Though these seemed thin on the ground too, no doubt because the school term had started and vacancies of that sort had been filled long ago.

Sibyl reviewed her meagre savings. It was beginning to look as though a leap in the dark might be the only answer. She did not lack courage but the thought of looking for private tuition work from rented accommodation was still daunting. As of the moment though it seemed to be the only way forward.

She took a decision.

'We're going to move to London,' said Sibyl to Mary.

* * *

54

When frostily informed of this plan, Davina Harding proved unexpectedly helpful.

She said, 'Your predecessor, Elfrida Halliday, might have some suggestions. She is, or used to be, employed by a girls' school.'

'Oh! Are you still in touch with her?' Sibyl was astonished. It seemed inherently unlikely given Mrs Harding's habitual lack of interest in other members of the human race.

'Yes, in a manner of speaking I am. By which I mean I believe I still have her address.' She frowned, trying to remember. 'Yes, I'm sure I do. Somewhere. When I find it I shall write.'

All in all it did not sound very hopeful.

Aloud, and gritting her teeth as she said it, 'That would be extremely kind of you, Mrs Harding. I should appreciate it very much.'

That same day, descending the back stairs towards the kitchen, Sibyl glanced out of the window which overlooked the orchard. The Harding boys, home for The Birthday, and Nettie and Mary making the most of a resplendent Indian summer were all lying on the grass under the trees which were heavily laden with superfluous fruit. There was no breeze at all. Long late afternoon shadows were amethyst and a dark, slanting sun burnished everything so that the apples, like those of the Hesperides, appeared to be made of gold. She paused. Godfrey said something to Mary. Watching her daughter bow her head over what might have been a daisy chain (it was hard to tell at that distance) Sibyl intuited that he had upset her. She wondered what it could have been. Godfrey was sometimes thoughtless but not usually deliberately unkind. The other thing she noticed was that William, sitting beside Jonty and a little way behind Mary, was staring at her daughter as though he could hardly bear to take his eyes off her. How ironic, thought Sibyl. Life and love, it seemed, but particularly love, were never simple. Thank heaven she was beyond all that. For a split second she allowed herself to contemplate her own romantic past as opposed to her sexual present. Even after all the years she still felt the pain. And the fury.

Look forward.

Never, never look back.

55

But she did.

She remembered another garden, particularly the white flowers. She remembered lilies and jasmine and roses and gypsophila but most of all she remembered the camellias, one in her hair and one tucked into her sash. And kisses, urgent stolen kisses, eyes closed, head thrown back. Oh, and the overwhelming scent of a shrub whose name she had never discovered, seductive, sexual, bringing to mind the possibility of all sorts of dangerous delights. Her last sight of it as he laid her gently down had been the glossy dark viridian of the leaves and the waxen, sculptured flowers crowding above her, shutting out caution, shutting out shame.

Afterwards there were crushed grass and leaves and a crushed camellia too and more kisses. (*Darling, oh, darling, you won't leave me, will you? Promise me you'll never leave me* . . . then *Sweetheart, I promise. I'll never leave you, never!*)

He had though.

Yes. And now, all that remained was the memory, though the scent of certain flowers still made her head swim.

7

Amazingly, Davina Harding did locate Miss Halliday's address. Even more amazing, Elfrida was still there. Punctilious as ever, she replied immediately to the letter, enclosing a telephone number.

'So there you are, Mrs Fox, now it's down to you,' said Davina, washing her hands of the matter. Sibyl, who had not expected a good turn from this particular quarter and was faintly suspicious, felt she had no choice but to get on with it and rang Miss Halliday. The two women arranged to meet the following weekend on Sibyl's day off.

Travelling up on the train she contemplated her life and the change it was about to undergo. She had been disappointed too often to not be a realist. She had no very high hopes that anything would come of the encounter, although the odd way in which it had all come about indicated that maybe an unseen hand was at work.

Elfrida lived in a small pleasant flat in Brixton. Watching her as she made them each a cup of tea, Sibyl estimated her age to be about fifty-five. When they were finally sitting down, Elfrida said, 'Now, dear, what can I do for you?'

'Probably nothing,' replied Sibyl frankly, 'except maybe give me the benefit of your own experience of this situation. It's very nice of you to see me at all.'

'Tell me, why are you leaving? According to Mrs Harding's letter you have been with the family for a long time.'

'Quite simply my usefulness is at an end,' said Sibyl, with a shrug.

'Ah, yes.' Elfrida sipped her tea. 'That is the lot of governesses everywhere. Indispensable one day, up the creek without a paddle the next. What's happened to the children?'

'Godfrey and the twins are at university, and Nettie is soon to go to finishing-school. Ergo, I am now redundant with a daughter to support. I have to say I knew it would happen eventually. Mrs Harding was perfectly frank the day she offered me the post.'

57

'How old is your daughter?'

'Mary is the same age as Nettie. The girls virtually grew up together.'

'I see. It will not be easy for her. She is not only losing someone who must feel like a sister to her but she is also losing her home.'

'I know.' Sibyl's face darkened. Elfrida felt sorry for her. She wondered what Mrs Fox's background had been. Probably much the same as her own. Gentility, followed by poverty, followed by needs must. It was a tough world for the have-nots.

'You must have liked the family to stay as long as you have.'

Unable to gauge the other woman, Sibyl was at a loss as to how to answer this, but without waiting for a response Elfrida said, 'It was my considered view that Davina Harding was daft. I thought so then and if I met her again I'd probably think so now. And as for Geoffrey Harding! Do you realize he's one of the ones running this country? My blood runs cold whenever I think about it!' Elfrida cast her eyes to heaven. 'Do have a scone or would you prefer a sandwich?'

In spite of herself, Sibyl laughed out loud. Goodness, that quite transformed her, thought Elfrida. If she took a bit of trouble with herself and ditched the bluestocking look she could be a very pretty woman. Those eyes are quite extraordinary.

'Bring me up to date on the children. What about Godfrey? And William? William was a sweetheart, I remember. Though they were all very young when I knew them, of course.'

Sibyl thought for a minute.

'Godfrey, who is middle-of-the-road academically like the others, has become very handsome and I mean *very* handsome. Now that he is up at Oxford he doesn't come home very often. William? Well, William is good-looking, as is Jonty, but both lack Godfrey's star quality. And, yes, William *is* still kind hearted. More so than Jonty, in my view. Jonty takes after his father, I'm afraid. He's got all Nettie's certainty without the charm.'

'Dear, oh dear,' remarked Elfrida, digesting this. 'That's a shame.'

'On the plus side though,' added Sibyl, feeling the need to qualify what she had just said for, after all it was very hard on anybody to be directly compared with Geoffrey Harding, 'He's very loyal to his siblings. And he'd go through fire for William!'

'And what about Nettie? Nettie always did have a lot of character!'

'Still does. Nettie has been very good for my daughter, who tends towards being quite reserved and bookish. Though Mary has reflective qualities which Nettie has benefited from as well. She calms her down and makes her think. All in all I think the girls have been good for each other.'

Yes, Elfrida dared say they had. Nettie had certainly needed calming down.

'In my day the Harding children were like little savages. Nice little savages, mind you. It sounds as though you may have civilized them.'

'Not really. The only one I can really take any credit for is Nettie and I don't think anyone will quite tame her.'

No. This struck Elfrida as very perceptive. On the other hand, given her privileged start in life, all Nettie would need to get by was a smattering of education and the thinnest veneer of civilization.

'I should have liked to have kept in touch with them all,' Elfrida sounded wistful, 'but Mrs Harding never was very good at that sort of thing. Out of sight, out of mind.'

Sibyl glanced at her watch. Elfrida had been hospitable and courteous, but in terms of ideas for a new professional incarnation for herself they did not seem to be much further forward.

'Getting back to my own job, or rather lack of one, I should be very grateful for any advice you might be able to give me concerning where I might go next.'

'Would you be prepared to entertain a change of direction?'

'The problem with that is that teaching's the only thing I know how to do.'

'No, I mean teaching in a school as opposed to a private house.' Elfrida proffered the cake plate and then took a small one with pink icing and a cherry on top for herself. 'I only ask because I am contemplating a *complete* change of direction. I'm getting married!'

It was the last thing Sibyl had expected to hear. Trying to conceal her astonishment, she said, 'That's wonderful. When?'

'Christmas. Edward, who is a widower, has a shop and I'm going to help him with the business. I'm very happy. I met him at a tea dance, you know. I must confess I never thought such a thing would happen to me at my time of life. But the upshot of this is twofold. Firstly, I shall be giving up my job at the school, and secondly, because we shall be living over the premises and I have a lease on this flat, I shall need a tenant.'

Sibyl stared at Elfrida. She wondered what was coming.

'Of course I can't offer you the job, that would be between you and the powers that be, but I am in a position to recommend. You would need to galvanize Davina Harding into a good reference, of course. What I definitely *can* do though, if you're interested, is offer you the tenancy of this flat at a very reasonable rent. Perhaps you'd like to think about it?'

Sibyl could hardly believe her luck. It was the answer to a prayer. *Seek and ye shall find!* God had been conspicuously absent up till now and suddenly here He was.

'I don't *need* to think about it. The answer is yes.'

Christmas came and went. For once life lived up to its responsibilities. Elfrida Halliday did marry her Edward and the school did offer her job to Sibyl Fox subject to a satisfactory reference from her current employer. The only person who was temporarily dissatisfied with this advance was Davina Harding.

'Nettie is not leaving for Switzerland until February,' said Davina, fussed. 'I must confess, Mrs Fox, I had hoped you would have deferred your departure until then.' The way in which this speech was delivered had more than a suggestion of pique. The words *After all I have done for you* were not actually uttered but might as well have been.

Sibyl Fox gave her employer a lynx-eyed look.

'I'm afraid I have no choice in the matter. I have agreed with the school that I will start on the first day of term and cannot go back on that now. But be that as it may, subject to a glowing reference from you, I'm sure something can be worked out.'

The solution was that Mary would stay on with the Hardings until Nettie left. 'The girls are very close. They will be company for each other. It will be one less thing for you to worry about,' said Sibyl. *And one less thing for me to worry about too.*

Since this appeared to be about as far as she was going to get, Davina reluctantly assented.

'It won't be quite the same, of course, but it will be better than nothing. Nettie is not at her easiest at the moment.'

No, she wasn't. Sibyl had noticed. It was, however, no longer her problem.

Jonty and William had said their goodbyes to Nettie before going back to university after Christmas. This year Godfrey had not come home for the festive season at all but had gone abroad to Italy instead for a cultural tour of the great galleries of Rome and Florence. At the beginning of February, as she had promised, Mary began to pen her monthly letter to William.

Dear William, she wrote,
This house seems very quiet without you and Jonty . . .
She chewed the end of her pen.
. . . how I envy you both at university. Even with Mother's new job it is not something we could ever afford and I have decided to take a secretarial course so that whatever happens I shall always be able to earn myself a living. I'm also going to learn how to drive . . .

Mary liked that last sentence. It sounded intrepid, the sort of thing the new, courageous Mary would do, the Mary who was about to strike out on her own away from familiar things and familiar people.

I shall feel very strange leaving this house. It has been my home for so long, and, though I know you aren't really, you have all felt like my own family and as such I shall miss you and Jonty and Nettie and Godfrey more than I can say . . .

Godfrey.

This was an uphill struggle, probably because at the end of the day she was writing to the wrong brother. She racked her brains for something unharrowing to write about, which was difficult for they were comparatively isolated here and, as a result, very little happened. A tear fell onto the page, followed by another. The ink ran and the paper crinkled, a small but telling testimony of her distress. Damn and blast! Mary screwed up the sheet, threw it away and started again:

Dear William . . .

For the first time in her life Sibyl found herself properly paid and with her own roof over her head. It felt like a break from a curdled past, a fresh start, and in some ways it was, but Sibyl also recognized that the older one got the harder such a thing became to achieve. Too much destructive detritus from the past came too. And now Mary had accrued some of her own in the shape of a naïve infatuation with Godfrey Harding. She would, of course, get over it. She would have to. It was a good thing that they were out of the Harding house. Hopefully with geographical separation would come forgetfulness. Although, if she was honest with herself, Sibyl was forced to admit that she had never got over the love of her own life and its loss. Even today the only way she felt she could cope with her memories was to disregard them.

Better not to think about it.

Despite all this, in many ways it still seemed to both women that there was much to look forward to, although a fault line in this hard-won, precarious security was the growing menace abroad. Each knew that should it escalate into the cataclysmic earthquake of war, small worlds like their own would be shattered, and each feared it.

On March 15th 1939 Hitler marched into Czechoslovakia and then, on September 1st, into Poland. In anticipation of the worst, there was mass evacuation of children from the major cities to the country and, as a result, Sibyl Fox found herself with no one to teach. Yet again. The rent still had to be paid and she was forced to take a clerking job in the City until something better turned up.

Part Two

Survival

The sky is darkening like a stain;
Something is going to fall like rain,
And it won't be flowers.

W. H. Auden

8

September 1939

'This morning the British Ambassador in Berlin handed the German Government a final note stating that unless we heard from them by eleven o'clock that they were prepared at once to withdraw their troops from Poland a state of war would exist between us.

'I have to tell you now that no such undertaking has been received, and that consequently this country is at war with Germany . . .'

The time was 11.15 a.m. on Sunday, traditionally a tranquil, unthreatening day. Together with the rest of the nation Godfrey, William and Jonty at Oxford and Sibyl and Mary in London listened in disbelieving, stunned silence to the words of Mr Neville Chamberlain on the radio. In his house in Mayfair Rafe Bartholomew, although he had known what was coming, also tuned in. He was full of anger. Anger that it should ever have come to this and contempt for the man whose voice he was listening to. For Rafe the Munich agreement had been the last straw.

'Chamberlain is at best an innocent abroad, at worst criminally stupid,' he had said in despair to Geoffrey Harding and anyone else who was prepared to listen. 'Hitler is running rings round him.'

It was an unpopular point of view.

'Peace in our time, old boy, peace in our time,' Harding replied, unfazed and, despite the sinister accumulation of evidence to the contrary, unalerted.

'Yes, but at what cost and for how long?'

Being proved right was no consolation. The future loomed ahead blood red. Once again the flower of the nation's youth, young men like Godfrey, would be sent off to fight and would be cut down in their thousands. There would be slaughter and mutilation, widows and orphans. Worst of all, in the wake of so much sacrifice, it could all end in defeat and the occupation of Great Britain by a brutal enemy. It did not bear thinking about.

The broadcast was drawing to an end. Now that it had finally come to this, for once he found himself almost in tune with the Prime Minister.

'. . . may God bless you all. May He defend the right. It is the evil things that we shall be fighting against – brute force, bad faith, injustice, oppression and persecution – and against them I am certain that the right will prevail.'

Bartholomew was not so certain. Outside the weather was sombre. Suddenly, like the keening of the banshee, the wail of air raid sirens could be heard in the empty streets.

9

From then on, the Damoclean sword of war hung over the whole country. The news from abroad was deeply depressing. Every night, Sibyl and Mary listened to it on the radio. The German advance in Poland continued and during the last days of September Warsaw capitulated. The Nazi juggernaut moved inexorably across Europe; through Austria and on towards the Low Countries. It was beginning to feel as though shortly Hitler would be on the doorstep.

By now serious reservations were being voiced by all parties concerning Chamberlain's conduct of the war. On May 8th 1940, Rafe Bartholomew sat in on a heated debate on the matter in the House of Commons which culminated in uproar. Two days later the Prime Minister resigned and was succeeded by Winston Churchill, who handpicked his war cabinet from all political persuasions and designated himself Minister of Defence as well as Premier.

'At last! Thank Christ for that,' exclaimed Rafe Bartholomew, openly jubilant. '*Now* we'll show them!' Brave words but it was beginning to feel as if it all might be too late. Apparently unassailable, the Nazi hordes pushed on through France and on May 21st reached the Channel. On May 25th, the first German bombs since World War 1 fell on England.

Winston Churchill summoned Rafe Bartholomew to his office in the Admiralty. This in itself was not unusual. Bartholomew had always been known to be Churchill's man. Geoffrey Harding, out in the cold, wished he had been as perspicacious. If he had then perhaps he too would be on the inside track. As things stood he was reduced to insinuating unconvincingly to anyone who would listen that he was, in fact, in the know but could not talk about it.

Sitting opposite the Prime Minister, Bartholomew listened intently.

'Nobody else must know what has been said in this meeting,' said Churchill. 'Nobody. Do you understand?'

'Yes, I do,' said Rafe.

Churchill leant back in his chair. 'Because if they knew what your brief was, or even suspected what it was, your cover would be blown and you would be of no further use to me. You have a subtle mind, Rafe, and an instinctive grasp of the machinations and nuance of politics and power, global and otherwise. As my eyes and ears, my Francis Walsingham if you like, you will be invaluable. We both know that the Secret Service as it is presently constituted is under-valued and consequently under-exploited. I want all that to change and I want you to be one of the architects of that change. I want the Secret Service to become one of our most potent weapons.'

He stood up.

'Do you want to ask me any further questions?'

'No, sir,' said Rafe. 'Not at present.'

'Then that will be all for now. Come and see me again when you have formulated some thoughts on the matter, but make it soon. They are closing in. Time is short.'

'I will,' said Rafe, preparing to take his leave. Outwardly calm, he was inwardly in a state of high excitement. Here it was, the chance to make his own contribution to the defence of the realm in terms peculiarly suited to his particular talents, and he would not fail.

Late that night, unable to sleep and sitting in his drawing-room, Bartholomew tried to analyse his complex emotions concerning the task he had just been given. It seemed to him that all his life love and secrecy had gone hand in hand and now they were doing it once again, but this time it was love of his country rather than the more familiar physical variety.

Rafe poured himself a whisky. As he did so, the clock chimed midnight and the telephone rang simultaneously. Warily he picked up the receiver. A call at this hour usually boded no good.

'Yes?'

Godfrey said, 'Rafe?' and then without further preamble, 'Rafe, I've decided to enlist.' The worst news of all. 'Don't try to persuade me out of it. I have to do it.'

Yes, Rafe could see that. 'I'm not going to try to persuade you out of it.'

'Jonty and William are going to enlist too.'

All three Harding sons. It was a microcosm of what was no doubt happening to families all over the country. Rafe felt as though a dead hand had fallen on his shoulder.

He said urgently, 'I need to see you before anything else happens. If you can't get to London, I'll come to Oxford.'

'I'll come to London! I'll let you know what time I'll be arriving tomorrow.' The phone went dead.

His glass untouched by his side, Bartholomew sat on into the small grey hours of the morning. It was to be the forerunner of many more sleepless nights.

Nettie, who as William had discovered was a hopeless correspondent, had not written to Mary while she was in Switzerland. When she finally rang up after her arrival back, Mary took her to task.

'Nettie, you are a beast! All those letters I wrote you and not *one* in return!'

'No, I know,' said Nettie, sounding unrepentant. 'I kept meaning to and then I never did. In a sense though you were writing to someone who doesn't exist. I've changed my name!'

'What to?'

'Venetia. No more Nettie.'

In an odd sort of way it was one more nail in the coffin of childhood.

'I'm going to be svelte and chic from now on and one can't be either of those things called Nettie. I intend to entrap men with my sophisticated allure. I shall be a *femme fatale*! *La belle dame sans merci*, that'll be me.'

They both laughed. All the same, Mary would not have put it past Nettie to mean it.

'You'll never succeed if nylon stockings become unavailable.'

'Yes I will! I'll paint a seam up the back of both my legs if I have to!'

'Nettie, you're a scream!'

'Venetia! And I know I am. Plus I'll tell you a secret. If Father hadn't taken me out of Madame Vernier's finishing-school, they were going to ask me to leave anyway!'

'Why?'

'Men.'

69

'*Ah.*' Then, changing the subject, 'I think you'll always be Nettie to me. Let's meet for lunch.'

They met in the City. To Mary's eyes the change in her friend was astonishing. Apart from anything else, Madame Vernier seemed to have instilled some dress sense into the tomboy that had been Nettie. Although it had to be said that Davina had always had a good eye for clothes.

Nettie, alias Venetia, was wearing a small hat tilted to one side which gave her a rakish air. Under it auburn hair which, though still wavy, was much less hectic than Mary recalled, was pinned in a shining loop. Her trim costume was belted with a knee-length skirt and with it she wore nylon stockings and narrow, brown leather shoes with laces and elegant heels. There was a racy confidence about her which marked her out and caused people, particularly men, to give her a second look.

'You look wonderful!' exclaimed Mary, meaning it.

'So do you!' responded Nettie, also meaning it. Mary had changed as well. Today, in common with a great many other women these days, she was wearing slacks and a cropped jumper with short sleeves. All in all, it couldn't have been called a becoming outfit but, Nettie saw, Mary Fox would have looked good in a sack. Slender height and a lovely though unfashionable face coupled with shy grace gave Mary the quality of a gazelle. There was nothing showy about her and yet, when she smiled, the effect was incandescent. I would die for eyes like those, thought Nettie. For the first time she noticed that they were green, like those of her mother.

The two women embraced.

'I love your scent,' said Mary, frankly envious.

'So do I!' came the answer. 'Wicked, isn't it?'

'Yes it is. Oh Nettie, it's so good to see you again.'

'Venetia, Mary, *Venetia!* Oh, I give up on it! I think aside from the family you'll have to be the only person in the world to call me Nettie.'

As they ate their lunch, Mary said, 'What are you going to do with yourself now you're back?'

'Father's London flat isn't big enough to house me as well as him and Mother and, strictly *entre nous*, I think Mother wishes it wasn't big enough to house her either.

In any case I don't think I want to go on living in the bosom of my immediate family. So I'm going to stay with Aunt Dorothy in Belgravia and then, as soon as I can, I'm going to get married.'

Mary raised her eyebrows. 'Doesn't getting married slightly depend on who you meet? I mean you don't want to marry just anybody, do you?'

'It isn't so much marriage I'm after as independence,' said Nettie frankly. 'Aunt Dorothy's a tartar. She's Father cubed. I want to get out from under as soon as I can. And let me tell you I'm a step ahead of the lot of them. I've already got someone up my sleeve.'

'Have you? Who?'

'You'll see!'

'How on earth did you manage that?'

'I knew him before I went to Madame Vernier's establishment. Randolph. He's a friend of Jonty's. Don't you remember him? Actually, on second thoughts, I don't think he ever did stay at The Hall. Anyway, Switzerland isn't the end of the world, you know. He used to come over and see me every so often. We had assignations. I slipped out at night.'

No wonder Madame Vernier had been keen to see the back of Nettie!

'Look, while I don't want to put a damper on all this romance, do you think this is wise? Rushing into marriage, I mean. Why don't you share a flat with someone instead?'

'Because Father is keeping me on a short financial rein. He wants me to have a chaperone. He "doesn't want me on the loose in London", I quote. Marriage is a completely different equation. Then I'd be my husband's responsibility. See?'

Mary saw. All the same it seemed a drastic and contradictory step to take in order to be your own woman.

'Why don't you get a job?'

Nettie rolled her eyes. 'A job? Well, I suppose I could.' She did not sound very keen. 'Do you have a job?'

'Nettie, of course I do. Mother and I both work. If we didn't we wouldn't have a roof over our heads. You *know* that.'

Nettie seemed disinclined to pursue it. 'Well, we'll have to see . . .' was her vague response. And then, 'I'm going to

71

a party on Saturday night. At the Dorchester. Why don't you come?'

'What about the dragon that is Aunt Dorothy?'

'It's people she knows and therefore feels will look after me. I'm their responsibility for the duration.'

'I'd love to go with you but I don't have anything to wear.'

'I'll lend you something!' It was suddenly just like the old days. 'Oh, go on, do say you'll come.'

'Of course I'll come!'

Courtesy of Nettie and her social contacts, the Dorchester party was to be the forerunner of many others for Mary and, in November, she attended a particularly grand one at the Ritz. When she entered the band was playing 'The Way You Look Tonight'. There was caviar, champagne and dancing. The only indication of a world under threat was the high proportion of men in uniform mingling with those in evening dress. The Ritz was *en fête*. Mary, who had gone there prepared to wallflower, found herself constantly asked to dance. Across the ballroom she could see Nettie, flirting outrageously and probably rather drunk. Eventually they lost sight of each other in the throng. Then, suddenly, like a revenant from a former life, she saw William, leaning against the wall with a glass in his hand and apparently on his own. She did not think he had seen her.

The young man in RAF uniform with whom she was currently foxtrotting followed her gaze.

'Someone you know?'

'Yes, a very old friend! He must be on leave.'

The music stopped and then almost immediately started again.

Silver Wings in the Moonlight.

Her partner said, 'May I claim one more dance before I go?'

Mary smiled at him. 'Of course.'

'You really don't mind?'

'I really don't mind.'

At the end of it, he said, 'Thank you for that. You'll never know how much it meant to me.'

Perplexed, she looked at him.

'You see, I know I'm going to die. Quite a lot of the people here tonight are going to die as well. The difference between them and me is that I know it. Would you like me to escort you to your friend?'

Devastated by his words, she nodded. When they reached William her partner did not wait to be introduced but gallantly kissed her hand and went. Mary watched his tall figure threading its way through the dancers until eventually he was lost to sight. She was never to see him again and never to know what happened to him but saw no reason to doubt his precognitive look into his own clouded future.

At the sight of her William's face lit up with pleasure. He was also wearing uniform. It occurred to Mary with a thrill of anticipation that maybe Godfrey was here as well.

'Mary! I had no idea you were coming to this party. Nettie didn't tell me.'

'I had no idea I was going to be here either until two days ago.'

He had an intense desire to put his arm around her waist, even take her in his arms and kiss her. There was one obvious way to get at least part of the way there.

'May I have the pleasure?' He swept her onto the floor. Nettie quickstepped past them, laughing loudly presumably at something her partner had just said to her. There was a glitter about Nettie probably produced by champagne.

William frowned. 'I wish my sister would be more discriminating.'

'Who's she dancing with,' asked Mary, 'and why don't you approve?'

'His name is Randolph Huntington and he's an upper-class lush.' William was short. 'He's been turned down by just about every decent woman in London.' His arm tightened around her waist. Mary stole a look at him. He looked suddenly puritanical. 'I'm afraid I don't always trust Nettie's judgement.'

No. Mary remembered the conversation she had had with her friend on the subject of marriage. It had seemed to her then that Nettie's reasoning was badly flawed and the end result of such an ill-advised course of action might very well be to remove her from one intolerable situation only to project her into another. She did not say any of this to

William but mentally resolved to have another go at making Nettie see sense.

Once again the music died. William was loathe to let Mary go. He said, 'Mary, there's something I've been meaning to ask you . . .'

'William!' His sister, flushed and slightly dishevelled with a florid-faced Randolph Huntington in tow, was heading towards them. She seemed to have a talent for turning up at the wrong moment. 'William, you know Randolph, don't you?'

'Yes,' said William. His curtness was lost on the effervescent Nettie. Mary noticed that her lipstick was slightly smeared.

'And this, Randolph, is my very old friend, Mary Fox.'

They shook hands. His felt fleshy and surprisingly soft. The signet ring dug into her hand and probably into his as well. In fact Randolph was fleshy all over though with the height and breadth of shoulder to carry it off, at least for the moment. She noticed that he smelt of spirits. Like William, he was in army uniform.

'Mary can be a bridesmaid,' slurred Randolph. 'How about it, Mary?'

As remarks go, this was so unexpected that nobody knew what to say. There was an embarrassed silence. Nettie had no qualms about ending it and announced, 'Yes, that's right, she can.' And then, clarifying the situation, 'We are engaged. Randolph has asked me to marry him and I've accepted. He's about to go back to the war so the wedding will have to be fitted in when we can.'

There was a defiance in the way she said it which Mary interpreted as an anticipation of opposition from her brother. Wisely, William did not take his sister on. He went for the oblique approach and addressed Huntington rather than Nettie.

'I presume you've spoken to my father about this.'

For the first time the other's bluff self-assurance faltered.

'Well, no,' and then, regrouping, 'but he won't object. He's a mucker of my old man. They were at school together. I think he'll be very pleased.'

Listening to it and remembering Geoffrey Harding, Mary thought, Yes, he probably will. William looked grim.

'Aren't you going to congratulate us?' asked Nettie, who seemed determined to aggravate her brother as much as she could.

'Congratulations,' said William in a toneless voice. He did not look at Randolph. 'It's almost midnight. I have to leave. I'll take you home, Nettie.' He turned to Mary. 'Would you like me to take you home too, Mary? I've got Godfrey's car.'

'That would be wonderful, but I'm miles away. I'm in Brixton.'

'Where?' said Huntington. 'Look, don't worry about Venetia. I'll look after her.'

'Yes, I'm sure you will,' rejoined William.

'Brixton is south of the river,' elucidated Nettie, partly for her fiancé's benefit and partly to skate over another awkward pause. To Mary and William she said, 'Randolph never goes outside Belgravia if he can avoid it.'

Eyeing the army uniform, Mary thought: No, but he's having to now, whether he likes it or not. She said, 'I'll get my wrap, or, rather, Nettie's wrap.'

When they were both in the car driving through the dark streets of London, Mary said, 'You know what Nettie's like. It'll probably never happen.'

'On the contrary. Because I know exactly what Nettie's like, I think it will.'

The thin shriek of the air raid sirens sliced through the night air. That August the Nazi planes had broken through the capital's defences for the first time, since when the attack had been relentless. It was very, very cold for November. The pavements had a glassy sheen. Tonight there would be a hard frost. There was the sound of an explosion and then another and then another, much closer this time and massive. The car rocked. As magnesium flares lit up the darkened streets they could hear the staccato rattle of anti-aircraft guns and then, with a roar, the sky ignited and sulphurous flames billowed high over a frozen capital. Fire and ice.

Mary said, 'It's the City. They're bombing the City.'

The two of them watched as searchlights, laser-like, pale and straight, strobed the skies criss-crossing each other, searching for the enemy and forming a spectacular aerial display as they did so.

'Bastards,' said William. 'Bastards!'

He stopped the car and for a few moments they both observed the spectacle in silence. Head tilted back, Mary's face was in profile. She did not appear to be afraid, though, like him, she probably was.

'We could go down into the Underground until the all clear, if you like,' suggested William, concerned for her safety.

She turned to him wearily. 'Oh, what's the point? This could go on all night. To tell you the truth, I feel quite fatalistic about what's happening.' The image of the young RAF pilot presented itself before her inner eye. 'Let's press on.'

Slowly he let out the clutch. As the car moved forward he wondered what would happen to them both and what she would say if he declared his love for her. In these dangerous days one had to take one's happiness where one could and a lot of people did. Including Nettie. Mary was cast in a different mould. There was a reserve, a fastidiousness about her which, while he found it attractive, also kept him at a distance. Suppose he took her in his arms. What would her response be? William could not begin to guess.

Another wave of bombers came over and another series of mighty explosions shook the capital, followed by bronze clusters of flames which opened up in the black sky like chrysanthemums. Mary said, 'You say this is Godfrey's car?'

'Yes,' replied William. 'He lent it to me. The idea is that I'll leave it in Oxford when I get my own marching orders.'

'What about Jonty?'

'He's gone already. Jonty's all action, he couldn't wait to go.'

'So where is Godfrey now?'

'He joined Bomber Command. He could be over Germany now for all I know.'

There was a brief pause. She might never see William again. With the exception of Nettie she might never see any of the Hardings again. As of now he was her only connection to the man with whom she was in love. It seemed the time to speak. Mary said, 'William, if I tell you something will you promise never to breathe a word of it to anyone else?'

Intrigued, he promised.

In a low voice, she said, 'I am in love with Godfrey. I have been in love with him for years.'

The shock was immense. Elaborately casual, William said, 'I see.' Forgetting to change gear in his disarray, he took a sharp corner in third. Although he said nothing further, indeed did not feel capable of saying anything further, she held up her hand as though he had.

Calmly but tonelessly she went on. 'Godfrey is not in love with me. I realize that. All the same I would be grateful if you could pass on any news of him that you might receive from time to time.'

Heart bleeding, 'Of course I will.' There did not seem, there was not, anything else to say.

Looking straight ahead he sensed her gaze upon him and knew that she was smiling at him in the dark.

'Dear, dear William. Where will *you* go next?' Although she did not make the connection, her words, kindly meant, echoed Godfrey's casual query the September before she and her mother left the Harding household. They cut William to the quick now, as they had cut her to the quick then.

'God knows!' And, thought William, in the light of what I have just been told, I no longer care.

He followed her directions to the house and stopped the car outside it.

Mary turned to him. 'You're most welcome to come in and spend the night on the sofa if you would like to. Mother would love to see you.'

'Thanks all the same, but I won't. I'd better get back.'

'If you insist.'

She leant forward and kissed him on the cheek and then got out.

He watched her walk away, tall and, to him anyway, beautiful, incongruous in floating chiffon and a fur wrap amid a ravaged world.

The all clear sounded.

10

The enemy assault escalated, firewatching became compulsory and Mary, feeling the need to do her bit, volunteered to drive an ambulance. There was no further communication from William concerning the fate of Godfrey. It was to be hoped that no news was good news. Risking her own life, although not on the battlefield as such, Mary felt closer to Godfrey, as though theirs was a shared endeavour. Like a talisman she kept a black-and-white photograph of him in her purse.

The air attacks on London intensified. Towards the end of November the nightly bombardment was constant. Probably because of this, the fear Mary experienced when she first drove the ambulance and its crew along the embattled streets of the city was gradually replaced by a fatalistic fortitude. Peace was a thing of the past. It was hard to remember what it had been like to sleep through the night. Assault and battery was now the norm and, of necessity, courage rose to meet it. After a realistic assessment of how much protection it was likely to afford, Mary wore her tin hat at a rakish angle and got on with what she saw as her duty. Her gas mask was relegated to the back of the vehicle. Under the soaring, watery arcs of fire service hoses they negotiated the bomb-blasted roads lined with heaps of rubble and the only flickering illumination of their progress was fire, as it leapt, like a live thing, from building to building. There was a desperate camaraderie in the ambulance. Nobody admitted to being terrified. Occasionally they would even arrive at their destination with the grievously wounded only to find that the hospital itself had been hit and doctors and nurses were sifting through the rubble, salvaging what patients and precious equipment they could. Daunting as all this was, it turned out to be only a rehearsal for what was to come next.

The blitz on December 29th hit London with terrible ferocity. It was hard to believe that four days earlier it had been Christmas Day. There had been nothing like this before. Phalanx after phalanx of Nazi raiders roared over, some dropping parachute flares which fell hypnotically slowly, illuminating potential targets during their drifting, lethal descent. Many of these were shot out by anti-aircraft gunners but just as many were not. As incendiary bombs showered down and the flames rushed to heaven, the purple night sky above the capital was split open like a ripe plum by a sulphurous blaze of yellow. There was an awful majesty about fire on such a scale. The noise was deafening. It was like nothing Mary had ever heard. This must be what Hades was like. Creeping the ambulance through the chaos she thought of all she had previously taken for granted, of hot tranquil country summers and love and friendship and a career to look forward to, and although to mourn their passing was premature, she nevertheless recognized that life would never be quite the same again.

The following morning revealed the extent of the carnage. A pall of black smoke hung over the city. Soot-covered ruins were still burning. Like broken teeth, fragments of buildings stood surrounded by debris and many streets were impassable. For those who worked in the City there was no way of knowing whether they still had jobs to go to short of struggling through the detritus to find out, and this in itself was hazardous for a significant part of what remained upright was tottering. After the tumult of the night before, the silence still seemed to reverberate. Mary accompanied Sibyl on her foray into the wasteland to discover whether her office had survived the attack. It had not. Only the façade was left. Sunlight streamed through windows empty like the eye sockets of a skull. On either side of it the buildings had been flattened. It was amazing, though, what had resisted the onslaught. Above the skeletal remains of the City, and against all the odds, like the great church of St Paul's, the statue of Justice had escaped the marauders unscathed. Blindfold she stood, arms flung wide with sword sternly raised and scales in balance. They stared at the lonely figure in sombre salute.

Mary thought: It's a sign that we will come through this, that right will triumph.

Suddenly shaky, she thought of Godfrey and Jonty and dear, dependable William all out in the field fighting for what

Chamberlain had called the right. For while Mary suddenly saw with great clarity that right *would* in the end prevail, she also saw with dread in her heart that millions might die before that happened.

That night she had a horrifying dream. She dreamt that the Thames ran red with blood, bright fresh blood the colour of poppies, in which thrashed and struggled thousands of people, crying soundlessly for help, arms raised in supplication. It was like a medieval painting of Hell. On the bank was a procession of bowed, hooded figures, of whom she was one, all swathed in long dark cloaks and all moving silently in the same direction. And then she saw Godfrey. Godfrey was in the water although how she was able to pick him out among so many was unclear. Electrified, Mary threw back her hood and stood, waving and shouting to him though as in a silent film she could not hear herself. The grieving endless procession of which she had been a part filed on past her. Godfrey did not appear either to see her or hear her and then a long flat boat glided eel-like from beneath the embankment on which she stood. At its prow stood a tall figure whose face was averted but who, nevertheless, seemed familiar to Mary. The boat slid through the hordes, some of whom tried to clutch at it as it passed but all slipped away. When it reached Godfrey the boatman bent towards him, took hold of his outstretched hands and pulled him on board after which the craft moved on until it was lost in the darkness. As though a light had been switched off the dream ended and Mary awoke to find her face wet with salt tears.

February 10th, 1941
Benghazi

My Dear Mary,
I am writing to you from Africa. I have no idea how things are going in Britain, nor do I have any idea whether this letter will ever get to you. I can only hope that it does. The smell of death is everywhere and it revolts me. Of course we have to fight this war. There can be no question of bending the knee to Nazi rule. I understand that but there are times when I think that I shall never see England

again (or you, my darling, he might have added, but did not). *I have no news of Godfrey, I'm afraid, or of Jonty. For all I know he could be out here somewhere in Africa, along with me. Probably the best way of finding out would be to contact Rafe Bartholomew or maybe get Nettie to do it for you. Write back. Letters from home are what keep most of us going. God save you and keep you,*
    Affectionately,
    William.

Mary went to see Nettie, who was still in Aunt Dorothy's flat.

'Not for long though,' said Nettie. 'I'm definitely getting married. Father has agreed. To tell you the truth I think he's quite relieved to shift the responsibility of my moral welfare onto somebody else. Mother, on the other hand, keeps urging me to wait, but after three months Randolph thinks we've waited quite long enough.'

Looking dubiously at her flighty friend, Mary said with as much enthusiasm as she could muster, 'Nettie, that's wonderful news! When?'

'Quite soon. In fact *very* soon, when Randolph next comes home on leave. I'm pregnant, so speed is of the essence.'

Heavens! Mary looked around Aunt Dorothy's ponderously over-furnished drawing-room, whose gracious moulded ceiling had a huge crack in it, courtesy, probably, of a bomb which had fallen uncomfortably close. Money was much in evidence, flair sadly lacking. There was a great deal of swagged and ruched teal blue velvet and, one on either side of the fireplace, a couple of positively threatening oils, portraits, presumably, of Aunt Dorothy and her husband, whom Mary had not yet met.

'Yes. That's my aunt!' said Nettie, unkindly, following her gaze.

Aunt Dorothy, who was large, looked exactly like Geoffrey Harding but in female attire. There was an unbecoming belligerence about her which had been lovingly translated into paint by the artist, possibly as a means of getting back at a bullying sitter. Uncle Dorothy, later revealed as Neville, was the same size but with a monocle and looked like a waxwork. Assessing the two of them Mary could definitely see that there was something to escape from here. But at what price?

'You must be thrilled about the baby!'

Nettie did not beat about the bush. 'Well, I'm not. It was very careless of Randolph.' She looked suddenly moody. 'Or maybe it wasn't. Randolph's an only child. He wants an heir and may have felt the time to get one started is before he goes off to the war. After it, depending on what happens to him, he may not be afforded the chance. Anyway, whatever the reason, I'm stuck with it.'

It sounded heartless put like that. Whatever had happened to love? More to the point, whatever had happened to Nettie? She used never to be hardboiled like this.

'Didn't you discuss it?'

'Discuss it? Randolph's a drinker not a thinker!' riposted Nettie. 'Look, do let's stop talking about my husband-to-be. I'm marrying him. For better or for worse. Full stop.' Getting off the subject caused her briefly to brighten up. Then, all at once anxious and going back to it again, she said, 'Mary, I know you don't approve, but you will come to the wedding, won't you?'

It was irritating, reflected Mary, to be told that she didn't approve (although Nettie was right, she didn't). It made her sound censorious and priggish. School-marmish even. That aside, however, it was too late to proffer an honest opinion on the matter. Support had to be the order of the day now. All the same, it was awful to have to stand by and watch the magnitude of the mistake she considered Nettie to be making.

'I don't approve or disapprove. I just want you to be happy. And of course I'll come. You're my best friend, Nettie. I'll do anything I can to help you.'

All at once sunny again and much more like her old carefree self, Nettie hugged Mary. 'It isn't the way *you* do things I know, but it's the only way I can function. I have to get away from the family and I can't live without money and position. Whatever you may think of his personal habits, Randolph is still a catch. But you are my conscience, Mary, believe me. I really care what you think. Before I do anything important I always ask myself what you would do if you were me.'

The idea of being cast in the apparently pointless role of Nettie's conscience, assuming such a thing did in fact exist, did not appeal to Mary.

'If I was you, no doubt I'd be doing exactly what you're about to do.' Mary was dry. 'My own opinion notwithstanding!'

Failing to follow her, Nettie was unabashed. 'Well, there you are. But nobody can say I don't try!'

'Getting onto something quite other, I wondered if you'd had any news of either Jonty or Godfrey. William I know about, I've just had a letter from him.'

'Have you? Well, he hasn't written to *me*,' said Nettie, sounding put out and then, with a resurgence of the old warmth, 'Poor William. Is he all right? What's it like where he is? Does he say?'

'You can look at the letter if you like,' said Mary, fishing it out of her shoulder bag. 'Here. At the time of writing he was fine, but it sounds like pure hell out there. He wants to know if Godfrey and Jonty are safe and so do I. He suggested that Rafe Bartholomew might have an idea as to where they are and, more importantly, how they are. Are you still in touch with him?'

'No, *I'm* not . . .'

Imagining she was following Nettie's drift, Mary thought of Geoffrey Harding. Of course! What an ass she was. *He* would be able to tell her. There was no need to go all around the houses trying to locate Bartholomew. It occurred to Mary to wonder why the same idea hadn't occurred to William. 'But surely, Nettie, your parents would know, wouldn't they?'

'No, I'm afraid not.' Nettie bit her lip. 'Father and Godfrey had an almighty row. Don't ask me what about, I don't know. What I *do* know is that Jonty took Godfrey's side. I think they were all still on non-speakers when the boys enlisted. I don't even know if William got to hear about it. But the other thing is that there has been a froideur between Father and Rafe Bartholomew. Again I don't know the ins and outs of it but it may have something to do with the fact that while Bartholomew's in the inside track, Father, who backed the wrong war horse so to speak, is currently out in the political cold. But with or without Father's help, somehow I'll find

Rafe's telephone number. He and Godfrey used to be thick as thieves. William's quite right, if anybody has the information, he'll be the one.'

Going home afterwards, it struck Mary as odd that it was she and not Nettie who was the prime mover where ascertaining the location and safety of Godfrey and Jonty was concerned. They were, after all, Nettie's kith and kin. Maybe, as one born into a substantial family, she took it for granted in a way in which an only child such as Mary never could. If I had a brother how I would cherish him, thought Mary. Nettie doesn't know how fortunate she is.

11

A few weeks later, as a result of her conversation with Nettie, at his insistence Mary was due to meet Rafe Bartholomew. At the Ritz.

'Really, all I need to know can be said over the telephone,' said Mary, embarrassed when he suggested it. 'Quite honestly, there's no need for me to take up any more of your time. You must be very busy.'

In common with the rest of the world she was unclear about what exactly he did these days. What she knew for certain, because Nettie had told her, was that he was very close to the centre of power.

'I *am* very busy, but I'd still like to meet you,' insisted Bartholomew. He was curious, in fact, to see what sort of person Mary Fox had turned into. Remembering that dinner in the ludicrous Geoffrey Harding's country house, Rafe laughed to himself.

Rabbit!

On the other hand, though, Fool's Mate. Where the chess game was concerned the laugh had been on him.

'What about a drink tomorrow evening? The Ritz? 6 p.m.?'

Listening to her polite acceptance, his acute social ear picked up the fact that she was dazed by the invitation, which she had not expected, and that she was reluctant.

He decided to be impervious to it. 'Splendid! I'll see you then.'

Restlessly he rose and began to pace up and down. The flat was very like Rafe himself: elegant, and at the same time discreet. Champagne-coloured walls were set off by dark green brocade curtains with sumptuously tasselled tie-backs. Large palms in blue and white chinoiserie planters graced polished floors scattered with Turkish carpets and the lighting was low. Above the marble fireplace was a magnificent painting depicting a sacrifice to Apollo amid a classical landscape. But the focal point of the drawing-room

85

and the *bête noire* of Bartholomew's housekeeper was something quite other. Within an arched alcove between two windows stood a lifesize marble statue of Antinous as Bacchus. It was Rafe's view that marble could look cold, funereal even. To counteract this the alcove had been painted a deeper shade than the walls so that without anything as crude as special lighting, the sculpture was pointed up, at the same time absorbing enough of the colour to endow it with a lambent lustre. Antinous was wearing nothing but a wreath of vine leaves on his head and held a bunch of grapes in one hand. But while the long-limbed, carelessly arrogant grace of the whole initially caught the eye, it was the head with its slight tilt which held it. Thick short hair curled close to the scalp. Over wide, sightless marble eyes the brows were straight and so was the nose. Beneath it the full, curving mouth with its short upper lip called to mind the voluptuous delights of the flesh and at the same time had a hint of cruelty about it. All in all it represented the Classical ideal of male beauty, an ideal shared by Rafe Bartholomew himself.

The first time Godfrey saw it he whistled.

'It's magnificent! Is it a real antiquity? Yes, of course it is. Silly question. Christ, Rafe, I knew you were wealthy, but not that wealthy!'

'Unlike certain others I could name, at least I *know* I'm privileged,' Rafe recalled elliptically replying to this. 'There are those who labour under the delusion that money and privilege go hand in hand with happiness but, never forget, there's a dark side to every sun. As to the Antinous, a perspicacious great-grandparent picked it up in Italy and quietly shipped it back to England. There weren't the restrictions then that there are these days.'

'Antinous was Hadrian's favourite, wasn't he? On the whole that sort of favourite doesn't last. Anno domini sees them off. What happened to him?'

'Antinous died young and therefore never lost those marvellous looks. He drowned swimming in the Nile.'

The Antinous was Rafe's most treasured possession. Now, with the greater part of the city he loved in ruins, his passion for a statue paled into insignificance. Rafe was a classicist and, as such, prized freedom, the greatest and most democratic privilege, above all else. It was the reason why, when Godfrey announced his intention of enlisting, there could have been no question of trying to dissuade him. Sacrifice on that level was universal. All the same not a day passed without Rafe thinking of him and, like Mary, speculating as to where he was.

These days the Ritz was looking somewhat the worse for wear, although it was amazing that it was functioning at all. The blackout, of course, did not enhance anything. Apart from himself, everyone was in uniform. Bartholomew got there early and took a table in the cocktail bar as arranged. Mary was late. When she arrived she apologized.

'I'm sorry. Getting across London is not easy at the moment.' That was an understatement. He suddenly realized that he had no idea where she lived and asked her.

'Brixton.'

Brixton! He had let her soldier in from Brixton on her own when he had a driver at his disposal. It was the sort of *faux pas* he practically never made. Rafe felt mortified.

'I'm sorry, I hadn't realized. I'll see you get back safely,' he said. 'What can I get you to drink?'

She hesitated.

'I'm going to have a champagne cocktail. Why don't I order you the same?'

'That would be lovely.' She smiled at him. The young girl he remembered had grown into a young woman. Unflattered by utilitarian clothes, the subtlety of her looks would, as he had once predicted to himself, have been lost on many but not on him for whom the obvious was anathema. The eyes were show-stopping though, green and clear. And very intelligent. There was a candour about her which impressed him. Rafe found himself thinking, I could use someone like this. I need discretion and I need to be able to trust.

He leant back in his chair and sipped his drink.

'Tell me what you've been doing. Since you left the Harding household, I mean.'

'Well, we had to leave, of course, when Nettie went to finishing-school. Nettie calls herself Venetia these days, by the way. Anyway, after that there was nothing left for Mother to do.' She frowned at the memory of it. 'By a stroke of good timing and with the help of a former Harding governess, she

87

got a job working at a school in Dulwich. Then, when war was declared, the children were evacuated and once again there was no job. Meanwhile I took a shorthand typing course and learnt to drive. Mother got a post as a clerk in the City which lasted until the offices were flattened by a bomb. After that she signed up with the WVS.'

'What about you?'

'I've been driving an ambulance.'

He stared at her for quite a long time without saying anything. She wondered what he was thinking.

'Don't you get frightened?'

There was more than a touch of impatience. 'Of course I was at the beginning. But not now. Now I'm inured to it and, in an odd sort of way, emotionally used up. The dead are all right, they're beyond it all, but the wounded . . . some of the injuries of the wounded are hideous. When you're dealing with that there's nothing left over for fear. Or self pity.'

No, he didn't suppose there was. He was silent. Mary looked haunted. Her drink stood neglected on the table. They both thought of Godfrey.

'You wanted to know about Godfrey,' said Bartholomew. 'And Jonty.'

At the mention of Godfrey's name she blushed and then shook her hair over her face to conceal the fact.

All at once, Rafe saw it.

Mary Fox was in love with Godfrey! It was the second time that evening that he had been slow off the mark. He must be losing his touch. *We are both in love with Godfrey Harding.* Unbeknown to her, this knowledge united them as nothing else could. For him it was secret love, for her, hopeless love. Though, for reasons other than the most conclusive one, she had probably worked this out already. He looked at her with respect and compassion. Giving himself a little time to think, he said, 'You haven't touched your cocktail.'

With resolution Mary picked it up and drank deeply. She hoped he had not noticed her confusion and then, sensitive to the nature of the man opposite her, decided he probably had.

'The fact is,' resumed Rafe, 'that there is very little I can add to what you know already. Troop movements are top secret. Frankly, it's amazing that William's letter got through in the form it did. At least because of it we know that, at the time of writing anyway, he was safe.'

At the time of writing anyway. Minute to minute there were no guarantees. 'What I *can* tell you is that Jonty wanted to go into a parachute regiment, and with that end in view was sent off for intensive training at an undisclosed destination before being posted. Godfrey's aim was the RAF and he underwent something similar. The last time I spoke to him he told me he thought he might be being posted. That's all I can tell you.'

Listening to him, Mary wondered if *that's all I can tell you* meant *that's all I'm allowed to tell you*. It struck her that in the circumstances William's letter had been amazingly informative about what had happened and where Wavell's armies were. 'The most we can hope for in the foreseeable future is irregular letters,' Bartholomew was saying, 'but with things the way they are, I don't expect too many of those. The best news of all is no telegram.'

He glanced at his watch and then gestured towards her empty glass. 'What about another of those? And then I'll get my driver to take you home.'

He signalled to the waiter. As he did so, a loud voice cut across the conversation in the bar.

'Well, I'm damned if it isn't Rafe Bartholomew!'

Rafe looked over his shoulder. 'Ah, Randolph.' He sounded less than ecstatic. A swaying Huntington lurched towards them. 'Allow me to introduce you to –'

'Miss Mary Fox and very nice too,' slurred Huntington, with something of a leer. 'Though I wouldn't have thought –'

Smartly, Bartholomew cut across whatever it was he had been going to say.

'I'm afraid I can't ask you to join us. Miss Fox has another appointment and I have to leave shortly too.'

Looking snubbed, as well he might, Huntington, who was still on the benevolent side of drunkenness, said, 'Oh. Oh, so you don't want my company then?'

'I'm afraid not.'

'Oh. All right. I'll go and pester someone else.' Looking puzzled and spilling his whisky as he went, he shambled off.

Turning back to Mary, Rafe said with distaste, 'How on earth do you come to know *him*?'

'I don't really. I've only been introduced to him once. He's engaged to Nettie. They're getting married in a fortnight.'

Rafe looked disbelieving. '*Nettie Harding* is marrying Randolph! I don't believe it. Nobody's that hard up and certainly not Nettie, surely?'

He was clearly so appalled that Mary felt embarrassed on behalf of her friend.

'*Why?*'

Carefully, she said, 'Put it this way, I'm absolutely certain it will happen.'

He had a vision of Nettie wrapped in a horse blanket confronted by an apoplectic Geoffrey.

'Are you telling me she's pregnant?' he asked.

'I'm not telling you anything, Mr Bartholomew.' Mary was cool.

'Well, let me inform you that whatever the reason is, it won't last. I wouldn't put it past her to do it just to get away from her grisly parents.'

His disenchanted accuracy was interesting. She had assumed him to be a friend of the Hardings. 'I think she's doing it to get away from grisly Aunt Dorothy, if you really want to know.' Spontaneously they both laughed.

It occurred to Bartholomew that after Nettie and Huntington were married, once he had been posted (presumably the reason, or one of the reasons, for the hasty ceremony) she would be a free agent. Though a loose cannon might have been another way of putting it. That remained to be seen. But given the way naughty Miss Harding operates, he thought, like Mary Fox she could possibly be very useful to me as well, though for different reasons. They finished their drinks and both stood up.

'Thank you for the offer, but if your driver takes me home, how will you get back?'

'I'm very close. I'll walk. Besides, I need to think.'

Outside in the street he said, 'If I hear any news of Godfrey, I'll let you know. Perhaps you would be kind enough to do the same for me?'

'Of course.'

They shook hands.

It wasn't until she was sitting in the back of his very comfortable car being driven through the unlit London streets that she realized that towards the end of the conversation neither of them had mentioned Jonty, but only Godfrey.

In the wake of their meeting, Rafe thought a lot about Mary Fox. Because of her love for Godfrey he felt protective towards her, and also because of her love for Godfrey he felt guilty. Since she was clever it was possible to go some way towards redressing this on an intellectual level and recruit her into his own department. Nobody was safe these days, of course, but at least it would take her one step back from the firing line where the ambulance service operated.

Before he found time to put this plan into operation, on the night of April 16th the most aggressive raid on London to date took place. Hundreds of Nazi planes roared over, strafing the City as they came. Bombs fell like rain and the conflagration was terrible to behold. Hungry flames ran through buildings and shot high above the roofs, their hot amber light turning night into artificial garish day. To Mary, piloting the ambulance along the cratered streets, it was as though the whole world was on fire. This was in a league of its own. Clutching the steering wheel stopped her hands from shaking. Driving as fast and as carefully as she could she clenched her teeth and tried to shut out of her consciousness the groans of the wounded.

Endless, endless night.

The morning after the terror, the sun came out. Once again it shone wanly on drifts of matchstick-sized debris and the charred remains of once august buildings, its pale benediction an affirmation that, in the wake of wanton destruction, certain things were immutable. All the same, the carnage was terrible and indiscriminate. Hospitals, homes, schools, even churches had been blown to smithereens.

Bartholomew joined Churchill in a sombre walk around the smoking, ravaged city. They hardly spoke to one another, for what was there to say?

Three nights later it all happened again.

Nettie got married. As yet her pregnancy did not show. It was very much a wartime wedding with Randolph in military uniform and Nettie in a short fitted coat and a stylish hat with

91

a peacock's feather. The only concession to tradition was an elegant spray of lilies and roses organized by Davina Harding. Otherwise there were no frills and, at the end of the day, no bridesmaids. After the ceremony bride and groom walked through the main door of the church, where they stood at the top of the steps beneath the raised ceremonial swords of Huntington's brother officers and were photographed. Without Godfrey and William and Jonty the whole occasion felt odd to Mary. And odd to the Hardings too, no doubt. Though given what William thought of Randolph it was probably just as well he wasn't here. Nor, it struck her, was Rafe Bartholomew, indicating, possibly, that the row between him and Geoffrey Harding had not been resolved.

The reception took place at Claridges. During the course of it, Mary overheard Geoffrey Harding say to his daughter, 'I've had a word with Randolph and we've decided that while he's away at the front you should move back in with Dorothy and Neville.' Then, inadvertently scuppering her plans, 'After all, we can't have you running around London on your own, can we?'

Nettie could not believe her ears. *After all the trouble I've taken to escape. Even getting* married, *for God's sake!* Her jaw set.

She flexed the third finger of her left hand, now adorned with a plain gold band surmounted by a very large ruby encircled by diamonds, and then drank her champagne at a swallow. Looking her controlling parent straight in the eye, she said, 'I have no intention of doing any such thing. Let me add, Father, I am now a married woman and, as such, would prefer you not to interfere in my affairs, with or without the connivance of my husband.' By the door, unaware of the uncompromising stance being taken by their niece, she could see Dorothy and Neville eating sandwiches and talking to the Huntingtons who, in an odd sort of way, looked very like them.

Harding went brick red. 'Now, look here my girl –'

'No, Father, *you* look here –' At this point the groom made the mistake of strolling over. 'Ah, Randolph!' Nettie sounded less than affectionate, combative even.

Impervious to it, 'Yes, my love?' said her husband.

'Am I to understand that you and Father have been deciding my immediate future with no reference to me?'

'Love, honour and obey, old girl,' said Randolph, who seemed to have no concept of the trouble he was in. He sounded very jocular but, Mary suspected, was not in fact joking. Nettie hated being called *old girl*. Mary knew this for a fact because Nettie had told her so and furthermore claimed to have stood down one particular admirer because he insisted on doing it. Now Randolph (. . . until death do us part . . .) was doing it too.

'Don't call me old girl! And don't rely on Love, Honour and Obey either!'

Randolph recoiled. His bride was plainly very cross indeed. Fuddled with celebratory champagne topped up with generous slugs of whisky, he was unsure what he had done wrong. In an effort to retrieve the situation, he slurred, 'Would you feel better about it if I said it was all my idea and nothing to do with your father?'

'No, I wouldn't, and by the way I don't like being patronized! If I'm old enough to get married, I'm old enough to take my own decisions. I want my own home. I don't want to go and live with Aunt Dorothy and Uncle Neville! Is that clear?'

He had to admit it was. Very clear. And it raised the question of what had happened to the sweet, compliant young woman he thought he had married. This one was all bad temper and insubordination. Casting round for the reason, he put the character change down to pregnancy. Better not to have a fight in front of everyone when they had only just tied the knot. Out of the corner of his eye Randolph could see his own formidable mother bearing down on him from the other side of the room, swooping and diving through the other guests, an unstable plate of complicated canapés apparently glued to her right hand. Soothingly he said, 'Well, of course, darling, if you feel like that about it . . .'

(Very snappy) 'I do!'

The point having been conclusively made, Nettie looked around her and became aware that a small audience had gathered. Collecting herself she bestowed on it an all-embracing social smile of great brittleness. 'Floor show's over for now, I'm afraid!' There was polite laughter and an outbreak of nervous speculative conversation. Nettie left Randolph and her parents standing together. She went across to Mary and took her friend's arm.

'You'll help me find a flat, won't you, Mary?'

'Yes, of course I will, but where are you going to live until you do?'

'At the Ritz, of course,' replied Nettie. 'Where else? Though I suppose there is the Dorchester too. This is my honeymoon, don't forget.'

Mrs Huntington senior reached her son.

'What on earth was all that about?'

'Nothing, Mother, just a discussion on the practicalities of what Nettie and I do next.' (Would it were as simple and unthreatening as that!) 'No, I won't have a canapé, thanks.'

'Randolph, you're about to go off to the war. You really must eat properly.'

He felt as though he was five. *God save me from bossy women.* The uncomfortable feeling that he might have just married one refused to be dislodged.

'Yes, Mother.' He selected and ate an angel on horseback. Going off to the war, which Huntington was frankly nervous about, was beginning to seem like an easier option than addressing his marriage.

'. . . and I should go easy on the whisky if I were you.'

(Grinding his teeth) 'Yes, Mother.'

Observing his son-in-law with disfavour, Geoffrey Harding seethed.

'That was outrageous! Outrageous! Randolph shouldn't have let her get away with that. Nettie was bloody rude!' This was said accusingly to Davina. The old *it's your fault* ploy. Nettie had moved beyond his authority. He could not get at Nettie so he was attacking her instead.

'I'm afraid she was, dear,' said Davina. It was a small but satisfying revenge after years of marital bullying both to agree with Geoffrey and secretly celebrate Nettie's defiance at the same time. As she spoke the words, she thought for the nth time: Why on earth did I marry him?

Still on the hunt for a culprit, Geoffrey want on, 'There are times when I wonder whether Randolph is a man or a mouse!'

'Thank you, yes, I will have another glass of champagne,'

said Davina to the waiter at her elbow, placing her fifth (or was it her sixth?) empty flute on the tray and taking another full one. She debated with herself whether to answer Geoffrey's rhetorical question and then, filled with Dutch courage, decided she would. *In vino veritas.*

'I definitely don't think his manhood's in question, dear. For one thing, Nettie's pregnant.'

What! His little girl!

Wondering if he could have heard her correctly, Harding turned a beetle-browed look on his wife.

'It is, of course, a secret,' added Davina, 'and as I don't have to tell you, the baby, when it arrives, will be premature.'

They both momentarily stopped talking, distracted by the loud laughter of Randolph, the father-to-be, who was sitting at one of the tables with a bunch of his army cronies. A bottle of malt whisky was being passed around. Nettie was nowhere to be seen.

'Do you realize I'm paying for all of this!' Geoffrey swept his arm around the room. 'Why am *I* the last to know?' He was clearly very put out.

(Mellifluous tones, enjoying the spectacle) 'You aren't, dear. If I had to guess I'd say you are the third to know. In other words, *almost* one of the first. Nettie is bound to have told Mary. She only confided in me because I asked her why on earth she was marrying him. *That's* when she told me.'

'But nobody told *me*! And why shouldn't she marry Randolph? Apart from the fact that he's seduced my only daughter, his credentials are impeccable. His father and I were at school together.'

'Nobody told you because Nettie thought you might make a fuss.'

As always Geoffrey was very consistent.

'Make a fuss! Too bloody right I'd have made a fuss! Fellow ought to be horse-whipped!'

'I don't think people do horse-whip each other any more these days,' said Davina vaguely, 'but your reaction is the key to it. *That's* why she didn't want to tell you.' Having proved the point, she felt triumphant. It felt good to be on top for once. Such a pity there weren't copious glasses of champagne on offer more often. 'I don't know why you're so upset. Randolph's made an honest woman of Nettie. What's the problem? Have another drink, why don't you? I'm going to.'

Two weeks later, Randolph was posted to the front leaving Nettie at the Ritz. Three weeks later, still at the Ritz, she miscarried. Even by then, Nettie was unimpressed with her marriage.

12

As Rafe Bartholomew knew but could not disclose to Mary, Godfrey had been initially posted to Yorkshire. Living quarters were a lot better than they might have been since the crews of this particular squadron were living in a large country house which had been commandeered for the purpose, complete with antique furniture and paintings. The contrast between elegance such as this and the freezing, cramped discomfort they all endured on bombing missions was stark. Being part of Bomber Command taught Godfrey, insulated child of rich parents, a great deal about how the other half lived. Old social taboos broke down in the light of the fact that they were all risking their lives on a regular basis, and there were times when he felt that his real education had only just begun. At first, in between raids, there had been long periods of standing by. For those crews on duty this involved sleeping in the plane, in an uncomfortable state of limbo which combined boredom with jumpy anticipation. Off duty, which was seldom, there were girls and hectic partying culminating in binges where a great deal of beer was consumed. Eat, drink and be merry for tomorrow we may die . . .

A lot of them did.

As time wore on the mission casualty rate became alarming. Some young pilots arrived only to be lost the very next day. Others, among whom Godfrey so far counted himself, seemed to lead charmed lives. It would not have been an exaggeration to say that his own survival was a constant source of amazement to him.

'We'll go in the end,' said the gunner Alfred, a man with a mordant sense of his own vulnerability. 'The statistics are all against us.' This sort of unwelcome intimation of their own mortality did not curb Godfrey's love of flying. In fact fear probably heightened it. Before the war he had learnt how to handle an aeroplane and had developed a passion for it, but this was something else again. This was high-risk living for the moment, often missing annihilation by a whisker. The physical proximity of Rafe Bartholomew apart, the heady unpredictability and sheer insanity of it all thrilled him as nothing else could.

This evening, on a June mission, piloting the Whitley towards the coast, he felt the old familiar exaltation. Riding high and very queenly, the pale moon was a tilted crescent. Rich as the roof of a sultan's tent, a night sky bedizened with glittering galaxies and planets arched to the far horizons. Gnat-like the planes shot through the airy vastness. The splendour and infinity of the universe was both wonderful and humbling to behold.

If I get out of this war alive, thought Godfrey, I'll never take anything for granted again . . . *if* I do . . .

The pessimistic gunner Alfred, currently uncomfortably segregated in the turret in the tail of the aircraft, was probably right though. Odds were they probably wouldn't get out of it alive in the long run, even if they got away with it today. It was interesting how dicing with death on a regular basis enabled one to contemplate such an outcome dispassionately. Cruising at around 8,000 feet, Godfrey, part of a crew of five, including the navigator Bill and the second gunner, Peter, all faced the possibility in their different ways. It would be around about three and a half hours before the action really began.

Wondering as he did so if he would live long enough to attempt to get it published, Bill wrote poetry. He liked Godfrey but was puzzled by him. It was not that Harding was unfriendly, quite the reverse, but the essence of the man remained elusive. So far as Bill knew, he had no women and never talked about his private life. Maybe there was a girl at home. His bravery was not in question though. They had all been stalked by death too often for that to have been in doubt. And he appeared to be lucky, so far anyway. Luck in these dangerous days was a prized commodity.

Time passed monotonously. Isolated within his turret at the back of the Whitley, though wrapped in a top coat with hat, gloves and multitudinous scarves, Alfred was very cold. His was a lonely journey. At least at the front of the aircraft the rest of the crew had each other for company.

In the fullness of time they passed over the coast. The first sign that they were approaching their destination was the searchlights, which located the plane in their lunging, swinging beams and, having caught it, pinned it like an iron butterfly to the backdrop of the night sky. It was bright as day in the cabin.

'Fuck!' said Godfrey. He sent the Whitley into a steep dive, brought it up again and then began to duck and weave. Barrelling on he shot out of the light. A Messerschmitt, seeming to come from nowhere, roared into the attack causing the formation to spread out and then begin to lose cohesion. In a dazzling pyrotechnic display, shells began to burst all around so that the Whitley was surrounded by an aureola of fire. A sudden mighty explosion at the back of the plane caused it to lurch dangerously. There was a strong smell of cordite. Managing not to panic, though his heart was in his mouth, Bill shouted, 'We may be over the target!' So primitive was the way it all worked, it was hard to be sure.

Godfrey did not turn round. 'Open the bomb doors and let 'em have it and then let's get out of here!'

'Watch it, here comes another 109,' yelled Peter. 'Christ, and more where he came from! Come on you buggers!' The gunfire was continuous, the din tremendous. Bullets struck the Whitley with a dry rattle like hailstones. 'There's one to the rear! What the fuck's Alfred doing?' Scrambling around in the back, Bill shouted, 'Alfred's wounded!'

Time to go, definitely time to go. Godfrey banked, turned and ran for the coast. He checked the fuel gauge. It was low. There must be a slow leak from the tank. If so it would be touch and go whether they made it back. They flew into a bank of cloud and eventually burst out the other side into an empty sky. It was a liberation. The pursuers fell away. All at once they were over the sea and going home.

Fortune was still with them. The fuel finally ran out over the English countryside.

'I'm going to have to ditch her!' shouted Godfrey, thinking, Christ, it would be ironic to die like this after what we've just been through. They braced themselves for the impact. After a huge jolt and an initial sensation that the Whitley was going to capsize, it settled down, ran through a fence and finally juddered to a halt.

They were in a cornfield. The sun was out and birds were singing. It was a cool, crystalline English country morning. Dazed with exhaustion they all sat in silence for a few minutes, too mentally and physically drained to move. Once again they had made it. Finally Peter wearily got to his feet and went to the back. There was a pause and then, 'Oh, my God! Alfred's dead!' He began to cry.

Bill joined him at the back of the plane. In the hell-hole that was the rear turret, Alfred's body had slipped sideways and was slumped over the gun. Godfrey did not move nor did he answer. He remained sitting where he was, expressionlessly staring straight ahead. It suddenly seemed to him that it was imperative he see Rafe again before it was too late.

Rafe sounded out Mary Fox about work at the War Office. Although she did not say so, it occurred to her to wonder why he was taking such a personal interest in her welfare. She supposed that the sensitive nature of the job made it better to employ someone who was known rather than take a chance on an outsider.

'Before you give me an answer, I have to say it strikes me you've done your stint on the ambulance front,' said Rafe, 'and this is more important. I'm not saying life and limb isn't, but this involves the survival of the nation. And it's top secret. You can't tell even your mother what you do every day or where you go.'

'Assuming I take up the offer, what am I going to tell her?'

'You'll think of something.'

'Yes, I expect I will.'

'Do I take it that's an acceptance?'

'Yes.'

'Excellent!' He was visibly pleased.

'I probably won't be living with Mother for very much longer, by the way. Nettie has found herself a small house in Chelsea and has asked me to share it with her while Randolph's away. She lost the baby, you know.'

No, he hadn't known. His eyes narrowed. So Nettie was on the loose and unencumbered.

'For God's sake don't tell Nettie any of this.' I've got something entirely different in mind for Mrs Huntington, he thought.

Mary said with a flicker of amusement, 'Of course I won't. If my own mother isn't allowed to know, I'm hardly likely to tell Nettie.' There were times with her when he felt as though he was dealing with an equal, rather than someone years younger than he who was, moreover, about to become one of his subordinates.

'That's it then. Welcome aboard.' He stood up and so did she. They shook hands. 'We'll expect you to report for duty, as they say, on Monday morning at 9 a.m.'

Going home on the bus afterwards, Mary put her book to one side and considered her mother: I used to think we were close, that we must be just because she's my mother. Now I don't think we've ever really been close. Mother had never been maternal, she now recognized. It had taken her a long time to realize this because, given the way they lived, there had been no one to compare her with except Davina Harding and she wasn't maternal either. Do I love my mother? wondered Mary. Does she love me? Mother's pathological secrecy concerning family history seemed symptomatic of a remoteness which chilled closeness. More or less pushed into it by Nettie, she had made several attempts to learn more about her unforthcoming parent's past and therefore her own, and each time had been deftly deflected.

'I don't understand why you won't tell me,' said Mary, bewildered.

'I won't tell you because I don't *want* to tell you, Mary!' Sibyl was tart. 'What I *will* say is that there will come a day when you will know everything.'

That had been the end of it. One couldn't force somebody to talk if they were determined not to, and it seemed Mother was determined not to.

Against all the odds, Godfrey and the crew of the Whitley returned from another bombing raid. If anything, survival increased superstition and luck was jealously guarded. There was a tacit agreement among themselves that, because his had self-evidently run out, Alfred's name was never mentioned and when his grieving widow, Betty, moved away from the base as all the widows did sooner or later, they were not sorry to see her go. Death was all around. No one needed reminding. It had become a silent travelling companion, sitting beside those who were still left, and all were aware of it. For Godfrey and his crew Alfred's demise was one death too close, and fostered the unnerving idea that the eye of the grim reaper had finally turned in the direction of their Whitley.

Godfrey hitched a lift to London with three other young airmen who also had the unusual distinction of completing a tour. The hood of the Morgan was down and two of them sat up on the back of it. They were all euphoric and, as they drove, they shouted and sang. It was good to be alive. No, more than that, it was *miraculous* to be alive. The warm August wind rushed past them and the sweet smoky smell of late summer was intoxicating. Rippled by the light breeze, bronze fields of corn shot with scarlet poppies undulated to the far horizon. Away from the battle for a few brief, precious days, Godfrey suddenly realized that he was very very tired.

They dropped him off at the end of St Martin's Lane and Godfrey walked up to Leicester Square where he tried to telephone Rafe. As he had expected, given the time of day, there was no answer which did not matter as he had a key. He trekked on, past the end of Shaftesbury Avenue and the statue of Eros and up Piccadilly. The Ritz looked the same as usual and so, green trees crowding, did the park. Godfrey went into it and sat down on a bench. All at once he felt nauseous and, although there was no mission to be completed that evening, afraid. It was possible that this brief return to a sort of sanity had been a bad idea, that it only pointed up the madness of what he and the rest of the crew were doing, night after night. Unwilling to be alone with his own thoughts any longer, Godfrey stood up. Sitting doing nothing was destructive. He saw Alfred's face in his mind's eye, and other faces too. Dead men's faces. Better not to dwell on it. Thinking sapped the nerve.

102

When he reached the house he rang the bell. Still no answer. Godfrey let himself in. He put his bag down in the hall and went into the drawing-room where he opened one of the windows, letting out a trapped butterfly in the process. Everything was as it always had been. Books littered the sofas and an empty whisky glass stood on the mantelpiece in the exact place where it was Rafe's habit to lean, with the magnificent Claude Lorrain painting behind him. He went into the study to see if there was any message for him and found a note. *Returning around 8pm. R.* The top of the desk was totally clear which was odd, rather as though the person who habitually used it had mentally moved out. Left with the greater part of the afternoon to deal with, Godfrey briefly entertained the idea of going to see Nettie and then dismissed it. Fond of her as he was, he did not feel up to his effervescent sister today.

He wandered back to the drawing-room and, as always, his eye was drawn to the statue of Antinous. Eternal youth. He moved across the room towards it. It was exactly the same height as he was and in other ways too a mirror image of himself. On impulse he stepped forward and kissed the cold marble lips.

Rafe Bartholomew arrived back half an hour later than he had expected and found Godfrey lying fully dressed on one of the capacious cream sofas. To Rafe's eye his lover looked leaner and older. The graceful youth had become a man. Godfrey lay on his back with one arm dramatically outflung, like the death of Chatterton. His eyes were darkly shadowed and his cheekbones jutted. So profound was his slumber that he neither heard the front door nor sensed another presence in the room. Sleep had erased expression so that the face before Rafe was a beautiful blank. Not for the first time he wondered what, if anything, was behind it. Maybe, at the end of the day, Godfrey himself was a beautiful blank. Studying perfection, the recognition of such a possibility did not inhibit love, Rafe discovered, rather it added another dimension, that of protectiveness. As he watched the eyelids stirred and opened.

With a slow smile, 'Hello, Rafe,' said Godfrey.

Much later they took themselves out to dinner at Rules and talked, or tried to. Tried to because it became apparent that for the time being each was living in a world that the other could neither share nor even properly comprehend.

'I think of you all the time,' said Rafe. 'Just try to tell me what it's like.'

'Most of the time I'm scared shitless, and yet I'm seduced by it. It's the most thrilling thing I've ever done. It's a drug. I suppose it's a combination of flying, which I love, and the sheer bloody unpredictability of it all. Really, the closest I can get to it is Russian Roulette. We're hostages to fortune. And the feeling, coming home at the end of a mission, when you know you've got away with it once again . . . the only word for it is sensational, orgasmic even. It may sound an odd thing to say but, apart from meeting you, in some ways I feel it's the only time in my life that I've been properly alive.'

Fine words and true but, listening to himself going into it, Godfrey was aware of exhuming latent dread, thereby upsetting the fatalistic equilibrium which had kept him going on mission after mission without apparently turning a hair while others had nervous breakdowns. Fear in the heat of the action was one thing but this was quite another, an undermining secret thing which could destroy him if he let it get out of control. Maybe coming to see Rafe had upset a vital survival rhythm. He hoped not.

Because I don't want to die.

It was as though a thin, cold, bony finger had been drawn lightly down his spinal column. Involuntarily Godfrey shuddered.

Determined to shake the feeling off, he sipped his wine. 'God, it's good to drink a decent vintage. All I ever get is beer these days. But what about you, Rafe. What exactly are you doing?'

Undeceived, Rafe was dry. 'You don't want to talk about it and I can't.'

'What, not even to me?' Godfrey sounded piqued.

'Especially not to you. You could get shot down and end up in enemy hands don't forget.'

'If that happens I'm more likely to end up dead than in enemy hands, believe you me.'

'Before we leave it, tell me: what sort of success rate do you think the bombing is having?'

Godfrey shrugged. 'It's hard to tell because we never get any feedback plus it's a less than exact science. With no evidence to the contrary, I can only assume it is succeeding. I hope so because if it isn't we're all risking our lives for nothing.' It did not bear thinking about. Changing the subject, 'Tell me, do you ever see Father these days?'

'In the distance,' replied Rafe. 'Incidentally, what do you think of your delectable sister's marriage to the unappealing Randolph Huntington?'

'Nothing to think!' said Godfrey. 'It won't last. Nettie always was impulsive. Have you heard from Jonty lately? Or William?'

'Jonty, no, William, yes in a roundabout way. I ran into Mary Fox and she told me she'd had a letter from him. According to her he is, or rather he was, in Libya with Wavell's lot. I'm surprised *you* haven't heard from either of them.'

'Oh, you know our family,' said Godfrey vaguely. 'We've always been hopeless at keeping in touch, even at times like this. What's Mary doing now?'

'Not sure.' Rafe skated over it. 'Nice girl!'

Ignoring this because he was not *au fond* very interested in the doings of Mary Fox, Godfrey raised his glass. 'Here's to us. Let's enjoy the time we have left.'

They spent two intense days together through which, elegaic and poignant, ran a vein of desperation.

Some time after Godfrey had gone, a gloomy Churchill handed the Butt report on Bomber Command to Rafe Bartholomew.

'I want you to read this paper urgently. Assuming what it says is accurate, and I have reason to believe it is, it's extremely serious!'

Rafe sat up most of that night studying it and was appalled by what he found. Among other damning conclusions Mr Butt stated that only a very small percentage of the bombs dropped were anywhere near their allotted targets. Some missed by miles and miles. If what it said was true, young lives like Godfrey's were being lost in droves every day for nothing. The burden of this depressing knowledge was a heavy one and one that there could be no question of sharing with Godfrey. Godfrey's best chance of survival, Rafe realized, given that the whole exercise was going to carry on in its present form for a while yet, was to go on believing that what he was doing was mainly, if not wholly, effective.

Wearily Rafe rose to his feet and walked into his bedroom. Tomorrow he was due at Bletchley.

It was while he was removing his cufflinks that he noticed an extraordinary thing. Resting on the polished surface of the serpentine-fronted mahogany chest of drawers was a very large moth. Rafe, who had had a schoolboy passion for lepidoptery, knew it to be *Acherontia Atropos*, otherwise called the Death's Head Hawk Moth. The skull on the thorax was unmistakable. What was less clear was what it was doing here. Such exotic lepidoptera did make their way to Britain occasionally but a visit from this one, which originated in Africa, was particularly rare. Though not a superstitious man, Rafe was aware that such a sighting was commonly regarded as a portent of disaster. Struck by the moth's immobility, he stooped to look at it more closely. Curiously he put out a finger and gently touched it. Part of the wing crumbled into ghostly fine grey dust. With a chill of trepidation he realized that it was dead.

Part Three

Venetia

Give me mine angle; we'll to the river: there –
My music playing far off – I will betray
Tawny-finned fishes; my bended hook shall pierce
Their slimy jaws; and, as I draw them up,
I'll think them every one an Antony,
And say, 'Ah, ha! you're caught.'

Antony and Cleopatra

13

Nettie's small house in Chelsea proved to be not so small after all. Displaying considerable flair, presumably inherited from her mother, she redecorated it from top to bottom and furnished it with a judicious mixture of Harding and Huntington antiques. Then she set about entertaining. Mary wondered who was paying for it all. The absent Randolph, probably. Nettie did not appear to miss her husband, who wrote spasmodically. If Nettie ever penned a letter back, Mary did not see her doing it. Meanwhile every evening the house was full of mainly male guests. In the dark winter mornings when Mary left very early for work, her friend was still in bed. What she did with herself all day remained a mystery.

'How on earth do you keep yourself occupied?' enquired Mary. 'Don't you get bored?'

'No,' was the succinct answer.

'You could be doing something for the war effort. Join the Women's Volunteer Services, that sort of thing.' With mock severity, Mary wagged her finger.

'Darling, I'm already doing something for the war effort!' Nettie gave her a sly look.

'What? Keeping the British Armed Forces happy?'

'Certainly. It's very hard work.' Disgraceful. All the same it was impossible not to laugh.

'What are you going to do when Randolph comes home? You can't carry on like this while he's here.'

'Don't I know it! Wait for this. I got a letter this morning and, *quelle horreur*, he's coming home on leave in two weeks' time. Among other things he wants to have another shot at a child.' Nettie looked embattled. 'He goes on and on about it. I'm beginning to feel like a brood mare.'

'So you don't want one.'

'Of course not! I'm having a good time. Pregnancy would cramp my style. I didn't want a baby the first time around and I sure as hell don't want one now. And I don't want him either.'

'I'd better move back in with Mother while he's here, hadn't I? I mean he hasn't seen you for ages. He won't want me around.'

'No, but *I* will. For God's sake, Mary, don't leave me on my own with Randolph!'

Mary was amused.

'Nettie, he is your husband, after all!'

'Yes, and you were right in the first place. I never should have married him! The moment I'd done it, I knew I'd made a mistake!'

'Oh, come on! You'll feel different when you see him again.'

Nettie looked moodily out of the window. 'I doubt it.'

For different reasons they each pinned their hopes on Randolph's leave being cancelled. It was not. He arrived on a Sunday night, missing by minutes the departure from his own house of a young RAF pilot on whom Nettie was particularly sweet. 'Here comes purdah,' muttered his wife as she closed the door on one and shortly thereafter opened it to the other.

'Darling!' said Randolph.

'Randolph!' returned Nettie.

'Here's your husband, home from the war. Aren't you going to give me a kiss?'

Without waiting for an answer and still wearing his great-coat, he lunged at her with such enthusiasm that Mary, who was standing in the background, feared he was going to sweep his wife off her feet and rush straight up to the bedroom with her. However, Nettie stopped him in his tracks with the one diversionary tactic certain to appeal: 'My love, you must be exhausted. Why don't you let me fix you a drink?'

Randolph subsided immediately.

'Good idea! Whisky and soda and go easy on the soda.'

Helping him off with his coat, it occurred to Mary that he had probably had one or three already. When they were all sitting holding whiskies, Nettie said, 'I thought we'd all go out to dinner tonight, to celebrate your first night at home. I've booked the Mirabelle and after that I thought we'd go on to the Café de Paris. Darling, you haven't *lived* until you've danced to Snakehips Johnson and his band.'

110

'That's all very well,' said Randolph, 'but how are we going to get there? And back? There's a war on, don't forget.'

'It's all organized,' replied his resourceful wife. 'The Rely on Us taxi service is taking us.'

'Not me!' said Mary hastily. 'I have to be up very early tomorrow morning.'

Randolph, who plainly had other ideas on how to celebrate his first night at home, dickered and finally assented, reasoning that he would have to eat at some point and, that being the case, it might as well be at the Mirabelle. As they were finally leaving, he said to Nettie, 'Good idea of yours to ask Mary to act as chaperone. You're a brick, Mary!'

Mary was startled. *To act as . . . ?*

Behind her husband's retreating back, Nettie gave Mary a broad grin and a little wave.

Mary raised her eyebrows.

Proceeding down the steps, Randolph blithely continued, 'Your father was quite right on that one. Can't have a comely young woman living on her own in London without tittle-tattle . . .'

'Yes dear, no dear,' she heard Nettie say.

He was still going on about it, his voice receding, as they climbed into the taxi and slammed the door.

Mary was woken by the front door bell ringing very persistently. What time was it? Rousing herself she put on the light and picked up her alarm clock. Three a.m. She got out of bed, put on her dressing-gown and opened the window. Below on the frosty pavement stood Nettie together with someone Mary had never seen before.

'I need help, Mary,' called Nettie. 'I've mislaid my key.'

Mary went down.

'This is Mr Tripp,' introduced Nettie, 'doorman from the Café de Paris. Mr Tripp has very kindly given me a lift home which is divine of him because he lives in the East End and, as you know, the East End is in the opposite direction.'

'What happened to the Rely on Us taxi?'

'Somebody else hijacked it.'

And where was Randolph?

Correctly interpreting Mary's questioning look, Nettie said, 'He's still in Mr Tripp's car.' She gestured towards a battered old Morris. 'We're going to need help getting him out.' Mislaying the key was turning out to be the least of the problems.

'What on earth have you done to him?'

'It's not what I've done to him, it's what he's done to himself,' said Nettie.

'I'll get my coat,' said Mary.

Randolph was comatose, half in and half out of the car.

'Leave me alone, I want to go to sleep,' mumbled Randolph and then, 'Where am I anyway?'

Between them they managed to lever him out of the vehicle. He stank of whisky and the resultant relaxation made him very heavy.

'All hands to the wheel. If you two ladies can support him on one side, I'll try to hold him up on the other,' said the small but muscular Mr Tripp. 'Once we've got him more or less upright he'll probably walk automatically.'

They did get Randolph upright, at which point his knees buckled and he slid to the pavement nearly taking the three of them down with him. In the same fluid movement he put one hand under his head, drew up his knees and prepared to drift back to sleep on the freezing pavement.

'I'm very tempted to leave him here!' said Nettie.

'Come on ladies, never say die,' chided the indefatigable Mr Tripp. 'Once more! Heave!'

They got him up again. As if speaking to a somnambulist, Nettie hissed in her husband's left ear, 'Walk, Randolph, walk!' When the knees threatened to sag again in response, she smacked his face very hard. Shocked into mobility, he straightened up and gave his wife a hurt look.

'What did you do that for?' asked Randolph.

Mr Tripp, who appeared to be deeply fond of clichés, said, 'Sometimes you have to be cruel to be kind. Quick ladies, quick, let's strike while the iron is hot!' This time they hauled him up the steps along the hall and into the drawing-room.

'Get him to the end of the couch while he's still upright,' instructed Mr Tripp. 'Now . . .' he inserted an expert foot behind the knees, 'Timber!' Randolph toppled backwards onto the *chaise-longue*.

'Or maybe you'd prefer me to help you get him up to bed?'

asked the saintly Tripp. 'After all, you don't want to leave him there all night, do you?'

'Oh, no thank you, Mr Tripp,' said Nettie hastily. 'That would be beyond the call of duty.' She put her hand into the inside pocket of Randolph's coat, took out his wallet and extracted a note. Munificently pressing it into her benefactor's hand, she said, 'Thank you, Mr Tripp, you've been wonderful!'

Dazzled, he departed. Minutes later they heard the Morris backfire before it reluctantly started. The two women faced each other over the supine Randolph.

'What on earth are you going to do?' said Mary. 'You can't go on staving him off for ever.'

'Just watch me!' said Nettie.

'How long's he here for anyway?'

'A week. He thinks!'

He thinks. What did that mean?

Mary gave up on it. 'Look, I've got work in the morning and I've got to get some sleep. Do you think you can manage now?'

'Absolutely!' responded Nettie, secure in the knowledge that if anybody had to get up early it was not going to be her. 'First though I'm going to be the perfect wife by taking Randolph's boots off. Let nobody say I don't work hard at my marriage. And then I'm going to bed as well.'

In the morning Mary left before either of them was up. Which was a relief. Despite a strong element of farce in last night's alarums and excursions, it was obvious to Mary that Nettie's marriage was a disaster, and furthermore that having made her bed she had no intention of lying in it. Thank God for the War Office! At least it kept her out of the house all day.

It did not, however, keep her out of the house first thing in the morning. Two days running, at a time when Mary would have preferred to see no one at all, she found Randolph, morose and sorry for himself, in the kitchen. Red-eyed and shambling in a checked woollen dressing-gown he was not at his best. As she made them both toast, out of the corner of her eye she could see him wandering restlessly around, apparently unable to settle anywhere, a breakfast Flying Dutchman. On the second day, able to bear it no more, she said, with one eye on her watch, 'What's the matter, Randolph?'

The answer was simple and heartfelt and dreadfully frank. 'I'm not getting my oats,' he said.

Mary, who had not set eyes on Nettie since the Mr Tripp episode, wished she had not asked. When she left in the mornings, Nettie was still in bed, and when she got back at night, often quite late, nobody was there at all. Mary had assumed that Randolph and Nettie were out on the town together. It now began to transpire that they were out on the town separately.

'Venetia is engaged on sensitive secret work,' explained her mopey husband, 'so sensitive that she can't even tell me what it is. The result is that she isn't here for *me*.'

Unwilling to hear any more of it, Mary drained her teacup and picked up her bag, 'Randolph, I'm afraid I've . . .'

Undeterred, he continued, '. . . well, of course I under-stand all that, Mary. War on. Security of the nation. That sort of thing.' Here he drew himself up and for one mad moment Mary thought he might be about to salute. 'But now, on top of that she says she has Women's Troubles, the curse as she calls it, and the upshot of *that* is nothing doing between us for at least four days. Well, I rejoin my regiment in three days and I want to crack on . . .'

'Crack on?'

'With producing an heir . . .'

Put like that it did not sound very romantic.

'. . . I'm the only son. If I got killed in action what would happen?'

'I don't know. Look Randolph, I must . . .'

Gloomily answering his own question, 'Money, property, it would all go out of the family. To a cousin! A *cousin*, Mary! God, I wish I had a whisky!'

A whisky? It was only 8 a.m.

'But you'd be beyond caring by then anyway.'

Suspiciously he stared at her and, for a moment, Mary feared it was one flippant remark too far. 'Dynastic matters have to transcend the grave,' Randolph pronounced pompously, having apparently decided not to take offence, for who else was there to listen to him if he did? 'Curse or no curse, I think I might insist. It's Venetia's duty!'

'Randolph, take some good advice from me and don't start pointing out to Nettie where her duty lies. It won't help. As you rightly say, there is a war on and all our lives are fractured to one degree or another. Why don't you put procreation to one side for the time being and just enjoy each other. After all, you have to admit that Nettie's already done her dynastic bit once –'

'Yes and lost the child!' The censorious way in which this interruption was delivered made Nettie sound careless.

'Nettie was quite ill!' Mary was short. 'Randolph, I must go!'

Still explaining his point of view he tracked her along the hall. It was very like having a dialogue with a limpet. No wonder Nettie had had enough of it.

That evening, when Mary returned home expecting an empty house, she was surprised to find Nettie in the drawing-room wearing a chic black dress and a small sequinned hat with a veil.

'Come on, Mary, I've been waiting for you. Where have you been?' she said, 'Go and get changed and hurry up about it, we're going out.'

'What, with Randolph?'

'No, *not* with Randolph.'

Mary asked the perennial question. 'Where *is* Randolph?'

'Out for the count, upstairs!' Nettie was terse. 'Oh well, if you *must* know . . .' She raised the veil which also had sequins on it. Beneath was a spectacular black eye.

'Oh, Nettie!' Mary was horrified on her friend's behalf. 'He didn't . . . ?'

'He did do this,' (pointing to the bruise) 'and he didn't do *that*. He couldn't raise it. Too drunk. But because he couldn't he got very belligerent and hit me instead.'

Probably still shocked, Nettie suddenly dissolved into uncharacteristic tears. 'You were quite right, Mary, I shouldn't have married Randolph but I was so desperate to get away from the family.'

Reflecting that at least the family hadn't knocked Nettie about, Mary remembered her recounting the story of how, after she had been caught *in flagrante delicto* with Joshua the stable lad, her father had beaten her and had appeared to enjoy doing it. Where some were concerned it was beginning

115

to look as though having a family could be almost as much of a cross as not having one.

There was the sound of movement upstairs.

Galvanized, Nettie brushed aside the tears and dropped the veil. 'No time to change. Quick, let's go!' Together they stole across the room and noiselessly let themselves out, after which they ran. Once round the corner and out of sight they stopped, laughing hysterically, and faced one another.

'Look, this is all very well, but what are you going to do tonight?' asked Mary.

'If the worst comes to the worst, I'll go to a hotel. But the worst won't come to the worst, I've got lots of options.' By now they were at the King's Road. 'Taxi!'

'Yes, but there's the night after and the night after that . . .'

'No there isn't. Randolph goes to rejoin his regiment tomorrow.'

Mary was astonished. 'I thought he was here until Saturday.'

'So does he. What he doesn't know is that tomorrow he's going to receive a telegram. Recalling him. I prevailed upon a brother officer who was at school with Godfrey to send it. Since Randolph's as popular in his regiment as he is with me it wasn't very difficult. By the time he realizes it's a hoax, it will be too late. So apart from the fact that there's a war on, it's back to normal.'

Rafe Bartholomew was one of those unobtrusive figures who seemed to be everywhere. There were those who assumed him to be a fixture at the War Office because his tall figure was often seen tacking along its corridors, and others who, for the same reason, thought Bletchley Park was his principal stamping ground. Yet another faction considered him one of Churchill's principal lieutenants and privy to the old man's innermost thoughts. In a way all these things were true for Rafe's roving brief took him into all the secret stratas of spying and intelligence. Liaising and fixing, assessing and recommending, he slipped seamlessly between them and the Prime Minister, working particularly closely with the urbane Stewart Menzies, Director of the Secret Intelligence Service, and

116

ensuring that the Armed Services and the Navy pulled together.

The war rumbled on. London remained under siege. Firebombs cascaded, destroying everything they hit. The Dorchester replaced the Ritz as a favourite haunt for Nettie and her crowd because the walls were built of reinforced concrete, in theory affording more protection for the inmates.

As the air raids continued, it was becoming difficult to remember what life had been like before the war. Mary continued to write to William but only received one more fragmentary letter back.

'Why does my brother write to you and not to me?' Nettie wanted to know.

'Because *I* write to *him*,' was Mary's answer. 'When did you last put pen to paper, Nettie?'

Nettie tossed her head and did not answer.

Since she felt she should, rather than because she wanted to, Mary went to visit her mother fairly regularly. Occasionally during the course of these meetings Sibyl alluded to the pre-Harding era but, when pressed by her daughter for details, tantalizingly and maddeningly refused to elaborate. Sometimes Mary suspected her enigmatic parent of playing a game, or maybe it was just that the past was more in the forefront of her thoughts lately. Whatever the reason, Sibyl was still not prepared to unburden herself to her daughter, though these days she was prepared to be more forthcoming than before about Mary's father. Avid for knowledge, Mary probed.

'You must have been devastated when he died.' Mary tried to imagine the phenomenon of her father leaving one morning, apparently on track for a perfectly ordinary day, and her mother receiving the news an hour later that he had had a fatal heart attack. The shock must have been immense.

'I was. Charles was the only man, apart from my own father, whom I felt able to trust. Our relationship was similar in other ways too, in that although I depended on Charles and felt affection for him, I was not in love with him. My father died young too. It was like a repeating pattern. For the second time in my life I had no one to turn to, but this time I had a child to support as well.'

The last words were uttered in an unemotional tone of

voice. *A child.* This is *me* we're talking about, thought Mary. Not for the first time it struck her that somewhere along the line Mother's ability to express, and maybe even feel, love had been cauterized during the course of her secret girlhood. The news that her mother had not been in love with her father came as an unpleasant shock.

Possibly because they were no longer living together she noticed that her parent looked older. Even the extraordinary hair had lost its electric crackle and, like a fire that has been damped down, the personality appeared to have lost its spark as well. Left with no diversion other than the war effort, Sibyl was peevish and bored. Lethal even. And deeply disappointed in her daughter who could have been, no *should* have been, such an asset. As it was, Mary's looks (although in Sibyl's view she did not make the best of them) and brains (alas they had not been able to afford to make the best of those either) were neutralized by the sort of lack of guile and manipulation which infuriated her mother. Since she had been subtly trying to mould her daughter throughout childhood without success, trying to make a sow's ear out of a silk purse now was unlikely to prove rewarding. Life being what it was, her strategy had, of course, worked with Nettie who did not need it. Most galling of all was that although she had achieved half her aim in that William had fallen for Mary it was a lost cause because Mary had not noticed and, even if she had, would not have been calculating enough to take advantage of it. Which left them both still out in the social cold in the wake of the Harding era. Geoffrey Harding had sporadically tried to make contact and, while Sibyl had not encouraged him, hedging her bets she had not discouraged him exactly either. For who knew what could happen? Davina might be flattened by a doodlebug thereby creating a job vacancy for Sibyl, although until that happened she could see no point in enduring sexual congress with Geoffrey. Let Davina take the rough with the smooth – in so far as there was any smooth where Geoffrey was concerned.

Sibyl had given up working for the Women's Voluntary Service and had taken another unrewarding clerking job in one of the few City offices that was still standing. Barren evenings enlivened only by air raids were a problem which she had solved by beginning to write her memoirs. For after all, thought Sibyl, what else do I have to fall back on? There were days when life felt as though it had come to a full stop.

Sitting opposite her during one of these visits, as they shared a very unappetizing meal, Mary could see that her mother was in a sulk.

'You say you never see anybody, so I don't know why you gave up the WVS,' pointed out Mary.

Sibyl bridled. 'Team work has never been my forte.' She did not go on.

Silence.

In the end, more to fill the void than anything else, Mary told her the story of Nettie and Randolph. At the end of it her mother said, '*Nettie's* always had gumption!' The way this remark was delivered it was hard to escape the inference.

'If that's the case, I can't see where it's got her,' protested Mary. 'She's married to a man she despises –'

'Where it's got her,' interrupted Sibyl Fox, bile welling, 'is away from her poisonous parents with a free rein on the London party circuit, insofar as that currently exists, and a new lover every night if that's what she wants. And what have you got? What have you got, Mary? I'll tell you! A censorious attitude, no man and no prospects either.'

The sudden vituperative spitefulness of the attack caught Mary off guard.

'Oh, I watched you,' jeered Sibyl, 'I watched you making calf's eyes at Godfrey Harding when you should have been setting your cap at William or the other one. What a missed opportunity! Godfrey Harding was never going to notice *you*. You're a fool, Mary. A fool! We could have ended up back in that house which meant so much to you, as part of the family if you'd had the wit to play your cards right.' Sibyl stopped abruptly. Perhaps she had run out of breath or maybe she had let out more than she intended.

Shocked and mortified by the revelation that her secret love for Godfrey had apparently been public property, Mary could think of nothing immediate to say. Her mother's ridicule of something so deeply precious to her felt like a desecration, and the idea that she might set her cap, as her mother had put it, at another brother just because the one she was in love with was not interested was repulsive to her.

119

Mary stood up. Her icy dignity was such that even Sibyl Fox was abashed.

'Where are you going?' And then, clutching at the mundane, 'Mary! You haven't finished your cup of tea.'

In silence her daughter gathered up coat, shoulder bag and book.

'Goodbye, Mother.'

Sibyl heard the sound of footsteps in the hall and then the immutable quiet closure of the front door.

Outside the sirens struck up. Listlessly, she turned her head towards the window.

Having driven away the only person who might have cared for her and been her solace, Sibyl Fox was left sitting by herself, a prisoner of her own disappointments and wilful desires. As the darkness gathered around her, she felt herself absorbed into it and, finally, in a strange way, part of it.

14

On the evening of December 7th 1941 Rafe, who had been at Bletchley Park that day, arrived late for dinner with Churchill. Among others also present were the American ambassador, the President's special envoy, Averell Harriman, and a young ambitious aide called Kyle McClaren. Without appearing to do so, as he ate Bartholomew studied McClaren. McClaren was a high flier or he would not have been where he was and, as a result, was no doubt privy to the sort of top secret American intelligence that Rafe would have given his eye teeth to possess. A patrician American, he was intelligent and attractive with a slightly reckless air which probably appealed to Churchill.

A plan began to form in Bartholomew's head.

It was now just after 9 p.m. and, as was his habit, the Prime Minister switched on the radio. Electrified, they all heard the news that the Japanese had mounted an attack on the American Navy. Assuming the report was accurate the consequences would be momentous. Rafe, who was staring intently at Churchill, thought he caught the briefest flicker of an expression he found difficult to interpret. In the end he pinpointed it as smug satisfaction, triumph even, as if something expected had come in on cue.

Well, well! Perhaps the old fox had known what was coming all the time and had kept it all to himself, not even telling Roosevelt. Or rather, Rafe corrected himself, especially not telling Roosevelt.

Rafe knew that the intelligence sources of both sides had expected some sort of Japanese strike; it was obvious from the reactions of the Americans present that none of them had had any idea where or when. But come to that neither had the British, or so he had thought. But if his surmise was correct, someone at Bletchley Park must have known. The Japanese linguist Malcolm Kennedy was a possibility. For the time being Bartholomew gave up on it. What mattered was that America now *had* to enter the war.

The Admiralty confirmed the news.

Churchill left his guests and went off to telephone the President. When he returned he told them that the assault had been on Pearl Harbour.

'It is the President's intention to ask Congress for a declaration of war on Japan,' stated Churchill. 'Gentlemen, raise your glasses to the beginning of the end.'

Rafe Bartholomew organized a large dinner party. He held it in his own house and among the guests were Miss Venetia Harding and Mr Kyle McClaren. On arrival he made sure that they were part of the same conversational group, but he did not seat the two of them together for the duration of the meal. Rafe saw that these two perversely thrived on overcoming all the odds; making it difficult for them to communicate for most of the evening would mean that a coming together later was certain. Half to his amusement and half to his irritation, he was proved right for when they finally all went into dinner Kyle McClaren took a seat beside Nettie. Quite rightly, Rafe noticed, passing behind them both. Somebody had swapped the place cards.

Nettie, who was looking as though butter wouldn't melt, was particularly peachy this evening. Appetizing was the word. Rafe thought it was doubtful whether Nettie's looks would last and it therefore behoved her to make the most of her youthful bloom and, self-evidently, she did not need him to tell her this. Plump white shoulders and creamy cleavage were set off to advantage by a black velvet *décolletage*. Round Nettie's neck was a single string of what Bartholomew thought of as débutante pearls. The contrast between blatant advertisement and the demure was perfectly judged. Here is a lady who is available but, nevertheless, a lady, went the message. She had taken off her wedding ring, he noticed.

McClaren was plainly bowled over by her. The two heads, one blond and one auburn, inclined. With total absorption and execrable manners, Nettie and McClaren ignored those to the left and right of them and concentrated on each other. It struck Bartholomew that he had mounted a big production in order to achieve something which at the end of the day had taken all of five minutes to ignite.

122

Staring at her place card and making up his mind to take it with him when he left as a memento, hopefully together with her telephone number, McClaren said musingly, 'Venetia. I just love your name, Miss Harding.'

He looked into her turquoise eyes. She tilted her head and slanted a smile at him, reminding him all of a sudden of the coquettish southern beauties of his boyhood who had also had magnolia skin and who also knew how to tease and entrance a man.

Miss Harding. Seeing it for the first time, it occurred to Nettie to wonder why she had been billed as Miss Venetia Harding rather than Mrs Randolph Huntington. Rafe Bartholomew could have given her the answer. As far as Rafe was concerned, Nettie was bait. He divined that in Kyle McClaren there just might be an old-fashioned sense of honour which could have prevented things going any further because her husband was an officer fighting for his country at the front. Let her ensnare him first and then tell him about her marriage if she felt like it.

Nettie did not feel like it. It was glorious to be Miss Venetia Harding again and, for one night at least, without the millstone of Randolph round her neck.

'Thank you, Mr McClaren,' said Nettie, eyes modestly cast down at smoked salmon and well aware as she spoke that an impeccable response was called for in the light of the come hither look that had gone before it. Preliminary bow and curtsy. This was a ritual dance that Kyle knew all about and, as he prepared to step out, it occurred to him that through his charming fellow guest he might learn more about their enigmatic host.

'Rafe Bartholomew, Man of Mystery,' said Nettie in response to his query. 'That's how I think of him, anyway. He is, or was, a colleague of my father's until they fell out. Rafe is Churchill's man and Father never was. He's very, very wealthy and according to my brother Godfrey, whom he befriended, very, very clever. As such he's one of London's most eligible bachelors. Also according to Godfrey there's no family to interfere either. He's an only child whose father is dead and whose mother lives in a certain degree of splendour in the country. More I cannot tell you. Why do you want to know anyway?'

'Oh, you know, we're trying to work together,' said Kyle easily. 'I just wondered . . .'

One of London's most eligible bachelors. Remembering the magnificent classical statue in the drawing-room, he sent his host a speculative look. 'Antinous,' Bartholomew had said, 'as Bacchus,' in answer to his question. Hmm. But never mind about that.

'You are very beautiful, Miss Harding!' Kyle would have liked to have taken her hand and kissed it but this was not the time or the place. Chicken Florentine arrived, temporarily giving them both something else to think about. Picking up silver knife and fork, he continued, 'But I expect men tell you that all the time.'

'Put it this way,' replied Nettie, 'I never get tired of hearing a handsome man say it.' There was laughter in her eyes and, at the same time, a slight set to her mouth which might have indicated impatience. *I know where I stand. What about you?*

Encouraged by her oblique compliment, Kyle said, 'Before I mend a fence by engaging the lady on my right in meaningless conversation, will you allow me to escort you home tonight?'

Without exactly answering him, she gave him a bright-eyed droll look. 'Actually, I wasn't thinking of going straight home afterwards,' said Nettie. Leaving him to think about it, she turned to her left.

They went to the 400 which in common with everywhere else was blacked out. It was an odd, surreal existence reflected McClaren. The band was playing, the drink was flowing and outside there was a war on. Dancing with Nettie, he tightened his arm around her waist and as he did so recognized her scent.

With exquisite timing the sirens began.

'Christ!' Anticipating the undignified rush to the cellars or wherever, but more importantly the end of the romantic moment, Kyle swore.

'What's the matter?' Nettie turned a serene face up to his. 'I love dancing! I'm not going anywhere until the band downs instruments.'

Unable to resist it he bent his head towards her and kissed

her on the lips, tentatively at first and then, when she did not object, with gathering passion.

Much as she would have liked to, Nettie did not ask Kyle McClaren into her bed that night, although she did allow him to escort her home.

'I'll phone you in the morning,' promised Kyle, prior to kissing her again.

'It *is* the morning, so not too early,' said Nettie.

In fact he was not the only one to telephone her. Rafe Bartholomew rang as well.

'Heavens, you haven't given me time to write and thank,' said Nettie.

'Never mind about that, I need to see you!'

Really? Nettie was intrigued.

'What about lunch?'

'I can't do lunch,' said Nettie, who had just committed herself to Kyle. 'What about a cocktail? Here if you like.'

'All right, but I'd like this to be a confidential talk.'

Curiouser and curiouser!

'Mary never gets home until after seven. Why don't we say six?'

'Six it is!' He took down her address. 'I'll be there. If I'm delayed, I'll ring. Oh, and Venetia . . .'

'Yes?'

'I'd prefer it if you didn't mention this to anybody. And I mean *anybody*.'

Agog by now, 'I won't tell a soul,' promised Nettie and she didn't. Not even Kyle, with whom she had, as she was to tell Mary, the most divinely flirtatious lunch.

Rafe Bartholomew arrived five minutes late and before he rang the doorbell paused for a moment looking at the outside of Venetia's little house which was part of a pretty, early Victorian terrace. He assumed it to be rented, presumably with Randolph footing the bill. She answered the door. Taking off his hat, Rafe stepped inside.

Her sitting-room was attractive, with lamps, little button-backed velvet armchairs and fresh flowers everywhere. A butler's tray groaned under the weight of a great variety of spirits. He wondered where she had got it all from. The black market? Inside Venetia Huntington's house it was very easy to forget there was a war on. While she made the drinks Rafe inspected some silver-framed photographs which were standing in a cluster on a mahogany side table. There they all were, all except Randolph, he noticed. Nettie, as she then was, on her first pony; all the Hardings in the garden; Geoffrey Harding glowering ferociously out of another one with Davina slightly out of focus by his side and, beside this, one of just the four children. With a lurch of the heart he found himself face to face with a young Godfrey in an Eton collar, standing at the back of the group, aloof and unsmiling and at the same time heart-breakingly handsome. Even at that early age it was possible to see the twins' looks beginning to diverge: as if a film was developing, Jonty's resemblance to his autocratic father was already registering, while William's oval face echoed that of his mother. Nettie, on the other hand, was very much her own woman and had succeeded in stamping her personality so vigorously on the lens that everyone else, even Godfrey, was upstaged. Absently taking his drink from her, Rafe tried to work out what it was about his hostess which was so potent and decided that there was a quality of wilful engagement there, a fearlessness: *Anything goes!* said the look. That being the case, she could be exactly right for what he had in mind. The question mark remaining in Rafe's mind was over Venetia's discretion.

There was another matter that needed clearing up too.

'How's Randolph?' asked Bartholomew.

Venetia rolled her eyes. 'Don't talk to me about Randolph. That was a mistake. I've decided I'm going to cut my losses and divorce him, though not yet since while he's away I don't have a problem. However, he's paying the rent and a separation leaves open the question of what I do next. I certainly couldn't afford to go on living here without a financial blood transfusion.'

'What about your father?' Bartholomew sipped his whisky. 'Couldn't he give you a helping hand?'

'He could but then he'd want to control me. Quite frankly I don't want Father in my life on that level ever again.'

That certainly made sense and at the same time opened the way forward.

After a pause for thought, Rafe said, 'I may have a proposition that would interest you and solve the financial

126

aspect. But first, and this will sound like an odd request, may I see the rest of the house?'

'Of course!'

The dining-room was in the basement. It was a long narrow low-ceilinged room, most of which was taken up with a D-ended table which could probably seat twelve. Again with rich wallpaper and swagged, elegantly-draped curtains, it was a seductive room. Venetia seemed to have the gift of intimacy with interiors as well as with men. Late at night, Rafe could imagine candles and flowers and the table encircled by mainly male guests at the end of a meal, all talking over brandy and port and cigars and, assuming they were all on the same side, swapping confidences.

'You can see the bedrooms if you like,' suggested Venetia, with a sidelong look. Was it an illusion, or was there the faintest trace of an invitation for more than just a viewing?

'No need for that.' Rafe was dry. 'Let's go back upstairs, shall we, and I'll tell you what it is I have in mind.'

When they were back in the drawing-room, he said, 'How would you like to help the war effort?'

Help the war effort? Oh, God. Nettie's eyes glazed. Helping the war effort sounded like getting a dreary old full-time job. Watching the reaction, Bartholomew was diverted.

'Let me explain. Now that the United States has entered the war, American top brass will be passing through London. They will need entertaining and cosseting and I will need someone to do it. Because they come from the allegedly democratic, classless land of the free, most of them will be impressed by the British upper class which is where you, Venetia, with your connections on that level come in. You would be the ideal hostess. The rent on this house plus all other expenses would be paid for.'

A calculating look crossed Nettie's face.

'I can see what's in it for me,' said Nettie, 'and up to a point what's in it for you, but only up to a point. There must be something more in it for you.'

'There is,' said Bartholomew.

Nettie raised her eyebrows enquiringly.

'Information.'

Nettie was puzzled. 'But surely they tell you everything now they've entered the war. We're allies after all.'

'Would it were so,' said Rafe.

'But how do you suggest I go about it?'

'All the introductions will be in place for you courtesy of me. I will brief you on the sort of thing we are looking for. How you go about it, as you put it, after that is up to you and none of my business. I need hardly add that this particular social operation is top secret and at the first hint of any indiscretion on your part, the arrangement would be terminated with no appeal.' He lit a small cigar.

Listening to him, Nettie observed, 'I may not be very brainy, like Mary for instance, but I'm perfectly capable of keeping a secret. I'm also fully aware at this stage of my life on which side my bread's buttered.'

It was more or less the answer he had been looking for.

Then, as an afterthought, she added, 'But what about Mary? She lives here too! How do I keep all this secret from Mary?'

'Leave it to me,' said Bartholomew. 'By the way, what did you make of my friend Kyle McClaren? Kyle, as I'm sure you know, is close to the centre of power as well as being a very personable fellow.'

'You want me to spy on Kyle.' It was a statement, not a question.

Rafe was pained. 'Not *spy*, Venetia, and not just McClaren either. Provide the ambience. Get the right people together, draw them out, listen. That sort of thing.'

'And report back to you!'

Bored with it, Rafe extinguished the cigar. 'And report back to me.'

Nettie was silent. The idea of being Chelsea's answer to Mata Hari appealed. Perhaps it *was* time she did something towards the war effort. She remembered Kyle's questions about Rafe himself. This could be a two–way street, Nettie recognized.

'What if they ask me about the British side of things? What then?'

'You won't know anything so there won't be a problem. Although what I'll almost certainly do is to give you the odd apparently strategic piece of information so that you can guilelessly pass it on to them. Just so that they feel

128

they're getting something too. Everyone a prizewinner as in the caucus race in *Alice's Adventures in Wonderland*.'

He leant back in his chair.

'I'd like an answer in the next day or two.'

'No need to wait a day or two,' said Nettie, 'the answer's Yes. I need the money. Can I get you another drink?'

Rafe glanced at his watch. He did not want to be there when Mary Fox returned. 'No, thank you. I'd better go. I'm expected somewhere else at eight.'

As he was leaving, he said, 'Have you heard from Godfrey lately?'

Nettie was shamefaced. 'I haven't, but as everyone knows I'm a hopeless correspondent. Have you?'

'Yes,' said Bartholomew. 'About a week ago. He's fine.' A sudden, disconcerting memory of the Death's Head moth surfaced. Shaking its spectre, he said, 'I'll be in touch with you within the next few days.'

She saw him out onto the pavement. It was dusk and the air was very still. Fine snow was slipping down out of a slate-coloured sky and just beginning to settle. When she had closed the front door, Nettie went to the window and watched Rafe Bartholomew's tall, spare figure in astrakhan-collared coat and black homburg hat stride along the street and finally turn the corner. She wondered where his car was and was not to know that in the interests of anonymity it was waiting for him two streets away. Turning back into the room and deciding to get into the spirit of the proposition that had just been put to her, Nettie picked up the empty glasses and the ashtray and took them downstairs where she carefully cleared away all evidence of Rafe's visit.

The Wednesday after his visit to Nettie, Mary Fox was asked to report to Rafe Bartholomew's office. She knocked on the door and then entered.

He was writing but immediately stopped.

'Do sit down, Mary.' He gestured towards a chair on the other side of his desk.

'Thank you, Mr Bartholomew.' She sat and waited. Not for the first time she tried to decide how old he was. Probably only about ten years older than she was. Hard to tell.

'Mary, how do you like being at the War Office?'

129

'I like it very much.' And then, with a certain degree of alarm, 'I hope my work's up to standard –'

'Your work is very good. To the point where I would like to offer you a promotion. At Bletchley Park we have finally been given the go-ahead to recruit more sorely needed staff. I would like you to be one of the new recruits.'

He waited to see what she would say.

Mary was startled. 'But isn't Bletchley miles away?'

'Sixty miles away to be precise. It would mean that you would have to live there and naturally accommodation would be found for you.'

There was a significant pause.

Kindly, Bartholomew said, 'You're worried about your mother perhaps.'

'No. In actual fact Mother and I have not seen each other for some time.'

Surprised, Rafe revised his ideas as to what that particular relationship was all about. He had assumed the two women were very close. Mary did not enlighten him.

'I was thinking more of Nettie. I don't want to let her down. If I go she'll be on her own . . .'

'Look, why don't you sound her out? Don't tell her what the job is but tell her you've been offered a transfer. You never know, you might be surprised by her reaction. That's assuming you're interested in it in the first place.'

'I *am* interested. Thank you very much. All right, I'll see what she says.'

She tackled Nettie that evening.

Impressed by Rafe's speed, Nettie said, 'Look, Mary, don't worry about it. There's a war on. We all have to do our bit. And whenever you come to London there's always a bed here for you if you need it.'

Half this speech sounded like Nettie and half did not.

'What sort of job is it anyway?'

'Oh, just more of the same old boring secretarial work,' replied Mary, side-stepping, 'but I rather fancy being in the country for a change.'

'Do you?' Nettie was frankly amazed. 'Wild horses wouldn't drag me back there. I've had enough of the country to last me a lifetime. But I will miss you. When are you going to go?'

130

'I haven't accepted it yet. I wanted to talk to you first, but soon I should think.'

The French ormolu clock on the mantelpiece struck eight. Nettie leapt to her feet.

'Oh Lord, is it really that late? I've got that heavenly American turning up to take me out to dinner in fifteen minutes, the one I told you about, and I'm not even changed. Why don't you join us? He's got the sort of crucial job where he'll probably have to leave early anyway.'

'It's a tempting offer but I won't,' answered Mary, who intended to write to her mother that evening. 'I can't keep the sort of hours you do and still get up at six-thirty and function properly. What I will do is sit him down with a drink and entertain him until you deign to reappear.'

Mary liked Kyle McClaren. He was personable and good mannered with an informal openness that she thought of as very American. Whatever it was it was very appealing. Pity Randolph was not more like Kyle.

'How did you and Nettie meet?'

'Nettie?' He looked nonplussed. 'Oh, you mean Venetia!'

'Nettie's what the family call her. It's a childhood name and probably about time she was promoted to Venetia.'

'We met at a grand dinner party given by Rafe Bartholomew . . .'

Ah! Mary's brow furrowed. Rafe Bartholomew. Again. The man was everywhere. She had a strange intimation of some sort of pattern forming itself, but when she tried to work out what that was, kaleidoscopic it dissolved and formed another.

'. . . Venetia and I hit it off straight away,' Kyle was saying. It was plain he was crazy about her. Listening to him, she wondered if Nettie had told him she had a husband. Probably not. Nettie reappeared, svelte in red. Recognizing the signs, Mary realized it was seduction night. Kyle McClaren would, of course, think he was doing it but he'd be wrong.

When they had gone, she went to the little writing desk, extracted a sheet of paper and an envelope and began to compose a letter.

Dear Mother,
It upsets me that there is this coolness between us and

131

that I have not heard from you since the night of our quarrel. Perhaps you don't realize how much you hurt me. Of course I realized that Godfrey Harding would never take any notice of me, much less ever fall in love with me. I could have and indeed have lived with that, though it was not easy. But to hear you dismiss my love for him in the sort of terms you did, as though it was some sort of laughable aberration on my part, hurt and offended me more than I can say. I would go further and say that I found the idea that I should transfer my affection from Godfrey, because he was not available, to one of the others (it did not apparently matter which) in the interests of making some money, abhorrent. This may seem unworldly to you but, for me, love is not a bargaining chip. You are my mother, (here Mary hesitated) *I love you and have not lost sight of the fact that I owe you a great deal. I want to repair this breach but felt I could not until all this was out in the open between us. Now it is. In conclusion I should tell you that I have a new job and, as a result, shall be moving to the country for the forseeable future. I should very much like to see you before I go, for in times like these who knows what could happen next? I shall be contactable on Nettie's number for at least another week.*

    Your loving daughter,
    Mary

Mary reread the letter and decided that while it was stern, it was also fair. She addressed an envelope, put the folded sheet inside and stamped it. Now it was up to Mother.

Kyle and Venetia were in the middle of dinner when a bomb fell near by. Along with certain other robust diners they had heard the warning and had decided to ignore it. The explosion was close enough to bring down a substantial amount of the ceiling of the room they were sitting in and to blow in a large proportion of the windows. The next might be a direct hit.

'I think we should leave,' said Kyle.

'Where to, though,' cried Nettie, gathering up her fur and bag post-haste and preparing to follow him. 'Shall we jump under the table? No, what about the Underground. It's literally fifty yards.'

As they raced for it the world seemed to ignite around them. There was another deafening explosion, again very close. Behind the black buildings the sky was incandescent. Nobody spoke. The clatter of running feet was all around as the population streaked for cover. Arriving breathless, Nettie and Kyle found the tube platform crowded with a mixture of those who were there for the night with their bedding, the lucky ones lying on bunks along the walls, and other birds of passage like themselves. There was an atmosphere of camaraderie in the face of shared danger. One resourceful group was making tea in a watering can and stirring it with what looked like a broom handle. A woman handed Nettie a steaming mug.

'Fancy a cup, love?'

'Yes! Thanks!'

She took it with alacrity and was disappointed. It tasted mainly of hot water and powdered milk. Nevertheless she took a deep swig. Heaven knew when any more sustenance would be on offer. Nettie's fashionable attire in an era of clothing coupons attracted a certain amount of attention.

'Who's your lady friend?' someone asked Kyle.

'That's no lady, that's my wife.' It was the oldest joke in the book but still they all laughed and so did Nettie. I wish I was married to Kyle and not Randolph, thought Nettie. She turned to him.

'Assuming we're still alive, what shall we do when the raid's over? No point in going back to the restaurant, the food will be cold. Would you like a sip of this?' She proffered the mug.

Kyle was both admiring and amused. 'No thanks. Are you usually this flippant in the middle of emergencies?'

'What else is there to do?' Nettie was insouciant. 'This has been going on since 1939. As far as I'm concerned it's become a way of life.'

'I can see that. To answer your original question, why don't we go back to my hotel? It's much closer than Chelsea.'

'Can you guarantee hot food?'

'Certainly can. Don't you think of anything except your stomach?'

'Depends what else is on offer.' She shot him a mischievous glance.

'Plenty.'

Venetia Harding is delicious, McClaren thought. She's got that independent-minded sparkle that reminds me of certain American girls I've known, and all coupled with that sexy English voice and English look. He took her arm. 'There's the all-clear. People are starting to leave. Let's go!'

Later on, in bed together after they had made love, he watched her solicitously as she slept. It struck him that sex came as naturally to Venetia as eating candy. Not only was she very good at it, but she got fun out of it too which in Kyle's experience some women didn't. He lifted back the sheet to enjoy the sight of her body once more. Trying to think which painter she reminded him of, he came up with Fragonard. It was only too easy to imagine her being a very naughty girl in the louche atmosphere of the court of Louis XV. In her sleep, Venetia raised one hand to her cheek and then let it fall again. As she did so he noticed something about the third finger of her left hand. Where there might have been a ring but was not, the skin was a paler shade. He dropped a kiss onto one smooth shoulder. Sleepily she opened her eyes and he was startled all over again by the depth of their colour.

'Venetia,' said Kyle, 'are you married?'

All at once alert and wondering if he had enjoyed himself enough to overlook the fact that she had not told him before, Nettie said, 'Yes.' Brief pause. 'After a fashion.'

'So am I,' said Kyle.

15

Six months later and still alive against all the odds, so that he was regarded as a crack pilot as a result, in 1942 Godfrey found himself posted to a crack squadron and flying a different sort of plane. A lot had changed. Area bombing was now regarded as the way forward and to Godfrey, who had long been sceptical about the target success rate so far, probably did make sense. Of the first cohorts of young pilots who had flown the Hampdens and Whitleys in the early days of the war only a handful remained. The era of the Lancasters and the Stirlings was beginning and with it came a more scientific approach.

On this particular clement evening in July the sky was the colour of a duck egg. Vaporous blue ground mist rose, infused with the scent of hay and wild flowers. It felt good to be alive and without the dark shadow of the war would have felt even better. Godfrey and the crew climbed into the plane. Their destination was Hamburg. It was not until they were well under way that he realized with a chill of the heart that he had left behind his mascot. The photograph, which was probably sitting beside the book he had been reading just before they left, or maybe tucked inside it, was of Rafe. On the back in the familiar black, spiky hand, was written a Shakespeare sonnet. For a moment a superstitious dread gripped Godfrey. It was an inauspicious beginning to a very risky raid. On the other hand it could be argued that they were all risky. With no alternative he cruised on and told no one what had happened although all would have understood because all had their personal rituals and life supports where luck was concerned. Since nothing could be done about it, there was no point in spreading alarm and despondency.

Evening deepened into night, and freewheeling through the starry firmament the old familiar elation took over and the need to concentrate on survival cancelled out fear. Flying the bomber towards Germany Godfrey thought a lot about his family, some of whom, though not Father, he had made a point of seeing during his last short leave. But mostly his mind dwelt on Rafe.

As usual, the searchlights were the first indication that they were almost upon the target. Once they were spotted, refulgent sunbursts of flak began to scintillate all around. Storming over the port in the wake of the Pathfinder aircraft, they dropped their bombs. And then the plane was hit. The Stirling bucked and lurched. Like the tail feathers of some exotic bird, amber flames streamed from the rear of the aircraft, underpinned by pungent black smoke.

'Harry's been hit!' shouted someone. 'Christ, so have I,' screamed someone else. There was pandemonium. The fire took hold. In an effort to put it out, Godfrey spiralled into a steep dive. He did not succeed. Pulling out of the plunge was a minor miracle. The German fighter, which appeared to have come from nowhere, stuck to them like a lion separating a buffalo from the rest of the herd and hit them again. Fuel was pouring away. By now the Stirling was garlanded with fire. Crippled and losing height rapidly, they limped towards the sea and, once over it, took the decision to bale out. It was that or be incinerated. Before veering away, the fighter waited around long enough to see the blaze extinguished in a hiss of steam as the bomber plunged into the waves.

Drifting down towards the shining black surface was eerily dreamlike. The chances of survival in this particular situation were probably nil. As Godfrey struck the water, the parachute slowly collapsed and the white silk wound itself around him like a shroud. Encumbered by fleece-lined flying jacket and boots and the rest of the paraphernalia, he found himself gradually waterlogged and then dragged down by the weight of it all. Struggling to stay afloat, a combination of exhaustion, the freezing cold and shock made the prospect of dying not just inevitable, but almost desirable. Death meant an end of the tension and the terror and the unrealistic exhilaration of having made it once again, the brief respite before yet another kamikaze op. Consciousness came and went. *All the same, I don't want to die! Dear God, don't let me drown!* Still fighting it, as the sea washed over him for the last time, Godfrey's final mental image was of

Rafe Bartholomew standing in the darkened doorway of his bedroom at The Hall.

The right room.

Antinous drowned too.

Rafe Bartholomew woke up with a start and an unnerving conviction that he was not alone. He was not. Godfrey Harding stood at the end of his bed. Or did he? The figure before him was not wraithlike or transparent but appeared to be made of flesh and bone. And was streaming with water. Flying jacket, hair, everything was saturated. There was a sepia immobility about what confronted him which put Rafe in mind of the Death's Head Hawk Moth. Transfixed, he waited but Godfrey neither moved nor spoke but only looked at him. He was aware of an emanation of intense sorrow and instinctively knew that if he stretched out his hand to touch his lover, as he had touched the moth, there would be nothing there.

Pain flooded through him.

Rafe said, 'I will never love anyone else as I have loved you.'

As if in response, the visitor began slowly to lose definition. Very gradually it simply faded away and where it had been the familiar things reappeared. Afterwards the silence was profound.

Missing, presumed dead.

The only one with nothing else to do, a grieving Nettie travelled north to collect her brother's few belongings. Without the benefit of the sort of visitation experienced by Rafe Bartholomew, she allowed herself to hope forlornly that Godfrey was out there somewhere, a prisoner perhaps in enemy hands. In her heart of hearts, she did not believe it. Putting heartbreaking personal items in a small suitcase, Nettie came across a dog-eared paperback book. She opened it. Poetry. As she did so, something fell out onto the floor. A bookmark, presumably. Nettie picked it up. It was a photograph of Rafe Bartholomew. Curious, she turned it over. On the back was written, *For Godfrey.* Underneath this, in the same stylish hand, courtesy of Sibyl Fox's uneven teaching Nettie recognized a Shakespearian sonnet.

Since brass, nor stone, nor earth, nor boundless sea,
But sad mortality o'ersways their power,
How with this rage shall beauty hold a plea,
Whose action is not stronger than a flower?
She let her eye run down it.
O fearful meditation! where, alack,
Shall Time's best jewel from Time's chest lie hid?
Or what strong hand can hold his swift foot back?
Or who his spoil of beauty can forbid?
O, none, unless this miracle have might,
That in black ink my love may still shine bright.

But weren't those sonnets written to a young man and not to a dark lady at all? Or maybe just some of them were. Nettie wished she had listened more closely at the time. Whatever gender this one had originally been aimed at, it was an extraordinary choice to pen on the back of a photograph given to Godfrey of all people.

Ah! All at once, Nettie saw it and wondered that she had never put two and two together before. How could she have been so obtuse? She who prided herself on her worldliness and sophistication. Probably because it was the last thing she expected. Homosexuality had not entered a sheltered country existence, and in London Nettie had been hell-bent on the heterosexual. While Godfrey . . . Sitting holding the image of Rafe Bartholomew, Nettie began to remember. She remembered how withdrawn her brother had been at school and Jonty and William's odd, embarrassed attitude to his progress ahead of them at Eton. And then Rafe had entered their lives and virtually taken Godfrey over.

'Rafe has become Godfrey's mentor,' she remembered Mother saying, presumably blithely unaware of what was really going on. There had been all those Christmas and Easter holidays when Godfrey had not come home.

Godfrey is doing the Italian art galleries with Rafe, Mother had said, and then, vagueness personified, at least I think it's Italy. Or is it Paris? Anyway, never mind, so sweet of him to take Godfrey under his wing like that.

Latterly there had been the cataclysmic row between Godfrey and Father and then Rafe and Father, after which Rafe had not been invited to her wedding to the odious

Randolph, whereas all his other cronies had been. Perhaps either Father had twigged what was happening or someone else had told him. At Rafe's dinner party where she had first met Kyle McClaren, Kyle had taken a great interest in the statue of Antinous to the point where she, Nettie, had looked at it more closely than she might otherwise have done. Now, seeing it again in her mind's eye, she recognized in the graceful marble youth more than a passing resemblance to her own brother. All at once her eyes filled with tears. Nettie saw that she had never really known Godfrey and also perceived that after an ambivalent, sexually confused boyhood, the years of his liaison with Rafe had probably been the best of his life. Nettie had transgressed enough of society's rules herself not to be judgemental, but was not about to underestimate Father's rigidity. Father, the man with *Forbidden Fruit* hidden at the back of one of the drawers of his desk, was a hypocrite and had probably been apoplectic when he finally discovered the true nature of the friendship between his eldest son and Rafe Bartholomew. Dabbing her eyes, Nettie carefully put book, photograph and the rest of Godfrey's small cache of personal belongings into the little leather suitcase and closed it.

After the death of Godfrey Harding, for Rafe Bartholomew it was as if an inner light had failed. Rafe existed rather than lived. He received his own photograph back from Nettie together with the book of poetry.

'I thought you would like to have these,' said Nettie.

In a very English way nothing else was said. She knew and he sensed her unspoken sympathy.

'Thanks, I'll treasure it,' said Rafe. He wondered how Mary Fox was bearing up under the tragedy and was astonished to learn that Nettie had not yet told her. Mary was now at Bletchley Park.

'I can't contact her,' said Nettie. 'I have to wait until she contacts me. She's coming to London at the weekend and I thought I'd rather tell her face to face.' It was not the only unpalatable conversation in the offing. Randolph was due home at the end of the month. I'll tell him our marriage is over in Quaglino's, thought Nettie. At least he won't be able to assault me in the middle of a restaurant where everybody knows him. She wondered crossly how he managed to organize himself so much leave when she and the rest of the family had seen neither hide nor hair of either William or Jonty since their departure. Deciding that she would cope with Randolph as and when she had to and meanwhile not think about him, she said, 'I'm holding the little soirée we discussed later on in the week, guest list as stipulated by you and all asked by Kyle at my suggestion, but I'll need briefing on what it is you're looking for.'

'Don't worry, you'll get it. And any other delicacies you might need, plus drink. Drink's the key to it.'

'Among other things,' said Nettie, who had not restricted her sexual favours to Kyle McClaren and whose intention it was to tackle with gusto her role as Venetia, Temptress in Aid of the War Effort.

Mary Fox did not hear from her mother before she moved to Bletchley, but given the temper her parent had been in the last time they had met this was not entirely surprising. In the light of further, calmer reflection, Mary decided she was not going to let it go at that. Mother's behaviour had been appalling, but the fact remained that Sibyl was on her own. Accordingly she rang Nettie and made an arrangement to meet her for lunch, after which she planned to go on to Brixton.

Nettie said, 'I think it might be better if we met at the house for lunch. There's something I have to tell you.'

That she had definitely decided to divorce Randolph, presumably.

'How very mysterious you are! Why can't you tell me over the telephone?'

'I'd really rather not.'

'All right. I'll be there at 12.30 on Saturday.'

Telling Mary when she herself was still very upset was one of the hardest things Nettie had ever had to do. Before delivering the tragic news she poured them both a stiff drink. Upon hearing it Mary went very white and for one minute Nettie thought her friend might be about to faint.

'I know that for you Godfrey was just as much family as he was for me,' said Nettie beginning to sob, 'and I just couldn't do it in a letter. I wanted to be here with you when I told you.' Weeping, the two of them clung together and in common with others all over the country mourned the loss of one of their own. Finally, unable to keep the Rafe/Godfrey story to herself any longer, Nettie told her friend about the photograph. Thunderstruck, Mary listened. In conclusion Nettie said, 'I know many would, but I can't find it in my heart to condemn Rafe though Godfrey was young when they met. I think they loved one another and who's to say that is wrong?'

Like Nettie before her, Mary remembered certain things which she had been at a loss to explain at the time. The secret tears in the nursery, for instance. 'It's something I have to work out by myself. There's nothing anybody else can do,' Godfrey had said. 'I want it to be our secret.' Aware at the time that there was another secret underlying the one he was talking about, Mary had spent weeks wondering what it could possibly be that had upset him so much. Now, years later, she knew. Paradoxically an extraordinary lightness of being engulfed her. For the knowing of it is my salvation, thought Mary. Now I realize that Godfrey did not reject me *as* a woman but *because* I was a woman. And that knowledge has set me free. She raised her eyes to meet Nettie's and Nettie was amazed by what she saw. Mary looked transfigured, radiant even.

'Nettie, how did Godfrey die?'

'They think his plane went down over the sea.' Nettie began to cry again.

With an unpleasant jolt Mary remembered what Rosa had said.

'Nettie, will you forgive me if I don't stay for lunch today? Maybe we could meet up tomorrow instead? I need to go and sit somewhere quiet by myself.'

'Of course I understand,' replied Nettie, aware that she did not and that some crucial change had taken place where Mary was concerned and she did not know why.

After she left the house, Mary walked the London pavements for a long time. She had no idea where she was going. The day was warm but overcast, with a tarnished silver sheen to the sky. Eventually she came to the Embankment and leant for a long time on the cool marble parapet. Like a handful of flung gravel, a flock of brown birds soared heavenwards and then swooped towards the opaque water.

Before her rose the graceful structure of the Albert Bridge whose sweeping curves had been delineated in less perilous times by a thousand lights as evening fell. And will be again, thought Mary, when all this is over. She was conscious of a complex fusion of mourning and joy within her, and that out of an ending might come a new beginning. Staring into the river as it unwound below like a bolt of dark, watered silk, she remembered the day she and William had gone to feed the carp and the koi and the brilliant flashes of red and orange and yellow as they darted through the dark depths of the pool. In an odd sort of way the dramatic splendour of their fleeting appearances reminded Mary of Godfrey. She stood there for a long time.

16

Mary Fox did not go and visit her mother that weekend as she had originally intended. She did not want her current buoyancy to be deflated by her parent's cynicism. I will go and see her, Mary promised herself, but only when I have properly come to terms with what has just happened to me. There is a dreadfully destructive side to Mother's character and while I have no intention of telling her very much, apart from the shattering fact of Godfrey's death, I just don't feel up to it. Maybe the answer was to write instead when she got back to Bletchley. In the end that was what she did.

Venetia Harding's select dinner parties became famous among the powerful Americans who either lived in or were passing through London. The hospitality was lavish, with the sort of food and drink that most of the country had not seen since the commencement of the war. Certain uncharitable, not to say envious, acquaintances asked each other how she did it and the words black market were bandied around though never by Venetia herself.

'Gifts! All gifts!' said Venetia blandly. 'What a lucky girl I am!'

Another source of uncharitable comment was the fact that the beneficiaries of her entertaining were mostly men. Venetia Harding, it seemed, did not have too much time for her own sex. There was a certain amount of speculation as to how many lovers she actually had on the go, who they were and whether they knew of each other's existence. Nettie's habit of flirting with everyone provided a useful smokescreen and the fact that all were married meant that those who were invited into her bedroom were very discreet about it. As Rafe Bartholomew well knew, the fact of the matter was that there was a regular triumvirate of powerful men, one of whom was Kyle McClaren, and each of whom was paying the rent on the little house in Chelsea.

Which makes four of us paying Nettie's rent, thought Rafe,

with a wry smile and not a trace of condemnation. No five, because she hasn't got shot of Randolph yet so presumably he's still forking out. She must be really coining it! Well, it's nothing to me. So long as I get the information I want I couldn't care less what Nettie does.

The deftness with which she kept her influential lovers apart was impressive too, especially when one took into account the fact that there was a lesser coterie with whom she also indulged herself if she felt like it or, more importantly, if Bartholomew indicated that the fruits of pillow talk with one or another might be useful to him. On certain fronts Nettie was proving herself an organizational genius and, all in all, her activities were producing more information regarding American attitudes than Rafe Bartholomew had ever dared hope for. It was also a very effective way of planting ideas as well as culling them, one such being the British endorsement of area bombing as opposed to precision bombing. Nothing could have been easier than for Venetia to instigate a debate on the matter with a clutch of American generals seated at her D-ended dinner table, one of whom was the top bombing commander and her lover. ('I must be the only woman in the world who talks about military strategy between the sheets,' said Nettie) Altogether, in Rafe's view his unorthodox investment was paying dividends.

'It's wonderful to meet somebody with whom I can talk about my work,' said the Major General, proceeding to kiss Venetia's white breasts, unaware that the person he was really talking to at the end of the day was Winston Churchill. Over the top of his grizzled head, wishing she was in bed with Kyle instead, Nettie murmured assent.

Kyle McClaren was a different kettle of fish altogether. He was nearer her own age and, insofar as she fell in love with anyone, Nettie felt that she had fallen for Kyle. This did not inhibit the subtle pumping of Kyle for information, all conducted under the guise of conversation, but it did make the whole process much more enjoyable.

The third of the strategically powerful American lovers was quite simply a trial. Without going into detail, Nettie said as much to Rafe.

'There's more ways than one to skin a cat,' observed Rafe mildly. 'If you can obtain the same brilliant results without getting so close to him physically, that's fine by me.'

It transpired that this was not possible. Jock Cummings was a skilled negotiator who was trusted by Roosevelt, and because of this was deployed to have top-level discussions with the Russians concerning Lend-Lease shipments of food supplies to the embattled British. He was also a social boor with no manners at all. 'No wonder he gets on so well with Stalin,' complained Nettie, bracing herself for another unimaginative and frankly repellent night. Attempts to coax strategical received wisdom plus Cummings' own views of where the war was currently at proved fruitless, despite copious slugs of whisky. The man had an iron head for drink. In bed, it was a different story. In bed, between bouts, Cummings was positively loquacious. It seemed she had no alternative but to get on with it.

In the fullness of time, Randolph came home on leave and was baldly told in a very expensive restaurant, over a dinner paid for by himself, that his marriage was finished. Convincing him of this fact took longer than Nettie had bargained for.

'I don't understand it!' moaned Randolph, himself the child of a loveless dynastic marriage.

Effortlessly Nettie captured the moral high ground. 'Randolph, you *struck* me!'

Lower lip trembling as she touched her eyes with a small, lace edged handkerchief, she was the epitome of wronged womanhood and looked very fetching with it. An unnerving vision of his wife in the divorce court witness box telling a besotted, dotty old judge all about it in graphic detail passed before Randolph's inner eye. Social death would be his lot if that happened. Keen to prevent such a thing happening at any cost he said, 'Why can't you just do your duty and provide an heir. Afterwards we can go on being married and no scandal. We don't actually have to *see* very much of one another. It's what everybody else does.'

Tears evaporated. 'Just tell me one thing, Randolph!' Very aggressive, Nettie squared her jaw. '*Why should I?*'

Recognizing that there was no change to be got out of trying to answer that one Randolph did not even bother to try but, impervious, pressed on.

145

'Look, I need an heir . . .'

Very flinty, 'That, Randolph, is your problem! You've got heirs on the brain,' snapped Nettie.

'Dash it, Venetia, I'm risking my life for my country –'

'And I feel I'm risking my life living with you,' she interrupted. 'Why don't you just accept that our marriage was a war-time mistake. Plenty of those about. Get somebody else to give you an heir.'

'How am I going to do that in the time I've got left? I've got to go back to my regiment the day after tomorrow and may never come back!'

Nettie thought it unlikely. On the whole it was the Randolphs of this world who did come back.

Feeling himself to be getting nowhere, Randolph tried another tack. 'And, anyway, what are you going to do for money if you sack me?'

Venetia did not enlighten him.

'I'll get by somehow.'

'I'm not going to go on paying for little houses in Chelsea you know!'

'There is no need to, I will take on the lease!'

Astounded, Randoph paused with his fork half way to his open mouth.

'Look, old girl –'

'Don't old girl me!'

The waiter hovered, waiting for a lull in the hostilities in order to dart in, head down, and remove the plates. It came sooner than he expected. One of the protagonists stood up.

'I'm not staying here to be insulted,' announced Randolph.

'Well, don't forget to do the gentlemanly thing and pay the bill as you go out,' said Nettie, unabashed. 'After all you don't want to come across in court as being mean as well as violent, do you? That's if it comes to that sort of confrontation.'

The inference was clear. Defeated, Randolph sat down again.

'All right. What do you want?'

'I want a civilized divorce. No publicity. I don't want any money –'

'That's just as well,' said Randolph, 'because I've no intention of giving you any!'

'– but I do want to keep the ring.'

146

'What!' Randolph was outraged. 'It's worth a small fortune. It's a family heirloom!'

'It may well have been but it's mine now. *With this ring I thee wed* you said.'

'Yes, and I want to stay wed! It's *you* who wants to get unwed!'

'That's beside the point. Point is I want the ring, and I'm going to have it. Take it or leave it, it's your choice. As I've said I don't *want* to have a fight about it.' *But I will if I have to.* The words were not spoken aloud but might as well have been.

'Get me a whisky, a stiff one,' said Randolph to the waiter, giving up on it and wondering mournfully as he did so how it had come about that one couldn't give one's woman a clout these days without getting taken to the cleaners.

17

The death of Davina Harding's eldest son caused her to re-evaluate her life and her marriage. Particularly her marriage. After the first storm of grief subsided, a dreadful, leaden depression set in and it seemed to her that the only way to cope with this was to talk to Geoffrey, who had also lost a son. Instinctively Davina knew that to cauterize the acute pain she felt she had to externalize it and, by confronting it, learn to live with it. For it would never entirely go away, she recognized. It became apparent that, in common with everything else in their less-than-satisfactory life partnership, grieving was one more emotion that had to be dealt with separately. My marriage is arid, thought Davina, arid. It was not that Geoffrey did not care about Godfrey, not at all. Davina knew that. It was just that he could not communicate or maybe simply felt no need to do so. And if neither of us is able to shore up the other in the face of common tragedy, then what are we doing together? she wondered.

After the telegram arrived, Geoffrey spent long hours closeted in the library, emerging only for meals which took place mainly in gloomy silence. What she did not know was that her husband's sorrow was complicated by his knowledge of, as he saw it, the shameful fact of their son's homosexuality. A man hidebound by convention, Harding had been unable to come to terms with this while Godfrey was alive and, now that he was dead, saw no prospect of ever doing so.

In the absence of any support from her husband, when Nettie visited Davina talked to her daughter long into the night. Listening to her, Nettie realized that her mother had no idea of Godfrey's sexual orientation and did not enlighten her although it was probable that Mother, who had cultivated a certain flexibility in order to cope with her dire marriage, would have taken it better than Father evidently had.

For Davina, the last straw was the memorial service she wished to hold for Godfrey.

'I think it's a good idea,' said Nettie, who was of the opinion that a period of public mourning would help everyone, herself included.

'Not a huge gathering,' Davina said. 'Just family and close friends.'

She drew up a list of those she wanted to attend and then sought her husband's agreement.

'Yes, all right,' said Geoffrey, but in the course of checking the invitees crossed out the name of Rafe Bartholomew.

Watching him do it while her mother was out of the room, Nettie said, 'Father, please don't do that. Couldn't you stretch a point, just for Mother? She doesn't know –'

'Out of the question!' Father was abrupt. 'Fellow's a blackguard. And how do *you* know, anyway?'

Blackguard. Nettie sighed. It was a throwback from the same sort of era as horse-whipping.

Deciding not to go into it, she replied, 'I guessed.'

'You *guessed*! In my day gently brought up young ladies had never heard of such a thing. Disgraceful! Absolutely disgraceful!'

In high dudgeon he got up and left the room.

On her return, Davina picked up the list.

'Did your father suggest any additions?'

'No. One subtraction.' Uncertain what to say next, Nettie waited for her mother's reaction.

Wonderingly Davina said, 'Rafe Bartholomew? I can't believe it! Why would Geoffrey do that? He must have made a mistake. I'll take it up with him. Rafe was so kind to Godfrey, such a good friend –'

It seemed there was nothing else for it but to tell her. With no idea what the reaction would be, Nettie said, 'Mother, Father won't change his mind. It was more than good friends. Rafe was in love with Godfrey and Godfrey reciprocated it.'

There was a very long silence. Finally, in even tones, Davina said, 'I see. Well, these days it is my view that we must all take love where we can find it.' Arrested by her quiet dignity, Nettie stared at her mother with new respect. 'If Geoffrey insists on presuming to denigrate theirs by refusing

149

to invite Rafe, the one person who *should* be present, there will be no memorial service. Godfrey wouldn't have wanted it and nor do I.'

And there wasn't. It was the death knell of the marriage.

At Davina's insistence sex between herself and her husband, never very frequent, totally ceased. I do not want to have to go on enduring Geoffrey in bed, thought Davina and said so, though not quite in those words. What she said was, 'I am the mother of your children and shall continue to run the houses and be hostess to your friends . . .' (This was not particularly onerous as Geoffrey did not have very many) '. . . but that is as far as it goes. No doubt in that respect we shall be no different from many other married couples we know.'

No doubt.

All the same that did not stop it being a bleak prospect, and it was as a direct result of this uncompromising statement of intent that Geoffrey laid renewed, desperate siege to Sibyl Fox. Here the balance had changed. Since she was no longer living in his house and therefore dependent on his largesse as her employer, Sibyl could have blown the whistle on their arrangement at any time. Because he did not want to lose her, Geoffrey found himself obliged to reciprocate in kind and so there were nylons and discreet suppers in dark corners of good restaurants and even, on one occasion, after sexual delectation of a particularly creative kind, a pair of diamond earrings.

It was after one of the dinners when Geoffrey was rather drunk that he let the cat out of the bag concerning his elder son and Rafe Bartholomew.

Well, well! thought Sibyl. There always had been something indecipherable about the urbane Rafe. Now she knew what it was. And the mystery around Godfrey and the twins' curious reaction to her questions concerning his school career was cleared up at the same time. At school there had presumably been romantic but unfulfilled friendships and a certain amount of sexual confusion all accompanied by rumour. Until Rafe Bartholomew had come on the scene, that is.

Sibyl wondered how Geoffrey had discovered what was happening.

'I found a letter,' he elucidated, pursuing the subject and

unwittingly answering her unspoken question. 'Or rather my wife did.' His brow darkened remembering it. Although she did now, Davina had not had a clue then as to what had really been going on.

'Look, isn't this *sweet*? Rafe has been so kind to Godfrey, one could almost say a kindred spirit,' Davina had said, handing it to him, the woman of no education missing all the classical innuendo which had pointed to only one conclusion. The resulting rows with Godfrey and then Rafe had been unsatisfactory as well. The first had been defiant and the second disdainful. 'Tell anyone you like!' said Rafe, apparently unfazed by blustering threats of exposure. Stymied and looking for outraged sympathy elsewhere, Harding had recounted the scandal to Jonty who of all his sons was the one most like himself, and to his chagrin had got no support there either. Furthermore, counselling discretion as the better part of valour, Jonty did not seem very surprised or very disapproving.

'I should leave it alone, Father. There's nothing to be done and what does it matter? You've got three sons, not just one, so it's not as if the line is going to die out.'

What does it *matter*?

A father cast in the Marquis of Queensberry mould, Harding felt as though he might be going to have a seizure. It was bad enough that in his own house Nettie . . . ! But of course one had to make allowances for women. They were frail creatures, easily led astray. At least Nettie was now safely married to Huntington's son. But Godfrey . . . !

'And I shouldn't bruit it about, either,' advised Jonty. 'You'll only end up hurting Godfrey as well as damaging Rafe's reputation. What's the point?'

When he cooled down, Harding had to concede to himself that, although as a course of action it went against the grain, Jonty was probably right. He did not even tell William. Maybe he would be afforded a chance to do Bartholomew down at some later date. Godfrey and he had not met again and now never would. Out in the political wilderness, doing an uninfluential job, he had had plenty of time to think about it and had come to no useful conclusions whatever. Meanwhile, infuriatingly, Bartholomew prospered.

Watching her dinner companion scowl at his plate, Sibyl

was privately amused. When she had finally got rid of him later that night it would all go into her notebooks. Since she had taken Geoffrey Harding back into her bed, Sibyl had started writing about the present as well as the past, for who knew when such reminiscences would come in useful? The story he had just recounted concerning Rafe Bartholomew and Godfrey was no exception. Sometimes secret knowledge could be lucrative knowledge.

Though outwardly, going about his work he appeared the same as usual, inwardly Rafe Bartholomew was bereft, assailed by the sort of stark despair that there was no shaking off. Ironically the war, source of his misery, became his lifeline and as sombre day succeeded sombre day, work was both his refuge and his solace.

By the end of 1942 there were times when Rafe thought the tide was turning and times when he thought it was not. What was certain was that it was all to play for. Bartholomew was one of very few people who knew one of the best-kept secrets of the war, namely that for the past two years Britain, the States and Russia had been collaborating on the formation of an audacious and ambitious battle plan whose aim was a massive offensive against Hitler's Fortress of Europe.

The time for its implementation had now come.

While all this was going on Mary Fox, who, unlike Nettie, liked the country, continued at Bletchley Park. Of all the beautiful country houses which graced the green fields of England, it seemed a great pity to Mary that GC&CS had chosen this particular one. The Park was a depressing Victorian mansion whose grim aspect was not enhanced by its barbed wire defences and the cluster of dingy huts within which they all worked, often in freezing conditions. Presumably it had been selected because it had intersecting rail links and therefore good communications; it certainly wasn't chosen on aesthetic grounds. The work was interesting though and on the whole Mary liked the people she worked with, including one in particular, a young cryptanalyst called Francis Stafford.

The privations of Bletchley might have been easier to bear if home had been a little more comfortable. Mary's billet was a room in the house of someone whose husband worked on the railway. It was poky. The walls were painted cream and the paintwork dark brown. Still, reasoned Mary, it could have been worse, she could have been the victim of a hectic wallpaper. Because the house was a small one there was little privacy and this was compounded by the fact that Mrs Gibbs, her landlady and a devotee of the latest popular music, constantly played *Forces' Favourites* very loudly.

Francis Stafford, on the other hand, had fallen on his feet where accommodation was concerned, for while his room was as dingy as Mary's, it was in one of the local hostelries, a public house called The Lamb Chop where rationing did not appear to exist.

'If you leave Bletchley, get seconded somewhere else, that sort of thing, don't forget to let me have first crack at your room,' said Mary. 'I'd rather be at the butcher's than working for the railway.'

'Why wait till then? You can move in now if you want to.' Francis, who had fallen for Mary the first time he saw her, was half teasing, half serious.

In answer to this sally Mary shot him a look he found hard to interpret. In fact his words, lightly spoken, raised in her mind the possibility of a love affair with Francis. In the end she said nothing but simply smiled what Stafford thought of as her Mona Lisa smile. Though it had to be said that, in his opinion anyway, Mary was much prettier than the original.

It transpired that Sibyl Fox was destined never to use her secret knowledge concerning the Hardings or anybody else. In April 1944 a flying bomb hit the City of London and in the process blew up the omnibus in which Sibyl Fox was travelling home after a particularly dull day at the office. She was identified by means of her handbag which survived the blast intact and contained, among other things, the name, address and telephone number of her daughter Mary.

Still in a state of shock, Mary travelled to London on compassionate leave to sort out her mother's affairs.

The flat in Brixton was just as it always had been. It was hard to believe that Mother would not walk in at any moment. Never very domesticated until she had to be, she had left her breakfast plates unwashed on the side in the kitchen. A paperback book with an orange and white cover was draped open across one arm of the chair. On the mantelpiece stood two empty glasses, one with a lipstick imprint and one without. Mary was surprised. Mother must have had company. Male company, for a cigar had been stubbed out in an ashtray on the little kneehole desk. Apart from that, a pile of books and a fountain pen without its cap on, the surface was empty. With a heavy heart Mary looked around. Everything would need to be sorted and cleared. It was hard to know where to begin.

Feeling shaky all of a sudden, she sat down in front of the desk. Probably the way to do it was to go through Mother's papers, such as they were, immediately and then progress to the more personal things, like clothes and jewellery. The first drawer she opened contained a lined writing pad and a packet of envelopes. Its opposite number on the right was locked. Mary looked for the key and eventually found it dropped into a small blue and white *cache-pot* on the desk. Within was a pile of large notebooks, all with marbled covers, and a Manila envelope. It also contained Mother's battered little jewel case. Mary lifted the lid. Apart from a string of seed pearls, a coral ring and a cameo brooch, all of which she recognized, there was a small, square box which she had never seen before. In it was a pair of diamond drop earrings. Perplexed, Mary stared at these for some time before deciding to look at the notebooks first. Perhaps they would hold the secret behind the earrings.

She opened the top one and was confronted by her mother's flowing, impatient handwriting. She turned the next page and the next. As she did so something fell out. Mary leant over and picked it up.

It was a pressed white camellia.

Part Four

The Notebooks of Sibyl Fox

Love, oh love, oh careless love,
You fly to my head like wine . . .

'Careless Love Blues'

18

Before tackling the notebooks in earnest, Mary opened the manila envelope. Inside it she found a small collection of assorted memorabilia. There was a dance card, so faded that it was hard to decipher although, peering at it, Mary made out what looked like the name Gerard entered several times, also a photograph of a society wedding, a young girl's fan, a pair of white kid gloves and, most mysterious of all, a parrot's feather. Mystified, she held this up to the light. It was red and green. Interestingly, the years had not destroyed its brilliant sheen nor made it brittle. Where had it come from? Mary went back to the first page of the top notebook. The first entry was dated 1943.

I should begin by saying that these reminiscences are for you, Mary, who have a right to know all the things I could not bear to talk about, even after thirty-three years. Talking and writing are different though, are they not? Writing is telling at one remove and means not having to confront the candid gaze of my only daughter as I do it. By the time you read these pages I shall be defending myself against another, higher scrutiny. And it is a way of passing the endless, solitary evenings. There is a limit, I find, to how much one can read or, for that matter, listen to the depressing news on the wireless. At present the war feels as though it might go on for ever. It has become a way of life to the point where I no longer fear the sound of the sirens, shortly to be followed by yet another bombing raid, but simply continue with what I am doing. Anyway, enough of all that. Let's get on with it!

I was brought to England from Rome when I was thirteen. The Adare family sent a lawyer out to fetch me. A lawyer! It was my first experience of the lofty arrogance of the British upper class. Not my last though.

My parents met in Italy in 1896 when my father, Philip

157

Adare, was doing the Grand Tour. My mother was an actress, slightly older than my father and a member of the *demi-monde*. In short she was everything that a family like the Adares, with all their pretension and their money, deplored. Deplored as an adventuress and were afraid of for the very same reason. And rightly so as it turned out, since she enticed away (as they saw it) my father, their only son, who stayed on in Italy and, despite all their representations, declined to come home because of her. Finally he married her. The following year, 1897, I was born.

Though I have no photographs of her (the family made sure of that) I remember my mother very well. She was of Italian and English descent and tempestuous. Her colouring was unusual, which was to say it was the same as mine. Though she described herself as such, as far as being an actress was concerned I never heard of her doing such a thing, except socially. My mother never walked into a room, she Made An Entrance. And when she left she Swept Out. She was vivacious, *outrée* and clever in a smart sort of way. To my father, used to the sort of well-bred, mannered English ladies among whom I was subsequently brought up, she must have seemed irresistible. The other side of my mother was that she was heartless and the circles in which she moved raffish. Her verbal cruelty was both capricious and gratuitous. My father, who was exactly the opposite, adored her as much as he was allowed to. He was enslaved by her. When I was twelve, he died. Of Roman Fever.

Our house, in Trastevere, was always full of people, whereas Grandmother's house hardly ever was. In her house I was treated like a child and expected to go to bed early. In Mama's house I was allowed to stay up till all hours, and wore evening dresses with my hair properly dressed and was treated like an adult. I was petted and indulged by artists and writers and courtesans and there, always in the forefront, was my highly strung, highly competitive, high pitched, stagy mother, cigarette in holder (scandalous!) and dressed for the Bohemian kill. In particular I remember a purple cloak with a huge standing collar like an Elizabethan ruff and rings

158

on her fingers with stones the size of pigeons' eggs. And her Byzantine face crowned with that startling hair. She was painted too, though I forget by whom, wearing a turban coiled snakelike around her head (Medusa!) and a slithery slippery dress spangled with stars. No bustles for Mama. Oh, there was something about Italy which seeped into the bones, a sort of world-weary sophistication that, once experienced, is there for life like a stubborn stain.

What did my father think about it by the end, I wonder? Father was background music to Mama's play. Apart from the money, that was about all.

When he died the money ran out. The family had discontinued his allowance the day he married my mother, but there had been another allowance from a deceased maiden aunt that they could do nothing about. The day he breathed his last, so did that and Mama was left with nothing.

I did not want to leave Rome. Mama might have been sharp as a scalpel but she was all I knew. However my grandparents were determined to have me. As far as they were concerned I was an Adare. And they got me, Mary. In effect, my mother sold me to them in exchange for a regular and generous allowance. Their lawyer brokered the deal and it was he who took me back to England. And so I went to live with strangers in a large country house where I arrived, aged thirteen, with probably more carnal knowledge at my fingertips than all the rest of the women there put together.

The first thing they did was to change my name. Or rather they substituted my middle name. So, because my mother's name, like mine, had been Francesca and nobody could bear to hear it, I became Sibyl.

Here Mary's face registered amazement. *Francesca?* She was beginning to feel as though she was reading about a distant acquaintance and not her mother at all. Fascinated she read on.

I missed Rome dreadfully. The vibrancy, the freedom, the golden glaze of the warm days and the aromatic evenings, the late nights and early afternoons. There, no two days were alike. Here, they were all the same.

After my father's death, I actually heard my mother say, 'Now, I shall need a new protector!' Oh, she was hard-hearted. But nobody came forward. Perhaps they all knew her too well for that. Father was my rock. Father was good and true. As a young girl, I instinctively knew that. When he died, I was devastated. For a while, life went on as before, but I was aware that for me a centre of gravity had been removed. In that milieu virginity was held cheap and, after he had gone, mine was no exception.

Filled with compassion, Mary laid the notebook down for a minute and tried to digest what she had read so far. The words were chilling. Through them she felt her mother's vulnerability, which had culminated in the cynical exchange for money of one who was, when all was said and done, only a child. Eventually she resumed.

When I first arrived in England I was viewed with curiosity. The ladies of the house were too well-bred to let this show but nevertheless I sensed it and saw them looking at me. The servants were not so subtle. I heard one of them say to another, 'Miss Sibyl's a deep one with all those funny little foreign ways of hers. They say her mother was a . . .' Here the voice was lowered, but I could guess what was said and it wasn't actress.

It was very difficult to go from one culture to another, especially from one so lax to one so stiff. I came to guard my tongue. More than once at the beginning I made the sort of observation which would have amused my mother's friends and here was greeted with a prune-faced reproof, followed by stony silence. As I say it was very difficult. Eventually, in self defence, on the surface I became like the family, but only on the surface. Inside it had all gone too deep and besides I did not want to change. In Italy I felt alive, in England I felt as though I was dead. I suppose some would have said I had been spoilt by too much freedom at an early age and no supervision. Now I was supervised and moulded all the time. Whatever happened to individuality, I wonder?

Miss Buckley, the governess, was kind to me though. For

different reasons we were both socially one down. Sometimes I thought she envied me my Italian existence. Miss Buckley, I suspected, had never been beyond Folkestone. Although she was employed to teach me, she seemed to me to know very little. It was possible that I had learnt more in the school of life than I was ever going to learn from my governess. Still, there were compensations. I loved dancing and I loved singing and playing the piano, all of which she taught. Through reading I escaped, in my mind at least, from the drab, privileged world in which I found myself. I wondered what my mother was doing now and whether she ever thought of me. My fourteenth birthday passed and I heard nothing from her. If she married again and therefore had no need of the family's money, would she come and fetch me?

I had three aunts. One was married and the other two were not. Maiden aunts. What a depressing prospect. Both were dependent on my grandmother who ruled the roost and would do so until the day she died. The aunt who was married and who was a beauty lived across the valley and had a son who was being groomed to inherit the house and estate following the death of my father. His name was Gerard and I longed to meet him. These days I hardly ever met anyone of the opposite sex. When I did they were ancient and avuncular and condescending. Sometimes at night I remembered Danilo, who looked like a faun with his curly black hair and sloe coloured eyes. Danilo was twenty or thereabouts, and seemed very old to me at the time. The profligate son of a profligate count, he used to lounge around the house all day and he came to all the parties.

No parties in Grandmother's house. Lots of church-going though.

I remember I used to see him coming out of my mother's bedroom and then, one day, he entered mine. Mother and daughter. Two for the price of one. When he left, I, at the age of twelve, was no longer a child in the physical sense.

Now, Mary, you see why it is easier for me to write this rather than tell you face to face.

I asked Miss Buckley if she would like me to teach her Italian, but she hastily refused, saying that, in the

161

circumstances, it would have been deemed inappropriate. In the light of what had happened, they all wanted to pretend that the Italian incarnation had never taken place. All the same, this puzzled me. After all, nobody need have known. It could have been our secret.

Sometimes I peered into the looking-glass and my mother stared back at me. I piled up my hair the way she used to do it for me and I did not look fourteen any more but grown up, with a strange, fey beauty which might win me a well-heeled husband one day. For that, I supposed, was the object of all of this.

Grandmother's house was very formal. To look at, I mean, as well as to live in. There were valuable things. Even I, who was not at one with it, could see that. What was missing was life. And exuberance. The house in Trastevere had an abundance of that. During the day it looked shabby, but at night it looked wonderful. At night the tarnished velvets and peeling gilt and the beaded fringes of the lampshades came into their own and there were candles everywhere, whose heavily scented smell was like that of certain lilies. And cushions, huge sumptuously-tasselled cushions, in rich fabrics. Cerise and scarlet and purple. It was not a very large house, but the mirrors made it seem so. My mother loved mirrors. I would see her catching her own reflection in them as she chattered and flirted. Like the house itself with its marble floors they were old, and in their grey spotted glass the pale candle flames, shooting and undulating in the draughts, were reflected again and again, from one glass to another. It was perhaps a miracle that nothing ever caught fire.

Do you know, looking back Mary, I think it was the age of Rome which was so potent. Past centuries seemed to lean heavily on this one as if reluctant to give up past glories. Maybe, along with my glittering mother, that was what my poor father found so seductive about it. Certainly I would have given anything to be back there, to pass again from the street, through the outer gate into the small stone courtyard with its one lemon tree and to hear the sound of the water in the fountain . . .

19

Taking up the pen again two days later.

The year I'm about to write about is 1911. At this point it occurs to me that perhaps it would be as well to start with a description of the other members of the household.

Rank dictates that I begin with Grandmother, Mrs Laetitia Adare, Grandfather having died two years prior to my arrival in England. I suppose Grandmother was the driving force behind retrieving me from Italy. Oddly enough, having succeeded in this aim, she hardly appeared to notice me unless, as constantly happened when I first arrived, I said the wrong thing. For example the day I asked whether either of my aunts smoked. Truly I had not realized what a heinous breach of manners this was. In Rome most of the women in my parents' circle did. As it was I thought Grandmother was going to have a fit.

'Ladies do not smoke,' she pronounced, very rigid. There was no room for debate. It was stated as a fact. And then, as if to clear up one more possible source of embarrassment, 'Nor, NOR, do they paint their lips, Sibyl!'

My mother, of course, had done both.

In the drawing-room there was a painting by Sargent of my grandmother in evening dress, bustled and stayed. Despite its grandeur, it had a wooden quality, I noticed, indicative of the artist having been bored by his subject. Nevertheless, in it she was as beautiful as jewellery and couture could make her (which was not very) and still could not hold a candle to my own eccentric parent. Even at my age, I recognized style when I saw it. Sargent would have enjoyed immortalizing Mama!

Grandmother did not exactly bully Aunts Margaret and Dorothea but she left them with no doubt as to who was in charge. In Rome, they would have had

163

admirers, in England, I was beginning to think, nobody was allowed to admire anybody. Margaret and Dorothea were up-to-date versions of Grandmother. Grandmother herself was clothed in the fashions of yesteryear. The wonderful clothes of Paul Poiret had passed her by though she could well afford them. They had passed by Margaret and Dorothea too. With all their money, not one of these women knew how to dress. Here I am conscious of sounding like my critical mother. Miss Buckley showed me pictures of Monsieur Poiret's fashions and they were like nothing I had seen before. He had introduced a walking skirt called a trotteur which showed the ankles (!) and culottes(!!). And his evening cloaks were sumptuous. Just looking at them made me think of Mama. If I managed to write to her, I wondered if she would write back. Though even if she did send me a letter I would probably never have received it for I'm sure my post would have been opened and read by Grandmother before being passed on to me. Or not passed on to me, as the case may be. So far as I was aware no one had written to me since I had been in England, but then who would? And how would I have known if they did?

Getting back to the family, at this point in time Aunts Margaret and Dorothea were both in their thirties and I wondered why it was that neither had married. If I had been them I would have wanted to live in London, not remain buried in the country. In fact I could not have borne it! Another thought struck me, that maybe Grandmother did not want them to marry and she held the purse strings. For if they did she would have been left on her own. I would not have put it past her. There was a sort of imperious selfishness about Grandmother which reminded me of Mama.

So far I had seen only photographs of Helena, the married sister. Helena was stylish, no doubt about that, with a handspan waist. Pictures showed her wearing a fashionable hat, festooned with fruit and flowers, and a flowing coat and holding a vast muff. It was not difficult to see that Helena had dash. She also had a husband who was a local landowner, and the unassailable trump card called Producing An Heir. Helena could be dressed by Poiret to great effect. Maybe she was for all I knew!

I could not wait to meet her. And her son.

In turmoil Mary put the book to one side, stood up and began to walk up and down the room. Every word of this part of her mother's narrative breathed privilege at the frozen heart of which was isolation. In the light of what she was reading, a lot was becoming clear.

Aunt Helena arrived to take tea with us. She came alone and I watched her alighting from her carriage. She looked graceful and proud and, unlike the other two, I suspected had never bent the knee easily to her formidable mother. Now she did not have to.

China tea, cucumber sandwiches, Gentleman's Relish and very small cakes were served. The insubstantial late February light made little impact on the drawing-room. Outside, in the park, rags and tatters of mist streamed through the bare branches of the trees. The sun was a low red orb. Appearing to listen, I let my mind drift away and was brought to myself by Aunt Helena saying, 'Would my niece like to accompany me on a walk before it becomes too dark? I should like both the exercise and the company!'

Aware that to have said Yes with alacrity, which was what I wanted to do, would have been construed as being forward in this house, I looked at Grandmother who said indulgently for once, 'Of course. Run along.'

Once outside, Aunt Helena did not speak for quite some time but was one of those who could do this without awkwardness. She had wrapped herself in a magnificent fur, whose lively sheen was such that it might still have been on the back of its original owner. I longed to stroke it, but did not dare. In profile, my aunt's face was delicate and patrician. The tulle-swathed, broad-brimmed hat atop her tall, slight figure gave her the look of a hot-house flower. I thought her exquisite.

Abruptly, she said, 'Are you happy here, Sibyl? Though it isn't Sibyl, is it? Not really. It is Francesca. Such a pretty name.' Here she stole a look at me.

My confusion was absolute. Everybody else in the family seemed to assume that I must be happy, for I was surrounded with wealth, was I not? As for my name, nobody had asked me about it. I had simply been told what I would be called.

'You may talk to me,' said Aunt Helena. 'I am very discreet.'

Dazzled by her as I was, all the same I did not quite believe it.

'Very happy, Aunt,' I said.

She nodded her head minimally, as though the tone rather than the words themselves had told her all she wanted to know. There was something remote and mysterious about her which intrigued me. Thinking about it afterwards, I decided it was something oblique, not quite straightforward.

'Tell me all about your father. My brother went off on the Grand Tour with his tutor and I never saw him again. I need to know.' There was no getting out of it. It was a command not a request and it suddenly struck me as odd that no other member of the family had made the same request, not even his mother.

So I told her. The sun went down as we talked. It became very cold in the park and with the chill came a sort of sadness. My aunt listened intently and then said, 'And what about your mother? Tell me about her too. As I am sure I don't have to tell you, she was regarded as a sorceress in this house.'

A sorceress, Mary! It conjured up visions of Grimm's fairytales.

Once again I told her. Not everything though. I did not describe the way of life in Trastevere, where day was night and night was day. At the end of my selective account, she unexpectedly said, 'I envy your mother. I envy her freedom. I was stifled in this house. Stifled! Now I live across the valley in another one rather like it. It's escape of a sort, I suppose. I got further than Margaret and Dorothea at least. Philip got furthest of all and, in an odd sort of way, it killed him.'

I said nothing. My mother would have liked Aunt Helena's money and position, or thought she would.

166

Aunt Helena yearned for the Bohemian life, with no idea of its poverty and insecurity. Each saw only the dream and none of the reality. I, who had known both, could see both sides.

'Families like ours are very cruel to those who do not conform. They cast them out!'

'Then why did they want me back?' It was a question which had long exercised me. 'Why did they not leave me where I was?'

'Because,' said my aunt, 'you are Philip's daughter and therefore they took the view that you belonged to them and must be brought up as one of them. Anything else would have been unthinkable.'

I did not like the sound of this. It made me feel like a chattel.

She shivered. 'It is getting very damp. Let us go back.'

Down the years, I've thought a lot about what she said. On one level Aunt Helena did not know what she was talking about. I suspect she envisaged herself in Rome, or wherever, with all the privilege and all the freedom too. The indolent, penurious days and gaudy nights did not enter her equation at all. What I don't understand to this day is why families such as this one lived in this way when they did not have to. The straitjacket, it seems to me, was one of their own making.

A tea party was arranged so that I might meet the daughters of some of the other county families. Mary, I was not confident, although I would have liked to have had a friend. What would they think of me? And, more to the point, what would I think of them?

On Grandmother's instructions, Aunts Margaret and Dorothea assembled six girls of my own age, each of whom looked as though she had stepped out of a bandbox. The English seem to have an obsession with tea, which has always struck me as one of the duller meals. Predictably, it was not a success for we had little in common. To me they all seemed very young and, truth to tell, rather silly. Breeding seems to inhibit spontaneity and quite often brains too, come to that. Conversation was stilted. Of course they asked me all about Italy though there was very little I could tell them. Or very little of interest, rather. Not even the fact that Mama was, or said she was, an actress. Actresses at that level of society were regarded as little better than prostitutes.

Grandmother warned me off that one: 'I need hardly tell you not to mention your mother's profession, Sibyl.' (Said with something of a sniff)

(Appearing guileless) 'But what shall I say if they ask me about her?'

'There is no need to say anything because ladies, on the whole, do not *do* anything. They do not have to. That is the definition of the word lady. The other girls will understand that very well. They will not pursue it. You should give the impression of one who has been brought up in the highest Roman society.'

But I hadn't been brought up like that, of course. This was my first encounter with hypocrisy. Regular as clockwork, Grandmother went to church every Sunday and would have described herself as a good Christian. She was not, however, above encouraging me to foster a false idea of the life which had been mine to date. It did not seem to occur to her to ask herself how this made me feel.

There were further excruciating teas, since all the girls assembled by the aunts had, one by one, invited me back. Otherwise nothing happened, though one morning there was a powdering of snow, something of a novelty to me. Time passed at a snail's pace. Just as I was beginning to feel as though the ennui might drive me mad there was An Excitement. Aunt Helena invited me to visit her for a Friday to Sunday at the beginning of May to meet my cousin Gerard and Grandmother gave me permission to go. I could hardly wait!

May came at last. With a lift of the heart I saw that the weather had changed for the better. It was warm, though not as warm as Rome of course, and the hedgerows were bridal with blossom. I filled a large Doulton china jug with it and set it in my room, but Miss Buckley said it was unlucky to bring May into the house and made me take it out again.

The countryside was lush and green and starred with wild flowers. Wood anemones, lady's smock, violets, ragged robin, primroses and cowslips were all in bloom and the smell of summer was in the air. Aunt Helena was to send a carriage to collect me. For the first time since my arrival I was almost happy and I looked forward to the journey.

It occurs to me that I should record my astonishment at how fresh all this is in my memory. Perhaps because I have done my best to look away from the past and have not scrutinized or analysed it the way many do, it is uncontaminated by interpretation. It is rather like opening a box within which lies a dress, bought and never worn. You remove layer after layer of tissue paper and there it is, out of date but exactly as it was. That is precisely how I feel about my memories, most of which have lain undisturbed all these years. My spy glass into the past reveals everything with clarity and, to my surprise, dispassion. I recall conversations, nuances, even smells, evocative underpinnings of the set piece events which were the framework of the bigger picture.

The weekend I went to visit her, Aunt Helena had a house party, a fact I suspect she did not tell Grandmother. Luckily I had brought my muslin with me, and the silk so, to my relief, I would not be disgraced in terms of what I wore. Aunt Helena's husband, Cosmo, was indistinguishable from all the other Englishmen I had met, being moderately good looking, moderately interesting and very rich. My aunt was sometimes impatient with him, which caused me to wonder how content she was within her marriage, but she was never impatient with her son on whom she clearly doted. Gerard was twenty and like her to look at, though whereas Helena was blonde, he was dark. There was a restlessness about him which echoed hers. I found him very handsome and very attractive.

I dressed carefully for dinner. The muslin, which was

the colour of ivory with an emerald sash, was simple but effective. For once I was pleased that I was not yet allowed to put my hair up. It fell in loose Titian curls to my waist, like that of a warrior queen, and its auburn burnish set off my pale face and long neck perfectly. I stared at my own reflection in the glass. My eyes looked huge and very green, like those of a cat. On impulse I took some lip colour out of my portmanteau where it had been secreted since I left Italy and smeared a little on my lips, after which I blended it in so that the cupid's bow of my mouth was emphasized but only the very sharpest of eyes would have suspected artificial colour. Then I pinched my cheeks and took an ivory camellia out of the bowl of flowers on my dressing table which I tucked in my hair. Pleased at the effect, I went downstairs.

With satisfaction I noticed that my cousin Gerard could hardly take his eyes off me. (Such is the power of beauty. You do not make the most of yours, Mary.) As I listened demurely to what the man on my left (the local vicar) had to say and then turned to the other on my right (yet another landowner), though directed at them, all my smiles were for Gerard. Every so often I tilted back my head too, so that the length of my neck was highlighted, and then angled my face, just as I had often seen my mother do, presenting a flawless profile. It was wonderful to flirt again, even at one remove like that.

On Saturday morning, at Aunt Helena's suggestion, I went for a walk around the grounds. To protect my skin from the sun I wore a wide-brimmed straw borrowed from her and tied on with ribbons and, as I made my way along, the lightest of light airs caused my skirts to billow. Striding out, I felt free. As gardens go, this one had more character than Grandmother's. It was like a palazzo garden. Classical statues abounded, many life-size and standing on plinths, and there were urns out of which depended ivy and other trailing plants. If I married well I too could belong to this sort of world. The question was, did I want to? It did not seem to have made Aunt Helena very happy.

In the wilder part of the park, just beyond where

the formal garden ended, I came across a pet cemetery. *Ranter, beloved bulldog, died 1843*, I read, then, amazingly, *Buttercup, faithful servant, 1890, provider of 5,475 gallons of milk* (who was counting, I'd like to know). Beside the prolific *Buttercup, Gone But Not Forgotten*, lay *Prince, King Charles Spaniel, 1902* and, further on, *Dependable Welsh Molly, aged 26, 1876*, a pony, presumably. There was even a parrot.

I wondered whether Grandmother would let me have a pet. Maybe if I had something of my own to love I would not be so lonely. Or so sad.

Dinner that evening was a glittering affair. Not just the house party and the odd local stalwart, such as the desperately earnest vicar attended, but others from further afield.

Aunt Helena decreed, 'Tonight, Sibyl, you must put your hair up,' and sent her maid to help me do it. Grandmother would have been horrified. My aunt, I was coming to see, was her own woman. One of the gentlemen in the house party followed her every movement with his eyes. It occurred to me that maybe Aunt Helena had lovers.

Once the hair was out of the way my neck needed adornment and she lent me a strand of pearls and matching earrings.

With the aid of this expensive finery the silk looked surprisingly sophisticated. It was dark green, the colour of one of the glossy camellia leaves. Green was my colour. 'And a touch, though only a touch, of that lip colour,' decreed my eagle-eyed, worldly aunt. 'It suits!'

This time I was seated beside Gerard.

'Mother says you will be a beauty, Sibyl,' said Gerard. 'It is my view that there she is wrong. You already are a beauty.'

Beyond polite conversation with the gentleman on my left, the curate this time, and more of the same sort of flirtatious banter from Gerard, nothing much else happened. But just being part of a grandly elegant evening was wonderful. I felt elated. It was hard to get to sleep that night!

The following day, after lunch, I was due to go home.

There was a conservatory in Aunt Helena's house, I remember, with palms in jardinières, and a huge white domed birdcage in which were maybe fifty parakeets and macaws. Their shrieking brilliance as they flew and darted was dramatic to behold. Once again I was reminded of my mother. I sat there alone for quite a long time, trying to make sense of what was happening to me.

Mary picked up the feather. With one finger she traced its brilliant curve. It was like touching an apport from the past. She laid it down again.

My cousin came to see me off and handed me into the carriage.

Gallantly, he kissed my hand, saying, 'I am sure we will meet again before too long, Sibyl.'

I noticed my aunt looking at me inscrutably as he did so. After I thanked her she embraced me. 'Yes, you must come again soon, Sibyl.' Warm words, but all the same I thought I detected a slight reserve and wondered whether she meant them.

She smiled her subtle smile.

Later I was to think of it as her Borgia smile.

June came and went. That summer was one of the hottest on record, with blazing soporific days. The garden was garish with reds and yellows all in bloom at once and the sun, hard and bright like a diamond, floated in a haze of heat. Probably because she was as bored with the worthy as I was, Miss Buckley took it upon herself to teach me Shakespeare. Almost for the first time, she had captured my attention. I was fascinated by the cadence of the verse and the intrigue, which reminded me of Italy. In Shakespeare people do not always get their just desserts and quite often it is the innocent who suffer. Now as then. We read *A Winter's Tale* (Exit pursued by a bear, Mary. Remember?) and then made a start on *Romeo and Juliet*. For the first time in months I began to feel alive again. There was no word from Aunt Helena and I thought that maybe she had forgotten me. I was beginning to resign myself to the thought that nothing would ever happen to me again and that my fate, like that of my aunts, was to moulder endlessly in the country when suddenly, in August, there came amazing news.

Aunt Dorothea was engaged! To a doctor. Despite what she said, I suspect that Grandmother was not best pleased. Maybe because she was informed rather than asked, or maybe because she did not want to take her claws out of my aunt. Perhaps we were back to property again. Whatever it was, there was a steely determination about Aunt Dorothea that I had not seen before. It was not a particularly good match but adequate and I did not think she would let this chance of independence pass her by. It transpired that she had been quite clever about it; I heard one servant saying to another, 'She's a dark horse!'

Dark indeed, Mary. Well done, Aunt Dorothea.

I speculated on Aunt Margaret's view of this development. She would be left on her own with Grandmother. Or maybe she had a suitor in her closet too. A thought crossed my mind: if ever there was an attempt to make me my grandmother's companion I must resist it with might and main. Life was for living, not pandering to the whims of rich old ladies whose heyday was past.

Of course the engagement also meant that there would be a wedding to which the county would come and which Grandmama would have to be seen to do in style. Status demanded it and one upshot would be that I would meet my cousin again. I looked forward to this more than I can say.

The enervating heat went on.

The wedding was to take place in the first week of September and my aunt was to be married from her own home. This was my birthday month. Fifteen. Without much hope, for the umpteenth time I wondered whether I would hear from my mother and at the same time knew in my heart of hearts that it was unlikely. Rome was beginning to seem like a dream . . . even my Italian,

173

a language in which I had once been fluent, seemed to have deserted me.

I met Aunt Dorothea's fiancé. He was, or seemed to be, a kindly man, a widower who was ten years older than her. The change in my aunt was remarkable. She bloomed and had become positively handsome, whereas Margaret had a starved, wan look. It was almost as though the happiness of the one was being syphoned off from the other. The honeymoon was be taken in Italy! I saw my grandmother fold her lips on receipt of this news. Not Rome though, Venice, where I had never been.

At this point Mary briefly stopped reading. It all explained much about Mother but the main question exercising her mind was what had happened to them all? The family must still be out there somewhere and yet Mother appeared to have severed all contact with them. Avid for more, she went back to the story.

September came. I was to be a bridesmaid, together with two of Aunt Dorothea's god-daughters. My aunt and uncle were invited to stay at the house and so was Gerard. There was to be a ball on the Saturday and the marriage service was scheduled to take place on the Sunday morning. It was hard to concentrate on my lessons with so much happening all around and Miss Buckley was equally distracted. Had *she* ever had a beau?

A week before the event, I had the final fitting for my ball dress. I had persuaded Aunt Dorothea some of the way towards the Poiret look, despite a frontal assault mounted by Grandmother to try and take over all such decisions ('after all, I am paying for this!') which was smartly repulsed by my aunt. Forced to retire to her tent, so to speak, Grandmother was demonstrably huffed and at dinner pointedly addressed all her remarks to her other daughter. This was of scant comfort to Margaret, no doubt, since she was going to be the recipient of them *in perpetua* once Dorothea had gone. For my birthday I was given a string of pearls, which I intended to wear with the new ballgown, my first. Once again this special day passed with no word from my mother. Aunt Helena gave me pearl earrings to go with the necklace and Miss Buckley presented me with a copy of the poems of Mrs Elizabeth Barrett Browning, with a fond inscription on the flyleaf.

Saturday, Mary, was one of the happiest days of my life.

After dinner we all repaired to the music room which had been cleared for the ball. My card filled up rapidly with Gerard insisting on every other dance. I saw Aunt Helena watching us and felt uneasy. I sensed that she did not like the attention he was paying me. With osprey feathers in her hair, diamonds at her neck and wrist and a magnificent gown of prussian blue silk, she herself was in constant demand. During the course of a gavotte, Gerard leant towards me and whispered, 'Let us slip away together after this. I long for the fresh air.'

I looked for the vigilant Aunt Helena but, for once, she was nowhere to be seen.

'Yes, I should like that,' I said.

It was cool in the garden. Like phantoms we flitted across the dark lawn, I lifting my skirts because of the dew. Behind us the house was illuminated, a house brought to life though not for long, alas. The double doors to the garden were open and light flooded out onto the terrace, its golden surge accompanied by the sound of the orchestra. Standing on the grass, I felt both part of the celebration and outside it. Perhaps it would always be like this for me.

Gerard turned away and I was just about to follow him when I saw a couple come out onto the terrace. She was as tall as the man she was with and the osprey feathers and her drifting, gliding walk caused me to recognize Aunt Helena. The man she was with was not my uncle. Recklessly, I say recklessly because anybody could have walked out and seen them, he pulled her to him and kissed her. In the event, apart from myself, the only witness was the stone Juno at the end of the balustrade. I saw Aunt Helena pull away and apparently

175

remonstrate after which he kissed her again and this time she let him.

I turned and followed Gerard into the area that was park rather than formal garden. Flowering shrubs of considerable height lined the rides and here the scene on the terrace was repeated as he kissed me. Remembering Danilo and all of a sudden hungry for love, I kissed my cousin back.

Writing this, it occurs to me to wonder how he dared do what he did. If I had screamed and denounced him, he would have been disgraced. I was, after all, only fifteen. Perhaps he had seen something in me which caused him to think I would not object and, if so, he was quite right, I did not. But what had he seen?

Maybe it was the corruption of innocence.

Frightened by the intensity of my own response and the fact that I had given myself away, I tried to step back a pace and, while he did not attempt to stop me, he still took my chin between finger and thumb and tilted my head so that the moonlight fell on my face. I closed my eyes and waited for him to kiss me again. He did not. In the end I opened them. After looking intently into my face for a while he said, 'Sometime, Sibyl, you must tell me all about your life in Rome.'

So that was it. He had seen beyond the well-bred veneer and sensed the secrets within, though he did not know exactly what they were.

Abruptly, Gerard said, 'After the wedding, we travel home. We are leaving in the early evening, I believe. It may be some time before you and I meet again, Sibyl. In the light of that fact, there is something I want to show you. Will you promise to meet me here tomorrow after lunch?'

Thinking how handsome he was, especially in evening dress (have I ever told you, Mary, how I adore men in evening dress?), a study in black and white, with a lock of his dark hair falling across his forehead, I said, 'Yes. At what time?'

'Let us say at three o'clock.'

'It will be difficult for me to get away unobserved,' I said.

176

'Not if you complain of a headache and announce your intention of retiring to your room to rest for an hour or two. If you do that, no one will disturb you. Then instead of going there you can slip out of the back of the house and make your way here. Meanwhile, I think we should return to the ball separately.'

His arm around my waist, he escorted me to the end of the lawn and vanished back into the park. This time there was nobody on the terrace. I skirted the edge of the grass and ran up the side steps, where I stopped for a moment to compose myself. Then I walked back into the music and the light. Stately in violet, Grandmother motioned me over with her fan.

'Sit down, Sibyl.' She indicated the chair beside her. 'Where have you been? I have just sent Miss Buckley in search of you.'

'I was very hot, Grandmother,' I replied, not quite lying, 'I went into the garden to get some air.' Then, preparing the way for tomorrow, 'I had a slight headache. I get them from time to time.'

'Well, it has been a great deal of excitement for a young girl to cope with and you are not used to champagne.' How my mother would have laughed at that. 'There is another full day ahead tomorrow so maybe it is time for you to go to bed in order that you may enjoy it!'

'Yes, Grandmother,' I said dutifully.

'Before you retire, find Miss Buckley and inform her that you are found.'

'Yes, Grandmother.'

Once in my room, I opened wide the window so that I could still hear the music and then sat with my elbows on the sill and my head propped on my hands, dreaming of tomorrow.

Mary stared into the middle distance. At that point in her life, despite the constraints of an Edwardian upbringing, Mother had had everything to look forward to. Her reminiscences abounded with spirit and with the hope of something better. Where had it all gone wrong? Mary glanced at her watch. Lunchtime. She rose and went to inspect the kitchen cupboards in search of something to eat. One powdered egg omelette later she went back to the large armchair, tucked her legs underneath her and prepared to resume. Prior to doing so, though, she looked at the photograph and tried to decide who was whom. The bride and groom, standing at the back of the group were obvious, the others less so. All stared solemnly at the camera. It might have been a wake rather than a wedding. 'Grandmother', radiating social aggression, was not hard to spot either. God, that jaw looks as though it's been set in stone, thought Mary. What a dragon! Ramrod straight, Laetitia Adare was queening it on a chair in the centre, flanked by (presumably) Margaret and Helena. On Helena's(?) right was a Bertie Wooster-ish apparition with a monocle, Cosmo probably, and on Margaret's(?) left a tall dark young man who might have been Gerard. Probably *was* Gerard. In front of the group, their bridesmaid's dresses charmingly bunched around them so that they looked like a cluster of peonies, knelt three young girls. The one in the centre was her mother. On the whole Mary thought she had got Margaret and Helena in the right order if only because Helena, the taller of the two and in danger of eclipsing the bride, was wearing a titanic hat and had a tiny waist only a little larger than her long narrow neck.

She returned to the notebooks, and to a description of the wedding itself.

Well, we all went off to the church, which was on the outer perimeter of the estate and was used by the local community as well as the family. The village ladies had filled it with flowers. My Aunt Dorothea was, it seemed, very popular and performed good works looking after the sick and the poor. *Noblesse oblige!* This was probably how she met her husband-to-be, so on all those days when, with Grandmother's blessing, she took the carriage, good works teamed up with romantic assignations. And why not? However much I was informed to the contrary (and I was, endlessly) I did not believe life was all about duty.

Together with the god-daughters I followed my aunt up the aisle. I carried the middle of the end of her train which was surprisingly heavy (the beading and

178

embroidery, I suppose), and the others the right and the left. When the ceremony was over, my new uncle lifted Aunt Dorothea's veil and kissed her full on the lips, a very carnal thing to do in a church. I looked at Grandmother straight afterwards. She appeared to be praying but the pursed lips and the way her hands worked told me everything.

The wedding over, my aunt was positively transformed. If this was what happiness did then it was much to be recommended. It was apparent that she was in love with her husband and he with her. Just as it was apparent to me, Mary, that my cousin was in love with me and I with him.

Waving and smiling, some of us secretly grieving, we all watched the newly-wedded couple leave on their honeymoon. How I envied them! I wished I was going back to Europe. Now the excitement was over, life would go back to normal, a prospect I frankly dreaded. I hoped it would not take me as long to escape as it had taken my Aunt Dorothea.

Now we are coming to it! Even after all this time I can hardly bear to write it down. Reawakened pain, I am learning, is capable of unsheathing its dagger to devastating effect.

To continue: Luncheon felt as though it went on for a very long time. Once again I was seated between two very serious clergymen, one of whom said Grace at the beginning. Perhaps Grandmother thought I was a brand to be plucked from the burning! At one point Gerard caught my eye and sent me such a droll look that I feared I might burst out laughing. When the pudding had come and gone I mentioned that I was feeling unwell and, to my horror, Miss Buckley was sent upstairs to look after me, though I finally persuaded her to let me simply lie down on the day bed. When she had gone, I rose and considered how to leave the house without being seen. The dangerous part was the first, for there was no way of escaping from here without descending the main staircase. In the end I braved it and slipped in stockinged feet down the polished stairs after which I

179

darted towards the back of the house and the kitchens. I could hear the servants talking and the clatter of plates and cutlery. Heart in mouth I passed through the great big old kitchen door and found myself on the cobbles of the courtyard. Here I put on my shoes and ran, taking a circuitous route to where we had been last night.

When I arrived Gerard was waiting for me. By this time I was very hot and my face was flushed. I noticed I had torn the skirt of my dress. I had probably caught it on a thorn. I felt my heart beating very fast.

'I brought you these,' said Gerard with a bow.

Two creamy camellias. I tucked one in my sash and put one in my hair.

'And now, come with me . . .'

I followed him into a part of the park where I had never been before.

'Close your eyes,' commanded my cousin. 'Don't be afraid, I will look after you.'

Obediently I did so. He took my hand and led me forward. I could feel twigs and earth under my feet and branches brushing against me. Then there was a different sensation, rather like walking on a carpet.

'You may open your eyes now!'

I did so and gasped. Beneath my feet was moss, thick curling moss such as I had never seen before with a viridian sheen that reminded me of devoré. We were standing in what felt like a natural temple: the clearing was almost perfectly round and walled by fleshy, glossy green leaves as big as dinner plates, and the whole was roofed with exotic flowers which looked as though they were made of icing sugar, and whose cloying perfume made my head swim.

I suddenly became aware that Gerard was kissing me and, at the same time, unbuttoning the high neck of my dress.

'No, no!' I said, trying to push him away. 'No!'

'No? Oh come now, cousin Sibyl . . .'

I was aware that he had eased the dress and what was underneath it off my shoulders and I could feel the warm summer air on my bare breasts, which were white and firm like the strange flowers crowding above our heads.

'No, please, please, no!'

Again I tried feebly to push him away, although I wanted him and I'm sure he knew that. He did not exactly force me, but he did not desist either. More kisses, and all the time the cloying, heady smell of the flowers. Garden of Eden flowers as I thought of them afterwards. It was then, as he laid me down on the moss, telling me how much he loved me, vowing he could not live without me, that I learnt the power the senses have over us for I did not resist any more but simply let him have what he wanted.

Afterwards, my head lying on the hollow of his neck, I said, 'You won't ever leave me will you, Gerard?'

As I spoke the words I became aware of the oppressive silence all around. It was very strange. No birds sang and there was an oddly threatening immobility about the flowers and the leaves, as though they were painted rather than real.

'Of course not, darling. I'll never leave you. Never.'

He kissed me.

Once again we went back to the house separately and once again I slipped up the back stairs. At the top I met Miss Buckley.

'Sibyl,' said Miss Buckley, 'where have you been?'

'I felt better and went in search of a glass of water.'

'Well, in that case, your aunt, uncle and cousin are shortly to depart and perhaps you would like to see them off.'

So he did leave me. Forlornly watching the diminishing carriage, oddly distorted by the shimmer off the drive, until it turned the corner and was lost to sight leaving only a plume of dust, I wondered when I would see my cousin Gerard again.

As a token, I pressed one of the camellias within the pages of a book. I still have it to this day. If you have not done so already, Mary, you will find it.

Everything returned to normal, by which I mean went back to being dull. There was no invitation to visit my Aunt Helena again and no word from my cousin either, strange behaviour from one who had professed himself so passionate. I had no one in whom I could confide, certainly not Miss Buckley.

October and November came and went. I did not feel at all well. One morning I was sick. Still no word from Gerard.

By the middle of December I was forced to confront the fact that I might be pregnant. In Rome such things were discussed rather than concealed the way they were here and so I knew what the signs were. Many other gently-brought-up girls probably would not have. The sickness, which I had so far managed to conceal from Miss Buckley, was not as bad as it had been, but my breasts were full and tender. I prayed for the curse which did not come. Trapped and frightened, night after night I cried myself to sleep. I could not understand why I had heard nothing from Gerard . . .

Mary felt a shiver pass down her spine. She remembered Rosa.

Rosa had said, 'Your mother had two conceptions . . .'

'Wrong,' had been her reply. 'I am an only child,' and then, after further thought, 'on the other hand she might have had a miscarriage, I suppose.'

'I'm not talking about a miscarriage. I'm getting a son and a daughter, both still on this plane. The daughter is sitting in front of me, so where is the son?'

'Are you telling me that I have a brother?' Just remembering the exchange, astonishment flooded through Mary all over again.

Rosa's reply had been elliptical. 'I'm telling you that your mother has quite a few skeletons in her cupboard. Perhaps you should have a long conversation with her . . .'

At the time it had seemed impossible. Mother, who was not prepared to talk about even the most mundane family history, would have thought she was mad. Now she was dead and it was too late. The only conversation to be had was through the pages of these notebooks.

In the end I told Miss Buckley. My governess was aghast, as well she might be since she was nominally in charge of me. She kept saying, 'Are you sure, Sibyl?' My dresses

182

and skirts felt tight. It could not be too long before somebody else noticed.

With the look of the condemned man approaching the scaffold, Miss Buckley said, 'We shall have to tell your grandmother. There is nothing else for it. I shall do it straightaway.'

Clearly quaking, she went and I was left by myself. Surely, I thought, Gerard would tell them how it happened, that it was not my fault. And Aunt Helena, who had lovers of her own, she would understand.

Outside it was snowing. The sky was low and ochrous over the park and the flakes were spiralling down, thick and fast. In a week's time it would be Christmas. I heard Miss Buckley returning. Oh, heavens! Now it was my turn . . .

Pity engulfed Mary. She picked up the wedding photograph again and studied Grandmother's granite visage before resuming.

Grandmother was in her small sitting-room. The door was shut and the only indication that anyone was inside was a drizzle of light which seeped underneath it and ran over the pointed embroidered toes of my velvet slippers. I stood outside in the dark corridor for a minute, summoning up all my courage, and then I knocked.

My grandmother was dressed in black bombazine and seated on a sofa by the window. To me she looked like the Lord High Executioner. I was not invited to sit down. In deference to the failing light, the lamps were lit though the curtains remained open. Outside the snow was falling more heavily. Tomorrow the grounds would be virginal.

'I am more shocked than I can say by what Miss Buckley has told me,' said my grandmother. 'And I cannot believe it. There must be some mistake. How could a young girl like you know if you were expecting a child? Well-brought-up young girls do not know anything about such things!' She was not entirely convinced by her own argument, however, for she then said, 'However, tomorrow I shall ask a doctor to examine you. That way we shall clear the matter up and need never refer to this ever again.'

Chance would be a fine thing and I had a feeling that, even in the unlikely event that I would be declared *virgo intacta*, the whole episode would not be dismissed as easily as that. I fervently hoped the doctor would not be Aunt Dorothea's husband. The same thought had evidently entered Grandmother's mind since she then said, 'Though he is retired, I intend to call in our old general practitioner, Dr Maddox, whom I know to be both competent and discreet. No word of this must be allowed to get out.'

I waited for her to ask me what had happened and who it was, but she did not. Maybe she was hoping against hope that there would never be any need to know. Or maybe she had her own suspicions.

'Go now, Sibyl. Your supper will be sent up to you on a tray.' She turned her face away from me towards the winter garden. There was an implacability about her profile which did not bode well for me.

Full of trepidation, I could not eat and I could not sleep either.

Dr Maddox was a kindly man who did not say much as he conducted his intimate examination, but I knew what the verdict was by the speculative look he gave me as he left to go and report his findings to my grandmother.

The cat was now well and truly among the pigeons.

When he had gone, she came to see me in my room. Her demeanour was glacial and went well with the weather outside. This time she did want to know what had happened and, stumbling over my words, I told her.

'If true,' she said, 'this is disgraceful. You are only fifteen. I cannot believe that Gerard would do such a thing.'

It was my first inkling of what was to come.

'Helena must travel over here and bring Gerard with

184

her so that we can thrash this thing out. And decide what to do. Meanwhile, I have dismissed Miss Buckley. It is my view that someone so lax, so inattentive, is not fit to hold the responsible post of governess to a young girl!'

With that she left.

After her departure I wept tears of remorse. When Miss Buckley had gone I would not have one single ally left in this house and she would not find it easy to get another job either, unless Grandmama relented and gave her a half-way decent reference.

Two days later Aunt Helena arrived. I heard the wheels of the carriage from my room and Aunt Margaret came to confirm the news. The heavy snow must have made the journey a hazardous one. Gerard, it turned out, was not with her. Margaret had a pinched look and had had ever since Dorothea got over the wall. I asked her about my governess and it transpired that Miss Buckley had already gone. Grandmother did not believe in wasting time. Quite possibly a glowing reference had been traded for total secrecy concerning what had happened. My grandmother would not want the whole county knowing of my condition.

After lunch which, as was now the norm, was served to me in my room, my presence was requested in the drawing-room. There I found Aunt Helena and Grandmother and, after an uncomfortable five-minute wait during the course of which nobody spoke except for the most perfunctory of greetings, my Aunt Margaret arrived looking harassed. Presumably all the household arrangements had fallen to her now.

My grandmother opened the proceedings by saying, 'You may sit down, Sibyl. I have told Helena the whole unfortunate story and she has confronted Gerard with it. Gerard has denied everything.'

Speechless, I stared at her.

Eventually I said, 'Gerard would not do that! He would not lie. Gerard loves me!'

'Gerard *did* do that. And it is only as a cousin that he loves you.'

Aunt Helena, who had had her back to me, swung

round suddenly with a crackle of stiff silk. Her face was venomous. 'Gerard has told me, Sibyl,' (my name was spoken with a hiss) 'that you set your cap at him in a most forward and immoral way, that he was appalled and repelled by such behaviour in one so young and that he tried to point out to you the error of your ways . . .'

The treachery was comprehensive. I remembered his last kiss. Judas!

'Then why is he not here to say so himself,' I shouted, able to bear it no longer. 'Why?'

'Compose yourself, Sibyl!' Grandmother was intimidating. 'And pray do not speak unless invited to do so! Certainly do not raise your voice in my presence!'

Ordered to subside, I did. Nobody, it seemed, was interested in who the father of my child was. All that concerned them was that it should not be Gerard. Under attack from all sides, I experienced a sudden detachment of mind. Milky, chilly sunlight illuminated the room. Outside I could hear the noise of icicles cracking and falling. A thaw must have set in, though not in here.

In the event it was Aunt Helena who seemed unable to compose herself. She took a step towards me and raised her hand. Her face was contorted. For one moment I thought she was going to slap me and I shrank back. Margaret put a restraining hand on her sister's arm. Brushing it off and collecting herself, Helena said, 'Gerard could not bear to be here to witness your disgrace. His only concern is your welfare, Sibyl!' She was ugly with spite, all beauty dissipated. It was possible to see what she would look like as an old woman. The word disgrace flicked me on the raw.

'What about *your* disgrace?' I spoke in a high-pitched unsteady voice. 'What about *your* morals? I saw you on the terrace kissing one of your lovers the night before Aunt Dorothea's wedding!'

There was total silence.

Aunt Helena took a step backwards, as though I

had moved to strike her rather than the other way around. Grandmother went puce. Presumably it was not every day she heard the word lover in her well-ordered drawing-room, still less the phrase 'one of your lovers'.

There was a sliding sound, followed by a substantial fall of snow off the roof. I saw Margaret give her sister an almost jubilant look and realized in that moment that she loathed Helena.

Regrouping, though not, I noticed, demanding an apology, Grandmother said sternly, 'Go to your room this minute, Sibyl! I shall come and see you later.'

I went. What else could I have done?

Outside the door, however, I paused. It was typical of this family that no reference was made to the existence or otherwise of Aunt Helena's lovers. She, however, could not resist saying, 'Well, what can you expect? The girl's a slut! Bad blood will out!'

Bitch! I thought.

I was just turning away when I heard Aunt Margaret say quietly, 'It is my view that Sibyl may have been more sinned against than sinning. And you know what I mean.' Although I did not fully understand them, these, the first kind words I had heard for a long time, affected me deeply and when I got back to my room I wept.

The Christmas of 1911 was a dismal one. In the course of it my fate was decided, though with no reference to me. Part of me hoped that I would simply be shipped back to my much vilified mother but, despite all that had happened, they would have died rather than do that. What was proposed was that I would stay at the house as long as possible, i.e. until my pregnancy could no longer be concealed. Because I was a thin girl, they reasoned, this would be quite a long time. Increase of weight could always be put down to puppy fat. Afterwards, I was to be sent to a clinic to give birth, after which the child would be given away for adoption. When it was all over I would be sent away to school.

Out of sight, out of mind.

187

On that bleak note Mary felt obliged to leave her mother's narrative for the time being. There was still a lot to be read and none of the sorting out Mary had come to Brixton to do had even been started. Outside it was getting dark and tomorrow she was due back at Bletchley Park. Reluctantly she put the notebook aside, resolving to finish it tomorrow. She was just starting the melancholy task of emptying the wardrobe, prior to deciding what to keep and what to give away, when she heard the unmistakable rattle of a key turning in the front-door lock.

The hall was in darkness and the room in which she had been sitting was at the back. That plus the blackout curtains made it virtually impossible to know whether anyone was in. Whoever it was must have assumed the flat was empty. After a moment's hesitation, Mary snapped on the light with a view to slipping on the security chain. Too late. The door was already opening. Heart in mouth, she waited for the intruder to come in.

20

'Good gracious!' exclaimed Mary. 'Mr Harding!'

She bit back the obvious question and waited for him to explain himself. Harding said, weakly, 'Mary! What a surprise!' It put him in mind of the time he had ended up in Nettie's bedroom by mistake while stalking the late Sibyl Fox.

Neither was quite sure what to say next.

What on earth did he want? All at once she remembered the cigar stub which was still sitting in the ashtray. Harding must have been the visitor. More than a visitor though, to have been given the key to the door. It raised the question of whether he knew what had happened. It transpired he did.

'Please accept my condolences, Mary. Your mother's tragic death must have been a dreadful shock.'

'Yes. I'm here on leave to sort out her belongings. It's not a task I'm enjoying.'

'No, of course not. I'm most terribly sorry.'

Silence.

They were still standing in the hall. She wished he would leave but he showed no sign of doing so. In the end, she felt forced to ask, 'Won't you come in?' The tone in which this was delivered left him in no doubt that she did not want him to. On the other hand he must have come here for something. 'Or is there something else I can do for you?'

It was an invitation for him to explain his presence.

'I lent your mother a book,' said the visitor unconvincingly. 'I thought I'd just drop by to pick it up.'

Lame. If this was the best he could do no wonder he had been politically sidelined.

'Why don't we have a look and then, if you'll forgive me, I have to press on. I'm due back at my desk tomorrow.'

'Yes, of course.' She followed him into the sitting-room and stood by while he looked around inconclusively. Not surprisingly, Harding said, 'It doesn't seem to be here. Perhaps she took it to the office.' Watching his eyes stray towards the bedroom door, it struck Mary that the provenance of the diamonds was now revealed and that they were what he was really after. And maybe the notebooks as well, assuming he knew of their existence. Heaven knows what Mother had written in the rest. A further reading on the train to Bletchley tomorrow would, no doubt, illuminate all this. Whatever it revealed, she was determined he should not have the earrings. They had been given and accepted and that was an end of it as far as she was concerned. And should have been as far as he was concerned too.

'Well, I won't take up any more of your time, Mary. If there is anything I can do for you, you will let me know, won't you?'

She saw him back to the door and opened it. As she did so, giving him a level look, she said, 'Oh, if you don't mind, I think I had better take back the key. I have undertaken to give all of them back to the landlady.' This was true as far as it went though in fact Mary had determined to sound Elfrida out with a view to having the lease put in her own name.

His face fell. Very reluctantly, he handed it over. Both of them were conscious of a lot left unsaid.

'Well, then, goodbye.' Harding touched the brim of his hat.

Mary went back to her depressing task.

The following day, sitting in a window seat on the train as it rattled through the countryside, Mary took the current notebook out of her case and resumed her reading. This, along with Sibyl herself, had entered a thoroughly dismal phase. Alienated from the family, she appeared to have spent much of her time incarcerated in her room, apart from lessons taken with a flinty Miss Buckley replacement. It must have been dreadful. Mary felt for her mother. Unable to bear reading too much of it, she let her eyes run over the pages until she came to the confinement in the clinic. Apart from the county, there was no record of the actual address. Perhaps Sibyl did not know it. The only member of the family to come and visit her appeared to have been the stalwart Aunt Margaret.

Apart from offering moral support, it transpired that Margaret did have some information to impart as well.

The clinic was a cheerless place. All in my predicament went there, from the highest to the lowest, though the lowest had to earn their keep by skivvying despite the fact that some were as pregnant as I was. My own body disgusted me. My stomach was the shape and colour of a hyacinth bulb, so distended that I felt it should be transparent. My breasts were full and blue-veined. The rest of me was stick thin. Thin with unhappiness and uncertainty. Aunt Margaret came to visit me. She was the only one who did. There was a well-spring of compassion in her, I had discovered, which was mainly untapped by the life she lived. I suspect she envied me the child I was bearing. Aunt Margaret should have had her own house, filled with dogs and children and a very conventional husband. Instead it seemed she was doomed to spend her life pandering to a selfish, old woman while life passed her by. It occurred to me to say this to her, to tell her that she should leave while time was on her side (just). On the other hand her problem was mine. She came from a moneyed background, by which I mean that all was provided. The twist in the tale was that she had none of her own to spend. On that level she might as well have been a pauper. To quote the song, she was only a bird in a gilded cage, and so was I, with no independence of action whatever.

It was Aunt Margaret's kindness that was keeping me going and she had promised to be there for the birth if at all possible.

As she was leaving, she said, 'You are not the first, you know, Sibyl. This has all happened before with Gerard.'

Disbelieving, I looked at her. 'Then why did nobody listen to me when I told them the truth?'

She spread her hands helplessly. 'Helena dotes on Gerard and would believe nothing wrong of him. Mama, I suspect, knows better but likewise did not want to confront it. The estate is entailed. Since your father died, Gerard is the heir and the only one they have. In default of Gerard, it would all pass out of the family. You have been sacrificed to an inheritance.'

Do these women have any rights at all? At least my mother lived life on her own terms.

191

As she left, my aunt kissed me. I wanted to say, 'Don't leave me, please don't leave me,' but I did not.

Mary could hardly bear to read it. She skimmed the next few pages, intending to study them in detail later, and finally came to what she was really looking for.

The baby, a son, was born prematurely. And taken away. I felt ill and wretched. Caught by surprise, as we all were, dear, staunch Aunt Margaret was not due to visit until the following day.

Profoundly moved, Mary looked through the window at the countryside passing by. Rosa was right! I am not on my own, she thought. Somewhere out there I have a half-brother. The emotional upheaval caused by this knowledge was complex. It was a sea change. Mary was aware that she would never be the same again.

She went back to the notebook.

My aunt and I wept together. I for the loss of my child, though I had not wanted it in the first place, and she, I would have thought, for children she would never have.

'What will happen to him?' I asked her.

'It is all arranged,' replied Margaret, holding me. 'He is to be adopted by a well-to-do family who are unable to have children of their own. He will want for nothing. You must look forward now, Sibyl.'

But look forward to what?

Mary skimmed on.

When deemed well enough, Sibyl went home and shortly after was sent to school as an upper-class young lady of unblemished reputation, there to receive a thoroughly second-rate education. While she was away, her grandmother unexpectedly died of a heart attack (or maybe Aunt Margaret throttled the old bat, noted Sibyl). Gerard moved in and took control of his inheritance and Aunt Margaret was moved out to a house in the grounds. This proved to be a liberation rather than a deprivation for she subsequently married a local solicitor. It had not been too late for her after all.

Oh, I was thrilled for her, wrote Sibyl, who had been invited to the wedding on her aunt's insistence but could not face it.

Margaret was good and true and deserved to be happy. However it was not such a happy ending for me. My schooling was completed and after that I was cut off and no longer welcome at the family house. I detected Aunt Helena's hand at work here. I asked Aunt Margaret if she would advance me enough money to travel to Rome so that I might rejoin my mother and she agreed. What would I have done without her? Alas, before I could complete my travel arrangements, I received a letter from the family solicitor informing me that my mother had died. Consumption was cited as the cause and, when I thought of it, Mother always did look as though she was being devoured from within. There was a sort of famished, desperate gaiety about her, a lust for life which might have worn her out as much as it appeared to nourish her.

In the end, with no other prospect in view I decided to go back to Italy anyway.

The train drew into the station. Mary hastily threw the notebook into her case, pulled on her coat, searched for and found her ticket and got off. Apart from the bus ride, from here on there would be very little time for reading except at night, by which time she was usually dog tired. The notebook, on the other hand, was addictive. It was hard to stay away from it. In her room at eleven o'clock that night she opened it up and read on.

After leaving England, Sibyl had earned a precarious living teaching and had done some of this in Rome after travelling there to take out of storage her late mother's very few effects. Several pages were devoted to this period, making it plain that the Bohemian, hedonistic life she remembered from her childhood was still extant. Finally, two rackety years and quite a few lovers later, Sibyl returned to England. She did not record why she did this and there was no further mention of her child. The impression received was that she had done as Margaret advised her and put the whole episode behind her.

Then the pace quickened again.

In 1919, I met your father, who eventually asked me to marry him,

wrote Sibyl. She did not sound overwhelmed.

Maybe my experience of it so far had cut off my feelings as far as love was concerned. What was certain was that Charles adored me. Charles was intelligent and rather high-minded. He was an engineer and not, as such, very amusing. If I decided to accept, security beckoned, though not delectation. I would no longer have to work and, to be honest, I was very tired of the perpetual struggle which yielded meagre rewards most of the time. In the end I said Yes and on July 24th, 1920, we married.

Then, in October, 1920:

I discovered I was pregnant! Oh, God, it was all to be gone through again. The discomfort and the pain, not to mention the memories. Charles was over the moon, but then he would have been. As a man he did not have to endure it.

In June 1921 you were born. Charles wanted the name Mary in memory of his mother. I have to say that I would have preferred something rather more exotic but, for once, my husband insisted. So Mary it was. This time it was all as it should have been. I was a respectable married woman.

Sibyl did not trouble to record the next six months at all.

Presumably most of the time was taken up with the exigencies of having a baby in the house. When she took up her story again, it was on a sombre note.

With dreadful suddenness Charles died. He left the house and I never saw him alive again. It was a heart attack, in the street. When the police came I could hardly believe it. There had been no hint of failing health. Now, Mary, you and I were on our own and an appointment with a solicitor confirmed that my clever, unwordly husband had made no provision for such a happening. The house was rented. We were not yet destitute, but would be when the small sum of saved money ran out. I started to look for another teaching post.

There followed a substantial part of the notebooks detailing how Sibyl found positions and where she worked until, finally, they both ended up at the Harding house. It was evident to Mary that it had not been a smooth ride and Mother had not been an ideal employee. Some people seem to attract calamity, reflected Mary, and some both attract it and aid and abet it. Mother appeared to have been one of those.

It was one o'clock. She decided to reserve the Harding years for the following evening, though by now she had a pretty good idea of what they might contain.

The following morning, Mary bicycled to Bletchley Park. The weather was frivolous. White ribbons of cloud unravelled across the sky and, except for a skittish breeze, it would have been very warm for the time of year. Courtesy of a shower of rain the night before, the air was sweet smelling and fresh, which was more than could be said for the interior of Hut 3 in which Mary was employed as one of the index girls. No scent, no talcum powder and limited hot water had seen to that. However if privations such as these were one thing, the work itself was quite another. Everything which came from Hut 6, in the form of the first Enigma decodes, had to be minutely recorded thereby providing an invaluable system of checking and cross checking. For this she was paid the munificent sum of two pounds a week, most of which went on board and lodging. The work was meticulous, but fascinating in that the

195

information she was processing was only a few hours behind the often momentous events unfolding on the battlefront.

Francis Stafford, currently working in Hut 6, did become her lover. Losing, or rather, giving away her virginity had been partly an intellectual decision. It was Mary's statement to herself about the present, a confirmation that the past really was another country and one beyond whose frontiers she had now moved. There was a spirit of camaraderie at Bletchley which went hand in hand with a certain formality. In deference to it, during the working day they addressed each other as Miss Fox and Mr Stafford. While privately amused by this, Mary would not have been surprised to learn that there were those who observed the regulations in bed together as well.

Francis Stafford was the mathematically gifted son of a perfectly ordinary couple who had no academic talents whatever, and who ceaselessly speculated on where their extraordinary child had come from. In such a way was intelligence revealed as the most democratic endowment of them all. Serious and dedicated to what they were all trying to achieve, Francis fell for Mary the moment he saw her. It was, therefore, perfectly natural that he should ask her out for a drink. The work at Bletchley tended to be relentless and all consuming and therefore, in an odd sort of way, it was more relaxing to consort with someone who knew what it was all about than with someone who did not. The girls in the index section were privy to all of it, though as with every job, there were those who mindlessly typed and those who took a more active interest in what was going on. Constantly trying to keep ahead of the German codes, between chasing packs of U-boats themselves chasing Allied convoys across the North Sea, might have begun as the sort of cerebral exercise Francis relished, but running fights, which could go on for four or five days at a time, left them all depleted and tense. There was, he discovered, an air of thoughtfulness about Mary Fox which calmed him. At the same time he found her hard to read. Her centre of gravity eluded him and he sensed that, although she was sitting with a bevy of upper-middle-class girls, she was not exactly *of* them. Though it would probably have taken someone like Francis, who was not from that strata of society either, to spot it.

For her part Mary liked Francis Stafford's modesty, and the way the blackbird's wing of his dark hair fell over his round glasses when he was concentrating, all but obscuring what he was doing. She found him beguiling and when his tall, thin figure hove into view with its slight academic stoop, she was conscious of a feeling of pleasure but, she told herself, she was not in love with him. Without his clothes on, he was revealed as having a good pair of shoulders and a skin that was as white and smooth as that of a girl. Why physical and mental attraction did not tip over into love, Mary could not begin to guess. Probably, given the times they were living in, it was just as well. Nevertheless, she found the presence of a man in her bed at night a comforting experience as well as a sensual one, and the warmth of his proprietorial arm curved around her body made her aware of just how much her life had lacked male protection.

She was curious about Francis's background and asked him about it. In its way it was as unorthodox as the little she knew of her own.

'My father is a piano tuner,' said Francis, 'and my mother is a housewife. Heaven knows where the mathematical gene came from. Anyway, I was lucky enough to win a bursary to a minor public school where the maths department was particularly strong. I say lucky because my parents could never have afforded to send me there. Once *in situ* I had another stroke of good fortune, in that a member of staff, Carstairs, another ardent mathematician, took an interest in me and monitored my progress, finally pointing me in the direction of Oxford. I'll never forget what he said when I thanked him for his help and encouragement. He said, 'I've been teaching for years, Stafford. I enjoy it, but every so often a pupil comes along whose outstanding ability lifts my role into a different dimension. At that point my work becomes a privilege rather than just a way of earning money. You are just such a pupil. You have a rare and extraordinary talent. Don't squander it!'

Francis smiled shyly at Mary. 'Believe it or not, I've never told anybody that before.'

Mary was sceptical. 'What, not even your family?'

'Especially not my family. I love them, but on one level we have nothing in common. My passion for mathematics separated us rather than drew us together.'

Another lonely, only child, she replied, 'Then I'm honoured that you have told *me*.'

'I've told you because, though maybe not in quite the same way, I think you suffer from the same syndrome.'

'Yes,' said Mary. 'Maybe I do.' And then, changing the subject, 'How did your recruitment for Bletchley come about.'

'I was quite simply contacted one day by somebody I'd never met before, but I've always suspected that my old mentor, Carstairs, was the instigator. What about you?'

'Oh, same sort of scenario,' replied Mary vaguely, without offering to elucidate. Then, deliberately digressing, 'Did you know that Lavinia Ponting was recruited to Bletchley from Cairo because she was known to be a crossword wizard?'

They both laughed.

Recognizing her reticence, Francis did not pursue his question, but filed her evasion away in his memory. It was one more question to be added to the others surrounding the mysterious Miss Fox.

The Park was a little world in itself. It had its own rhythms and hierarchies and, although they were theoretically all working towards the same end, its own cabals and secrets. Rafe Bartholomew was frequently there and sometimes dropped in on Mary. Churchill, although a huge admirer of the work they were doing, only visited once.

'You've got connections in high places,' remarked Francis, referring to Rafe. 'How do you come to know Bartholomew?'

'It's a long story,' said Mary. 'I don't know him very well.'

'They say he's one of Churchill's closest confidantes.'

'No doubt they say a lot of things. He's a man who's very hard to read.'

Puzzled, Francis thought: And he takes more than a passing interest in Mary Fox.

Since she was obviously not going to tell him any more, there was no point in pursuing it and their talk turned to other things. Still, the glamorous connection added another brushstroke to the portrait of Mary that he was trying to paint for himself. He did learn that Rafe Bartholomew had recruited her for Bletchley and was aware that unless her credentials had been deemed impeccable this would not have happened. So the connection must go back quite a long way. Mary did not tell Francis about her mother's past either. Having just discovered her own family history, she was still trying to come to terms with it and did not as yet feel like sharing it with anybody else.

That night, after a meagre ration-book supper, Mary settled down to read the rest of the notebooks. Sibyl's view of other people and, in particular, her own station in life, made her daughter wince more than once.

> Even after all these years, I have not forgotten the way I was treated. Nor have I forgiven it. The damage remains. Because of it for me romance is a thing of the past. Though not sex necessarily, I hasten to add. Sex is useful for barter and these days men no longer interest me unless there is something to be got out of them. Since I had no power and therefore no redress, I was forced to work in the houses of the rich, the sort of houses which once received me. Latterly, to earn my daily bread, I taught as little as I could get away with. Arithmetic, English, drawing, a little history, a smattering of French. Geography, the most boring subject on earth, if I had to. Oh, and singing and playing the piano off key, of course. Still, heaven knows why, very important. However, it is all I knew how to do and things haven't changed much. I educated the children of the upper classes, if one can call it that, just as I myself was educated by other governesses in the days when I assumed that privilege was my birthright.

Also instructive was Mother's acerbic account of her first meeting with Davina Harding:

> On September 12th 1928, I travelled to Framwell and from there by taxi to the Hall to be interviewed by Mrs Harding. Davina Harding turned out to be a type with whom I was all too familiar, a vapid, pampered, under-employed member of the upper class whose husband spent most of his time in London. It is probable that this arrangement suited him, for while his wife had been a beauty and still, rather like her own surroundings, retained a faded elegance, she seemed to me intellectually uninhabited. Furthermore, and more importantly, she struck me as devoid of the

199

sort of undercurrent of sexuality which, once tapped into, might have continued to command the attention of a man on the loose in London with an otherwise atrophied marriage. Though sex, Mary, it must be said, can be a two-edged sword. In my case it has been variously my solace, my weapon and, ultimately, my social destruction and my cross . . . What would the ladylike Mrs Harding have said, I wonder, if she had known the truth about my past? She might have fainted. She looked the type. She would not have employed me, that's for sure. Luckily for me it appeared that she was not a very dedicated reader of references. Either nuance escaped her or, more likely, she saw only what she wanted to see.

Deferentially attending to her inconsequential ramblings during the course of the interview, as befitted the perfect would-be live-in employee, I learnt a great deal. I learnt, for instance, that the Hardings could not keep staff. Which is no doubt why the lukewarm recommendations from former employers were glossed over. For once, it appeared, my prospective mistress's need was greater than mine. The sigh of relief when I accepted her offer of the post, plus the pittance she offered me (which I had every intention of trying to push up) was practically audible and emboldened me to raise the subject of my daughter. Implicit was the possibility that, regretfully, I should have to turn down the job if you could not be accommodated. Reluctantly Mrs Harding assented. *Au fond*, she did not want to, but still she did it.

Another straw in the wind.

'Provided the probation period works, the position will be a long-term one,' said Mrs Harding.

Listening to her, it was obvious to me that if I played my cards with subtlety and outward submission the opportunities might be limitless. In the beginning, of course, it would be a watching, waiting discipline. Later, though maybe much later, a greater game plan might be called for. We would see.

I'm closing this entry, Mary, with a favourite verse written by the ill-fated Marquis of Montrose for no better reason than that I like it! Ill-fated or not, his view is mine.

'He either fears his fate too much,/ Or his deserts

200

are small,/ That puts it not unto the touch/ To win or lose it all.'

Because the Harding era was familiar territory to her, Mary was preparing to skip through it, intending to read it all in depth later, when the phrase: *sexual liaison* coupled with the name *Geoffrey Harding* caught her eye. Alerted, she read the following and was discomfited to find her mother's disenchanted eye turned on herself:

Since you, Mary, proved a disappointment in the romantic stakes, I'm sorry to say I was forced to conduct (or should I say endure?) a sexual liaison with Geoffrey Harding as my last throw. Before I embarked on this, once again I considered suggesting to you that you should transfer your affections from the oblivious, unattainable Godfrey to the more ordinary and available William who, I suspected, had a soft spot for you anyway. Still has for all I know. In the end I rejected the idea. If Nettie had been my daughter I would not have thought twice about doing so, but you are quite different. You, Mary, believe in Love, an unpractical predilection you must have inherited from your unpractical father. You certainly didn't get it from me!

Which left me servicing Geoffrey. In bed Geoffrey was energetic but that was about it. It was easy to see why Davina Harding suffered from migraines on a regular basis when he was at home. In her place so would I.

The question was, what would happen next?

Quite soon the predictable Hardings would want to send Nettie off to be finished. Which would be the end of the mental slog for Nettie and the end of a job for me. I considered two options. The first was to snare Geoffrey into marriage. I have to say I did not favour this except as a last resort, since at that point I should have had to live with him. Joining the Harding family at one remove as William's mother-in-law (or Jonty's, come to that) would have been more congenial. However, as I say, owing to your scrupulous view of such things, this particular option was not on offer. Then it occurred to me that there was a third possibility. A little pressure on

Geoffrey, commonly known as blackmail, might do the trick and transform our rocky financial prospects.

Horrified, Mary nearly dropped the book. Blackmail! Ye gods!

Periodically, in between shouts of ecstasy and epic orgasms (his not mine) the words, 'Davina must never know,' were uttered.

Of course I said, 'And she never will. You may rely on my discretion.'

Speaking the words, I thought, If Geoffrey believes that he'll believe anything.

In the light of this, the push-you-pull-me with Davina, who emerged the undisputed winner, was interesting. Mary would not have thought Mrs Harding had it in her. A short, bleak paragraph underlined her mother's chagrin. Mary felt it extraordinary how much had been going on beneath the surface that she had not known about. Nothing had been as it seemed. In the light of what had happened at the Brixton flat, the liaison with Geoffrey Harding did not come as a surprise, though her mother's attitude to it did. The desperate scrabbling for some sort of foothold back on the ladder of privilege was unedifying but, for Mary who now knew the whole story, understandable. It seemed to her that, through no fault of her own at the beginning, Mother's had been a misfired life.

She went and got out the little jewel box, opened it up and took out the Harding earrings. She put them on and held the mirror up to her face. For one brief moment, Sibyl looked back. Fiery and pale, even by the dim light of a sixty-watt bulb the diamonds flared, symbolic of an aspiration that had never been realized. Mary took them off again and replaced them on the velvet in their own little leather box. The real jewel in the heart of all this was the knowledge that somewhere, hopefully still alive, she had a half-brother. Whom it must be possible to find. Not now, of course, with the war on, but when it was all over as, please God, it would be one day.

Mary closed the book. Though she was aware that the room had grown cold, she did not move but sat silently where she was for some time, contemplating the past and, more importantly, the future.

21

Kyle McClaren and Venetia Harding saw a great deal of each other. Kyle put the thought of his American wife to the back of his mind (despite his own behaviour he was old-fashioned enough to expect Allegra to be faithful to him) and concentrated on living life to the full in wartime London. After all, reasoned Kyle in common with a lot of other people, I might be dead tomorrow. Nettie, who had never felt the need to square her conscience, was certainly not about to start now. In the fullness of time she and Randolph would obtain a divorce, or rather she would, in the teeth of his opposition. Negotiating with Randolph was tantamount to conducting a war of attrition. Every time she thought the whole issue was cut and dried and safely buried, he would go quiet for a bit and then, like a dog with a bone, he would dig the whole thing up again and she would find herself back where they had started.

Finally: 'Fuck off, Randolph,' said Nettie. 'I am not returning to you!'

Thank heaven he was back at the front and the locks had been changed on the house in Chelsea.

Kyle was aware that he did not have his finger properly on the button where Venetia was concerned. When she was not with him he had no idea where she was or what she was doing. On the other hand, in the sensitive circles in which they moved, everyone was keeping everyone else in the dark concerning something. LOOSE TALK COSTS LIVES proclaimed the posters, thereby providing a useful mandate for a lot of loose living not directly connected with the war at all. Nettie liked Kyle and would probably have preferred to be in bed with him rather than anyone else, which was fine as far as it went, but eliciting information of the sort that Rafe Bartholomew wanted from crusty top brass took half the time in the bedroom than it would have done elsewhere. Since, almost without exception, they all had wives at home, discretion was maintained and there was no bragging about the carnal delights on offer in Chelsea. There was, however, a certain amount of sour female comment.

Nettie, who was aware of it, though the fact rather than the detail, could not have cared less. Two-timing Kyle presented no moral problem whatever. In fact it was her *duty* to do it. All in all, against all her expectations, the war effort was proving a great asset and could be usefully cited to support almost any sort of behaviour.

Casting around for a new diversion, Nettie hit on the idea of going to see the celebrated clairvoyant Rosa Murphy about whom she had been told by a friend. She wanted Kyle McClaren to go with her.

Kyle refused.

'It's mumbo jumbo,' he said, loftily dismissive. 'I've got more important things to do.'

'Where's your sense of adventure?'

'Not electrified by the prospect of travelling overland to Stepney!'

Nettie did not give up easily. 'What about an advance into the unknown? A foray into the future? Darling, how can you resist?'

'Quite easily, so no thanks.'

In the end Nettie went on her own.

By now it was early May. The trees were greening and the blossom was out. It was probably better to be going without Kyle who had looked all set to put a dampener on the whole thing. On arrival she was shown into a large room. Deceptively narrow at the front, the house must have been one of those which went back a long way. Four other people were already present, seated around an oval table. All nodded to Nettie but none introduced themselves. Apparently anonymity was the form at seances. The curtains were drawn. Nettie took the last seat.

When Mrs Murphy entered the room Nettie was struck by how small and sparrow-like she was. She took the chair at the head of the table and requested that they all held hands.

'There are no guarantees,' said Rosa, 'but it is perfectly likely that my spirit guide Stanley will materialize. Sometimes he does and sometimes he doesn't.' This speech was delivered in the same way as she might have said, 'It is perfectly likely that my Auntie Doris might drop in from Stoke Poges.'

'It is also possible that loved ones of your own who have passed over may join us too,' she continued. 'Meanwhile, I should like to ask you to remain very quiet while we wait.'

They did remain very quiet. It would have been possible to hear the proverbial pin drop. Nettie tried to forget that she was holding the moist hands of two people she had never met before and concentrate. An air of expectation prevailed.

Mrs Murphy began to breath deeply, fast at first, and then, presumably as she settled into trance, slowly and stertorously. It was Nettie's impression that the lights had dimmed slightly, but since no one was anywhere near the switch (she looked round to check) it could not have been the case. There was no sign of Stanley. Instead Rosa began to speak. She began to go the round of the table, speaking to each in turn often in varying voices, as if others spoke through her. According to the responses she received, her hit rate seemed high. But then, thought Nettie, whose turn had not yet arrived, it would take a lot of nerve to shout out in the middle of a seance, 'You're off beam there, Mrs Murphy!' Do not be flippant, Nettie, she chided herself.

When Rosa finally got to Nettie, there was a long silence. Then she said, 'A man is here. A pilot. He was young when he passed over.'

Alerted, Nettie sat up. Not so off beam after all. On the other hand, given the horrendous casualty rate of Bomber Command, to take just one example, there were probably a lot of pilots out there in the ether wanting to make contact.

Mrs Murphy slipped into the first person and said, 'Shot down! I drowned in the sea!' It couldn't have been, of course, but to Nettie's startled ears the voice sounded just like that of Godfrey. 'It's the turning point now,' the voice went on. It seemed to Nettie that it was beginning to fade as if there was a faulty connection. Tears started to her eyes. Please God Jonty and William were not out there with him but still in this world.

There was quite a long silence. Nobody moved or spoke.

When Rosa resumed speaking it was once again in a man's voice, though not that of Godfrey this time. The

205

elusive Stanley perhaps. If so, he picked up from where her brother, if it *was* her brother, had left off.

'Yes, the turning point. France. Attack from the sea. A huge enterprise and very successful. June is the month!'

Nettie, whose incarnation as spy had honed her powers of recollection no end, memorized all of it, though her real interest was reserved for Godfrey. The light in the room appeared to increase. Rosa shook her head and opened her eyes.

It was over.

They all released each other's hands. Nettie furtively wiped hers on her skirt and then reached into her handbag for some money.

Nettie was due to see Rafe Bartholomew the following day to be debriefed on the latest dinner party. Rafe was looking older these days. Not cynicism exactly but disillusion or maybe just grief underlay the urbane manner. This had set in after Godfrey's death, Nettie recognized and raised the question of whether to tell him about what had happened during the course of her sitting with Rosa Murphy. An up-front personality, Nettie decided that she would.

Rafe listened. If he was upset by her account of Godfrey's presence there, he did not show it, in fact, if anything he did not appear to take it seriously. He had, it transpired, heard of Mrs Murphy. What Nettie did not know was that Churchill himself had had at least two private sittings with her and had told Rafe about them without giving away very much about what, if anything, had been divulged. The old man had been notably more cheerful afterwards though, he recalled. Maybe there was a mystical side to Churchill's nature which inclined him to probe such things, or maybe it was just an attempt to explore every available avenue for information. Whatever it was, it was not a way of going about things that he, Rafe, felt comfortable with, although Godfrey's visitation on the day of his death had shaken his assumptions. Hitherto a non-believer in an afterlife, Rafe was now not so sure.

'So,' said Bartholomew, 'what did you make of ectoplasm, Venetia?'

Nettie was nonplussed. 'Ecto what?'

'Never mind,' he said. 'Did Mrs Murphy say anything else?'

'Well, yes she did as a matter of fact,' replied Nettie and repeated it word for word.

Good God! To say Rafe was thunderstruck would have been no exaggeration. 'That was all she said, was it,' he probed carefully, letting no sign of his heightened alertness appear on the surface. 'You're sure?'

'Yes, quite sure.'

'Venetia, I want you to give me an undertaking not to speak to anyone else about this. And I mean anybody. It's a matter of national security!'

Nettie stared at him. 'Yes, of course.' In the light of the fact that her privileged lifestyle depended upon her discretion, Nettie had become more adept than she had ever believed possible at holding her tongue.

When she had gone, Rafe sat assessing the implications of what he had just been told. It was imperative that he put a stop to what could have been a catastrophic breach of national security.

The question was how.

In the end, he rang Mrs Murphy and made an appointment under an assumed name to go and see her. Speed was of the essence.

When she answered the door, he was surprised at her ordinariness, a petite, black-haired, blue-eyed woman in a pinny. Apparently clairvoyants did the washing up just like everyone else.

'Come in, Mr Wentworth!' She stood aside to let him in. It occurred to Rafe as she did so that given the apparent extent of her strange powers, she probably knew, or should have done, that he was not Mr Wentworth. As he passed her, he noticed her looking sharply over his shoulder and wondered what could have attracted her attention. Mrs Murphy took the lead and preceded him into a long, narrow room with a table in it. This must be where she held her seances. It was cluttered with the sort of twee bric-à-brac that Rafe detested. He tried to picture Venetia Huntington in it and could not.

'Cup of tea, Mr Wentworth?' offered Rosa.

'Thank you, no,' said Bartholomew.

207

He wondered how to begin. It was not every day he had to warn seers about contravening the Official Secrets Act.

Watching his hesitation, she said, 'Why don't you just say it, whatever it is?'

'All right. You held a seance in this room quite recently, on Wednesday to be exact. Someone who was present told me about it –'

'That would have been the posh one,' interrupted Mrs Murphy. 'Crocodile-skin handbag and a fur. She came under an assumed name too.'

Flushed out, Rafe decided to ignore this remark and soldier on, '– and during the course of it you delivered to the assembled company some information classified as top secret. I would like to know where you got it from.'

'I got it from Stanley.'

'Stanley?'

'Is my guide.' She held up an imperious hand. 'And before you panic, Mr Wentworth, I do not know what I'm saying in trance. You are from the Ministry, I take it?'

'In a manner of speaking, yes.'

'And I assume that whatever it was Stanley said was accurate, otherwise you wouldn't be here.'

Deciding not to answer that directly, Rafe said, 'The fact that you may be passing on highly sensitive information in trance, in spite of the fact that you say you had no idea what it was, could render you liable to prosecution under the Official Secrets Act, not to mention the absurd 1735 Witchcraft Act.'

If what Mrs Murphy said was true and she did not even consciously know what she was saying, he had an added complication on his hands. Neither of them had any point of reference. All the same it was imperative that he stop her.

'So what do you suggest I do?'

'I suggest you give up staging seances until the war is over, otherwise you could find yourself in prison for endangering the State.'

'I don't want to endanger anything,' said Rosa fervently. 'My son's out there somewhere, fighting for this country. But this is my livelihood we're talking about. I used to do the fairs, you know, and since my horse went to the knackers I've no other way of earning a living.'

'I could arrange a pension,' suggested Bartholomew.

'I don't like the idea of taking money like that,' said Rosa at last. 'I've always paid my own way.'

Bartholomew leant forward. 'Nevertheless, Mrs Murphy, I urge you to do it. Just for the duration. If you can give me some idea of your average income, I'll arrange it. I assure you it would be on the generous side.'

She took a decision. 'Very well. But just for the duration, mind you. I don't want charity.'

Relieved, he leant back again.

'Now what about the others who were present at the same sitting. I'll need to talk to them. Do you know who they were?'

'Every last one. All local and come quite often. The only stranger was Miss High and Mighty.' There was the ghost of a smile. 'No German spies there. If you'll take my advice, don't stir it up again and you won't muddy the waters. Just let them forget what was said. On the whole people come to me to hear about themselves, they aren't interested in other folk's messages.'

Rafe had no way of knowing whether this was good advice or not. On the other hand, gut feeling told him that what she said did make sense. He stood up and proffered his hand. She shook it.

'The first payment will be immediate. After that every week.'

As he was putting on his coat, at the same time making for the front door, Rosa said conversationally, 'By the way, a young man followed you in. A pilot in flying kit. Handsome. Very. He's been standing behind your chair all the time we've been talking. There's a message for you. He says it was the right room and he's waiting for you.'

By this time they were on the step.

'I have no idea what he means, but I expect you do. Goodbye, Mr Wentworth.'

22

In June, the brilliant strategy of D–Day enabled 250,000 troops to land on the bare coast of Normandy, thereby taking the German army by surprise. It was the beginning of the liberation of France as foreseen by Mrs Murphy's guide, Stanley. On August 25th, Paris was liberated. ('Oh, good,' said Nettie, '*now* maybe we'll get some decent frocks.')

Successes abroad did not mean that the heat was off at home. German flying bombs, agents of random destruction and death, ravaged the south of England. As time went by, Mary resigned herself to the fact that her odyssey in search of her lost brother looked like being indefinitely postponed. Hardest of all was not knowing if he was alive or dead, and it did cross Mary's mind once or twice that it was a pity she had no idea where Rosa and her horse were these days because Rosa would have known the answer. It was Nettie who casually brought this wheel full circle one day when they met for lunch in London. Nettie said, 'I must tell you! I went to see Mrs Rosa Murphy the clairvoyant and, you'll never guess, Godfrey came through!'

Mary was taken off-guard. Godfrey? And *Rosa*? Surely there could be only one Rosa who told fortunes. On the other hand Mrs Rosa Murphy, celebrated London clairvoyant, was a significant promotion from Madam Rosa, gypsy seer. Cautiously, Mary said, 'What did Mrs Murphy look like?'

Surprised, Nettie said, 'What did she look like? Well, she's small, blue–eyed and black–haired –'

'Did she have a crystal ball?'

'No, I didn't see one of those,' recalled Nettie. 'But I've since learnt that I made a mistake by going to a seance, rather than a private sitting. As it was I had to share her with several other people. I might go again sometime.'

'Where did she live?'

'Stepney,' said Nettie, 'where I've never been before. Doesn't Mr Tripp live in Stepney? Remember Mr Tripp who helped us haul Randolph into the house one of the many nights he was paralytic? Why, were you thinking of going?'

'Maybe,' replied Mary non-committal, since the last thing she wanted to do was make this particular excursion with Nettie in tow. 'How is Randolph, by the way?'

'Still turning up in London,' Nettie replied. 'Strutting about Having a Good War. Still banging on about producing an heir . . .'

'I thought that was all over!'

'It is but I can't get it into Randolph's thick skull. The problem is we aren't yet divorced so he can't fall on one knee and propose to anybody else . . . And, boy, does he complain! As soon as the war's over I intend to get shot of him very quickly.'

'You don't have Mrs Murphy's address on you, do you?'

'Possibly.' Nettie rummaged in an impressive crocodile-skin handbag and finally, in exasperation, tipped the contents onto the table. She leafed through a tattered little black book. 'Yes, here it is!'

She dictated the address to Mary.

Shovelling everything back into her bag and watching her friend write the address and telephone number down as she did so, she observed, 'I thought you were much too level-headed to go in for that sort of thing.'

'So did I. I probably won't do anything about it, but thanks all the same, Nettie.'

But she did do something about it, of course.

Mrs Murphy's initial response was disappointing.

'No more sittings or seances for the foreseeable, dear,' said Rosa.

'I don't really want either,' said Mary. 'I really just wanted to see if you could enlarge on something you told me years ago.'

'Probably not,' answered Rosa. 'If I didn't tell you whatever it was you wanted to know at the time, it's because Spirit didn't tell me. I can only pass on what I get. Anything else and I'd be guessing. But come anyway. I'll have a go! Where was it that we met?'

Mary reminded her.

'Oh, yes, I remember. When would suit you?'

'Today, if possible. I'm only in London for the day.'

'OK. Come along *now*,' said Rosa.

It was at a party at the 400 that Nettie saw someone across the room whose face was familiar. Rack her brains as she might, she was unable to put a name to it. Finally she asked a friend.

'That's Josh Kellaway who's made himself a fortune out of the war. Munitions is the name of his particular game.'

'He looks very young to have done that so quickly.'

'If I simply say he's a young man on the make who married the boss's daughter, all of which is true, by the way, I'd be selling him short. He's actually got a very good head for business. Plus a ruthless reputation. So watch it, Venetia.'

It all sounded very attractive. 'I'd like to meet him!'

'I'll introduce you.'

The moment they connected physically, though only with a handshake this time, Nettie knew who Josh Kellaway was.

'Joshua!' said Nettie. 'Do you remember me?'

'Miss Nettie!' The delivery was ironic and self-assured. Joshua had evidently come a long way socially since his stable days. 'How could I forget?'

Always a looker, he had acquired a glaze rather than a polish, Nettie decided. The hair was slicked back and the suit was double breasted and a bit too sharp. He was smoking the sort of cigar her father favoured. His fingernails, she noticed, were manicured. He probably had a camel-hair coat. With exaggerated shoulders. Everything about Joshua was very expensive and socially not quite right. Except the money, of course. There was also an indefinable aura of being outside the law about him which appealed to the rebel in Nettie. Probably always had.

Smiling up at him, she said, 'Is your wife here?'

Parrying, he replied, 'How do you know I'm married?'

'Because I researched you before asking to be introduced.'

'Did you?'

Unabashed, 'Yes. So! I repeat: is your wife here?'

'No, she isn't. My wife's in the country out of harm's way with the children. What about you?'

'My husband's out of harm's way at the front!'

It spoke volumes. Joshua laughed. His eyes appraised her.

212

Nettie Harding, who had always known what she wanted, had turned into a *soignée* young woman who probably still knew what she wanted. And usually got it.

It occurred to him that maybe once again she wanted *him*.

Not at all averse to the idea, though this time it would be on his terms not hers, he said, 'Why don't I take you out to dinner? For old times' sake.'

'Yes, why don't you?'

Later, with a starched tablecloth and a bottle of champagne between them, Nettie asked, 'Tell me what happened after you left us. Where did you go?'

After you left us. It was a euphemism that amused him. After you were thrown out by my unpleasant father would have been more like it.

Joshua proffered a gold cigarette case and then lit Nettie's cigarette for her before extracting one for himself.

'Well, I reckoned that as far as the local area was concerned, I was a dead duck. Seducing the daughter of the most important man in the neighbourhood isn't exactly a passport to another job.'

'I thought *I* seduced *you*!' Nettie was not about to let that one pass.

'Whatever.' Joshua preferred not to address the issue. 'Am I going to be allowed to finish my story without being interrupted?'

'Yes, of course. Sorry.' Not at all contrite, Nettie grinned at him. 'Go on.'

'So I decided to try the big city instead, and I went to Birmingham and got a job in a factory. From there, having got some experience under my belt, I went to another one. At the time war was declared I was working in a munitions factory. By then I knew my way around and I got promotion and then I had a stroke of luck. I met the boss's daughter . . .'

Nettie wondered what the boss's daughter was like.

'. . . and then war broke out and the rest was history. I've made a pile. Furthermore, I've discovered that I've got an instinct for business and a quick brain. I may have been ignorant but I'm not stupid. Although I suppose it's true to say that if your father hadn't booted me out, I might have been mucking out stables all my life. As it was, I was forced in a different direction. Though, despite the happy outcome, I'm still not prepared to nominate him philanthropist of the year.'

No. Nettie had no difficulty in endorsing that one.

'What about you?'

'Me? I'm known as Venetia Huntington these days. My husband, Randolph, is a walking disaster. When he's upright, that is, which is seldom.'

'You say your husband's away at the front, so what do you do with yourself all day?'

'That I'm not allowed to talk about.' There was a brief silence while Nettie tried to resist the temptation to give Joshua a clue and failed. Eventually she came up with, '. . . in a manner of speaking, I suppose you could say I liaise . . .'

Liaise! It was a good word. She congratulated herself.

Liaise? thought Joshua, also considering it. It could have covered anything from prostitution to running the Foreign Office. The latter he dismissed as highly unlikely but was not inclined to dismiss the former quite so readily. Remembering the lissom delights of Nettie's adolescent body, Joshua decided that this time he would be the one to do the seducing. Preferably tonight.

'What happened to the governess and her daughter?'

He had not had much to do with either of them, but remembered Mary as a gravely beautiful girl. She and Nettie had been like chalk and cheese, yet had appeared to get on well together. The mother had been another kettle of fish altogether. Fox by name and foxy by nature. An edgy redhead with a beady green eye.

'Sadly, Mrs Fox is dead. Killed by a bomb,' said Nettie. 'Mary remains one of my best friends. After all, we were like sisters for years. But never mind about them. What about *us*?' There was a rapacity about her which was arresting.

No beating about the bush with Nettie.

Determined to regain the initiative, Joshua took a chance.

'Your place or mine?'

It paid off.

'Mine,' said Nettie.

'That's right. You're the one who came from nowhere wanting a glass of water,' said Rosa Murphy when she

214

opened the door to Mary. She did not take her visitor into the seance room but into her own small sitting-room instead. The sun was on the back of the house. Striking through the dusty window-pane, it threw a square of light onto the patterned rug. The room was stuffy and the only sound was that of a bluebottle crawling up the glass before falling back and starting again. Invited to do so, Mary sat down.

'Now!' said Rosa.

'The last, the *only* time I've seen you,' said Mary, 'you told me I had a half-brother whom I knew nothing about. I'll be perfectly frank and tell you that after I got over my amazement at what you said, I wrote it off as nonsense. Since when I've discovered that you were absolutely right . . .'

'. . . and you want to find him!'

'In a manner of speaking, yes, but first I want to know if he is still alive.' Thinking of Godfrey, Mary bit her lip, 'So many young men have died in the war . . .' Her voice trailed away uncertainly.

Rosa concentrated.

'But I get the feeling not this one. Not yet. Maybe you should set about your search sooner rather than later.'

'I'm afraid I can't do that.'

'Then do it as soon as you can.'

Mary decided to share the burden of her secret with Francis Stafford. He listened intently and finally said, 'What an extraordinary story. In the light of the family cover-up it may not be so easy to trace your brother though. A lot would depend on who is still alive and remembers the sequence of events. Plus, if what you say is correct, your mother hasn't exactly been lavish with geographical information, not even the name of the clinic and, given the circumstances, I wouldn't place too much store by parish records either.'

Concern for his lover was paramount. Francis discovered that he could not bear the thought of Mary being hurt.

'The other fact that you should come to terms with if you do succeed in tracing your brother is that you and he may have nothing in common.'

'I've thought of that and I still want to do it. Whoever he was, he's my only living relation. I'd go further and say that for my own peace of mind, I *must* do it.'

215

He took her in his arms.

'Of course you must.'

Rafe Bartholomew wondered from time to time whether Mrs Murphy was keeping her word. As a good judge of people, it was his view that she probably was but one never quite knew. D–Day had come and gone but the war went on and there was a lot of other strategy and battle-planning being formulated all the time concerning which absolute secrecy was equally vital. His mind was to be set at rest in an unexpected way.

At the conclusion of one particularly long meeting of the War Cabinet and closely involved others, Churchill asked Bartholomew to remain behind. It had been a belligerent, bad-tempered discussion with the old man clearly out of sorts. Maybe one of the dreaded black dog depressions was in the offing. Familiar by now with the debilitating sadness that had stalked him since Godfrey's death and from time to time threatened to drag him down totally, Rafe hoped not. Ultimately responsible for the security of the nation, Churchill's was a lonely responsibility and to perform his job properly he needed all the faith and optimism he could muster. And the energy. As Rafe knew to his own cost, depression sapped energy.

The problem, it turned out, was Mrs Murphy.

'I rang her,' grumbled Churchill, 'to arrange a sitting. It's important to keep all lines open, you know, Rafe. Anyway, she ticked me off! No more sittings for the foreseeable, said Mrs Murphy. A Mr Wentworth from the ministry has forbidden them and didn't I know there was a war on! I, the Prime Minister!' The great man's chagrin was comical to behold.

'Leave it with me,' said Rafe.

23

In September, 1944, the Harding family suffered another blow. By now the Allies were storming through Holland, aiming for a bridgehead over the Rhine delta. A plan was formulated to drop thousands of paratroops in the vicinity of Arnhem and Nijmegen in order to capture the two main tributaries. If the risk was huge, the rewards could have been equally great and shortened the war by months. They came within a whisker of success. The Nijmegen objectives were achieved but those of Arnhem were not and a combination of severe weather preventing air back-up, and the magnitude of the German resistance, defeated what had always been a hazardous enterprise. The 1st British Airborne Division, of which Jonty was a member, made a heroic stand before finally being withdrawn. Of the eight thousand men originally parachuted in, only around three thousand came back and Jonty was not among them.

Mary comforted Nettie, who was very distressed.

'Jonty has been posted missing, Nettie, not dead. He could be a prisoner of war. Don't despair so soon.'

Neither of them quite believed it, but the need to keep Nettie's spirits up caused Mary to mourn alone. The loss was made all the more bitter by the fact that it looked as though the end might be finally in sight. All their prayers now centred on William but month after month passed without news. Suddenly, the following March, another letter arrived.

My dear Mary,

I am writing this from the Western Front, under the command of Field-Marshal Montgomery. It seems we are prevailing, but the fighting has been grim. I am not allowed to go into any of it in detail, so would only mention one particularly savage battle, without being specific as to when or where, during the course of which we won a particularly bloody victory over some German paratroopers. They fought like tigers and I could not help thinking of Jonty. We are all very tired, maybe weary is a better word. This notwithstanding, Montgomery is inspirational and there is a feeling of optimism in the air, of victory within our grasp. I hope I survive to see it. It would be ironic to die now, when the end may be so near.

When I have time to myself, I think of home and of all those English summers we spent together as children. I remember the apple orchard. Oh, Mary, I need to know that at the end of all this horror it will all be as it once was. I have a dog-eared volume of Rupert Brooke's poetry with me and I read it constantly. Do you remember sitting beside the pool, watching the carp and the koi. Do you? 'Green as a dream and deep as death . . .' I long for all I once took for granted, the sharp, sweet tang of an English spring, Oxford in the summer and those tinder-dry blazing autumns when one dark gold day succeeded another. Most of all I long for the peace and the certainty for there is none of that here. Promise me, Mary, that if I make it back you will have dinner with me, if only to talk over a shared childhood.

I need to know that some things at least are constant.
William

It raised the question of what to do for it was almost a love letter. It would be unthinkable not to pass on the good news that William was safe but then they would all want to see it. In the end Mary passed on the good news to the Hardings and to Rafe Bartholomew, and in answer to the cries of *May we see the letter?* said that she had temporarily mislaid it.

Kyle McClaren's wife Allegra arrived from the States.

Her husband's letters had become repetitive, offhand even, as though his mind was not on what he was doing. They smacked of automatic pilot. On the telephone, though she could hear him perfectly well, he sounded disconnected in a personal sense. Allegra, an equine American with an impeccable pedigree who had jumped this fence before, formed the opinion that there was a lot he was not telling her. She voiced her fears to her formidable socialite mother-in-law, a bejewelled, blue-rinsed matron who understood her son very well.

'Oh Lord! Better get over there quick, honey!' was the

advice on offer, followed up by, 'and get pregnant while you're at it.'

Bossy old trout! Nevertheless, Allegra went.

Once in London, she sized the situation up quickly and that was the end of Kyle and Venetia. Wisely, Allegra did not make scenes but she did make sure that during his leisure hours she was always by Kyle's side. Without the need for words, female semaphore accompanied by dazzlingly insincere social smiles conveyed to Nettie the unmistakable message: Steer Clear Of My Man. On the whole, though she was heard to say 'That woman's got a face like a tomahawk', Nettie felt disinclined to make a fight of it. Which was a relief to Kyle, who had known the game was up the moment his wife set foot in London and did not feel like being torn to pieces by two strong women.

Joshua Kellaway who, it turned out, did have a camel-hair coat, picked up where Kyle McClaren left off. Part of Nettie was frightened of Joshua. The shy youth who had once idealized her had gone and been replaced by a man who had earned his own place in the world and felt himself beholden to no one and certainly not to the Harding family. After the initial courting ritual, Nettie found herself treated as something akin to a concubine. All the black market perks she had become used to were on offer, but not the sole rights to Kellaway. Nettie's response to not being in control for the first time was to fall in love. And very inconvenient it was. Being in love meant waiting for the telephone to ring and ringing him if it did not. It also meant wondering where Joshua was when he was not with her. Jealousy was an unpleasant revelation. As if this wasn't enough, she was required to work harder for the rent in order to fill the intelligence gap left by the corralling of Kyle McClaren.

'You can't blame me if his possessive wife lands on these shores and snatches him back,' said Nettie to Rafe Bartholomew. 'Nothing I could do about that.'

'No, of course not.' Apparently initially reasonable, Rafe followed this up with, 'but as I'm sure you'll understand, I must have value for money. Kyle's pillow talk was *very* valuable. You need another Kyle McClaren.'

Flushed out, 'I'm already sleeping with almost everybody else who could be useful,' said Nettie tartly and immediately wished she hadn't.

Rafe looked pained.

'As I've said before, it's no concern of mine how you debrief our American cousins. I just want the information.'

There they had left it.

A week later she heard from him again.

'You're in luck, Venetia,' Rafe said. 'The highest-ranking American naval attaché is going back to Washington with his wife and being replaced by another one without his. See what you can do! Over and out.'

All this entertaining did not impinge on Nettie's arrangements with Joshua for the reason that Kellaway made it plain that he preferred their assignations to be at the weekend. What he did with himself from Monday to Friday remained a mystery. Nettie supposed that he ran his factory in Birmingham or wherever it was and returned to his wife and children at night. When he made it plain that he did not appreciate being asked about his movements, feeling that she had no choice Nettie desisted and found herself forced to settle for the fact that on Saturdays he came to London to go out to play and see her. She did not like it, but, having let the initiative slip as comprehensively as she had, she was at a loss as to how to retrieve it.

Quite often she asked herself why it was that she had fallen so comprehensively for Joshua, who was not quite right in every social sense and who, moreover, did not treat her very well. In common with lovers all down the ages, Nettie was unable to come up with an answer to this. Love, it appeared, was irrational. What was certain was that she had been much happier before Cupid started interfering in her affairs.

By now it was the end of April. Since William had written his letter to Mary the Allies had surged on, driving the German army before them, and Cologne had fallen. In March there was a massive airborne landing east of the Rhine. This time success was total. The Arnhem débâcle was not repeated and the way was now open. There was still savage fighting but euphoria began to overtake exhaustion. For the first time William dared admit to himself that he might get out of this alive and that victory in Europe was within their grasp. Morale among the troops was high. Buoyed up by it, he thought of Mary and his family and for the first time in years entertained the thought that he might soon see them again.

Leipzig, Nuremberg and Bremen all fell as the attack was pressed home and the Allied armies rolled inexorably on. By the end of April the German Army in Italy had capitulated and on May 7th Field Marshal Keitel, Chief of the German Army, signed the document of unconditional surrender. The war in Europe was over.

On the following day, VE Day, in all the towns and cities the people poured out onto the streets. Amid the outpouring of emotion the only one who looked beyond it and could see nothing, or at least nothing for him, was Rafe. Before he met Godfrey Harding he had been self-sufficient, the cat who walked alone. Now he feared the silence the end of the war would bring and recognized that, as a result of their doomed love affair, he was no longer that person. Going forwards, to live alone after Godfrey, was unthinkable and at the same time the idea that anybody else could take his lover's place was repugnant. It looked as though there was no solution.

Francis kissed Mary with passion and sensed restraint. It had been his intention to ask her to marry him. As a result he did not. And probably never would. A mathematician to his fingertips, Francis understood logical progression very well and was aware that for whatever reason it was not happening now.

Elsewhere, Kyle and Allegra were also part of the huge ecstatic crowd which was so dense and so single-minded that it seemed to surge and billow like a following sea, carrying them towards the palace. Floating along with it and facing the prospect of a return to life as he had known it before he came to London, Kyle's thoughts were of his mistress and all were regretful. I've been a fool. I love Venetia Harding and it is not too late for her and me, thought Kyle, conscious of the fact that his wife had put her arm through his. Absentmindedly he squeezed her hand. He would leave her and stay in London with Venetia, or maybe both of them would move to New York. Fantasizing on, he became aware that Allegra was speaking to him and bent towards her in order to hear what she was saying. As he did so, he heard, 'Kyle, I'm pregnant! I'm going to have our child! Isn't it wonderful?'

By now they were at the palace. Amid cheers, the royal family appeared on the balcony and were joined by Winston

Churchill. The sheer drama of the moment and the roar of applause gave Kyle a moment to collect himself. If Allegra noticed the faintest of hesitations she did not comment on it. He faced her. 'That *is* wonderful news, honey! Just wonderful!' He kissed her, aware that the pace of his reaction was one beat behind what it should have been and also aware that she had probably sensed it. *So, not Kyle and Venetia but Kyle and Allegra after all. A life sentence. He should have told his wife right at the beginning. Now it was too late.* In his mind he heard the cell door clang behind him.

'But are you *sure?*' asked Kyle.

'*Quite* sure!' said Allegra. 'I think we should ring your mother tonight and tell her, don't you?'

A similar conversation was taking place in another area of the jubilations.

Nettie said to Joshua, who appeared more than usually preoccupied, 'I've got something to tell you.'

Joshua, whose mind was dwelling on the fact that he was an arms manufacturer without a war to manufacture for, merely grunted. Factories, of course, could make different things. Money, on the other hand, evaporated unless you built on it. The question was what to concentrate on next.

'I'm pregnant!' said Nettie.

He turned and stared at her blankly.

'What?'

'I'm pregnant. Aren't you pleased?'

Kellaway, who had thought Nettie of all people understood the rules of the game they had been playing, was not. He turned to look at her. The ebb and flow of the crowd which had separated them, now pitched them together. Nettie threw her arms around her lover's neck. 'I want to know when you are going to make an honest woman of me.'

'I already have an honest woman,' said Kellaway. He disentangled himself from Nettie. 'You've forgotten about my wife, whom I have no intention of divorcing, by the way. Anyway, how do I know it's mine?'

Nettie was outraged.

'Well, of course it's yours.'

He wondered if she was telling the truth about being pregnant, never mind about whose it was. Joshua's attitude to women was very akin to that of Geoffrey Harding. There were virtuous women of unblemished reputation, sometimes dull, and loose women, usually not dull. Despite all her high-falutin connections and airs and graces, Nettie was firmly in the second camp. All mixed up with it was a desire to rub the collective Harding nose in the dirt.

'You can't pin it on me,' said Joshua. 'You're on your own with this one!'

Nettie slapped Kellaway's face hard.

Kellaway slapped her back.

'You bastard!' shouted Nettie. In the middle of the crush, nobody noticed.

He turned away from her and began to shoulder his way through the mêlée. Nettie was left standing where she was, a tragic figure caught up in the exuberance of everybody else's fresh horizon.

After Kellaway left her, Nettie stood, blinded by tears as the throng surged around her. What on earth am I to do, she asked herself. With her usual view of life, which was that if you pushed hard enough for what you wanted things would eventually fall your way, Nettie had assumed that taking the initiative with Joshua would win the day for her, that it would be a *fait accompli*. It was not. Quite the reverse, in fact. And not only that, but a whole way of life was over with the German defeat. The American contingent would begin to drift away from London and she couldn't see Rafe Bartholomew continuing to pay for a lifestyle which was now redundant. There would probably be a month or two's grace, but that would be it. Uncharacteristically dejected and unable to see a way forward, Nettie stood uncertainly for a while and then, buffeted and at times lifted off her feet by the crowd, decided to go with the flow and began to move along Whitehall.

When she finally got back to the Chelsea house, there was a letter waiting for her. Nettie recognized the handwriting. It was from Randolph. She turned over the envelope, slit it open and began to read. It was a perfectly OK communication, though Randolph never had been one to bear grudges. Most slights, Nettie suspected, got lost in a haze of alcohol.

My dear Venetia,

I shall be returning to London in the early part of next week and would like to suggest that we meet. I am well aware that certain matters are still unresolved between us. Now that the war is over we should, perhaps, tie up the loose ends. What about dinner at Quaglino's?

I shall be in the country until then, but you may contact me there.

Yours ever,
Randolph.

Nettie blinked. He seemed to have forgotten his last humiliating encounter with her at Quaglino's. And then she had an idea. Yes, what about Quaglino's.

She took the Huntington family ring off her finger and held it up to the light. Large enough to have belonged to a nabob, the ruby seethed with inner fire and because of its impressive size was not overshadowed by the peerless diamonds which, like magnificent courtiers, encircled its sulky splendour. Randolph wanted an heir. She, Nettie, was pregnant. They were still married. All in all, for the first time, it was a perfect fit. Better not to dally though.

She rang the number and Randolph answered. The quality of her voice took him by surprise. Venetia sounded huskily seductive, cordial even. At her insistence they arranged to meet for a drink or three at the Chelsea house before going out to eat. Putting down the receiver, Nettie wondered if she still had the telephone number of the gynaecologist, the one she had intended to use the first time who had been prepared to fudge the dates. In the event it had not been necessary. This time it would be not just necessary but essential.

On the appointed day, Randolph arrived early together with gladioli. Nettie, who did not like gladioli and especially not bright red gladioli, exclaimed with delight and then hid them in the kitchen.

'What can I get you?' she asked on her return.

'The usual,' said Randolph, 'and go easy on the soda.'

With her back turned to him so that he could not see what she was doing, Nettie went easy on the whisky. There was a fine line to be walked here. Experience had taught her that three whiskies made Randolph amorous. Beyond that

224

he became unpredictable in terms of performance, though there was some way to go before, like a darted bull elephant, he became comatose.

Nettie had dressed carefully for this occasion and her husband did not fail to notice. He eyed her trim but full-breasted figure, *soignée* in a fitted, claret-coloured velvet coat dress. With accessibility in mind, Nettie had chosen something button through which, with long sleeves and a daring neckline, was designed to titillate as well as tantalize. Her nylons were sheer and the heels of her pointed suede evening shoes were high and slender. Since clothes rationing was still in force, it occurred to Randolph to wonder how she did it.

As she passed him on her way to fetch an ashtray, he could smell her sharp, seductive scent. She must be wearing a lot of it, it made him feel quite dizzy. Or maybe that was the two whiskies he had imbibed before he ever got to the house. Though Nettie did not realize it, this for Randolph was the *moment juste*. Luckily for her he did recognize it. As she handed him the ashtray, he caught hold of her wrist and pulled her onto his knee.

Nettie had never liked sitting on anybody's knee. It reminded her too much of her father. This was not, however, the moment to complain.

'Randolph!' cried Nettie, affecting skittish surprise, 'What *are* you doing?'

It was perfectly obvious what he was doing and Randolph felt no need to explain himself. He ran his hand up one shapely leg. Thinking, If he ladders my stocking, I'll kill him, Nettie let him. The other hand began to unbutton the claret velvet.

'No, Randolph, no!' cried Nettie, with just enough conviction to make her husband feel impetuous and masterful.

'Come on, old girl. You know you love it!'

Old girl!

With token resistance from Nettie he undid two more buttons and then a front-fastening brassière so that two creamy breasts were revealed, underpinned by velvet. After a brief moment of appreciation and before swooping on them, Randolph took time off to observe, 'You always did have the most glorious breasts, darling. They're even bigger than I remember.'

And so they were. Over his bent head Nettie stared at the wall and hoped he did not put two and two together. Though her

225

experience of Randolph was that even if he did he was still likely to come up with five. By now he was getting quite rough. Mindful of the coatdress which had cost Kyle McClaren a packet and which she did not want to get torn, Nettie said, 'Why don't we go to bed?'

At the end of it she had achieved her aim. Once Randolph was asleep, Nettie picked the dress up off the floor and hung it up until she should need it again when they finally went out to dinner. She got back into bed again and snuggled up to her husband.

'Randolph, are you awake?'

He opened one eye.

'Randolph, I've been thinking about our marriage. I've been a silly girl. Very silly and very headstrong! I realize that now. I'd like us to get back together again . . .'

By now both Randolph's eyes were open.

He had always known that she would come round to his point of view.

Her left hand was lying across his chest and his eye fell upon the ring on her third finger. Venetia and the ruby back in the family. It had all come full circle. Next stop a Huntington heir.

'Let's put it all behind us,' said Randolph magnanimously and then, so that there should be no mistake, 'and you know what I want most of all, don't you?' He added hastily, because Venetia could be very funny about that sort of thing, 'Apart from you, that is.'

'Yes, dear,' (shades of her mother) 'an heir,' murmured Nettie dutifully. 'And you shall have one, I promise.'

So that was all right then. Randolph could hardly believe how easy it had all been.

'Darling!'

'Darling!'

They kissed. As ever, his breath smelt of Glenfiddich.

'Come on, let's go out and celebrate,' said Nettie, who was very hungry by now and who felt she deserved a square meal at the end of all her endeavours.

'Go and pour me a whisky while you're getting dressed, there's good girl. You women take forever getting ready.'

Going to get it for him and resenting the sweeping generalization as she did so, Nettie reflected that it looked like being a repetition of the Mr Tripp evening. Never mind, she had got what she wanted. Extraction could come later.

24

Mary Fox requested an interview with Rafe Bartholomew.

'It's just that, at some point, I'd like some time off. A week would probably do it.'

Rafe, who knew about the liaison with Francis Stafford, wondered if she had decided to marry him. Apparently not, for Mary then said, 'I need some time to sort out my mother's affairs.' Misleading and at the same time quite true.

Rafe shrugged. 'I have no problems with that. The one to ask would be your immediate boss.' It came as a surprise to him that Sibyl Fox's estate, which he had assumed hardly existed, needed as long as a week. Leaning back in his chair, his thoughts apparently elsewhere, he considered Mary and wondered what she would do next. After six years of it, the war had become practically a way of life. All were thankful that it was over but few, Rafe suspected, had as yet looked too closely at the future. What was certain was that the privations of war were not about to cease just because the battle had. For the victors as well as the vanquished there would be tough times ahead. He wondered how long it would be before disenchantment with the government, currently hero of the hour, set in.

'I take it there has been no further news of Jonty.' Certainly the last time Rafe had asked Nettie there had not been.

'No.' Mary looked down at her hands and twisted a coral ring that had belonged to her mother round her middle finger. 'I told Nettie he could still be all right.'

She frowned.

'But you don't really think so.'

It was a statement, not a question.

'Not really, no. But Nettie was so distraught I felt she needed time to come to terms with it. William wrote. At least one of them's safe.'

It occurred to Mary that because ostensibly nobody had known about the love affair between Rafe and Godfrey, Rafe had been left grieving alone, for whom could he talk to? Alone at night, she wondered how he was bearing up. Presumably he realized that Nettie knew, but this was an intensely private man who was not about to divulge the extent of his personal pain to Godfrey's flighty sister. What was certain was that there was nothing she, Mary, could do, much as she would have liked to.

She stood up and so did he.

'What do you think you'll do now it's all over?' he asked.

'It's something of a pipedream, but if I could, I'd like to try and put myself through university. As I'm sure you realized we never had the money to afford anything like that.'

A vision of the diamond drops suddenly came into Mary's head. What about those? She wondered what they were worth and made up her mind to find out. Harding had come in search of them so maybe their value was substantial. Certain it is, thought Mary, that I'll never wear them. Maybe, and ironically, Geoffrey Harding, the man who did not believe in too much education for women (or, quite possibly, *any*) would turn out to be the unwitting means to her particular end.

They shook hands.

'Good luck and *courage*,' said Rafe. 'It must be harrowing sorting out the affairs of the dead.'

Was there the faintest of inflexions on the word *affairs*?

Mary had a sudden jolt, a feeling that perhaps he had noticed the earlier *double entendre*. If so he gave no further sign of it.

Obtaining leave proved harder than Mary had anticipated and it was not until the autumn that she was able to get away. The evening of her departure, Francis said to her, 'Would you like me to come with you? For support.'

On one level support would have been welcome, for who knew what she would discover. Worst of all, maybe she would not discover anything. Nevertheless, on reflection Mary said, 'It's such a kind offer, Francis. But do you know, I thought I should try to do this on my own.'

His disappointment was evident. Her reaction rather confirmed what he thought he already knew.

Mildly, Francis, brilliant mathematician and latterly

cryptanalyst, said, 'I'm very good at solving puzzles, you know. Everyone says so!'

Mary laughed out loud.

'I know you are –'

'– and besides I don't want to lose sight of you for a whole week.' Which was true and concealed his real fear, which was that he might never see her again.

'It's not such a long time!'

Impossible to tell him, of course, but Mary felt that, among other things, she did need some time away from Francis to assess a relationship that had begun in a war and now was about to enter a completely different phase.

'Look, I promise I'll telephone if I need you. But this is so near the bone for me, I feel I have to confront it alone, at least to begin with. Please try to understand.'

'I do understand. I just want to be with you, that's all. More than you want to be with me apparently.' He sounded miffed.

'I'm not sure about that,' protested Mary, who really was not.

'At least let me help you with some prior sleuthing so that you know you're starting in the right place.'

'All right!' Mary pushed her hair back from her face and sent him a luminous, sidelong smile. For Francis it transformed the room.

He thought, I don't want to lose this woman and yet I feel her slipping out of my grasp and I don't know what to do about it.

The end of the war also changed life for the senior Hardings.

While Geoffrey had been otherwise occupied trying to remake his number with the government and Winston Churchill in particular, Davina had met an army colonel playing bridge and rediscovered the joys of sex. Or maybe rediscovered was pitching it a bit high, for, thought Davina, there really isn't much joy to be had with Geoffrey.

After knowing each other for two months, much against Davina's better judgement she and her colonel had finally gone to bed together. Given their relatively mature ages and, in her case anyway, the ongoing sexual disaster that had gone before, to say Davina was dreading it was an understatement.

There was no getting out of it though.

'Look,' said Peter Flamborough, 'I am in love with you, Davina, and I believe I can make you happy but I am not prepared to settle for a sexless marriage. That's the bottom line. Otherwise we might as well be just friends.'

Davina did not want to be just friends. Being just friends probably meant staying with the disappointed Geoffrey, who was getting crankier by the day. She was conscious that in Peter's company her fragmented personality integrated. She bloomed. The nervous tics occasioned by her husband's presence disappeared and she looked better too. Even Nettie, currently distracted by some dalliance of her own, noticed it.

'You're looking wonderful, Mother,' said Nettie, noting that her hitherto downtrodden parent had become positively frisky. 'What's Father been doing to you?'

Nothing to do with Father. Davina sent her daughter an inscrutable look and did not enlighten her. It was probably this conversation though which made her decide to go for broke romantically. If it didn't work, *tant pis*.

The following evening Geoffrey was attending some sort of all-male gathering at his club and Peter had invited her out to dinner. A sensitive man, Flamborough realized that there would be no second chance. He took Davina to a favourite restaurant and at the end of the meal, as they were drinking the last of the wine and he was considering how to broach what was on his mind, she said, 'Your place tonight I think!'

Ah! No point in throwing a spanner in the works with cries of, 'Oh darling, are you sure?' when he knew very well she was not. Peter leant across the table and took her hand.

'Then let's go, now.'

His flat was small and comfortable, a distillation, no doubt, of the house he had once lived in with his wife before she had run off with a brother officer. There was the faint smell of cigar smoke, with which Davina was all too familiar, and one or two good paintings. More in hope than expectation there were fresh flowers in the bedroom and, though Davina did not know it, a bottle of champagne on ice in the kitchen.

'Peter, would you excuse me for a minute?'

She went into the bathroom taking her small case with her.

Once inside, Davina took off all her clothes and anxiously appraised herself in the full-length mirror. Stomach and breasts once firm had not improved with age and the birth of four children, but she still had a waist and attractive face, which was presumably what Peter had noticed first. He certainly hadn't fallen in love with her self-confidence. Davina sprayed herself with scent, and then slipped on a silk kimono embroidered with exotic Japanese flowers. She did not tie the sash. No more hesitating. This was do or die. She opened the bathroom door and, black silk billowing, stepped out across the bedroom.

That autumn was one of big skies, across which sailed stately fleets of cumulus clouds. On the ground, crisp drifts of fallen leaves were the colour of gingerbread and crumbled underfoot, while those still to fall flamed yellow and crimson and cinnamon. At sunrise the light streamed through the mist, transmuting it into golden gauze as it drifted through the bare branches of the trees. It was on just such a morning that Francis Stafford put Mary in search of her roots on the train to the North and wondered whether he would ever see her again. After doing all the right things, such as buying her a newspaper and settling her into her seat and then (final futile gesture) running along beside the open window of her carriage waving and grinning like an idiot until he could no longer keep up with it, he turned away, bereft, and went in search of a cup of tea.

Railway stations, normally repositories of soot and noise, were at their best at 6 a.m. decided Francis. The crowds had not yet arrived in force and a clot of sunlight was concentrated in the lofty roof, where it irradiated the grimy panes of glass and allowed an incandescent glow to creep through the rest of the huge, dusty interior. Even the hissing jets of steam from the engines seemed to be lit from within. To Francis, standing by a kiosk drinking insipid tea out of a white china mug, King's Cross was rather like an industrial cathedral in its airy, soaring vastness.

It was an odd sensation, he reflected, being right at the end of the wartime incarnation and not yet embarked on the next stage. Unsure about what was going to happen next, like a fly petrified in amber, he found himself to be in a sort of

231

mental and physical limbo which felt as though it might go on for ever. Despite the fact that he was in love with Mary Fox (the one thing he *was* sure of), all his instincts told him to forget her. Mary was a complicated young woman, with her own agenda which at present anyway did not appear to include himself. One-sided love was of no use to anyone. Perhaps, thought Francis, I should go back to university. In his heart of hearts he knew that there was no perhaps about it and that he was probably destined to be an academic.

By now the remainder of his tea, which had never been very hot in the first place, was stone cold. He tipped the dregs onto the platform and put the mug on the side. In that instant he took a decision. He would withdraw from Mary's life leaving the door open for her to come to him if she so desired, and he would do so by letter. To compensate for the pain of this romantic amputation he would pursue his other passion, that of pure mathematics, preferably at Oxford if he could.

With something of a sigh, Francis turned up the collar of his shabby coat. A solitary dark figure defined by the dazzle of light all around him, he walked, slowly at first and then more briskly and with resolution, towards the exit.

25

Geoffrey Harding received a letter he could have done without. It informed him that his stockbroker (a personal friend) had been at best incompetent and at worst fraudulent. The sum of money involved was gargantuan. Because the malefactor had been an old school chum and old school chums did not do that sort of thing, Harding had not kept as close an eye on his own affairs as he should have done. But after all, with a war on there had been a country to be run, justified Geoffrey to himself, though he had in reality been doing no such thing, and personal affairs had been of secondary importance compared with that. Whatever the excuse, it did not alter the fact that the money had gone and worse was to come for, running his eye down the page, he discovered that the broker in question was dead, a fatality of the last air attack on the City, and that was what had brought the whole thing into the open. In circumstances like these it looked as though there would be no financial redress for him.

Harding considered the future and found it wanting.

The house in the country would probably have to be sold. He wondered how he was going to break the news to Davina and, feeling badly in need of some sympathy (what were wives for if not to provide a shoulder to weep on?), decided to do it straight away by taking her out to lunch.

'Get Mrs Harding on the telephone would you,' he said to his secretary.

This apparently simple task took longer than he had anticipated.

'Geoffrey, what a coincidence,' said Davina, whose line had been busy for something like twenty minutes, 'I was going to suggest the very same thing. There is something I have to tell you.'

Whatever it was it couldn't be as important as what he had to tell *her*. They arranged a time and a place. Rather to his surprise his wife opted for a sandwich and a walk in

Kensington Gardens. When they finally met, before finding a suitable park bench, they tramped along in silence for fifteen minutes or so, each trying to decide how to deliver their news. True to form, as they unwrapped their lunch Geoffrey said, 'Right! I'll kick off, shall I?' It was a statement rather than a question.

Davina held up an imperious hand.

'No, Geoffrey, *I* shall!'

No, Geoffrey?

Harding knit his brows. He stared at his wife, who was presenting him with her profile while throwing part of her sandwich to some rapacious starlings. There was something different about her and in the end, never having properly understood that other people, even wives, might be entitled to opinions of their own, he put it down as defiance. Racking his brains, he tried to think of the last time Davina had said No to him and came up with his first proposal of marriage. She had said No then.

With thunderous expression, he waited.

'I'm leaving you,' said Davina.

She took a dainty bite from the remains of her sandwich.

Surely, he could not have heard right.

'What do you mean?'

Patiently Davina repeated, 'Leaving you. Going away.' And then, so there could be no possible misunderstanding, 'With another man.'

This was a bolt from the blue. Harding was stupefied.

'But why? *Why* Davina? We've been happy, haven't we?'

The new Davina was not about to let this go.

'No, we haven't been happy, Geoffrey, or at least *I* haven't been happy. You may have been.'

Never mind about insubordination, suddenly recollecting that he had a rival, and male pride demanded that he and the marauder lock horns, he blustered, 'Who is it? I order you to tell me!'

Davina waited for him to threaten to horse-whip whoever it was and he did. Reflecting that there was something sadly stunted in such predictable knee-jerk reactions, she said, 'It is of no relevance who it is and I have to tell you, Geoffrey, that my mind is quite made up. I shall not change it.'

Serenely she turned her face up to the sun which was

still quite hot. Oh, it was heady, being decisive. Groups of uniformed nannies with large prams strolled by them, interspersed with pairs of lovers and little elderly ladies with little elderly dogs on leads. Or maybe the little elderly ladies were on leads. It was amazing how certain things had so quickly gone back to normal. Sitting beside her, her husband silently smouldered. Davina looked at him. Geoffrey looked volcanic. Had there been a hole in the top of his head hot ash would no doubt have been shooting into the air and lava pouring through the flower beds of Kensington Gardens. His lower lip projected in the belligerent way she recalled all too well.

In an attempt to cheer him up, Davina indulged herself in a masterpiece of understatement. She said, 'Now I've had my little say, what about you?'

Deciding to overlook the domestic mayhem about to be caused by her 'little say' (that was if he couldn't persuade her out of the extraordinary course of action she seemed set on, something he had every intention of trying to do that evening), Harding said through clenched teeth, 'Courtesy of the blundering idiot Charlie Fanshawe, we've lost all our money!'

'You mean *you've* lost all *your* money, dear,' corrected his wife, thinking with affection of the comfortably-off Peter Flamborough. Then, impressed by the scale of it, 'What *all* of it?'

'Almost all. The country house will have to go.'

Harding's shoulders slumped. First his money and now his wife. It was not, as they say, his day.

Davina thought, Thank God I got in first! I couldn't have said it in the light of what Geoffrey has just told me. It would have looked as though I was leaving him because he was broke, whereas a million pounds would not induce me to stay.

'I *never* liked Charlie,' said Davina. 'He was oily.'

'You didn't say so!' Harding was accusatory.

'You never asked me, dear!' This smart retort could have been the epitaph on the tombstone of their marriage.

Harding looked at his watch. He had a meeting at 2.30. They both stood up.

'I'm going in that direction,' said Davina, indicating the

opposite one to the way Geoffrey would probably want to go.

'Look, old thing, I think we should talk this over tonight . . .' Geoffrey's attempt to mollify was hampered by the fact that he was plainly still in a very bad temper. Davina, who regarded the term *old thing* in more or less the same way as her daughter regarded *old girl*, said 'If that's what you want, dear,' and did not enlighten her husband with the news that she intended to move out of the flat that same afternoon.

They parted. After she had walked about fifty yards, Davina turned around and followed his portly figure with her eyes as it strode off into the distance. Going, going . . . He turned a corner . . . gone!

'Goodbye, Geoffrey,' said Davina out loud.

There was a sudden chill in the air. She pulled her coat around her. The hot-house Davina of yesteryear would not have liked the drop in temperature. This one found it invigorating. As she walked along a path bordered with massed late flowers, asters and dahlias and chrysanthemums, a blaze of bronze and hot yellows and pinks and purples, she was conscious of a spring in her step. Hers was going to be a late flowering too. But it was never too late, Davina realized, never. She left the park by the Alexandra Gate, hailed a cab and went back to the flat to pack.

As Mary's train steamed north, the weather began to deteriorate. Bright morning gave way to a sulky, overcast day and finally they ran into driving rain. The carriage had no heating. All the same it was exciting to have embarked on her quest at last. The memory of Francis Stafford's receding figure as the train drew away was a poignant one though and caused Mary to re-evaluate her feelings for him. How did one know if one was in love? Francis evidently did but maybe it had been on display more for him as a child than it ever had for her. The whole Godfrey episode, for instance, had been suspect since on that occasion she had considered herself in love with someone only to find, on closer inspection, that that person did not exist. More importantly, Mother had been tricky. Having had her fingers burnt at a very early age, Mother had been the ultimate enigma where love was concerned in that she had been in need of it, Mary suspected, but distrustful of it and with reason. Which leaves me, thought Mary, without a point of reference.

Francis had been very helpful though. The analytical brain had found it hard to accept that somewhere in the Adare notebooks there was not another geographical clue to exactly where the whole sequence of events had taken place.

'Unless Mrs Fox was *deliberately* trying to conceal it, and I can't see why she would.'

'Well, I think she might have been,' observed Mary. Mother covered her tracks as a matter of course . . . It was instinctive with her.'

'Maybe.' Francis did not sound convinced. 'Gut feeling tells me that there is something there. I'd offer to go through the books for you, but I'm sure you'd rather do it yourself.'

On that level the past had lost its power, Mary discovered. She no longer minded sharing it with somebody else, especially if that somebody was Francis.

'No, you go ahead!'

Once started, he could not put the notebooks down. It was an extraordinary story of manipulation and betrayal and explained much about the clever, beautiful, unconfident girl that was Mary Fox. But Mary, Francis saw very clearly, would have to exorcise her ghosts before she could possibly embark on a serious, long-term relationship with him or anybody else for that matter. On the further information front, he had to confess himself baffled. As Mary had said, there was nothing. Unwilling to give up because he could not rid himself of the feeling that the knowledge they were seeking was there all the time, he flicked through the notebooks one more time and, as he did so, became aware that one of the pages was weightier than the rest. On closer inspection it was found to be two glued together.

Preparing carefully to prise them apart, Francis braced himself for a second pressed camellia, although on the whole he doubted it. A flower, even a pressed one, dry as a bone after all these years, would have been bulky enough to be obvious. With Mary watching, he steamed the top of the two pages open, so that he could look in between them, as into an envelope, and was disappointed to find nothing.

'Nobody glues two pages together like that for nothing,' said Mary. 'Steam open the other two sides.'

He did and together they bent over the open pages.

In ink were written the words, Holden & Macaulay, 2/3 The High Street, Lamprey. Beneath, and almost indecipherable, Sibyl had penned *They know*. There was nothing else.

Know what?

Francis was very intrigued.

'Curiouser and curiouser. Could be a solicitor. Or an accountant, maybe. Whatever it was, it narrows the search. Why don't you try and get them through the operator and I'll locate Lamprey on the map.'

He found it. It looked as though it might be a small market town. There was country all around including, according to the contour lines on the map, a large valley. Aunt Helena had lived on the other side of a valley. Putting the phone down, Mary said, 'There is no Holden and Macaulay at that address according to the operator. Hardly surprising when you consider how many years have gone by since it all happened.' She sounded very disappointed.

'It's my view that we've got as far as we can here,' said Francis. 'And having got this far, you'll just have to go there. You'll never rest unless you do. Once on the spot you could crack it very quickly. I'm willing to take a bet that Holden and Macaulay is still a solicitors' office, or whatever, but with different partners and therefore a different name. Furthermore, if you ring the operator again and ask for the number of the Lamprey Arms, you could book yourself a room, rather than arriving cold.'

'How do you know there's a Lamprey Arms?'

'I don't. It's just a hunch. Try it.'

She did, and there was. Mary booked a room.

'I suspect you of having a crystal ball. No wonder you were so good at chasing U-boats all over the Atlantic!'

And now here she was, going there. Mary pulled out the notebooks and began to reread them very carefully. She wondered how many of the original players were still alive.

26

The Lamprey Arms turned out to be a lot more pleasant than Mary had expected. For one thing there was a fire in the grate of the oak-beamed saloon bar which appeared to burn all the time. Clocks ticked unevenly, dogs dozed and, Mary was to discover, several of the regulars appeared to have (and were possessive of) what they regarded as their own chairs, most of which were lop-sided from a century of uneven flagstones.

On arrival Mary went straight upstairs and unpacked her small grip. Her room contained a single bed, a wardrobe, a chest of drawers and a chair. In one corner was a wash-stand whose pedestal was modestly concealed by a frilled, flowered curtain which matched the frilled, flowered curtain at the small window. On the bed was a cream crocheted spread and on the floor a rag rug. Without being in the least luxurious, the effect was charming.

With the intention of going for a walk around the town, Mary combed her hair and then went downstairs again. On her way out she booked herself an evening meal. There seemed to be plenty of food about. It was rather as though the war had passed Lamprey by. The town was small and, in places, the streets were cobbled. All around it could be seen the moors which at this time of the day and year looked bleak. The main thoroughfare, which was the backbone of the town, was not hard to find and led off either side of the market square, so that there was Main Street Upper and Main Street Lower. Choosing at random, she walked along Main Street Upper and right at the end of it came to 2/3. Exactly as Francis had surmised it was still a solicitor's office, though now, according to the highly polished brass plaque on the double front doors, the practice of Tapsell & Tapsell. Although it was only 5 p.m., the door was locked.

The light was beginning to fade. It occurred to Mary that rather than continue her tramp around the town she might postpone this until tomorrow and more usefully and comfortably spend her time in front of the fire quizzing the landlord of the Lamprey Arms about the local gentry. Accordingly, she retraced her steps and when she re-entered the saloon bar found her host together with his wife, both of whom were polishing glasses. Mary settled herself on a bar stool and opened the proceedings by asking how long they had been running the Lamprey.

'Ten years, give or take,' came the disappointing answer, followed by the more promising, 'but the pub's been in the family longer than that.'

'So you were born and brought up here.'

'Aye. There's not much about this town and surrounding country I don't know.' He upturned one polished glass and placed the stem in a slot above the bar, where hung a whole row of them, and started on another.

'There must be some wonderful country houses around here,' said Mary.

Speaking for the first time, 'There are,' said his wife whose name, it transpired, was Rebecca.

'You don't know of a family called Adare, do you?'

'Certainly. The Adare mansion was the grandest. Gloomy though. It's all shut up now.'

This news was a blow. It seemed that every time she thought she might be getting somewhere, she encountered a set-back.

The landlord gave her a keen look.

'You got connections there, have you?'

'In a manner of speaking,' said Mary. 'I'm curious to know what became of them, that's all.'

A group of customers entered the pub and the landlord (*Call me Dave. Everyone else does.*) went off to serve them

'The old lady died,' said Rebecca, adding, 'she was a real tartar and no mistake.'

'What about the daughters?'

'Well, there were three of them as I recall it. One of them had a son. She was a chip off the old block, that one. And then there were two others. As far as I know they're all still alive.'

Things were looking up.

'Are they all still living locally?'

'I wouldn't know. Now my mother-in-law, she would have had that sort of information at her fingertips . . .'

240

'Do you think she would mind if I asked her?' said Mary.

'Wouldn't get you very far,' said Rebecca. 'She's dead.'

'Oh, I'm sorry.' Mary was embarrassed.

'Don't be. She was a tartar too. Dave could find out for you. Why don't you ask him?'

When she finally got him to herself for a moment in the process of ordering a Gin and It, Mary did.

Mixing it, Dave said, 'The Adares kept themselves to themselves. They regarded themselves as London and County and had very little to do with the town. And apart from regular grocery deliveries, the town had very little to do with them.' There was a distinctly disapproving note here. 'The old lady ruled with a rod of iron but she couldn't continue to rule from beyond the grave. There were three daughters and a son who married an Italian chorus girl and died abroad.'

Italian chorus girl. Mary smiled. As usual tittle-tattle was part, but not all, of the way there.

'What happened to the daughters?'

'They must be in their late sixties or early seventies even. One's supposed to be mad, one married the local solicitor, and I don't know what happened to the other one, but as far as I'm aware, they're all still alive . . . Yes, sir?'

Dave was called away by another customer, but it was enough. With the exception of the dragon that had been Grandmother, they were all still there.

After supper, Mary rang Francis.

'I'm hot on the trail already,' said Mary.

'I thought you would be. What's the hotel like?'

'It's comfortable and mildly eccentric. Staying here is rather like stepping back in time. I honestly don't think they've even noticed that there's been a world war going on. But the main thing is that I am in the right place and according to mine host at least three of the original *dramatis personae* are still alive, though one is reputed to be gaga.'

'Sounds positively Dickensian!'

Mary laughed. 'It *is* positively Dickensian!'

'When are you going to see the solicitor? Assuming he's still there.'

'*He* isn't but as you surmised another one is, so I thought I'd go along tomorrow morning.'

'*Bonne chance!* Let me know how you get on.'

'I will.'

Francis replaced the receiver and stared down at the letter he had been writing when the telephone rang. He picked up his fountain pen and then put it down again and replaced the cap. The sound of her cool voice had undermined his resolution to step aside and get on with his own life. Now he wondered if he had the self-discipline to do such a thing.

In Lamprey, Mary was similarly moved. It occurred to her that Francis was the one dependable thing in the shifting sands of her personal life, the one person who knew all there was to know about her. Most important of all, with the possible exception of William and, though more remotely, Rafe Bartholomew, he was the one man who cared what happened to her.

That night Mary dreamt that she had found her brother. Her joy was intense, a transfiguring, radiant thing but as she opened her arms to embrace him, he slipped away from her and she was aware as he did so that she had never seen his face. Devastated, she remained standing where she was, willing him to come back to her, but he did not and instead it was Francis Stafford who moved to her side from the shadows, slipped his arm around her waist and led her away.

The following day dawned mild but damp. There was a yellow tinge to the air and drifts of autumn leaves idled along the streets. Dark vaporous cloud had settled like a frown on the brow of the moors, so that Lamprey was encircled by its lowering, diffuse presence.

Today Tapsell & Tapsell was open. The window blind was up and behind the panes of glass Mary could see a girl sitting typing, a secretary presumably. She rang the bell and walked in.

'Mr Tapsell senior is with a client at the moment,' said the girl in response to a request to see one of the partners.

'If you would be kind enough to give me an appointment, I could always come back later,' said Mary.

At this moment the other Mr Tapsell came out of his office, heard the last sentence and said, 'I've got fifteen minutes, why doesn't Miss . . . ?'

'Fox.'

'Yes, why doesn't Miss Fox bend my ear instead. Unless you've set your heart on seeing my uncle, of course.'

'I haven't set my heart on seeing anyone. Thank you very much.'

Inside his small office, most of which was taken up by a partner's desk surrounded by walls lined with law books, Mr Tapsell offered Mary a cup of tea and, when she refused, waited. Legal antennae told him that she was not a client in the ordinary sense of the word.

Trying not to give away more than she had to, for no doubt small market towns such as this one were hotbeds of gossip, Mary told him who she was, though not specifically what she was there for. At the end of it he leant back in his chair and said, 'I should start by confirming that this practice was once Holden & Macaulay. Mr Holden died and Mr Macaulay eventually retired. In the fullness of time he died too. His widow is still alive and lives outside the town. Her maiden name was Adare. My uncle and I took over the partnership in 1937.'

'Do you have any idea what happened to the Adare papers when that happened? Presumably they weren't destroyed.'

'Good Heavens, no!' Mr Tapsell was visibly shocked at the very idea. 'No, they are still lodged here, in the cellar. I think I'm right in saying that what we have mainly pre-dates old Mrs Adare's death.'

'I wonder whether it would be possible for me to see them.'

'With the permission of the family, yes. Without the permission of the family, no, I'm afraid.' Curiously, he wondered what it was she was looking for exactly. 'What I can do is to put you in touch with Mrs Macaulay,' he continued, 'though I should have to telephone and clear it with her first. Then you could ask her yourself. She's probably the best bet. As I'm sure you're aware there were two other sisters, one of whom is very forgetful, shall we say, and one of whom has frankly lost her marbles. They're all getting on you understand.'

'That would be very helpful. If you could put me in touch with Mrs Macaulay, I'll take it from there. I'd like to see all three of them if I can.'

'I'll ring Mrs Macaulay now, if you like.'

That afternoon Mary borrowed a bicycle from the pub and set off into the drizzling rain. Hopefully, she thought, battling uphill, there'll come a time when I don't need to use a bicycle ever again. There was a bus, but an infrequent one, and she had taken the decision that it was better to be self-sufficient. On the moors the mist was still low enough for visibility to be reduced and damply clinging, like a winding sheet, it wrapped itself around her. Here the leaves had mostly gone and the dripping trees were black and skeletal. The sodden bracken was brown. All in all it was a depressing time of the year.

Mrs Macaulay's house was in a hollow. The land rose steeply behind thereby protecting it from most of the weather and maybe most of the light as well. In front was a cottage garden which looked, in common with the rest of the sad landscape, as if it was bracing itself for the onslaught of winter. Mary shot through a small yard, scattering chickens as she went. She dismounted and by the time she got to the door Margaret Macaulay, wearing tweeds and a twin set was waiting for her.

'Just stand there a moment,' said Mrs Macaulay. 'I want to look at you.'

Mary did as she was told.

'When Tapsell rang I had my doubts but yes, you *are* Sibyl's daughter. Except for the hair it could be her standing in front of me. And one never encounters eyes like those twice in a lifetime.' Mrs Macaulay might have been speaking to herself. Maybe, thought Mary, they're all dotty.

The rain began to intensify. By now she was drenched.

In desperation, 'May I come in?' she asked.

Mrs Macaulay collected herself. 'Yes, of course! It's just such an odd feeling after all these years. Tell me, how is your mother?'

'I'm afraid she's dead,' answered Mary. 'She was killed during the war.'

'I'm so sorry.'

It was an odd detached exchange with someone who was a stranger and, at the same time, one of her only living relations. Margaret Macaulay was tiny, had no doubt shrunk with age, but still had a patrician indomitability about her. She also had something else in common with the English upper class: a brusqueness verging on rudeness. Draping Mary's sopping raincoat across an old-fashioned kitchen range, where it began to steam, she said, 'Why are you here, Miss Fox?'

Following her hostess into a small sitting-room where she stood by the fire in an attempt to dry out, Mary decided to be just as blunt.

'I'm here to find out about my half-brother.'

The rain rattled on the windows. Inside the room there was a profound silence but no denial.

'Ah!' said Margaret Macaulay. 'So Sibyl told you.'

'Not directly, no.'

'Well, how then?'

'Mother wrote a memoir.'

'Oh, did she.' Mrs Macaulay sounded wintry.

'It's all in that.'

'Not quite all, I think, or you wouldn't be here.'

'I'm here because I know the fact but not what happened afterwards. The notebooks also record that you were very kind to my mother during her confinement.'

Mrs Macaulay said simply, 'I was fond of her. She was not well served by her own family, of whom I was one. It was the least I could do. Money and privilege do not necessarily make for happiness, Miss Fox.'

Having had neither, except vicariously, Mary did not comment on this.

'Is my brother still alive?'

'I've never heard to the contrary. But after the adoption the child passed out of our lives and so did the family he went to. As far as I am aware there has been no contact since. Who they were was a secret closely guarded by Mother. It's ironic when one considers what happened next.'

'What do you mean? What did happen next?'

'Gerard, groomed to inherit, came into his kingdom and squandered the lot. I'm surprised that Mother did not come back to haunt him. He never married either, so there was no heir. Gerard did none of the things he should have done and all of the things he shouldn't have done. Helena ruined him, of course. Mother, who naturally did not foresee any of

245

it, took the secret of his illegitimate son to the family vault with her.'

Or maybe lodged it in the safe of Holden & Macaulay. Surely there must have been some sort of legal agreement worked out.

'Since I am unlikely to come back, I had hoped to visit both your sisters while I am here, but I'm told neither is in good health.'

'Helena's the way she always was, only more so,' said Mrs Macaulay, obscurely. 'She's bad rather than mad, though maybe slightly mad as well and maybe always was. She and I never got on, of course. Dorothea is very vague. If you can keep Dorothea's mind fixed on anything for more than thirty seconds, you're a better man than I am, Gunga Din. Right, shall we go?'

'Go?'

'Yes. I will drive you to Helena's house and, *en route*, we will visit Dorothea. It is high time I went to see them both.'

'Thank you very much, but shouldn't we let them know that we are coming?'

'Absolutely not! Helena will say No, given the opportunity. So let's not give it to her.'

The car turned out to be a little Austin 7 with a surprising turn of speed. It would have been no exaggeration to say that Mrs Macaulay drove like an elderly demon. Luckily, thought Mary clinging to her seat, they were not likely to meet too many other drivers travelling in the opposite direction on these country roads. On the other hand it only took one. Throwing the car from third down to second and up to third again as they cornered, Mrs Macaulay said, 'I should like you to call me Margaret. You are my great-niece. Mrs Macaulay is not appropriate. By the same token I shall call you Mary.'

After three quarters of an hour, narrowly missing the gatepost, they turned right and lurched up a driveway. At the end of it Margaret brought the car to a halt with a squeal of brakes. Dorothea's house was grander than Margaret's in that it was a small Georgian gem. A starched nurse opened the door to them.

'Good afternoon, nurse,' said Margaret briskly, 'and how is my sister today? This is Miss Fox, by the way.'

'I'm afraid we are hardly here at all today,' replied nurse, inextricably identifying with her patient.

'Oh really? Well, never mind! Lead on!'

Dorothea was sitting in a wheelchair in her drawing-room.

'You may leave us now, nurse,' said Margaret. 'No cups of tea, thank you, we shall not be very long.'

Nurse departed.

'Who are you?' said Dorothea to Margaret.

It was not an auspicious beginning.

'You know perfectly well that I am your sister Margaret! And this is –'

Dorothea was scornful. 'I know perfectly well who this is. This is Sibyl! What have you done to your hair, Sibyl?'

Stepping forward in an attempt to clear the matter up, Mary said, 'I am Sibyl's daughter.'

'Rubbish! Sibyl did not have a daughter. No daughters in this house, only sons. Daughters were superfluous. Mother says so. Where is Mother? Is she away? I haven't seen her for a very long time.'

'Dorothea, Mother is dead!'

'Dead? That was very sudden,' said Dorothea. She began to pluck at her pearls. Then, undeterred by this piece of information, 'She tells me Margaret is going to marry a ridiculous little man from Lamprey. A solicitor, if you please. It really won't do, says Mother, and I agree with her.'

Exasperated, Margaret said, 'You married a *doctor* for heaven's sake!'

'Yes and I haven't seen *him* for a very long time either. Where is everybody?' It was a dialogue of the deaf. 'Will somebody tell the maid I would like some tea, please!'

'I'll fetch the nurse,' said Margaret.

While her sister was gone, Dorothea appeared to fall into a reverie, with her mind presumably slipping between past and present. Mary studied her as she sat staring into the middle distance. Even though for all intents and purposes the mental light was failing, and Dorothea was much thinner, the facial resemblance to Margaret was marked. Her cheekbones seemed to be pushing their way through the skin, which was scored with a myriad fine lines and stretched over the skull as tight as a drum. Papery and transparent, like the leaves blowing across the lawn outside, her hands lay in her lap, all the rings loose on the bony fingers.

Mary could hear Margaret and the nurse returning from the far reaches of the house. She picked up her shoulder bag. Suddenly, disconcertingly, Dorothea turned and looked at her and, as she did so, slotted lucidly into the present. 'Sibyl's daughter, you said. I expect you're going on to see Helena aren't you? That's what Margaret usually does. She sees us both, makes an afternoon of it. Beware of Helena, Miss Fox. Helena is pure poison. Believe me, there is nothing more lethal than a disappointed old woman who was once the sort of fêted beauty my sister was. And even in those days she could not be trusted.'

Margaret re-entered the drawing-room.

Speaking loudly and slowly, as to a foreigner, she enunciated, 'We are going now, Dorothea.'

'There is no need to shout, Margaret, I am not hard of hearing!'

Ignoring it, and just as emphatically, she continued, 'The nurse is going to bring you some tea, dear.'

They kissed.

'Goodbye, dear.'

'Goodbye, Margaret.'

Outside on the gravel, Margaret said, 'You see what I mean?'

'Yes, I do,' said Mary, 'but while you were out of the room she suddenly became *compos mentis*.'

They both got into the car.

'What did she say?'

'She said, Watch Out For Helena.'

'That's good advice,' said Margaret, letting out the clutch. '*Very* good advice.'

Built of grey stone, with a venerable *magnolia grandiflora* growing over the porch, Helena's house was by far the grandest. It looked out across the valley. Mary wondered where the pet cemetery was. This time a housekeeper opened the door to them.

'Good afternoon, Madge,' said Margaret. 'I am here to visit Mrs Landseer.'

Madge looked fraught. 'Madam has given instructions that she does not wish to receive visitors today, Mrs Macaulay.'

'Stuff and nonsense,' pronounced Margaret. 'I've come a long way to see her and I don't intend to leave until I do. The sooner she sees me, the sooner she'll be rid of me. Go and tell her that. I'll wait. Oh, and while you're at it, tantalize. Tell Madam that I have another visitor with me. A face from the past.'

Madge departed. Watching her go, Mary had a feeling that this was a ritual which was repeated with every visit and that Madge knew the drill. Standing in the hall, she studied the paintings, some of which were very fine.

Madge returned. 'Madam says, Oh, very well.' The ungracious intonation was probably exactly the same as Madam's.

They followed her to another sister, another drawing-room.

Helena was standing up when they entered, with one elbow on the mantelpiece. There was a certain defiance about her stance and she was smoking a cigarette in a long holder. Even at her age there was a pliability about her figure which must had been supremely graceful when she was a young woman. But more than just pliability, Mary decided. There was the languorous coiled containment of a cat, which could unravel in a swift pounce if provoked. Vanity had evidently not deserted Helena in her twilight years and, despite the ravaging inroads of age, the rags and tatters of a superlative beauty were still extant, together with waved dyed hair in a bygone style. Her dress, which was a tailored affair of impeccable cut beneath whose hem ankles as thin and brittle as carnation stalks could be glimpsed, had a bygone air as well. It was as if, even in her seventies, Helena had never moved beyond the aura of her heyday, had never properly matured.

She must have been short sighted, Mary later thought, because it was not until they were very close indeed that her eyes properly focussed on her sister's companion. When they finally did the effect was instantaneous.

'Good *God*!' said Helena. 'I don't believe it!'

She balanced the cigarette holder on an ashtray and stared at Mary for a long time without speaking.

Margaret said, 'Helena, this is Sibyl's daughter, Mary Fox.'

By now the stare was aggressive. Helena was one of those people who could make the atmosphere dense with her own emotion, whether it was displeasure or delight. Though not much delight abroad these days, perhaps.

'Daughter, eh? Well, well! I have to commiserate. You do look just like her, however.'

Mary was shocked by the hostility. She remembered the notebook account of the spiteful, destructive role played by Aunt Helena in the ultimate betrayal and decided not to stand for it.

'Thank you for the compliment, Mrs Landseer. There is really no need for commiserations.'

Knocking the ash off her cigarette and then taking a deep pull: 'Where is your mother now?'

'My mother is dead.'

There was no discernible reaction to this, neither jubilation nor sympathy. Instead, Helena said imperiously to Margaret, 'Would you mind leaving us for a while? I would like to talk to Miss Fox on her own.' She turned away.

'Very well,' said Margaret, casting her eyes to heaven behind her difficult sister's back, 'if that is what you want, that is what you must have. I shall go and sit in the conservatory. You can come and find me there when you have finished.'

After she had gone, Helena walked to the window where she stood silently smoking for a few minutes with her back to the rest of the room. During the lull before battle recommenced, Mary took the opportunity to study a clutch of silver-framed sepia photographs which were grouped around a blue and white Chinese bowl on a sofa table. They were all of Helena. Among others, Helena riding side-saddle, Helena alighting from her carriage, Helena in full fig off to a party, shadowed by a blurred figure in evening dress who might have been her husband and, right in the middle and bigger than the others, a studio portrait of Helena with fur and cartwheel hat smiling into the lens with arrogant panache. There was no photograph of her son and none of the rest of the family either. The woman was an egomaniac.

Without warning Helena swung round. Mary was to learn that everything she did was theatrically exaggerated and almost certainly sprang from a deep-seated desire always to be the centre of attention. To drive home what she was about to say, she fixed Mary with a baleful, penetrating look before beginning to speak.

'Your mother came here as a guest of this family . . .'

Automatically springing to the defence of her parent, 'My mother came here as a *member* of this family,' corrected Mary, not about to put up with this, 'moreover she did not *come* here, as you put it, she was *brought* here!'

As she delivered this speech, she was aware that this was not the way to go about getting what she wanted.

Helena's voice became shrill and her face convulsed.

'Do not contradict me! Do not! Her gratitude for this act of generosity by Mother took the form of causing a lot of trouble. She was a cuckoo in the nest, a scheming devious little slut and, at the age of fifteen, fifteen mind you! no better than she ought to have been.'

'I would dispute that. But whatever her faults she was cynically betrayed by those she should have been able to trust and, according to what I have been led to understand, *you* were almost certainly the principal malevolent influence,' said Mary.

Unsurprisingly, it appeared that Aunt Helena did not like being referred to as a malevolent influence. Scattering burning flecks of cigarette ash in her wake she marched across the room until she was within a foot of Mary, who flinched before her precipitous rush. Out of control, she shouted, 'How dare you! How dare you! You know nothing about it! Nothing!'

At such uncomfortably close quarters Mary noticed that Helena still wore make-up and that her lipstick had seeped into the lines around her mouth. Elsewhere eye shadow had flooded into crowsfeet tributaries and there was a hectic spot of rouge on each high cheekbone. Like iron filings to a magnet, powder clung to her face and neck. It would have been better to let it go, Mary thought, though the effect from a distance was still dramatic.

She continued to fight her corner, 'On the contrary, I know a great deal about it!'

'Hah! Only what your mother told you, no doubt,' scoffed Helena. 'Your mother, Miss Fox, was a liar!'

'My mother did not tell me *anything* about it while she was alive. She never talked about her early life. I only found out about the events here from one of the notebooks she kept.'

For the first time, Helena looked disconcerted. 'Notebooks. *What* notebooks?'

Mary ignored this.

'Look, I'm not here for recrimination –'

'Maybe not, but *I* am and this is *my* house! Your mother came to England with all her fancy foreign ways. Butter wouldn't melt! We'll draw a veil over the role played in all of that by my brother's wife . . .' And then, apparently incapable of drawing a veil over anything, '. . . who was regarded as a whore by the rest of the family, by the way, Miss Fox. A whore! And her daughter was no better. Her daughter was depraved. Her daughter, aged fifteen, tried to seduce my son!'

Glittering with malevolence, Helena was beginning to shake. She was probably capable of violence. It was easy to see how the word *mad* could be applied. What was the expression? *Fit to be tied.* On the whole, though, Mary did not think Helena *was* mad. Like a five-year-old, Helena could not bear being thwarted and was prepared to scream and scream until she got her own way. To shock her out of it, though more out of an instinct for self-preservation than by design, Mary delivered a verbal slap in the face.

'Look, Mrs Landseer, I know about the child and I know whose it was.'

The silence pulsated.

Unnervingly, Aunt Helena began to weep stormy histrionic tears, walking around the room as she did so. It was rather like trying to conduct a social conversation with Ellen Terry.

'I did everything for him, you know, everything.' It was unclear to begin with who she was talking about, but it turned out to be Gerard, for then she said, 'The day he came into his inheritance, he cut me out of his life. Me, his mother!' As suddenly as they had started, the tears dried up. Now she was outraged.

'Where is he now?' Mary asked.

'He was forced to leave the country,' said Helena, 'there were debts. Every gentleman has debts, of course . . .' Here there was a surprising flash of cynical amusement, what Sibyl

252

had called her Borgia smile, '. . . but still the bank refused to underwrite them. I believe he went to Australia. Since then we have not spoken. To this day I have no idea if he is alive or dead.'

Betrayal and counter betrayal. At the end of it she was still making excuses for him.

'Do you know what happened to the child?'

'Oh, the *child*! I have no idea,' was the disparaging reply.

The woman was unbelievable.

'But he was your *grandson*!'

Patiently, 'Yes! But born on the wrong side of the blanket. Mother took care of all of that. Nothing could be allowed to compromise Gerard.'

Although Gerard had compromised himself later with no help from anybody else.

'The child was also my half-brother. I would like to make contact with him. That is all I want, nothing else.'

'I can't help you. As I said Mother took care of the whole thing and, as far as I know, the secret went to the grave with her. At the time I wanted nothing to do with it and I still don't.' The full, painted mouth turned down with an expression of distaste. Helena fitted another cigarette into the holder and lit it. Her hands were trembling, indicating that another emotional front was coming through. Mary decided to go for broke.

'It's possible that you *could* help me. Some of Mrs Adare's papers were lodged with a solicitor in Lamprey. It may be that the information I'm looking for is somewhere amongst them. However, Mr Tapsell will only let me go through them if the family gives permission . . .'

'Oh, I see. Quite right too. The answer's No,' said Helena. 'I don't want the whole thing raked up again.' She rang a bell. 'Now I would be grateful if you left and took Margaret with you. The conservatory is in that direction. Madge will show you out.'

Mary left through the door indicated without waiting for the materialization of Madge. There seemed nothing else to do. Owing to the cacophonous noise, the conservatory, which still contained the parrot aviary, was not hard to find and, as Sibyl had before her, Mary exclaimed with pleasure as she entered it. The domed birdcage was just as described in the

253

notebooks. Within its spacious contours brightly coloured, raucous birds swooped and dived and swung on perches. Margaret was sitting on a cast iron seat reading a magazine. Around her crowded tall palms and other tropical plants. The air was hot and at the same time damp and smelt of the lush greenery all around.

'Get anywhere?' enquired Margaret.

'No,' said Mary.

'I didn't think you would. You didn't exactly treat her with kid gloves. On the other hand, it quite likely wouldn't have got you anywhere if you had. Anyway, it doesn't matter. As the only surviving member of the family who's half-way sane, you can have *my* permission. Helena never goes out, never mind anywhere near Lamprey, so she'll never know. Shall we go?'

On their way out, in order not to encounter Helena again, they passed through a door at the other end of the conservatory and entered a music-room. At one end of it, by the door and behind a harp, hung an oil portrait. Struck by it, Mary paused.

'Margaret, who is that?'

'It's the waster, Gerard, in his twenties. It used to have pride of place in the drawing-room. Maybe Helena can't stand the sight of it these days. If so, I wouldn't blame her. Why do you ask?'

'Oh, no real reason. It reminds me of someone, that's all.'

Travelling back in the car, Mary said, 'What happened to Helena's husband?'

'Cosmo the dim? He left her. Actually, he caught her and a lover *in flagrante delicto*. Even Cosmo couldn't ignore *that*. He worshipped her, you know, but that was the end. After it he went to London. He was too gallant to divorce her though and she has the run of that house until she dies.'

'Do you know what I think? I think Helena was jealous of my mother.'

'I'm sure she was. Until your mother came along with the inestimable advantage of youth on her side, there was no competition.'

'I also think she was a little in love with her own son.'

'That wouldn't surprise me either,' said Margaret. 'But mostly she's in love with herself.'

They left it that Margaret would telephone Tapsell and Tapsell and formally give permission for the exhumation of the Adare files. Soldiering back to Lamprey on the bicycle, Mary reflected on her day. Thank God the rain had stopped. By now dusk was setting in. Over the moors the violet bank of cloud had lifted a fraction and bled like a watercolour into the pearly horizon. She felt exultant and at the same time a little frightened about what might be in store. There was a sensation of impetus coupled with inevitability. Whatever the end result should turn out to be, there was no stopping now.

At this hour the town was deserted. On reaching the cobbled section, Mary dismounted and walked. When she reached the square the lights were on within the church. On impulse she propped the bicycle against the wooden gate, walked up the flagged path between the gravestones and went in. It was illuminated by candlelight which picked up on the russets, chrome yellows and garnet reds of the autumn floral displays on either side of the altar. The pews were three quarters full and the organist was just commencing a hymn with what could only be described as crash and dash. Without being noticed, Mary sat down at the back. Raggedly at first, and then with gathering discipline, the congregation joined in.

It was a comparatively small interior and the sweet sound of untrained voices rose to the barrel-vaulted ceiling and swelled to fill the vacuum. There was the smell of incense. Pale and tall, each with its own aureola of light, beeswax candles bestowed a medieval ambience on the scene and then, as if angels had joined in, the pure treble voices of the choir soared in descant. Mary was not religious and yet the sight and sound of it touched her to the heart. In its way the scene spoke personally to her. As she perceived it, it was an affirmation that whatever she did or did not discover tomorrow, certain things were constant and always would be. With great clarity she saw that, if she let him, Francis Stafford would be one of those. She thought of Netty and Rafe Bartholomew and William, dear William, who would hopefully soon be home. But most of all she thought of her lost brother, who probably had no idea that she even existed.

27

Rafe Bartholomew decided to rewrite his will. Godfrey was dead and in default he did not want a large part of his estate to end up in the hands of Geoffrey Harding. Furthermore, in the light of his last meeting with Mary Fox, he had taken the decision that, in a sense in Godfrey's memory, he wished to do something for her. The money side of it was easy. Mary wanted to go to university and she should. It was, Rafe felt, the least he could do for her. But he desired to do something more as well, to give her something of value and of beauty that would be personal to her in a way in which money was not.

He dickered over a charming Fantin Latour canvas of old-fashioned roses but finally dismissed it as facile. In the end he settled on a small Bonnard which depicted a dark interior with an open window. Through the window, conveying an impression of distance, there lay a landscape. Sapphire sky met sun-baked red earth, cypresses and vivid flowers. Within the room, to one side of the painting could be seen the form of a woman. It was unclear whether she was looking in or looking out.

The reasons for his choice were complex and to a degree revolved around guesswork. Rafe intuited that when Mary Fox said she needed a week off in order to sort out her mother's affairs, it was entirely likely that she was, among other things, in search of her own family history. What was it Nettie had once said to him? 'Beyond the fact that Sibyl is her mother, do you realize that Mary knows nothing, but *nothing*, about her own family. I think that's extraordinary, don't you!' Extraordinary or not, it was transparently obvious to Rafe that before going forward into the Promised Land outside the window as depicted in the Bonnard, a personal point of reference was needed to know where you were going forward from. If Nettie was to be believed, Mary had yet to establish that benchmark and the ambiguity in the painting of the woman who was either looking out or looking in, but could not do both at the same time, was a perfect illustration of this. All the time the Promised Land, a lush garden into which she might one day step, enticed. But not until she had fully explored the past. Rafe wondered who would step into it with her. Whether it would be William Harding or Francis Stafford or neither of them.

When he explained his plan to his solicitor, a family friend, the reaction was one of disapproval.

'Are you quite sure about this? It's a unique work of art. May I be allowed to ask who Miss Mary Fox is?'

In the light of the fact that, as far as he was aware, Mary Fox herself did not know the answer to this, it was an impossible question to answer. And it was, of course, out of the question to say: I want to leave her a substantial sum of money plus a Bonnard because we were both in love with Godfrey Harding and that is what we have in common.

In the end, Rafe said, 'Mary Fox is an estimable graduate of the school of hard knocks. She is a close friend of Venetia Huntington –'

Here the legal eyebrows shot up in alarm.

'– but is nothing like her. I esteem and admire her and want to give her a helping hand. That's all.'

They both knew it was not all. Since it appeared to be the sum total of the reassurance he was likely to get and he had done his duty by urging caution, the solicitor was forced to let it go.

'Just so long as you aren't about to start giving away the rest of the collection to every Tom, Dick and Harry.'

'No, of course I'm not about to do that. Though I do have something in mind for the Antinous. I want it to go to the British Museum. Otherwise, if I should die before her, I want everything else to revert to my mother's estate.'

'Yes, of course, though that's hardly likely.'

'You never know,' said Rafe.

William came home from the war. In common with a great many others, he had nowhere to come home to. The first person he contacted was Nettie.

Nettie was very emotional, and not just at the prospect of seeing her only surviving brother. Pregnancy was causing hormonal uproar and every morning she thanked God that Randolph was currently away in the country.

On the telephone, William sounded very, very tired.

'Where are you?' asked Nettie, 'I'll come and get you.' It was a rash offer. She hoped he was not about to say Dover.

'Victoria. I'll get a cab.'

He arrived on the doorstep half an hour later and was still in uniform. Nettie caught her breath. The privations of war had refined her brother's looks. William looked exactly like Godfrey. Wordlessly, brother and sister embraced.

'I'll make you a stiff drink,' said Nettie.

Watching her as she did it, William said, 'I rang the flat before I rang you. I didn't expect Father to be there but was surprised not to get Mother.'

Astonished, Nettie paused in the act of handing him a whisky and soda.

'She said she was going to write to you. Didn't you get her letter?'

'I haven't had any letters for weeks,' said William. 'Why, what's wrong?'

'I'd better tell you the bald facts first,' said Nettie, dreading what she had to do and anxious to get it over. 'The first, and worst, is that Jonty has been posted missing after the Arnhem offensive.' She began to cry, only managing to pull herself together with an effort. 'The second is that Mother has left Father for another man and Father has lost a huge sum of money as well and the third, but keep this under your hat, is that Godfrey and Rafe Bartholomew were having a homosexual relationship.' Nettie could have added, but did not, that on top of all of this she was about to pass off another man's child as Randolph's much-desired heir.

Maybe because of all he had endured at the front, William did not panic on receipt of her catalogue of woe but took it one thing at a time. He felt protective of his sister, who looked washed out and who wouldn't with Randolph Huntington as a husband. There was, however, no point in going over old ground now. He had told Nettie what he thought of Huntington at the time. She had not been prepared to listen and it was too late now.

'Don't despair about Jonty until you have to, Nettie,' said William gently. 'A lot of men were made prisoners of war

258

and there's still chaos out there. The war may be over but the mopping up isn't. What I'm saying is that Jonty could still be OK. Let's not grieve until we have to.'

It was exactly what Mary had said.

'Tell me more about the parents.'

Nettie shrugged. 'Remember that buffoon Charlie Fanshawe, the stockbroker? And you remember that he was at school with Father sometime in the Dark Ages, so the Gospel According To Father says he must have been honourable and competent because he came from the right background? One of us? Well, a gaping hole seems to have opened up in the old boy network here, because he either lost the money or embezzled it. Nobody seems quite sure. Anyway, he compounded his crime by getting killed in an air raid so the money's gone and Charlie's gone and the country house is up for sale.'

Good God! The country house, their childhood home. It must be serious. William remembered Mary sitting on the lip of the fish pool trailing her fingers in the black water that idyllic summer afternoon when none of them had known of the six-year horror ahead of them. His first priority would be to find her again.

'Meanwhile,' Nettie was continuing, 'Mother took a lover.' She made it sound like buying a new hat. Maybe in Nettie's world everyone took lovers. William felt he had been away from England for too long to have any conception of what the norm was any more. 'Father, in desperation, graciously said he would overlook this aberration and Mother said she didn't want it overlooked because she wanted to be divorced as soon as possible.'

'What's he like?'

'Peter Flamborough? He's a good sort and obviously adores her. He asks her opinion about things and it turns out that she does have opinions!'

'Which, unless you agree with his, is not easy with Father in the offing. I'm amazed that wasn't crushed out of her.'

'I know. Anyway it's heartening to see that, like the phoenix, Mother has risen triumphantly from the ashes of her marriage and that's more than one can say for Father. Father still doesn't understand where it all went wrong. You'll get an earful when you see him. Do you realize

259

this is the first time we've ever talked frankly about the family's peccadilloes. Until I got out into the big wide world, I thought every family was like ours.'

At this point William, who had been speculating on the subject of Nettie's own marriage, enquired after Randolph. Nettie did not mince words. 'Now I'm in pod, I hardly see Randolph,' said Nettie, 'which on one level suits me, but because I'm pregnant I'm grounded. He goes off to his club every evening and when he comes home he's usually plastered and I've passed out with sheer boredom. I've never gone to bed so early since I was five.' Uttering these words, Nettie thought longingly of *louche* nights with Joshua, of whom she had seen neither hide nor hair since their quarrel, before resuming, 'Anyway, after the birth, he can have the baby and I'm off. If Mother can do a successful bolt at her age, so can I!'

If William was shocked by her attitude he did not show it. 'You'll feel differently once the child is born.'

'Want to bet?'

William knew there was no point in him arguing the toss with Nettie. Let Randolph field this one.

Instead, he said, 'I'm not surprised, incidentally, by what you had to say about Rafe and Godfrey. You know rumours were rife at Eton about Godfrey's sexual orientation. Rafe must have been devastated by Godfrey's death.'

'You never know with Rafe. But yes, I suppose he must have been. Before it happened, Father found out about the liaison and raised the roof. It was Jonty who neutralized him by pointing out that if he went public on The Outrage, as he persisted in calling it, the only person he would hurt would be Godfrey. Jonty actually said he couldn't see what all the fuss was about at which point, according to him, Father looked as though he might be about to have a seizure.' Nettie laughed.

At last William felt he could ask the question.

Casually, 'And where is Mary? Have you seen her lately?'

'Mary's away at the moment on some mysterious quest in the North. I didn't speak to her immediately before she left so I don't know exactly where. The person who just might be able to help you there is Rafe Bartholomew.'

'Really? Why would Bartholomew —'

'Rafe recruited Mary out of the blue to work at Bletchley

Park with all the boffin brains who were cracking the German codes.' Nettie did not enlarge on what her own role in the war effort had been. 'As of now she's still there so she must have asked for leave. Whether she told Rafe what she wanted it for was another matter, but it should be possible to find out how long they're expecting her to be away.'

Nettie thought her brother looked exhausted, poor lamb. She left him where he was and went into the kitchen to prepare some food for them both. When she returned to announce that it was ready, she found him asleep.

Before Geoffrey Harding even had the chance to put his country house up for sale, he was amazed to receive an enquiry about it.

'A Mr Kellaway,' said the secretary.

'I wonder how the devil he knew it might be coming on the market,' speculated Geoffrey. 'Who is he anyway?' It was inconceivable that someone who could afford to spend that sort of money should not be someone he either knew personally or had at least heard of. On the other hand, it occurred to him that a discreet private sale rather than a series of highly public advertisements in *Country Life* might be one way of keeping his straitened financial circumstances quiet. In the end, his instructions were, 'Tell him to come and meet me for a drink at my club. Seven o'clock this evening. If he can't do that, then the same time tomorrow.'

As he entered the august premises of Harding's club, Joshua Kellaway congratulated himself. Apart from the seduction of Harding's daughter, if one could call it that, the purchase of the Harding mansion was the apogee of his social ambition.

Geoffrey was sitting in a leather wing armchair moodily reading *The Times* when he was informed that his guest had arrived. Good God, the fellow was wearing a camel-hair coat! With shoulders which looked as though they still had a coat hanger in them. Geoffrey discovered he did not like the idea of the owner of such a coat strutting around his club let alone owning a house that had once been his.

They shook hands and then both sat down. Stiffly he said, 'What can I get you to drink?'

'A whisky would do it.'

'Two whiskies, one with soda,' ordered Harding.

Turning back to Kellaway, he said, 'What led you to believe that my house might be for sale?'

The temptation to reply, 'Your daughter told me when we were having a fuck,' was almost too much to pass up, but was resisted in the interests of not upsetting the applecart.

'I heard it on the grapevine,' said Kellaway.

Harding still could not work it out. The house had not been advertised and so far as he was aware he had not spoken to anyone outside the family about it. His estranged wife was a loose cannon, though. Maybe Davina and her fancy man had talked about it. Their drinks arrived and as each took the first sip, they appraised one another.

Joshua thought that Harding, the man about to become a country squire without a country house, had not aged well. Disappointment and irascibility had caused the jowls to become pendulous. The waistline had spread, the hair had thinned and his colour was hectic, though if the defection of Davina had dented the overbearing Harding self-confidence, there was no sign of it. For his part, Harding had the niggling feeling that he had met Joshua Kellaway somewhere before. Without the coat, Kellaway looked altogether more presentable, though the hair was too shiny and the nails too manicured. Because it was classless, the accent was alerting as well, though a man who smoked the same cigars as he did (Havanas) was probably fundamentally all right.

'What's your profession?' enquired Geoffrey.

'I own a factory,' was the unwelcome reply, 'more than one of them in fact.'

A factory! More than one! Industry! Appalling!

Regrouping after the revelation of this social horror story and coming to terms with the fact that he was having a drink with such a person within the hallowed confines of his very exclusive club, Harding could think of nothing to say. Undeterred by the glowering silence, Kellaway decided to press on.

'I took the liberty of going to inspect the house with an estate agent, just in order to get a rough idea of what it was worth,' said Joshua, unaware of the fact that the equally damning word *Trespasser* had now supplanted *Factory* in the forefront of Harding's mind. Harding had done the same

262

with a different agent, whom he had told he wanted a valuation for insurance purposes, so he too knew what the house was worth.

'What sort of figure did he come up with?'

Kellaway named a sum. Give or take, it was practically the same as Harding's estimate, though his own fellow had seen the inside of the property as well, of course.

Harding said, 'Obviously I could reasonably expect to get more on the open market. Nothing like competition to push the price up.'

'On the other hand,' riposted Kellaway, 'in these post-war days you might not even get your asking price. There's not that much money about and I wouldn't have said there was the demand for large country mansions that there used to be.'

Harding was silent. At last he said, 'All right! Why don't you make me an offer and I'll consider it overnight.' In an unreliable world this was, after all, the proverbial bird in the hand. He was inclined to think Kellaway was right. At the end of the day there might be nothing in the bush.

Kellaway wrote it down on the back of a business card and handed it to Harding. He then stood up.

'I'll look forward to hearing your decision tomorrow.'

Harding also stood up and saw his guest to the door, where they shook hands.

'Thanks for the drink, Mr Harding.'

'My pleasure, Mr Kellaway.'

With relief, Geoffrey watched the camel-hair coat enter the revolving door where it took up most of one segment before passing out into the street.

The feeling that he had met Joshua Kellaway before reasserted itself. The name rang a faint bell too. On the whole though he was inclined to dismiss it. Except for tonight, owners of factories simply did not cross Harding's social path. He must be mistaken.

On his way back to his wing armchair and his unfinished drink, he turned over the business card and was extremely put out by what he found. The sum offered did not even reach the lower end of his own estate agent's estimation. On that level it was derisory, an insult. Not for the first time that evening it crossed Harding's mind that maybe Kellaway knew how badly he needed the money.

263

28

As arranged, Mary presented herself at the office of Tapsell & Tapsell in order to go through the Adare file. The first thing she noticed about it as the file approached under the guardianship of Mr Tapsell junior was the smell. It reeked of mildew and stones long unturned and was an overstuffed, furry folder rather than a sleek modern file. The outside of it was spotted with brown, like an old hand. Taking it from him, Mary was surprised by the weight of it and supposed it due to a combination of the fact that it was damp and the fact that legal anything was always enshrined on thick paper.

'Do you have a spare room somewhere where I could go through all of this without getting in your way,' asked Mary, who did not relish sharing the front office desk with the secretary while she did it. It appeared they did not.

'Maybe I could take it to my hotel and go through it there?'

It immediately became plain that Mr Tapsell did not like that idea at all.

'I could sign for them,' she suggested.

It still wouldn't do. Dealing with the legal profession could be very like wading through deep water, Mary decided. Of course it had to be admitted that weighing the pros and cons of everything was what they were mainly there for, but this was verging on the ridiculous.

'Why don't you ring Mrs Macaulay? Ask her if she minds.'

He did so. There was a short, sharp exchange at the end of which Mr Tapsell's ears went pink.

'Mrs Macaulay says she has no objection,' he announced huffily, replacing the receiver. 'All the same, Miss Fox, I think you should sign for them.'

Mary did so. Back in her room at the Lamprey, with trembling hands she opened a window to let out the dank smell and then she opened the folder. What was inside was a mixture of old leases, presumably cottages on the estate, and private papers. Carefully unfolding and then refolding everything, she began to go through it all. Two thirds of the way down the pile she came across an envelope addressed to Mrs Laetitia Adare. Within it was a brief letter written in an artistic flowing hand. The address at the top of it was Minton House, Minton in the same county.

My dear Mrs Adare,
It is with gratitude that I write you this letter. The third party has accomplished his mission and I am now the happiest woman in the world. I shall fulfil my obligations with zeal and with love and I assure you that you may rely on my absolute discretion in this matter.
My husband joins me in sending our heartfelt thanks.
Yours sincerely,
Alice B.

That was all. But that was all she needed. With a surge of excitement, Mary knew she had the key to it in her hand at last. She put the letter, which was disintegrating along the folds, carefully to one side and continued going methodically through the rest of the pile. With the exception of a mysterious invoice dated around the same time as the Minton letter and claimed against Services Rendered, there was nothing else of interest. All the same, mindful of the extreme care with which Francis had gone through the Sibyl Fox notebooks not once but twice before ultimately striking gold, Mary made it her business to go through the contents twice more before putting the folder to one side. She did not want to be in the position of wresting it off a reluctant Mr Tapsell a second time.

That evening, full of triumph, she rang Francis Stafford. There was no answer. Not wanting to believe it, Mary let the phone ring and ring, a forlorn unacknowledged echo in an empty room. The extent of her disappointment and, if she was honest with herself, chagrin that he was not there surprised her.

Where was he?

To take her mind off it, she got out the map. Minton was on the other side of what was a very large county. It looked as though a train was going to be needed and then a taxi. For I've *had* it with bicycles, decided Mary. This time around I deserve a taxi. She had two days left and was due to return to Bletchley on the third. Clearly the way to tackle this was to spend one night and possibly two in Minton village at a hostelry, assuming such a thing existed. It did. Mary employed the Stafford tactic of asking the operator for the number of the Minton Arms.

'No Minton Arms,' was the reply, 'but I've got a Minton Inn here.'

'That'll do.'

Mary rang them and booked herself a room. While she was on the line she asked about the present incumbent of Minton House and was informed it was a widow, a Mrs Alice Fort. It might or might not be the same person. The name Alice sounded hopeful, but the signatory of the letter had written Alice B. Mary considered telephoning Mrs Fort before setting off and decided against it. It was preferable to arrive in Minton and do some research first rather than making a call out of the blue.

Instead of the infuriatingly absent Francis, she rang Margaret Macaulay.

'I may have found what I'm looking for,' said Mary, 'and I'm off to follow it up tomorrow. But whether it is or whether it isn't, I'm eternally grateful to you for all your help.'

Margaret sounded gruff. 'Well done you! Don't forget to let me know what happens.'

'I won't! Oh, and I'll make sure the Adare papers get safely back to the solicitor before I leave.'

'Yes, that man Tapsell's fretting nearly drove me mad this morning.'

'I know, I noticed.'

Francis Stafford got back to his depressing room at midnight. When Mary was in it the room was not depressing. Then it was a refuge, a place of succour away from the rest of an intrusive world. Now she was not there, its shortcomings were painfully apparent. Suddenly lonely, he looked at his watch. It was too late to telephone her and there was no way of knowing if she had tried to contact him. Wandering restlessly around the furniture, he wondered whether she

266

had had any further success with her research. And when she was coming back.

The letter had remained unwritten.

The last evocative relics of her presence there, a jug of Michaelmas daisies, had died but Francis had not had the heart to throw them away. For the moment they were all he had. The two of them had made no arrangements for her return. Unless Mary let him know what train she was proposing to take, he would be unable to meet her.

For Francis the illogicality of love was hard to come to terms with. It bore no relation to all the things he had hitherto seen as fixed points of the compass. It ought to have been possible for him to say: I am in love with Mary, Mary does not appear to be in love with me. Ergo I must look elsewhere, or, better still, stay away from this inconvenient emotion altogether. This was where irrationality came in (or was it addiction?), for he found himself incapable of implementing the dispassionate, sensible course of action. There was a rather bad unframed snapshot of his tormentor on the mantelpiece. While taking the photograph, Francis had cracked a joke. Mary's smile was wide. Head thrown back, eyes narrowed against the sun, she looked a fairly typical victim of an amateur cameraman. An uninformed observer would have said this was a carefree person. Francis knew better, which was why in its way it was a bad picture. The journey she was currently engaged on in the North would either lead her out of the desert of her past or take her deeper into it, to the point where he lost sight and track of her altogether. Whatever it did, Francis saw very clearly that there could be no question of not being there for her when she came back.

When he rang her at the Lamprey Arms the following morning, she had gone and had not left a message saying where to.

'But she did ask me about Minton,' revealed Dave, in response to repeated questioning.

Minton.

'Is that where she was going, do you think?'

'She didn't say, but she was very interested in where it was.'

Francis rang the operator.

267

'Could you find me the number of the Minton Arms, Minton, please.'

Long pause.

'No Minton Arms but there is a Minton Inn.'

'That'll do.'

He wrote it down.

As she sat on the train, Mary read her mother's notebooks yet again. Outside the temperature had steeply dropped and there had been an occasional dilatory flake of snow. It seemed to Mary very early for such a thing, but maybe as far north as this it was not. By the time the train steamed into her destination, snow was falling steadily and the low sky was dense with more to come. It was possible that getting a taxi to Minton would be problematical.

It was not. Up here severe weather was the norm and as a result nothing was held up because of it. Minton village turned out to be picturesque and the Minton Inn minuscule with another affable (*Call me George, everyone else does*) landlord. There were two guest bedrooms, the other one of which was empty.

'Nobody usually comes here at this time of year,' said George.

Mary asked him about Mrs Fort and Minton House. George was vague, not on the gossip ball like Dave. 'She's a widow,' was the reply, 'and does a lot of good in the local community. It's a type that's dying out,' he said with regret. 'Why are you interested?'

'I hope to meet her,' returned Mary carefully. 'We just may have a relation in common.'

George was impressed.

'I'm going in that direction tomorrow on my way into the town. I could give you a lift, if you like.'

'That would be very kind of you. I'll ring her now.'

A man's voice answered the telephone. The butler perhaps.

Mary asked to speak to Mrs Fort.

'Who shall I say wishes to talk to her?'

'Tell Mrs Fort that my name is Mary Fox, but my mother's name was Adare,' said Mary.

Mrs Fort came to the telephone.

In response to Mary's request to come and see her, she said, 'I've been half expecting this call for years,' and it was then that Mary knew she was finally on the right track.

'I'm getting a lift from the landlord of the Minton Inn,' explained Mary, 'so I shall have to find out from him when he intends to do his trip into town.'

'Depending on the movements of the landlord of the Minton Inn? I won't hear of it,' said Alice Fort. 'You must come to tea, Miss Fox. I shall send the car to pick you up. Shall we say 3.30? I look forward to meeting you. Goodbye.' The receiver was gently replaced.

Before attempting to contact the elusive Francis Stafford, on impulse Mary rang Nettie. Again, a man's voice answered the phone.

'I'm afraid Nettie's out at present –'

'Randolph?'

'No, it's her brother William speaking.'

'William! Oh, William you're home! It's Mary, William. Mary Fox!' Her voice was unsteady.

'Mary!' His joy at hearing her was audible. 'Don't forget that you promised to have dinner with me on my return!'

'I'd *adore* to have dinner with you. How long are you staying with Nettie?'

'At the moment I've nowhere else to go, so as long as she'll have me. Certainly until Randolph gets back. What are you doing wherever it is you are and when are you back?'

'Research!' was the guarded reply, 'and, in theory, the day after tomorrow.'

Research? Oh well, never mind, he would hear all about it when they finally met.

'Why don't you let me come and meet you off your train?' Mary thought of Francis.

'Better not. My plans are fluid. I'll ring you when I'm back. Give my love to your naughty little sister.'

'You know she's pregnant, don't you?'

Pregnant! Now it was Mary's turn to be surprised. The last time she had talked at length to Nettie, Allegra McClaren had just arrived on the scene from the States and the Huntington nose had been very out of joint. So far as Mary had known there had been no one else on the horizon then and certainly not Randolph.

'Randolph's over the moon apparently!'

Yes, well he might be but what about Nettie? Mary smelt a rat, but did not voice her misgivings to William.

'William, my money's about to run out. I'll ring you as soon as I'm back.'

Click.

She had gone.

Mary redialled.

Francis was not there again.

The following day no more snow fell but it was very, very cold. Too cold for snow, some would have said. Under an opaline sky the covering still remaining from the fall of the day before glittered, and swags of icicles refracted pale sunlight. The air was still and trees cast long blue shadows. Riding towards her destiny in the shape of tea with Mrs Fort, Mary tried to marshal her thoughts and in the end gave up on it. The main thing was to lucidly set out her own agenda and then wait for the response, whatever that might be. The very fact that she had been asked to go to Minton House at all augured well.

The drive up to the house was a long one. On either side of it the white drifts looped and curled like *crème anglaise*. Shrubs leaned low under the weight they carried and the car passed a large ornamental lake with a Neptune in the centre, whose opaque frozen surface, like a semi-precious stone, dully reflected the wintry light. A galaxy of surprised ducks skidded across the ice. Sitting in the back, Mary was sealed off from the chauffeur by a panel and was grateful for the barrier. For, thought Mary, I want to take all this in with no distractions. By now they surely must be getting to the house. Parkland was yielding to a denser, more formal layout and they suddenly entered a yew avenue. At the end of it stood the house. Mary caught her breath. Minton House was a medium-sized Palladian mansion of exquisite proportions. Set in the current snowy landscape it looked as if it had been sculpted out of Royal icing.

The car drew to a halt. The driver opened the door and Mary got out. She stood for a moment looking up at the house and then walked up the steps and rang the bell.

Later, recalling the encounter, Mary was to decide that

she had been privileged to meet Alice Fort. Unlike the equally grand but crasser Adares, here was dignity coupled with perfect manners and all underlined by the sort of steely integrity, goodness even, which did not cloy but nourished. In the old-fashioned sense of the word, Alice Fort was a lady.

Her hostess poured the tea and then sat back in her chair. The fire flared and there might have been some sort of herb among the logs, for as it did so Mary noticed an aromatic scent. Bay, perhaps. Apart from the spitting and crackling of the flames and the melodious chimes of a long case clock, the room was very quiet.

'Tell me your story, Miss Fox,' invited Alice Fort.

Mary did so. Apart from a certain amount of editing where her mother's rackety Roman childhood and subsequent adult career were concerned, she left nothing out, culminating in the notebook account of the birth. Mrs Fort listened intently and did not interrupt. At the end of it all, she said, 'So the secret I have kept all these years, even from my son, is out!'

'Not totally,' said Mary. 'You may prefer to leave things where they are.'

'Put it this way,' said Mrs Fort, 'in the light of all you have said and your own emotional interest in the matter, it is no longer mine to keep. You would like to meet your brother and it is my view that I should be failing in my moral duty both to you and to him if I were to stop you. If you had not come forward I should have felt no need to say anything but your existence, Miss Fox, concerning which I knew nothing, changes everything. All the same this is a delicate matter which will need delicate handling.'

'I know.'

'But before we decide what to do, first let me tell you my part in this story.'

29

With Randolph still away in Scotland and her brother *in situ* and a very useful escort, Nettie, who could not afford another scandal at this tricky stage, began to get out more. By this time the McClarens, she triumphant, had gone back to the States and so had other influential lovers. Now the war was over William noticed a certain re-alignment of society taking place and, because he had been away for as long as he had, probably noticed it sooner than those who had been there all along. There was, for instance, a new affluent class comprised of those who had made money out of the war as opposed to being bereaved or beggared by it. One such had bought the Harding country house, much to his father's disapproval.

'I don't like the idea of the fellow strutting about in my house,' said Geoffrey, moodily. 'Do you realize the man owns a factory!' Outrage escalating. '*More* than one!'

'It isn't your house any more,' pointed out William. 'It's his, so he can strut where he likes. And given your current financial situation it might be useful if *we* owned a factory. What's the name of the buyer anyway?'

'Kellaway. Joshua Kellaway.'

William, who had a good memory for minutiae, connected the name immediately.

'We had a stable boy called Joshua Kellaway! Don't you remember him?'

It was an unusual name. Surely there couldn't be two. There weren't two. The look on his parent's face spoke volumes. Father was thunderstruck.

'I thought I'd seen him somewhere before,' stuttered Geoffrey. 'Do you realize he came and had a drink with me in my club?' He seemed, if anything, more exercised by this than the trade connection. As if it was yesterday, Harding saw Nettie in the horse blanket accompanied by her proletarian lover and was further infuriated to remember that Rafe Bartholomew had seen it all too.

When he got back to the Chelsea house that afternoon,

William mentioned the incident to Nettie. Nettie, who had learnt discretion during her Bartholomew apprenticeship, did not comment. All the same, she was shocked. Nettie remembered lying in bed with Joshua and telling him that Father was strapped for cash and that the country house was going to have to be put up for sale. Running her hand adorned with the Huntington ruby over his bare chest, Do you recall all those divine tack-room assignations? she had asked and Joshua had said he did. What a shame that it's all going out of the family, had been her next remark. Yes, wasn't it, he had said, starting to make love to her again. Since when the bastard had not only thrown her over but had bought her family's house for himself without even telling her.

The following evening Nettie and William went to a cocktail party and Kellaway was there. It was interesting, mused Nettie, that when someone one hadn't seen for a while was in one's thoughts, they often turned up in the flesh around that time as well. It was almost as though thinking about them conjured them up.

'There *is* Joshua Kellaway,' whispered Nettie to her brother.

Interested, William looked across the room.

'He's obviously done very well for himself,' observed William without rancour.

'Yes, hasn't he!' Nettie tossed her head. Later, when her brother was talking to somebody else, she moved in Kellaway's direction. Catching her by her wrist as she passed him, thereby stopping her in her tracks, he said, 'Ah, Mrs Huntington. I've been meaning to contact you.'

'Really!' Nettie was withering.

'Yes, really. I want to talk about the child.'

'Why?' Nettie was astonished. 'You told me you weren't interested in me or it.' She looked around to see if anyone else was listening. No one was, all were braying and booming. The noise level was ear splitting.

'That depends.'

'On what?'

'On what sex it is. If it's a boy, I want it. If it's a girl you can keep it. I've already got two daughters.'

Nettie could not believe she was listening to this.

'Why can't your precious wife do her duty?'

'My wife had a hard time with the last birth. She doesn't want to go through it again.'

'Well, tough! You should have thought of that before. I've told Randolph it's his now. Besides, your wife wouldn't want to bring up another woman's child as her own.'

'My wife will go to any lengths to keep the marriage together.'

His wife sounded like Allegra McClaren, the woman with a face like a tomahawk.

'You'd never be able to prove it was yours!'

'I'd be quite prepared to go and tell Huntington that it was. Sow the seeds of doubt.'

'I think it would take a lot more than that for Randolph to remove the label HEIR from around its neck if it's a son. Apart from anything else, once he's finally got one he won't *want* to believe you. Anyway, what about your reputation?'

'I haven't got a reputation to lose,' said Kellaway. 'What about you?'

Neither, thought Nettie, if she was honest with herself, did she. What she did have to lose was the little house in Chelsea, the Huntington ruby ring and the status and protection afforded by the fact that, whatever the rest of the world felt about it, she was Mrs Randolph Huntington. No matter that the marriage as it stood was a bed of nails, she needed it to last the pregnancy in order to obtain a lucrative divorce so that she was properly positioned for the next round, whatever that might turn out to be.

Nettie felt that she had no alternative but to brazen it out. Across the room she could see William signalling that he wanted to leave. He had evidently decided against catching up with Joshua. 'I have to go, but I strongly advise you against the course of action you're proposing. It won't get you anywhere!'

'Maybe it will and maybe it won't.'

'An heir's an heir!'

'And a blood test's a blood test, sweetheart!'

'What! You wouldn't! No gentleman would do that!'

'We both know I'm no gentleman, and don't provoke me or we'll get onto the subject of whether you're a lady or not.'

Feeling like slapping him but recalling that the last time she had done so he had slapped her back, Nettie turned away.

As she did so she said, 'You might have had the courtesy to tell me that you've bought our old house.'

'I haven't bought it,' said Joshua. 'We're still haggling. *Au revoir!*'

When Nettie reached William, who was by the door, he noticed that her colour was high.

'What on earth were you talking about for so long? You looked so engrossed in it I decided not to interrupt you.'

'Old times, that was all.' Nettie's usual ebullience seemed to have deserted her. 'Let's go home, shall we?'

Elsewhere, in London, Rafe Bartholomew had no one to go and meet. He felt his emotional isolation to be complete. There was still work, of course, but without the peril of imminent invasion and war and days that merged into nights in the urgent effort to stay ahead of the enemy. Paradoxically that had been the ultimate opiate and with its help Rafe had pushed his depression and terrible loneliness to the back of his consciousness. Now he had what he most dreaded, time to think.

By himself in his flat in the evenings he thought of Godfrey and then it was that grief caught up with him at last and Rafe wept by himself for the loss of his lover. These days he could hardly bear the sight of the Antinous, once his favourite possession. People got over bereavement. Rafe knew that and therefore was prepared to concede, in the light of all the evidence, that he would, and yet there were days when he frankly doubted it. Hardest of all was the realization that there was nothing rational about the vortex of despair into which he found himself plunged. In the past the joined forces of courage and a first-class brain had provided an effective defence against whatever crisis he was currently having to face.

Not this time.

The memories were the worst. They were haunting and inescapable. Godfrey by the fire, leaning on the mantelpiece where he himself was in the habit of standing, the fine profile reflected in the old grey glass and reflected yet again in the inscrutable smile on the face of the statue of Antinous. Godfrey the willowy, beautiful youth with whom he had walked about the old streets of Rome and with whom he had shared his own passion for the classical antiquities of Italy and later of Greece. And right at the end, and most poignant of all, the last few days they had spent together, when in his heart of hearts Rafe had known that his lover was probably doomed, and this secret understanding had infused their time together with mourning as well as with joy.

One night, when bleakness threatened to overwhelm him, he took his small revolver out of his bedside drawer and balanced it on the palm of his hand, where it lay, shiny beetle-black and cold, the certain means to the annihilation of his torment. Though he knew she was hundreds of miles away, he was all at once aware of his beloved mother's presence. In his mind's eye he saw her, willing him not to succumb to his desolation but to fight it. Finally, reluctantly, he put the gun away and then, dreading the lonely sleepless hours before the breaking of another dawn, he put out the light.

Part Five

The Account of Alice Fort

30

'I was born in 1876,' said Alice Fort. 'I daresay to a modern young woman like yourself that must sound like a million years ago. I have lived through two world wars, two husbands and a great deal of social change. Do you realize that I have seen women win the vote? It seems inconceivable, doesn't it? That we did not have it all along, I mean.'

Sudden girlish laughter took years off her. She turned her head and looked out of the window. Her profile was a fine one which had tightened with age rather than the reverse. Long-fingered hands lay tranquil in her lap. There was an air of repose about Alice Fort which gave Mary the illusion of having come home at last. It was an illusion, of course, for, thought Mary, I have no real home. And yet there is something here for me. I sense it.

Resuming, Alice said, 'When I was twenty-one, I married. I was so in love, Miss Fox. It is an intoxicating experience at that age. One may fall in love again but never in quite the same way, never with quite the same intensity. Richard was fifteen years older than I was, some said too old, but if so I never noticed it. Everything seemed quite perfect. It wasn't, of course. Nothing ever is. Above everything I longed for a child and it was the one thing which was denied me. Well, the years went by. I amassed a prodigious number of god-children all of whom I adored, but still had no child of my own. With all the privileges that I had, you will think me a very spoilt woman when I say that this was something with which I never came to terms. It was an emotional hunger which never left me. These days women have careers and it is quite possible that this would have made a difference to me. But I was educated to be a gentlewoman, nothing more, and time hung heavily on my hands. Seeing it and understanding, my darling husband proposed that we should go abroad for several months. You see how privileged we were, Miss Fox. I was a very lucky woman but still not content. Others have to get on with it as best they may. I had all these consolations.

He promised to show me Rome and Florence and Venice, surely one of the most romantic places on earth.

'A month before we were due to depart, my maid was dressing my hair one evening and talking inconsequentially as she always did, Carrie was a great gossip, when I suddenly heard her say that there was a problem in the Adare household. The Adares, as you know, lived on the other side of a large county, so while I knew of them as another prominent family, we had never met. But Carrie had a sister who was employed there as a downstairs maid, and she had told Carrie that Miss Sibyl was *enceinte*. Below stairs was seething with the scandal. Nobody was supposed to know, but of course everybody did. Servants know everything, Miss Fox. Good servants do not pass it beyond the house they work for and, no doubt, as in this case, their nearest and dearest.

'Very casually, as I chose a decoration for my hair, I said, "Just assuming this is true, Carrie, what will happen to the child?"

'"What always happens, Madam. Miss Sibyl will go away to have the baby and then it will be adopted."

'"This one I think, Carrie. Does rumour tell us who the father is?" Already a plan was beginning to form in my head.

'"Mr Gerard," said Carrie without hesitation. "Though he denies it, as he would, wouldn't he?"

'"And Mr Gerard is . . . ?"

'"The old lady's grandson. My sister says Mrs Adare won't hear a word against him."

'"If this is true, I pity poor Miss Adare!"

'All the next day I thought about what Carrie had told me. Finally, after he gently chided me for not attending to what he was saying, I told Richard.

'"If it does indeed exist, I would like that child to be mine," I said boldly.

'He was visibly startled. "Alice, Carrie might be completely wrong and even if she is not, approaching the Adare family on such a sensitive and private matter would be impossible."

'"I have thought a lot about it," I said. "An approach would have to be made through a third party. There must be such a person. If Carrie knows, then the secret is not as well kept as the Adares would like to think."

'Some time later, when I brought the subject up again, Carrie was only too happy to talk to me about it. It transpires that although Dorothea Adare was married to a doctor, for reasons of delicacy he was not the one to confirm the pregnancy. That fell to their old family doctor, long since retired. It was obvious to me that this was the key to it and that Richard must go and see old Dr Maddox.

'At first he refused.

'"I would do anything for you, Alice," said Richard, "you know that, but you must see how very inappropriate this is."

'Inappropriate? I could not see it. I did not *want* to see it.

'If Carrie's sister was mischievous or merely mistaken, then the matter would not go beyond Dr Maddox's drawing-room. It seemed to me that there was nothing to be lost and everything to be gained. I was quite determined, Miss Fox. I wept, I begged, I pleaded and in the end, much against his better judgement, my poor, long-suffering husband agreed to do it. I did not, of course go with him. *That* would have been inappropriate.'

There was a faint smile and here, thought Mary, was a formidable woman.

'Well,' continued Mrs Fort, 'according to Richard, the upshot was that Maddox listened in silence to what he had to say and at the end of it wanted to know where his information had come from. Richard, of course, declined to say. To have divulged such a thing would have cost Carrie's sister her post. They left it that Dr Maddox would think over what had been said and in the light of whatever conclusion he came to would contact Richard anon. Which did not mean that at all, of course. It meant that he would go and see Laetitia Adare and in the light of whatever conclusion *she* came to would contact Richard anon.

'Which is exactly what happened. Except that the next time Richard met Mrs Adare at the Adare mansion and Dr Maddox was nowhere to be seen. "What was she like?" I said. "She's an old tyrant," replied Richard, "who can countenance nothing getting in her way. Sibyl deserves our pity for being caught up in such pointless ruthlessness."

'The word pointless caught my attention, Miss Fox. It

seemed to me that if I could nurture this unwanted child, I could go some way towards neutralizing this dreadful dynastic drive as epitomized by Laetitia Adare, with all its attendant cruelties. After all, at the end of the day what was it all about? It was all about a house. Just that. In my view houses should go hand in hand with families, along with love. They should not dictate the terms.

'Anyway, to get back to it, she was very interested in what Richard had to say. But mostly she was interested in secrecy. The scandal, you see. Today a child born out of wedlock is a scandal, but nothing like it was then.

'Richard said, "You may rely absolutely on our discretion, Mrs Adare."

'Apparently she nodded, and then said, "But if you and your wife suddenly adopt a child, there will be much speculation as to where it has come from."

'To which my husband replied, "I should tell you, Mrs Adare, that we are about to leave England to travel and shall be away for at least six months."

'She was onto it in a flash. "Then what I suggest happens is this: before she leaves these shores your wife lets it be known that she is pregnant. She returns with her child, born prematurely in wherever. In fact the handover will take place the day you come back to England, which will be dictated by the birth itself. After that the child is yours. There will be no formal contract or adoption and no contact between our families thereafter, in short nothing to connect us."

'"What if your niece does not want to give up her child?"

'"My niece will have no choice!"

'Richard told me he felt chilled listening to her. No doubt this woman was a pillar of the church but she displayed no compassion of any sort.

'Well, we did it Miss Fox. My pregnancy was announced, which at my great age caused something of a stir, as you may imagine. It had been arranged that Carrie should travel with us, but in the interests of maintaining the fiction and much to poor Carrie's disappointment, the plan was changed and we were to engage staff at our destination who knew nothing of any pregnancy. There is very little else to relate. The child was born, a boy, and, as arranged, was handed over to us by Mr Macaulay of Holden & Macaulay. Mr Macaulay's wife

Margaret, who was an Adare daughter, was never told of the arrangement and did not know of her husband's part in it. No doubt Mrs Adare pointed out to him that marriage and the secrets of the professional were to be kept apart.'

'I wonder then how my mother knew about Holden & Macaulay,' observed Mary.

'As I've said before, Miss Fox, nothing is watertight. Maybe somebody at the clinic took pity on her and told her. I've no idea, though I subsequently learnt that the Adare family was not popular in that part of the country, being regarded as high-handed and arrogant. Maybe that was the motive. What I can tell you for sure is that from the first moment that I held him in my arms, I adored that child and still do. Just as much as if I had given birth to him myself (and the agony and uncertainty surrounding his arrival made me feel as though I actually had). And Richard worshipped his son too. To us he was the best son in the world and to me he still is.'

'And presumably your son, my brother, took your first husband's name. May I ask what that was?'

'Ah, the last piece of the puzzle!'

Alice Fort's voice died away. She turned and looked out of the window at the frozen park.

There was a sudden suspension of normality, accompanied by a pulsating silence, not, Mary instinctively knew, a natural silence. It was a discontinuity of time and space, a psychic shift, as though the present had missed a beat. Into this vacuum savagely exploded the sound of a shot. Shocked, Mary looked across at Alice Fort and knew that she had heard it too. Neither of them spoke. Outside there was none of the uproar usually caused by such a thing. There was no echo and no clamorous flocks of startled birds rose. The stillness was profound.

With difficulty Alice collected herself.

So faint was her voice when she finally answered the question that Mary had to lean forward to hear what she said.

31

On her return to the Minton Inn in the wake of an extra-ordinary afternoon, Mary rang Francis, and once more he was not there. Where the hell was he? Unexplained absence heightened interest and unreasonably (she knew it) Mary felt slighted. He had, of course, had no idea when she might try to contact him so could hardly be blamed for not being there, but still she was irritated. On impulse she rang Nettie instead. Much as she loved Nettie, on this occasion her friend was a poor substitute. Dying to pass on momentous personal news and unaware of Nettie's role as establishment social spy which had honed her capacity for discretion, Mary felt she could not entrust her with her own sensitive secrets.

All the same it was good to hear her voice and Nettie, it transpired, had news of her own.

'Oh, Mary, such a pity you're not here! It's a celebration! We're opening the champagne . . .'

Mary forbore to observe that it took very little for Nettie to crack a bottle. It did not sound like the first one either.

Nettie effervesced on. '. . . We had a letter today from the War Office to say that Jonty is alive and about to be repatriated. You were right, he was captured. I don't suppose he's had a very nice time as a POW and heaven knows what state he'll be in when he gets home, but the main thing is he's safe . . .'

There was the sound of laughter in the background and the clink of glasses.

'Nettie, that's wonderful news! It sounds as though you've got quite a party going.'

'Not really,' said Nettie, whose idea of a party was min-imum fifty guests. 'Just Mother and Peter, who's a good egg by the way, plus the odd American. Oh, and William. William's here. Do you want to talk to him?'

On the whole Mary did not at this moment in time, recognizing that, assuming she succeeded in contacting him, she was in imminent danger of being met off the train by both Francis and William.

'No, no. Just give him my love. And Nettie . . .'

'Yes?'

'I'm *so* happy for you!'

When she had hung up, Mary tried Francis's number again.

Still no answer.

Unaware that she had tried to ring him, Francis Stafford rang Mary and missed her again. If he had not been so desperate to talk to her it would have been laughable.

'Tell Miss Fox to ring me tonight without fail,' he instructed the person who took the call. 'I'll be in all evening. I need to know what train she's travelling on so that I can meet it.'

Because the message was never passed on, Mary did not return Francis's call and when he rang her yet again it was to discover that she had left. By means of a not very difficult series of calculations with the help of a train timetable and some information from the landlord of the Minton Inn, he targeted the train she would probably be on and decided to go to the station on the off-chance. If she was not on that one, she would be on the next. He decided to take a book with him and prepare to wait.

Just as he was putting his coat on and about to switch off the radio, Francis caught the BBC news and was transfixed by what he heard. Christ! Surely the report could not be right! It seemed it was. On the streets the early evening editions had the story too. He bought a paper and, heavy of heart, scanned it, willing there to be some mistake but doubting it. When he got to the barrier he had just one minute to spare. Passengers streamed through and there was no sign of Mary. Francis was just beginning to give up when he saw her stepping along the platform. She must have been in the last carriage.

Even at that distance, Francis could see that there was something different about her, one might almost have said a sort of radiance, as though she moved within a light of her own. Ignoring the protests of the ticket collector, Francis pushed past the barrier and ran towards her and when he reached her, took her in his arms. Watching them embrace, the last couple on an otherwise empty platform, the ticket collector decided to take himself off for a cup of tea and, in so doing, turn a benevolent blind eye to the violator of the barrier.

Francis took Mary's grip from her, saying as he did so, 'You'll never know how much I missed you.' Then, after a moment's hesitation, 'But I'm afraid there's some very bad news.'

He was taken aback by the fear in her eyes. It was almost as though she knew what he was about to say. Now he had started Francis felt he had no choice except to go on. In any case it was on all the newspaper placards.

'I'm afraid Rafe Bartholomew shot himself yesterday.'

To his horror she slipped to the platform in a faint.

Shocked and unsure what to do about it, Francis tenderly gathered Mary up and laid her down on an empty bench where he knelt beside her, chafing her cold hands and calling her name. Gradually she came round and, as she did so, with consciousness came the memory of what he had just said. Incoherent and clinging to Francis, Mary wept hysterically. He had, of course, expected her to be very upset but the extent of her distress astounded him.

He wondered what to do. Getting her back to Bletchley in this sort of state was out of the question, but though he had never been there he knew of her mother's flat in Brixton. Unable to get any sense out of Mary, he went through her shoulder bag and found the address and a set of keys which were not the ones for her Bletchley digs, though those were there too.

'Darling, are these the keys to your mother's flat?'

He showed them to her.

Mute, tears streaming, she nodded.

'I'm going to take you there in a cab,' said Francis. 'Are you up to walking as far as the rank?'

Unsteadily, she stood up and half-carrying and half-supporting her he got her there.

'Brixton, please,' said Francis to the driver. 'Here's the address.'

*   *   *

286

Much later, by which time she had begun to calm down, he began to understand what had happened.

'The portrait of Gerard in Mrs Landseer's house was very like Rafe Bartholomew,' said Mary, 'but though I was struck by it, I still discounted any connection. I put it down to coincidence. I really couldn't believe it. Not until I met Alice Fort, Alice Bartholomew as she once was. After that there could be no doubt.'

In the face of this extraordinary story Francis was silent. Certain of life's wheels were always meant to come full circle, and here could be such an instance where the hand of fate appeared to be all around and spinning. Even so the denouement was a cruel one and, if there was a greater plan, *if* there was, seemed pointless. Francis gave up on it and turned back to the here and now.

What on earth was he to do? Mary had begun to weep again, silent agonizing tears redolent of dreadful inner torment. He remembered cautioning her against her search for her brother, essentially a search for self as well, and, despite her evident distress, decided that he had been wrong to do so. Wasn't it better to have loved and lost than never to have loved? On the whole it had to be. The rest was sterile. Mary had known Rafe. She had esteemed and admired him and, albeit for the very short time between Mrs Fort's revelation and hearing of his untimely death, had loved him as a brother. Maybe that was all anybody had a right to expect.

Francis was due back at Bletchley tomorrow. It occurred to him that Venetia Huntington, whom he had heard about from Mary but never met, might be able to help here. After another forage through Mary's address book he rang her. A male voice answered and then handed him over.

'Who?' said the crisp upper-class tones when he announced himself.

Mortified, Francis realized that Mary had told him about Venetia Huntington but had not told her about him.

Patiently he repeated his name and then explained some, but not all, of the problem.

'Mary is ill,' elucidated Francis. 'I have to go back to Bletchley tomorrow and it's my view that she should not be on her own.'

'On her own where?'

'Brixton.'

Appalled intake of breath at the other end. 'No, she certainly shouldn't. Mary can come here. I'll send William to fetch her.'

William? Who was William?

Francis was conscious of a stab of jealousy, though for all he knew William was a Harding lackey.

'I have to clear it with Mary first and then I'll come straight back to you.'

On being consulted, Mary said wearily, 'It's a good idea. I simply couldn't hack it back to Bletchley right now. Nettie and William will look after me. Oh, Francis, I feel so tired . . .' Tears began to fall again. She lay back on the pillows. 'Poor Rafe, poor, poor Rafe . . .'

Francis rang Venetia Huntington back and the arrangement was made. There was more talk of the mysterious William and what time he would arrive.

'Who is William?' asked Francis, able to bear it no longer.

'William is my brother,' said Venetia. 'He's known Mary for ever. He is absolutely devoted to her!'

Absolutely devoted to her.

Francis liked the sound of this less and less. He was beginning to wish that he had never involved Venetia Huntington, much less her threatening brother. There was no going back on it now, however.

'What exactly is going on?' she was saying. 'What's the matter with Mary?'

'You know, of course, about Rafe Bartholomew's death . . .'

'Yes. What a shocking thing!'

'Well, Mary has taken the news very, very badly.'

'Has she?'

There was surprise at the other end followed by the sort of silence which was questing for more information. It was difficult to know what to say and what to leave out.

'I'm sure she'll tell you all about it when you see her . . .'

William Harding arrived forty-five minutes later and his appearance fulfilled all Francis's worst fears. William was tall, good-looking and deeply concerned for Mary. It did not take a genius to spot that William was in love with her.

Once he had got over his shock at her fragile state of

mind, William sized up Francis Stafford. Certain exchanges indicated that he and Mary knew each other well. William was forced to confront the painful fact that they were probably lovers. Stafford had met her off the train, which was more than he had been allowed to do. During the course of the conversation, he learnt that his rival was, or had been, one of the cryptanalysts at Bletchley, which was presumably where he had met Mary. So, highly intelligent then. Watching Francis watching Mary, one did not have to be a great brain to spot that Stafford was besotted.

Well, thought William, Mary's going to be staying with us until she is properly back on her feet which gives me a location advantage over Stafford and I intend to make the most of it. It would be interesting to see if he kissed her when he saw them off.

Francis accepted a lift to the station and he did kiss Mary. William looked away. As they drove off, through the rear-view mirror he watched Stafford stand looking after them before finally turning away and walking into the ticket hall.

En route to Chelsea Mary did not say very much. She looked drained. William wondered what on earth could have happened to bring her to this but tactfully did not ask. Nettie, naturally, had no such inhibitions when they got back. They were hardly through the door before Nettie asked and Mary, who could no longer see any point in keeping it to herself, told them everything.

When she had gone up to her room, Nettie said to William, 'Well, well! What do you think of that? All along Mary's been one of us!'

William hated it when his sister talked like this. He was short. 'I don't know what you mean! To me she's always been one of us.'

'Yes, you do. You know exactly what I mean.'

'What I *am* certain about is that I'm in love with Mary!'

'Are you really!' Nettie raised her eyebrows a second time. 'Well, I have to say I thoroughly approve of that. But what about Francis Stafford? Where does he fit in and what did you make of him?'

William raised his shoulders and spread his hands in a gesture of despair.

'I liked him. He's in love with Mary too.'

'Mary's a lucky girl,' said Nettie.

After the inquest, conducted in a blaze of publicity of the sort he would have deplored, Rafe Bartholomew's funeral took place privately at Minton where he was buried beside other, less illustrious, Bartholomews. In attendance were a select few, led by a dignified Alice Fort.

Mary, still very ill, had been frantic to go.

'I *must* go, I *will* go,' insisted Mary, tearfully, 'even if it kills me.'

Her mental equilibrium was so precarious and her distress so acute that Francis feared it might. Putting his foot down, after the manner of a Geoffrey Harding, was not Francis's way. Instead, and without telling Mary he had done it, he rang Mrs Fort.

'Mrs Fort, my name is Francis Stafford. We met briefly in London. I hope you will not consider this an intrusion but Mary is determined to make the journey to her brother's funeral. She cannot accept the fact that she is too ill to do it.'

Alice Fort, who had sat beside the strained, thin Mary at the coroner's inquest, could quite believe it.

'And your connection, Mr Stafford, is?'

Intending to tell her about Bletchley Park, thereby explaining the thread which linked him with both Mary and Rafe, he was astonished to hear himself say instead, 'I am in love with her.'

Yes, of course he was. Alice remembered him. He had been at the inquest too, a serious young man with an intelligent face and a slight, scholarly list. Despite her preoccupation with her own grief, she had noticed both his solicitude for Mary and his tactful, self-effacing manner.

'I should also say that Mary does not know I have made this call,' added Francis.

'On no account must Mary make the journey,' said the quiet voice on the other end of the line. 'I, myself, will forbid it on health grounds. When she is fully recovered she can come to Minton to pay her last respects at Rafe's grave and stay here. Meanwhile, there is to be a memorial service in London and I am sure I can rely on you to support her through that. Is she still staying with that friend of hers, Venetia Huntington?'

'Yes, she is.'

'Very well. If you would be kind enough to give me the number, Mr Stafford, I shall telephone her there this evening.'

32

Over the next weeks Francis Stafford visited Mary as often as he could get away. Nettie decided that she liked him and said as much to Mary. Francis, on the other hand, was by no means sure that he liked Nettie but did not pass any of his reservations on to Mary. Her generosity and nursing of Mary were not in question but there was a hard ruthlessness about her, probably labelled sophistication by the set she moved in, which repelled Francis. Worst of all he suspected her of being shallow. Her pregnancy seemed an incongruity. He simply could not imagine Venetia Huntington as a mother and intuited that neither could she. Once when he was at the Chelsea house, Randolph was present. Huntington was everything Francis most disliked, a bombastic mediocrity and drunk who seemed to think himself a cut above the rest of the population. There was something about the way Nettie looked at her spouse from time to time which caused him to think he was not entirely alone in this tart summing up. Not for the first time he wondered why on earth she had married Huntington and, even more mysterious, why, having left him, she had gone back to him again. Francis might not have approved of Nettie but he still considered her worth a hundred Randolphs.

At the end of a fortnight, though still mentally shaky and prone to sudden tears, Mary was on the way to recovery. Maybe, thought Francis, the hurricane of grief which had hit her when he clumsily broke the news of Rafe Bartholomew's suicide had been the best thing after all. Emotional waters ran deep with Mary and there was no doubt that a trauma such as the one she had just suffered was better on the surface rather than suppurating within. While she was in London he thought about her all the time and resolved to ask her to marry him.

William did ask Mary to marry him and was gently turned down.

'Dear William,' said Mary, 'I'm honoured to be asked and

I love you but I'm not *in* love with you, so the answer must be No. As much for your sake as for mine.'

William told Nettie what he had done and what the answer had been.

'I'm hoping that Mary might change her mind,' said William. 'What do *you* think?'

Mindful of Young Lochinvar, '*Faint heart never won fair lady*. All the same, I think she won't!' Considering it, Nettie veered from the positive into a negative. 'Mary doesn't play games the way some women do. Besides, I suspect she's in love with Francis Stafford!'

'Well then, why doesn't he do something about it?' William was irritable.

'Maybe he's waiting for the *moment juste*,' hazarded Nettie.

The following weekend Francis turned up in Chelsea with a bundle of post for Mary. Most of it looked predictable, but there was one letter of the portentous vellum variety. Mary dealt with the dross first and then opened the grand one. There was silence as she read it and then, when she had done so, she said, 'Good God! I don't believe it!' She handed the letter to Francis. 'Read this and tell me if you think it's some sort of tasteless hoax. But even if it isn't I can't accept what's on offer. I've done absolutely nothing to deserve it.'

Francis read it and as he did so felt his heart plummet.

'It's not a hoax,' he said, 'and there can be no question of your not accepting it. Rafe Bartholomew never did anything without thinking it through. It would be an insult to his memory if you refused.'

'I *can't* take it. Francis, it's a *Bonnard*! Do you know how much a Bonnard painting is worth? Do you? Plus a huge sum of money.' Mary looked dazed.

Francis was patient. 'Yes, you can. You must. Look, at the very least I suggest you contact the solicitors and set up a meeting. Tell them you've been ill and leave it for a week if you don't feel up to it, but *do* do it! Promise!'

'All right, if you insist. I promise!'

It was ironic, thought Francis, that he was insisting she should do it when the upshot would be so disastrous for all his own hopes and desires. Mary Fox was about to become a very rich young woman and he, Francis Stafford, hadn't a bean. There could be no question of asking her to marry him now.

When Francis was leaving he ran into William. William thought Francis looked distracted, depressed even. Maybe he had asked Mary to marry him and she had turned him down as well. Although even if that were the case, it wasn't likely to advance his own cause.

That evening, over dinner, Mary passed her news on to Nettie. Nettie was frankly envious and then disbelieving.

'What do you mean you've got misgivings about taking it? You must be mad, Mary! As a result of accidents of birth people inherit money all the time without having done a thing to deserve it! I was hoping to be one of them until Father lost it all, so I should know. Besides, Francis is right, if Rafe wanted you to have the painting and the money, who are you to turn it down? In its way his bequest is as perfect an end as you could hope to get at the end of a tragic story.'

'Maybe you're right.'

'Of course I am!'

When Nettie told William about it, he whistled. And then, remembering Stafford's dejected look, said, '*Now* I see! Unless he has already, Francis will not propose to Mary now.'

Nettie was astonished.

'Why ever not?'

'Because he has no money of his own.'

'I don't understand what the problem is. Mary's going to have enough for both of them!'

'He won't want to appear a fortune hunter,' elucidated William.

'So what if he does?' replied his grasping sister. 'Honestly, they're like babes in the wood, those two. Mary doesn't think she should accept the money at all. Francis encourages her to do so but feels that, as a result, although he's in love with her, he now can't ask her to marry him. They need their heads knocking together!'

William smiled. Nettie's attitude to money had always been famously practical. His eye fell on the Huntington ruby. Even if the marriage fell apart again, he couldn't see Randolph succeeding in prising that particular bauble off the third finger of her left hand. There was no point in trying to explain scruples to Nettie. As far as she was concerned the concept of honour was a completely foreign one.

As the talk moved on to other things, William made a mental note to have a word with Mary and to alert her, if he got the opportunity, to what he was nearly sure was going on inside Francis.

Mary went to see Rafe Bartholomew's solicitor the following week. Meanwhile she rang Francis and asked him to go to her Bletchley room and bring her mother's jewel box to London with him when he next came. Her tenancy was about to expire anyway. It was better to get that sort of thing back.

'I am very undecided as to whether to accept this extraordinary bequest or not,' Mary informed the solicitor.

He was stupefied.

'My dear Miss Fox, my client, Mr Bartholomew was adamant about it. I have to tell you I argued against such a thing but he would not budge. His reply was, "I want Miss Fox to have enough money to put herself through university if she so wishes, but more than that, I want to enable her to enter the Promised Land!" That's what he said. I have no idea what he meant, have you?'

'No.'

'It was at this point that I stopped urging him not to do it. It seemed to me that whereas money is money, whichever way you view it, the painting is something else again and he gave me to understand that he wanted to bequeath it because he had some sort of message in mind specifically for you. What I'm getting to is that, apart from its value, it is not any old painting but one selected from a sizeable collection for you personally. To turn it down would be discourteous –'

'But what would I do with it? If I hung it, it might get stolen,' said Mary.

'Yes, it might. That's the sort of chance we all have to take, one way or another.' The lawyer was dry. 'Look, Miss Fox, I knew Rafe Bartholomew for years and I think I understood the way his mind worked. He was a very subtle man and not much given to the obvious interpretation. My view is that once you have seen the Bonnard and absorbed whatever it was he wanted you to see, what you do with it is up to you.

You could take the risk of putting it on your wall, or you could put it in a bank vault, such as the one in which it is currently incarcerated, or you could sell it to a gallery, the Tate, for instance, where it would be enjoyed by thousands. Any of those options would be acceptable *provided* you understand what it was he was trying to tell you, for *that* is the real point of it. Do I make myself clear?'

'Yes you do, and you're right. Of course I must see it.'

'Excellent. It shall be arranged.'

They shook hands. Seeing Miss Fox to the door, it occurred to him that he had dealt with some strange arrangements on behalf of his clients down the years but this was definitely one of the strangest. For her part Mary saw no point in telling the old man about her blood relationship with his client. It had, after all, no bearing on what they had been discussing because Rafe had never known about it.

Finally standing in front of his gift to her, she was conscious of a sort of wonder. It was all there. The luminosity of the light and colour outside the window was given extra vibrancy and depth by the darkness of the interior. But it was more than that, Mary recognized. The mysterious figure which she supposed to be herself stood poised between the two and might turn either way. The exorcism of a dark past was the key to the glory of the garden of the future. *If she wanted it to be.* And I do, thought Mary, I do. I'm going to pursue what Rafe wanted and I want too, and put myself through university with the money. Furthermore I'm not going to sell this sublime painting, which is a mirror of my life so far and maybe of my life to come as well. I'm going to insure it and hang it where I can revel in it every day. As she made up her mind, she had the odd perception that her brother was standing by her shoulder and applauding her decision.

Outside in the cold streets smoky-blue dusk was setting in and the lights were coming on. Mary felt invigorated. Soon it would be Christmas and shortly after that the beginning of a new year and a new life.

The simplicity of Rafe Bartholomew's memorial service as orchestrated by Alice Fort contrasted with the grandeur of the many guests. She and Mary Fox sat together, flanked by

Nettie and Francis and William. Behind them sat Davina and Peter Flamborough. The church was full.

Geoffrey Harding was not there.

That morning he had rung up his estranged wife. Without preamble and apparently still trying to order her about even though they were now separated, he announced, 'Davina, as Godfrey's mother, I expressly do not wish you to attend the service today.'

Davina was crisp. 'Geoffrey, as Godfrey's mother, I have every intention of attending. And now, if you will excuse me, I have to put my hat on!'

Click.

It was amazing, reminisced Davina, remembering the exchange with satisfaction as the marvellous music of Verdi's *Requiem* filled the church, how easy trouncing Geoffrey was. She slipped her arm through Peter's.

At the end of the service, Alice Fort and Mary stood up and wordlessly embraced. Alice gently put a hand to Mary's tear-stained face.

'My dear, the time has come to stop mourning. Rafe wouldn't have wanted it. He ended his life when *he* wanted to and who is to quarrel with that? It is the ultimate right. Besides, although I have lost a son, I have gained a daughter. *The Lord taketh away and the Lord giveth.*' Her smile was like a benediction and it was in that spirit that they left for a champagne valediction to a glittering, ultimately tragic life, as requested by Rafe Bartholomew in his last will and testament.

The following day, which was a Saturday, Mary informed Nettie that she felt well enough to leave.

'Where will you go?' asked Nettie. 'Not back to Bletchley, surely. They must have wound all that down by now, haven't they?'

'Yes, more or less. I have to clear out my room and get my stuff up to London. After that I intend to live in the Brixton flat while I sort out a university application.'

'Well, gently does it. There's no rush. And don't go without seeing Jonty, he's coming to tea tomorrow. Though before you do you should know that since he came home, he's not the person he was.'

'What do you mean?'

'According to Mother he has dreadful recurring nightmares and flies off the handle over nothing. It's as well to tread very carefully round Jonty these days.'

Nettie was conscious of a twinge of envy. Not over the prospect of university, heavens no. It was a twinge of envy for her own lost independence. She looked down at her distended stomach with distaste. Since their last encounter she had not heard from Joshua Kellaway but Nettie did not deceive herself that this meant he had decided to cut his losses and leave her alone to get on with her life with Randolph. Kellaway was a ticking time bomb. In so far as she thought of it at all, Nettie hoped the baby was a girl. Though even if it was, while this would solve one problem, it would raise another in that Randolph would want her to get stuck into another pregnancy straight away. The depressing Henry VIII scenario of daughter after daughter presented itself before Nettie's inner eye. In an effort to take her mind off it, she asked, 'What about Francis? What's he going to do?'

'I don't know. We haven't really discussed it.'

On impulse Nettie said, 'He's in love with you, you know!' and then followed up this small conversational hand grenade with, 'Are you in love with him?'

Mary blushed.

'You are!' said Nettie triumphantly, and for the first time Mary admitted to herself that maybe she was.

The following afternoon, as arranged, Jonty turned up.

Despite Nettie's warning, Mary was appalled by his appearance. Jonty was a shell-shocked, pale reflection of the exuberant youth she remembered. Of the three Harding sons the only one who had come through apparently unscathed was William. Seeing him gave Mary an idea.

Pouring him a cup of tea, she said, 'You're not going to see your father in the near future are you, Jonty?'

'As a matter of fact I am. Tomorrow. At his club. The sale of the house was completed today and he's very morose about it and wants some company. Since Mother left him he's been at something of a loose end. Why? Can I do something for you?'

298

'Yes, you could give him something if you wouldn't mind.'

'No, of course not.'

'What?' asked Nettie, very inquisitive.

'Aha!' said Mary.

She went upstairs, opened Sibyl's jewel box and took out the diamond drops. They glittered. Like slivers of ice they dangled from her fingers and brought the word heartless to mind. For the last time Mary held them up to the light and then, without regret, she dropped them into the black velvet darkness of a small bag whose drawstring neck she tightened and secured with a bow. It only remained to put them in an envelope which, after writing Geoffrey Harding's name on it, she sealed.

'For once,' said Mary to herself, 'thy need is greater than mine.'

She descended the stairs and, under Nettie's mesmerized gaze, gave the small parcel to Jonty.

'What is it? Do tell!'

'None of your business, Nettie!'

The day Mary was due to leave, William arrived at the house and found her packing.

'We never had the promised dinner,' he said, 'but let me at least take you out for a drink.' Noting her hesitation, he added, 'I promise not to propose again, though I admit that there is something I want to talk to you about.'

She smiled at him.

'All right! But I have to be back by two because Francis is picking me up then.'

Walking along the King's Road to The Man In The Moon, passing lovers on the way as they did so, William wished he had Mary's hand in his so that everyone could see that she belonged to him. Alas, it was not to be. He had accepted that but the knowledge did not extinguish his love for her. In time, no doubt, it would mutate into something more philosophical. All the same, because of it, he wanted to do one last thing for her.

The pub was crowded. William bought them each a drink and when they had eventually secured a table, he said, 'I gather you have decided to accept Rafe's bequest.'

299

'Yes. Yes, I have. Why? Do you think it's the wrong thing to do?'

'On the contrary, I think it's the right thing to do. But it wasn't you I was thinking about. It was Francis.'

'Francis!' Mary stared at him.

'Forgive me if this sounds impertinent. I think, no, I'm *sure* that he's in love with you. But I also think that because you are now a rich woman and he's an honourable man with no money of his own, he will feel that he cannot ask you to marry him.'

'Ah!' Unlike Nettie, though this had not occurred to her before, Mary understood perfectly. 'You're right. Of course, you're right!'

Hoping she wasn't blushing, she lowered her eyes and looked pensively down into her gin and tonic and then, unwilling to meet William's gaze, circled her glass so that the spinning ice cubes became prisms of refracted light.

Finally she did look up and when she did, took his hand.

'Thank you, William. You have done me the most enormous favour.'

It was then, heart breaking, that he knew she was irrevocably lost to him and admitted to himself that, up until now anyway, he had never quite given up hope.

'Let's talk about something else,' said William.

As the two of them travelled to Bletchley together that afternoon in an otherwise empty carriage, Mary said to Francis, 'I want to ask you something.'

Enquiringly he looked up from the book he was reading.

'Will you marry me?'

Part Six

Another Country

Love and scandal are the best sweeteners of tea.

Henry Fielding

33

1946

The wedding took place in the new year and Mary married wearing a gown designed by Worth.

'It's my present to you,' said Nettie. 'You only get married once!'

(Or do you?)

'Nettie, I really can't accept,' Mary had said.

Nettie cast her eyes to heaven.

'Mary, for God's sake, don't start that again! I *want* to do it and I'm going to.' Besides, she could have added but did not, though he doesn't know it, Randolph's paying. 'Your first fitting is next week. Tuesday at 2.30. Don't be late!'

On the day the little church was full. Elfrida came with her husband and so did a large ex-Bletchley contingent, one of whom, a very pretty girl called Celia, caught William's eye. Of the Harding family, all accepted except for Davina who had an awful vision of Geoffrey threatening to horse-whip Peter in the middle of the nuptials and decided that it was more politic to stay away. Margaret Macaulay and Alice Fort travelled there separately from different ends of the same county, sat at different ends of the same pew and, so far as Mary could tell, did not speak to each other.

As she sat watching Francis and Mary take their vows with Jonty on one side of her and Randolph, coaxed out of his club for the occasion, on the other, Nettie mentally bemoaned her fate. With dissatisfaction she stared down at her spreading girth.

I am vast, she lamented to herself, vast! I may never be the same again. Thank God the birth was imminent though she sincerely hoped the child did not choose today of all days to make its début. Only the other day she had taken a call from Joshua Kellaway, who had underlined the fact that he had not forgotten her.

'I shall be scrutinizing the births column of *The Times* daily from now on,' he said.

With this threat in mind, Nettie said to Randolph, 'I don't think anybody much puts notices in *The Times* these days, do you? I thought we wouldn't bother.'

Randolph was thunderstruck. 'Not announce the birth in *The Times*! Good grief woman, have you gone mad! Of course we must!'

The baby kicked Nettie hard, turned over uncomfortably and then kicked her again. 'Stop it, you little brat,' said Nettie under her breath. Her mind wandered to Kyle McClaren, now ensconced in New York with his possessive wife. The other day, on impulse, she had telephoned him and learnt that contrary to what he had been led to expect, Allegra had not been pregnant after all. Kyle had sounded very glad to hear her voice. She felt all at once nostalgic. We had such fun, Kyle and I, reminisced Nettie. Such fun! And now he was thousands of miles away in America, with all those other high-level contacts she had made during the war years, in America, Land of Opportunity, Land of the Free.

Suddenly Nettie saw what had been staring her in the face and wondered how she could have been so dense.

With gusto she sang the next hymn.

And thus it was that, one month later, London opened its morning papers on what was otherwise a slow news day to read in the tabloids: HIGH SOCIETY NETTIE HOPS IT! HUSBAND LEFT HOLDING THE HEIR and in the more circumspect quality dailies: SOCIETY BEAUTY VENETIA HUNTINGTON LEAVES FOR USA ON THE QUEEN MARY.

Reactions to this startling news were mixed.

Reading it over a cup of Darjeeling, a traumatized Elfrida said to her husband, 'I am *so* disappointed in Nettie. And *shocked*! *SHOCKED!* To *think* that I had a hand in her upbringing. Imagine leaving that little baby! How *could* she do it?'

This was pale compared with Geoffrey Harding's explosion of wrath over his Earl Grey. Who to blame, that was the question. Predictably he rang Davina. 'Have you seen the papers,' raged Harding. 'Have you? You have! This is all your fault, Davina, you showed Nettie the way . . .' There was quite a lot more in the same vein until he realized he was talking to himself and probably had been for some time because she had hung up on him.

Randolph, who had yet to hear from Joshua Kellaway on the subject of paternity, put a slug of whisky in his tea in order to help him come to terms with what had happened and, because he felt a fool, uncharacteristically made no public comment and was represented by out-of-date photographs depicting him marching about in army uniform and riding boots. Pictures of Nettie (described as 'hot stuff' by a former lover) abounded and the sobriquet Hot Stuff Huntington graced the next rash of headlines, offending close family and causing even the most loyal of friends to wince.

Mary said to Francis, 'I don't know whether to laugh or cry! I never thought she'd do anything like this.'

'Didn't you? It doesn't surprise me in the slightest,' was Francis's rejoinder. 'You'll find she's got a lover all teed up for when she gets to the other side.'

'I wonder if I shouldn't ring William.'

In an attempt to move his life on, thereby leaving behind him his doomed love for Mary Fox, William was in bed with the delectable Celia when he took her concerned telephone call and was equally unamazed.

'Good luck to her,' said William. 'Of course she shouldn't have left the child, but if you think about it Randolph's awful and chances are the baby's just like him. It will certainly be brought up just like him. Besides, she wouldn't have seen much of it. Nettie's just not the maternal type.'

No. Self evidently. There was probably nothing else to say.

Enjoying her own notoriety, Nettie herself was unfazed. As she reclined on a steamer chair, looking out to sea with her waistline back and the Huntington ruby on her finger, Nettie thought, I couldn't care less what they're all saying about me. I really couldn't. I'm on my way again, I'm my own woman and that's all that matters to me. Let Randolph and Joshua fight it out between them.

With pleasure she anticipated the rest of the voyage and, in particular, Kyle McClaren's presence on the quayside to welcome her when they docked in New York. There was everything to play for.

She sipped her vodka and tonic.

The water was aquamarine, the sun a brilliant sphere of light.

Oh, this is bliss. Bliss!

America here I come!

Part Seven
Full Circle

34

1965

The letter from America came out of the blue.

I learnt from some English friends who have just passed through New York that The Hall is up for sale again, wrote Nettie, a famously lackadaisical correspondent. *Mary, why don't you make a pilgrimage there on my behalf. And on yours, come to that. Go and say goodbye . . .*

Rather against her better judgement, Mary did go.

She drove there alone one summer's day. On the brow of the hill she stopped the car. The countryside was lush. Butterflies proliferated. Where there were nettles, handsome dandies such as Peacocks browsed. Elsewhere Brimstones, Red Admirals, Tortoiseshells, even a Purple Emperor, delicately danced from wild flower to wild flower attended by a *corps de ballet* of Cabbage Whites. It was very hot and the humming of insects was loud in the golden air. Below her in the hollow, wreathed in roses and rampant Virginia creeper, stood the house in which she had spent her girlhood.

Letting out the clutch, her feelings were complex, as she had known they would be.

The descent was a steep one. Memories came back of herself and Nettie hurtling down the hill on rusty bicycles, sandalled feet shot out in front, risking life and limb and shrieking with a heady mixture of ecstasy and terror as they did so. In this, a different incarnation, Mary drove slowly and with care. Just as she remembered the gradient flattened out and finally joined the road which led to the house.

The agent had assured her that the house would be empty. The curtains were drawn back though and Mary looked through one of the drawing-room windows. Disquietingly, the sofas and certain other items of furniture were the originals. Apart from small personal effects the room was

309

more or less as it had been. The Kellaways must have bought the place lock, stock and barrel. The sensation of revisiting a past life was eerie and strange. She walked on, round the corner to the back where the double doors of the dining-room led onto a stone terrace. Here the shutters were partly pulled across but it was still possible to see in and Mary was confronted by her own reflection in one of the two magnificent gilded pier-glasses which flanked the marble fireplace. It gave her an odd sensation of being inside the house as well as outside it, as though the past and the present faced one another.

More memories surfaced. In particular the last September she had lived there. In her mind's eye, once again Mary saw Jonty, William, Nettie, Godfrey and herself all lying under the apple trees in the sun-shot orchard, Godfrey lazily chewing a blade of grass. One brown hand shaded his brilliant blue Harding eyes with their straight dark brows, and his sunbleached blond hair spread around his narrow sunburnt face. Wearing white slacks and a white open-necked shirt, he had been the very embodiment of that last summer.

As if it was yesterday, she recalled him saying, casually and unexpectedly, 'What are you going to do next, Mary? Where will you go?'

Polite, interested even, but essentially disengaged, despite the fact that they had all been brought up together. He might as well have been speaking to an acquaintance. Or, maybe, just another sister. She recalled picking one daisy and then another and another and starting to fashion them into a chain in an attempt to conceal her own distress. Finally, she had managed to say in what she hoped was a neutral tone of voice, 'I don't know. I really don't know,' at which point she had raised her eyes just in time to catch Nettie furiously mouthing *Idiot!* at her tactless brother.

Mary turned away from the window and the past. In this house she and Nettie and the Harding boys had grown up together. Here she had fallen in love with Godfrey, or thought she had, and here she had first met Rafe Bartholomew, and Rafe had first met Godfrey and the rest had followed. As she slowly retraced her steps back to the car, she had an uncanny sensation of leaving her reflection behind, together with the

310

ghosts which had stood at her elbow for the last twenty years. Godfrey, Rafe and Sibyl. All stepped back a pace.

A sudden sensation of release engulfed Mary. Like balm it flooded her being and as it did so it nullified the feeling of regret which, like a fault line, had subtly undermined an otherwise idyllic present.

So, not a pilgrimage.

No.

An exorcism.

On her return home, Mary wrote to Nettie.

Dearest Nettie,

I did go back and am penning this in the wake of my visit. The Hall is very much the same. I couldn't get in, of course, but from the outside it looked as though the Kellaways hadn't altered it much. He has gone bust, by the way. That is why they are selling. Anyway, to continue, standing in the garden I suddenly had a revelation. I saw that ghosts only stay around as long as you let them, and that it was time for me to stop dwelling on what has gone and to let mine slip away. The lightening of spirit I experienced was quite extraordinary and, in an odd sort of way, has drawn a conclusive line under the past.

Turning to other matters, your news that you are getting married again in May is opportune. Francis and I had intended to travel to the States with children in tow in June but now we'll come earlier and will look forward to toasting you both. I hope you will be as happy as we are. It's a shame that you and Kyle didn't work out, but Third Time Lucky, as they say!

'And Fourth, and Fifth,' observed Francis, looking over his wife's shoulder as she wrote. 'I'll be very surprised if this is Nettie's last shot at matrimony.'

Ignoring the unhelpful interruption,

. . . And how on earth did you come to meet a film mogul?

'Same way she meets all of them. Between the sheets!' observed her incorrigible husband, still hovering.

'Francis, go *away*,' said Mary. 'Haven't you got any sums to do?'

Resuming,

. . . Well, you can tell me all when we meet. I'm dying to hear the gossip, but most of all I long *to see you. I should tell you, incidentally, that our daughter, your namesake, is agog at the prospect of seeing her outrageous godmother again. Mind you don't lead her astray!*

Oh, Nettie, I've missed you. Let's raise a glass to loyalty and friendship, but, most of all, let's raise a glass to the future!

With very best love,
Mary